# FRIENDS, LOVERS, & OTHER GASLIGHTERS

## 25 TALES OF THE MACABRE AND THE BIZARRE

### B.A. RIES

# CONTENTS

# FOREWORD

This work is the culmination of five years of sporadically writing horror stories in the little bit of free time work and life responsibilities permit me to have.

Most of the stories are fully self-contained, but there is one set of characters whose journey progresses, sometimes in the forefront and sometimes in the backdrop, throughout this collection.

I can only hope that you enjoy reading these stories as much as I enjoyed creating them.

**1**

---

# AFTER THE SURGERY (PART 1)

It's been ten months since I first remember meeting Brandon, but, according to the rest of the world, he and I became a couple three years ago.

It all started after the surgery. When I awoke from my anesthesia-induced sleep, I nodded groggily as the doctor listed common post-operative symptoms – like drowsiness, dizziness, and disorientation. Then, two nurses wheeled me down an elevator, through the main lobby, and outside the hospital.

Even though I'd arranged for my friend Mae to pick me up, the car that arrived was not her black sedan but, instead, an unfamiliar silver SUV. The stranger who emerged from it was a tall, well-built man with hazy green eyes and tousled red hair.

Panic rushed through me as he squeezed my hand and told me in a firm, deep voice that he was so glad that the operation had been a success, and that he'd be taking good care of me while I recovered.

I tried to scream. I tried to explain to the nurses that they were delivering me into the arms of an abductor. But, in my weakened state, all I could manage were weak whimpers and incoherent mumbles that the man and nurses dismissed as "side effects" and "temporary confusion" as they lifted me into the car.

The ignition started. As the hospital faded into the distance, I tried to beg the man to free me. With immense effort, I managed to croak words like "please," "don't," and "stop," but to no avail. If the man heard me, he gave no sign of it.

Meanwhile, a sense of absolute exhaustion gradually descended over me. The last thing I remember before darkness overcame me was the man's affectionate smile, and three words that haunted the frightening dreams that followed: *I love you.*

When I awoke the next morning, I found myself, to my immense relief, in the familiar location of the bedroom of my townhouse. For a moment, I wrote off what had happened as a dream, or a hallucination brought on by my semi-conscious state. Maybe Mae had picked me up after all.

Soon enough, however, the same man stepped into my room. He placed a tray with two slices of toast and a small fruit smoothie on a bedside table. Upon seeing that I was awake, he asked in a deep, caring voice, "How are you feeling, honey?"

The scream I uttered left him flustered and pale-faced.

"W-what's wrong, April?"

*He knew my name.* **"Get out, get out, now!"** I hollered.

He nodded and quietly backed out of my room.

I mustered what energy I had to leap out of bed and lock the door. I found my phone in its usual place atop a dresser.

The photo that displayed on the background of the phone screen caused me to drop it. A nauseous feeling ran through me as I picked it up and stared, wide-eyed, at the image of the stranger and me, smiling and holding hands. The sight of an ornate diamond ring on my finger in the picture – one that matched the gold band that he wore – made me dizzy.

With trembling hands, I dialed 911.

When the police arrived, the man – who identified himself as Brandon Harrison – spoke calmly as the officers interrogated him.

Everything he said checked out. He produced a marriage certificate, and his driver's license listed my home address. He showed the officers the numerous photos of us together that were displayed around the house. He repeated to them that he was just *so* worried about me, and that I'd never acted like this before.

"Don't listen to him," I begged. "He's *lying*."

One of the officers led me upstairs while her partner stayed behind with Brandon.

When I started to ramble again, she cut me off. "Look, ma'am, please try to see this from my perspective. You're still recovering from a medical procedure, and this man has everything – and I mean everything – to prove that he is, in fact, your husband, and that he lives here with you."

"You *can't* be serious," I replied. "You're not going to leave me alone with this, this man-"

The officer interrupted me again, asking me if Brandon had threatened me or tried to hurt me.

"Well, no, but..." My voice drifted off. "But, officer, I have friends, and family...they'll confirm what I'm telling you."

The officers left after my friends and family did the opposite. Every person I contacted swore to the same version of events: that I married Brandon almost a year ago, and that we'd been living together as a couple for even longer.

My own social media pages were consistent with the happy pictures of us displayed around the house. Post after post reflected us living and traveling together. My phone and text message histories, meanwhile, were filled with corresponding communications.

All of it left me absolutely baffled and confounded. I had no idea what to do. I just knew that I did not feel safe having Brandon in the house with me.

"It's my house too, you know," he replied when I asked him to leave. "But, okay, I'll go to a friend's place, or a hotel, or somewhere else until you figure out whatever is happening to you, if you promise to see a doctor in the meantime. I'm so worried about you."

"Fine. Just go, please."

Over the next few days, I met with practitioner after practitioner.

Many had records or notes reflecting my marriage to Brandon, such as me mentioning him in response to routine questions, and none could clearly explain what was happening. They all agreed that I exhibited no signs of mental or physical illness that could explain why three years of memories of my husband had somehow vanished from my mind.

I was sitting on my living room couch, tall glass of red wine in hand, when Brandon called. I hit 'decline,' took a big gulp of my drink, and leaned my head back against the wall.

*What the fuck do I do now?* I thought. The whole world was telling me something that I knew wasn't true. During a long call with my parents, my mother had insisted that I invite Brandon back, and my father had even implied that I was deliberately lying about losing my memories of him.

Logically, the only answer is that, somehow, everyone else was correct – this man really was my husband, and I was losing my mind, or in denial, or *something*. As much as I *felt* otherwise, no alternative explanation was possible.

And Brandon wasn't acting maliciously. Instead, he was complying with everything I asked of him, to the point that he was living out of a hotel despite having the legal right to reside with me here, in a house *he* apparently co-owned. If it were all some elaborate lie, then what was he gaining from it?

I downed another glass of wine and called him back. He answered right away.

We talked for hours. He asked about my health and the results of my recent appointments.

I asked him about how we met. He related how he'd used his old red pickup truck to pull my car out of a ditch during a blizzard. By coincidence, we'd run into each other at a bar a few weeks later, where I'd insisted on buying him a drink as a token of appreciation. We'd hit it off quickly and made plans together to meet again. Before long, we considered ourselves a couple.

He described leaving his apartment to move in with me, proposing to me in a park by the harbor, and planning our small wedding. He told me I'd never been as beautiful as I was when he saw me approach the altar.

"I don't know what's happening, April. But I do know that I love you with all my heart, and that we can work through this. We were happy together, and we can be happy together again."

I realized I was crying. He sounded so sincere, and I could sense real emotion behind his words. "I believe you," I said. "But try to imagine what it's like for me. To just be told, by everyone, that so much of my life happened differently from what I remember."

"Take as much time as you need. Just let me know when you're ready to see me again."

I tossed and turned all night. I couldn't shake the feeling that I was living a life that wasn't mine, like I'd slipped from one reality to another – one where I didn't belong.

Because no matter how patient and understanding Brandon acted...I couldn't change the fact that I didn't feel anything for him. I barely *knew* him, much less loved him. I thought about the pain he must be feeling, for his whole life to just be inexplicably upended one day, and I couldn't help but feel like I was somehow responsible.

I decided to call my mother again. "Honey," she told me. "I would never lie to you, ever, and you know that. So listen to me when I say this: Brandon is your husband, and you need to let him back into your life."

An hour later, I called Brandon and told him that I was alright with him moving back in, so long as he stayed in the guest room in the basement.

Months passed with us living together like roommates. At first, we handled our own meals, but after a while, we started cooking for each other. Sometimes we'd sit at opposite ends of the couch and watch tv.

I asked him questions about our time together, and he supplied me with plenty of stories – the early date during which I'd putted a golf ball so badly that it went spiraling over a fence and onto a nearby highway, the time he'd carried me for nearly half a mile after I injured myself during a jog, and our honeymoon on an Alaskan cruise. We had a natural chemistry, and he often made me laugh. At the end of the night, he'd retire to the pull-out couch downstairs.

We took many walks together at a nearby public park. These outings were generally uneventful, except for one occasion when Brandon intervened to stop a crazed woman from harassing me.

I'd been giving her dog, a sweet ridgeback who'd run up to me, some scratches and pets, when she started to scream at me. As I backed away from the dog, she made a hostile, guttural sound, and I noticed what looked like narrow streams of blood running down from her eyes as she wailed. She charged at me, but Brandon intervened, shoving her off me and telling her to leave me alone. Another bystander restrained her as we hurried away, and I thanked Brandon for looking out for me.

Otherwise, life fell into a mundane routine. We were watching a tense movie once when I realized I'd been gripping Brandon's hand. Afterwards, he told me his back was aching from all the nights he'd spent on the foldout downstairs.

I took a deep breath. "I'm being a jerk, keeping the bed all to myself. We should set up a rotation in terms of who stays there, and who is in the basement."

He replied that that wasn't what he meant – that, while the bed was more comfortable, what he really missed was going to sleep with me. He related how he had been having nightmares recently. In them, I was living my life without him. He would try to speak to me, but it was like he was a ghost, and I couldn't see him or hear him. He would then wake up in the basement, covered in sweat, and I wouldn't be there to comfort him like I used to be.

"I'm sorry, Brandon, I-."

"I just miss you so much," he stammered.

"Brandon, I'm just not there yet."

He sighed and told me he understood.

I finally asked him a question I'd been holding back for weeks. "Do you think I'm lying? About not remembering you?"

"No," he responded, abruptly. "Not at all. I don't know what it is – if it was some fluke side effect of the surgery, or some kind of undiagnosed condition – but I know that you would never lie about something like this. I wouldn't have married you if I didn't trust you completely."

As much as I appreciated his words, the exchange left me feeling terrible. We were a married couple, after all. I had to assume that we'd done plenty of things together. But, now, I didn't even want to fall asleep in the same room as him.

The truth was that I continued to feel no meaningful attraction towards Brandon. I'd developed an affection for him, sure. He seemed polite, self-sacrificing, and protective of me. Perhaps he was good-looking, too, in an objective sense. But he sparked no romantic interest in me. It made me feel awful, given how kind and patient he was being.

Maybe that would change with time – maybe, eventually, I'd feel towards him the way I must have in the photos displayed around the house of us kissing or embracing. But what if that never happened? I couldn't stay married to someone I didn't love, no matter how good he was to me.

Still, I figured the least I could do was return some of the kindness he'd shown me by switching out our rooms as I'd offered. I wanted it to be a surprise for him.

After he left for work the next morning, I set about moving the belongings he'd brought to the basement back up to the bedroom. I decided to wash the sheets and pillowcase he'd been using as well.

When I lifted his pillow, I noticed a slight bulge in fabric where the mattress met the back of the couch. Reaching my hand under the fabric and up the backrest, I felt something solid. I gripped it and slowly pulled it out.

It was an old, tattered book. A pattern was infused into its otherwise blank mahogany leather cover. A golden triangle stood in its center. Three charcoal ovals lay over it, each intersecting with one of the triangle's sides. At the top, just above the triangle's pyramid tip, was a half-circle. Tiny, unrecognizable characters lined its thin, sepia perimeter.

Its aged, browned pages were of uneven sizes. Curious about their contents, I tried opening the book, only to discover that it was locked by a narrow, metal clasp with a tiny key hole.

I didn't know what to make of it. I couldn't find the key for it, and when I looked online, I couldn't identify anything that matched the pattern on the cover.

It could just be something as innocuous as a vintage private diary, or a family heirloom. But the way Brandon had tucked it out of sight disturbed me. Clearly, he didn't want me to find it, and this was the first time, to my knowledge, that he'd tried to hide something from me.

For the moment, I elected to leave the book where I'd found it and not mention it to Brandon while I gathered more information. I had a friend who might be able to help me, after all. I took a picture of the cover, texted it to Mae, and carefully put the book back in its place.

I pulled up to the house that Mae, her boyfriend Casey, and her roommate Olivia rented half of soon after. She led me away from the closed door to Olivia's room, through the kitchen, and down the short hallway to where she and Casey, who was at work, stayed.

As we sat together on her bed, I noticed that Mae's once-small collection of cacti had expanded into an indoor garden that filled at least a third of the room. "Olivia's got one too, now," said Mae proudly. "I gave her a particularly prickly red torch cactus a little while ago, and she takes good care of it."

I asked Mae if she still named the cacti after people she knew. With a smirk, she pointed to one by her desk and asked me to guess what he called it.

When I answered 'April,' she shook her head and giggled. "No, silly, it wouldn't feel right naming one after you. This one's Brandon."

"*What*? You're ridiculous, Mae." Compared to the cacti and succulents around it, Brandon was smaller in size. Yet, on a closer look, I discerned that the clusters of spines that covered it appeared particularly long and jagged.

Once we settled down, I brought up the book I'd sent her a picture of. I explained how I'd found it and how I wondered if it had anything to do with why I had no memories of Brandon. "I *know* this is a ridiculous theory, Mae. I just don't know what else to think. You used to be obsessed with the occult, and I thought maybe you'd recognize the symbols on the cover." I felt my face grow red with embarrassment as I realized how unhinged I must have been sounding.

Mae put her arm around me. "April, I'm glad you came to me. Don't ever be afraid to talk to me, okay? I've seen some shit that defies rational explanation, so believe me, I'm not dismissing your theory offhand. But I don't recognize the image you sent me, and I turned up nothing when I researched it this morning. My best guess is that it's just a fancy diary of some kind. Nothing more."

This calmed me down. We talked for a while about other subjects, from Casey's shoegaze band, to Olivia's ongoing lawsuit against her former employer, to their landlord's efforts to find any excuse to hold them in breach of the fixed-rate agreement they'd been renewing for years – and I felt better the longer we chatted.

I was about to leave when Mae stopped me. I watched as she got to her feet and moved slowly toward her desk. Her steps were shaky and erratic, like her body was navigating contradictory commands. She removed a small business card from a drawer and tossed it in my direction. It flew past me and landed on the ground. As I turned to pick it up, I heard a tumbling sound, followed by a sharp cry of pain.

When I looked back, Mae's hand was covered in blood. To my shock, I realized it was stuck in a tight grip around cactus Brandon, with dozens of its needles protruding all the way through her palm and out the other side of her hand.

"What the hell!" I shrieked. "Mae, let me help-"

Her face had grown pale, and her expression was understandably agonized. She begged me to call 911.

Olivia and I followed the instructions the emergency operator gave us as we waited for assistance. When paramedics arrived, Mae repeated to them what she told us: that she'd slipped and fallen, and, when she tried to catch herself, her hand had landed on the cactus.

As they carted her away for treatment, I examined the card Mae had thrown at me. It displayed a name and an address: *Monsieur Herrmann's Occult Artifacts*, 6681 Cheshire Lane.

I didn't know what to make of it. I didn't know what to make of a lot of things. But once Olivia assured me I didn't need to wait at the hospital with her, I decided to follow this lead to its end.

Rainfall pounded at my umbrella as I hurried from my car to the door of 6681 Cheshire Lane. The store inside was lit primarily by scented candles that smelled vaguely of black cherry. Its shelves were lined with books with titles like *Encyclopedia of Demonology* or *Dark Magic and Incantations* separated by prop skulls and Baphomet statues.

I came across a bald man placing an ornately chalice on a top shelf. His name tag read *Jean*, and when he noticed me, he asked me if there was anything he could help me with.

"I, um, there's a symbol – a pattern – that I saw on one of my husband's books. I have a picture of it. I'm wondering if you might know what it means."

I passed him my phone. When he looked at the image, his eyes narrowed and his brow widened in a brief expression of concern. Then, his face softened, and he smiled as he returned my phone to me.

"It's meaningless," he said in an earnest voice. "There's a craftsman out of San Antonio who makes blank notebooks with this sort of cover and sells them online. The design vaguely draws from some pagan symbols, but it doesn't have any particular meaning." He asked if I had any other questions.

"No," I said, a mix of puzzlement and relief running through me, "I think not."

~

I didn't mention the day's events to Brandon. After we switched beds that night, I noticed that the book had disappeared from the couch downstairs. I decided it was likely just a diary Brandon wished to keep private and decided not to press him on it.

Mae left the hospital before long with an array of bandages around her hand. When I mentioned *Monsieur Herrmann's Occult Arti-*

*facts*, she indicated that she'd been there plenty of times before but insisted that she didn't remember giving me a card.

Over the next few weeks, the episode slipped from my mind. Brandon continued to be supportive, even giving me rides to and from work when my car needed minor repairs. I began to feel even closer and more comfortable around him.

One Friday night, he prepared a fancy candlelight dinner. He explained to me that it was the anniversary of the date we'd first met. I tried to picture the story he told me – me, stranded by the side of the road, and him driving up in his red truck to save the day. It was a good story, and I was ready to accept it was true.

We sat together after the meal. He asked me how I felt about coming upstairs and staying with him in the bedroom. He insisted it didn't have to be anything more than us sleeping in the same bed again.

I gripped his hand. "Yes, I'm okay with that. Brandon, I'm so sorry for what I'm putting you through. I just wish I knew *why* this is happening."

He insisted that it was all okay, and that he would always be there for me.

"Brandon, were we...did we have plans? Like, life plans moving forward?"

He described how we'd been trying to have a child. We'd had it all planned out: Hannah for a girl, Martin for a boy. "But, don't worry about that now, April," he said in a soft voice. "We can take things one step at a time."

I felt secure enough around him that I fell asleep quickly that night. I awoke several hours later to the sounds of Brandon having a nightmare. He was sweating, shaking, and making low, panicked murmurs.

I put my arms around him and whispered, "Brandon, it's okay, you're just having a bad dream."

He calmed down. "I love you," he mumbled in a groggy voice.

"I love you too," I whispered back.

He quickly went back to sleep as I realized what I'd said. I'd finally spoken those words, and I'd done so spontaneously. *Maybe things really are going to work out*, I thought as I dozed off again.

The next morning, I waited for the dealership's shuttle to arrive to take me to pick up my car. As I climbed inside the van, I saw that it had a different driver than before. I slowly realized, to my surprise, that it was Jean, the man who'd assisted me at the Occult store.

As he drove, Jean spoke to me in a frantic voice. "You need to listen carefully to me, April. We don't have much time."

"What are you doing here? How do you know my name?" I pulled out my phone.

He snapped at me to put it away. I realized, meanwhile, that he was driving at a dangerously fast speed in the opposite direction of the dealership.

"Look, *please* pull over, and-"

He cut me off. "We don't have time! Hear me out. Please. There's a reason Mae sent you to me."

That got my attention. I told him to start talking.

He spoke as he merged the van onto the interstate. "You have no idea how hard I've worked to pull this off. We only have a brief window before he catches on. If we're lucky, it'll be just enough time to reach Emma, and then the two of you need to get as far away from here as possible."

"Emma? Who the hell is Emma?"

Jean removed a polaroid photo from the glove box and passed it to me. In the picture, I was in an orange sundress in a park by the harbor with a beaming expression of joy on my face. A woman I vaguely recognized was kneeling before me. In one hand, she gripped a leash that connected to a ridgeback puppy. In her other, she held out a beautiful golden ring.

"Emma is your wife, April. She's waiting for us in a secure location. You should be safe there, for a little while at least."

"My *what*?" No, no, it couldn't be...

I realized where I'd seen her. She was the crazy lady at the park, the one Brandon had protected me from. "But...why, if that's true..." It was too much to take in. I started to feel light-headed.

Jean told me about an obscure text containing a legend about some kind of creature – a 'cambion', as he called it – named 'Grousel'. He explained how everything about the book in the image I'd shown him – the symbols, the lock, and the rest of the design – was something only the real Grousel would have. Nobody knew for sure, but the most common theory is that this book was where he recorded each alteration he made.

Jean continued as I tried my best to digest what he was saying. "Grousel casts illusions that are almost impossible to see through. And he can command people to do what he wants. It takes incredible willpower to even notice his influence, and even more to do anything about it. Even temporary resistance comes at the cost of severe physical punishment."

I remembered the blood running down the woman's – Emma's – face as she scrambled after me. Had she been trying to tell me who she – and who I – really was? I thought, too, about Mae's bloody 'accident,' just as she directed me to the one person who had the answers I was seeking.

"When you showed me the book cover," Jean said, "I had to pretend I didn't know anything about it. I arranged to pick you up, here, in circumstances that he wouldn't view as suspicious. As far as he knows, you're still on the way to the dealership. But as soon as he realizes you aren't where you should be, he will search for us, and if we're not far enough away from him, he'll find us."

"So, you're telling me that this *thing*, whatever you called it, is making all of this happen? But *why*? And if he can fool everyone else, why can't he just make me remember being married to him?"

"That's how he harnesses his power," said Jean, as he took an unfamiliar exit. "He latches onto a particular target, and there are limits on how much trickery he can use on that person. Sure, he can change pictures or legal documents, but he can't actually insert himself into your past memories. The more you choose to believe his lies, the stronger he gets, and the more elaborate his illusions can become."

"But why *me*, in particular?" I asked as the car turned down a dirt road that led through a thick forest.

"I can't say for sure," he replied. "But I suspect it's because you're a challenging target, for a lot of reasons. He could prey on the mentally unwell, or those easily susceptible to influence, but fooling them doesn't give him the kind of power he craves. He chose you because he knew how skeptical you'd be. If he behaves as the texts describe, he'll discard you in a few years, once he's sucked all the life out of you, and then he'll move on and find a new victim. April, I need to ask: how successful has he been so far?"

"What do you mean?"

"Well, prior to this ride, how convinced were you that he was telling the truth? That you were, in fact, married to him?"

"I dunno. I...we haven't done anything, really...But I was starting to believe it. Last night, I even told him..."

Jean turned to me, an anxious expression on his face, and asked, "You told him *what*?"

"Watch out!" I cried, pointing to the road. But it was too late.

The red pickup truck that I'd just spotted speeding out from the woods sideswiped the van. Jean cried out as the world flipped upside down. I remember the smell of smoke and excruciating pain as I lost consciousness.

~

When I next opened my eyes, I found myself in a hospital bed. My vision was blurry, and I felt sore everywhere.

A doctor leaned over me. He told me that I'd undergone emergency surgery to address injuries I'd sustained in a serious car accident, and that I'd been unconscious for nearly three days. He said it would take months of healing and therapy before I could walk again but that, with any luck, I'd eventually be able to make a full recovery.

"You're fortunate to have such a loving family," he continued. "They've hardly left the hospital over the last few days."

I lacked the strength or muscle control to say any of the things I wanted to say. I just watched, helplessly, as he opened the door to the hallway and called out that I was awake.

Seconds later, Brandon approached. He displayed a wide, toothy grin. "Martin and I were worried sick about you, April. But don't worry, I'll be by your side, every step of the way, for as long as it takes for you to get better."

A small, auburn-haired child emerged from behind Brandon. Anguished tears flooded my eyes as he placed his hand gently on my face and spoke four words: "*I love you, mommy.*"

**2**

———

# CLASS OF 2013

There's a saying in my hometown: *"Nobody leaves Copper Hill for good."*

For years, I'd mostly managed to defy it. In the decade that followed my graduation from Copper Hill High School, I hardly set foot in its vicinity.

Instead, I absorbed myself in my studies at an out-of-state university and, eventually, my career. I spent the little free time I had with my girlfriend, who I'd met as a sophomore in a chemistry lab, and her friends. When we eventually broke up, I lost not only her, but also what little social life I had.

It was in this state of loneliness that I found a letter from my old high school in the mail. This surprised me, as I hadn't realized that anyone there even knew my current mailing address.

I opened the envelope to find an invitation inside. Its design was fancier than I'd expected, complete with gold-colored glitter, a royal blue background, and a finely-drawn silver border. It read, in cursive letters: *Cheers for 10 Years! Zachary R. __, Please Join Us for the CHHS Class of 2013 Official Reunion.* It went on to list a start time and the school's address.

On its back, it even contained a personalized handwritten note: *I know you live far away, Zach, but it would mean so much to me if you can make the trip. Paul and I will be there, and Arthur may fly in as well. I'd love to catch up! Hope to see you soon – Vince K__, Co-Chair, CHHS Reunion Planning Committee.*

Vince had been one of my best friends, once. You see, Copper Hill is one of those rare small towns where you can easily graduate from high school alongside the same friends you first made in kindergarten – in my case, my buddies Arthur, Paul, and Vince.

I'd spent most of my youth with them. The four of us were in the same scout troop, played on the same sports teams, and took mostly the same classes. On weekends – and on weeknights, when we felt like sneaking out without permission – we often stayed up late together playing video games and drinking whatever cheap beer we managed to keep hidden from our parents.

We'd meant so much to each other once. So why, since graduation, had I neglected them so badly? I couldn't even remember the last time I'd talked to any of them.

Perhaps this reunion could serve as an opportunity for me to reignite friendships I'd let fade. At a minimum, I knew that spending time – even just one evening – with my old pals would do me a lot of good, especially considering how lonely I'd been lately. Accordingly, I resolved to attend.

~

By the time I reached Copper Hill, I was an hour behind schedule due to congestion caused by an accident. As I approached town, I observed amidst the fading evening light that it appeared even quieter and more deserted than I remembered. Bars that had reliably drawn decent crowds on a Friday night ranged from boarded-up to barely occupied. Meanwhile, the few other cars on the street drove lethargically at speeds far below the limit, and I spotted no pedestrians.

In my memory, the school was only a short distance from the courthouse, city hall, and post office that formed most of 'downtown,' but my GPS took me down a long, unfamiliar route bordered on both sides by tall cornfields. I was about to pull over and double-check the address I'd entered when, sure enough, my headlights illuminated a sign in the school's distinct black and red colors that stated: *CHHS: Home of the Patriots.*

The brick building that loomed behind it was just as I remembered, from its tall, towering middle section to the two narrower wings that stretched out to the left and right. Through the rectangular windows that lined the main building, I made out indistinct, shadowy figures milling about inside.

A banner displaying *Welcome – 10 Years – CHHS Reunion* stretched over the stairs that led to the main entrance. Underneath it, a familiar figure scurried towards the main entrance. "Arthur," I said to myself with a smile.

Seeing Arthur improved my mood. He was the only other member of our class to leave town after graduation, and I suspected that he might share somewhat of an outsider status with me.

*It'll be just like old times,* I reassured myself as I approached the building. Strangely, though, it still didn't *feel* that way.

For one, the air had a staleness to it that was difficult to describe. It felt artificial and thin such that, as I climbed the front steps, I found myself needing to breathe in more of it than usual to avoid getting winded.

Plus, the school's location still seemed *off* somehow. It didn't make any sense – it's not like a building this large could have been relocated. But, amidst the eerily quiet surrounding countryside, everything felt more isolated and remote than I remembered it being.

I tried to stop worrying. After all, with any luck, I'd soon be laughing and reminiscing with old friends who'd be happy to see me.

Inside, balloon garlands, multicolored streamers, triangle flags, and small banners welcoming attendees decorated the main corridor. I observed tables stocked with snacks, pamphlets, and information about fundraisers.

The only noise came from the intercom, which planned an era-appropriate Calvin Harris song. Everything necessary for a reunion was there, with only one notable exception: the people.

As I approached an unmanned table marked "Check In," I

wondered where everybody had gone. Perhaps the event had moved to a different room? I was late, after all.

As I added my signature to a sign-in sheet, my eyes scanned the list of other attendees who were marked as having already arrived. I recognized many names on it.

Like Alice, who'd shared a stand with me in orchestra. Our conductor was a hard-ass, a real disciplinarian who snapped at us constantly, and Alice was one of the many students he'd driven to tears on a semi-regular basis.

I'd had this petty fantasy of comforting her after class, and then mustering the courage to ask her out. But I never did it. It was Vince, actually, who'd ended up with her.

That had always annoyed me. I'd confided in Vince about how I felt about Alice and, soon after, the two of them were together. It felt as frustrating as it sounds. But, oh well, that's what I get for hesitating for as long as I did.

Drifting down the hallway, my eyes caught the words "Reception" displayed over double-doors that led to the gymnasium. It made sense as the main location for the event – that's where homecoming, prom, and plenty of major sports events were held, after all.

I could hear chatter, laughter, and the loud thump of dance music just beyond the gym doors. I approached it excitedly.

But, when I stepped inside, all the noise instantly cut out, leaving me in an eerie silence. Even more perplexingly, the room before me, like the entrance corridor, was entirely devoid of people.

A party had just been here, no doubt. I spotted a makeshift bar stocked with a standard assortment of liquor, tables holding half-finished drinks and refreshments, and an area cleared for a dance floor in the room's center, but there were no people around. Had I missed everyone again? Where had they gone?

"Hello?" I called out, to no avail, as I drifted around the room in a state of bewilderment.

As I did so, I came across the entrance to the boy's locker room. Just a whiff of the musty, sweaty smell emanating from it unlocked long-buried memories of the time I'd spent in there.

I remembered one occasion, in particular, where Paul had gotten *pissed* at me. Paul was usually a pretty low-key guy, but when he lost it, he went *wild*. On that particular occasion, he'd been angry with *me*, hadn't he? But why?

I recalled his hot breath as he got in my face and screamed at me. When I gently nudged him away, he responded by slamming a locker door into my head.

My memories from that moment forward were hazy. There was a growing pool of blood, the pain of his fist against my cheek, and the cheering of the classmates who had encircled us. They were egging us on to continue the 'fight,' as if my beating could be called that.

I hadn't thought about this event in years. How could I have forgotten something like that? My mind churned in confusion. Feeling dizzy, I took a seat on a bench that appeared to be part of a crude photobooth setup as my mind continued to replay this repressed memory.

As Paul had continued to pummel me, I'd spotted Vince among the gathered crowd. I'd begged for him to intervene. But neither he, nor our strangely absent instructor, had done anything to help me. It was only when Arthur got between us that Paul had reluctantly cooled off.

It had taken weeks for those bruises to heal. Had Paul ever been punished for it, or even apologized? Surely he must have. We'd remained friends, after all.

A strange pressure around my shoulder and a sudden bright light jolted me back to the present. The flash on the camera facing the bench I was sitting on had...gone off, somehow, even with nobody around to operate it. How was that possible? Maybe it was automated to go off every so often?

It didn't make sense, just like so much else that was happening. Where was everybody, and whose voices had I been hearing? I'd seen people from the road, and I'd even watched Arthur come inside, but, as far as I could tell, the event was deserted.

I texted Arthur asking if he'd found anyone. For all I knew, he could have changed his number in the many years that had gone by since I'd last used it, but I figured it was worth a shot. To my relief, he responded right away.

*Hey man, long time no see! Paul just called me. He says everyone's up on the third floor, in Mr. Minelli's old room. I'm on my way there now. Meet you there soon.*

I couldn't fathom why the entire event would relocate from the area clearly designated for it to the third floor. There wasn't much up there, after all, aside from classrooms and a few administrative offices.

Nonetheless, I resolved to head up there. Arthur was there, after all, and hopefully the rest of my friends would be as well.

Navigating off my memory of the building's layout, I hopped up a small set of steps that connected the gym to the second floor. From there, it would just be a short walk past a few classrooms before I'd arrive at the central staircase, which would take me to my destination.

I'd never seen the school quite this gloomy before. Each footstep echoed through the halls. The classrooms were weirdly empty, too, bereft of any decorations or other signs of use.

I recognized one as my calculus classroom. I remembered how, after class had ended one day, I'd come across a group of students congregating in the hallway.

Mary, Michelle, and Abby, like so many of my classmates, had grown up with me, and I'd always gotten along with them. But that day, they were harassing a shy girl – Morgan, I think. Calling her all sorts of names – 'slut,' 'whore,' 'bitch'. She was trying to get away from them, but they wouldn't let her leave. Their taunting of her became a regular thing, and it often left Morgan in tears.

What ever happened to Morgan? Like most of my friends, I'd known her since I was a little kid. She was quiet, but she was perfectly nice.

Then, one day, gossip about her started to spread. The type of nasty, embellished rumors that often make their way through high schools, full of sexist undertones and double standards. Her former friends shunned her, and she'd been subjected to taunting and ridicule as she walked to class and sat alone at lunch. And, one day, she was just...gone. I'd always assumed that her family had moved away, but was that *true*?

Growing up, Mary, Michelle, and Abby had always been sweet girls. I'd never seen them treat another person the way they'd treated Morgan. But Copper Hill High School had a way of bringing out the worst in people. There was just something about this building, this place, that ate away at their – at *our* – souls.

Had I bullied Morgan, too? Maybe not, but, once her mistreatment started, it's not like I'd made an effort to be kind to her, or ever invited her to sit with me and my friends in the cafeteria. I could have done more.

I reached the central staircase. With each step that I took up towards the third floor, a feeling of dread ran through me. I'd seen something terrible happen up here, hadn't I?

It was Paul and Vince. Arthur had done something to offend them. It could have been the rumors spreading about his reasons for never having a girlfriend, his diminutive size, or the way he'd reacted when Paul had beaten me half to death.

Whatever the reason, Paul and Vince – without my knowledge – had decided to subject Arthur to a cruel prank. After school one day, they'd lured Arthur up to the third floor, where they'd taken hold of him and tried to wedge him into his own locker.

Now, there's a reason this sort of thing occurs primarily on 90s sitcoms: most people simply can't fit inside of a locker. Arthur, as short and skinny as he was, turned out to be no exception, but this only made things worse for him.

As Arthur later related to me, Paul and Vince laughed rowdily as they slammed him repeatedly into the metal frame. By the time they finally relented, Arthur had bruises all over his body.

There were other horrible acts, too. Other victims, other beatings. It dawned on me that this place had been an absolute hellhole. It's no wonder I – and Arthur, too – had gotten as far away from it as we could at the first opportunity.

The peculiar thing was that, in the years that had passed, I'd somehow forgotten all of this until just now. Instead, my recollections of high school were all happy, all positive. Had false memories of camaraderie and friendship drawn Arthur back as well?

Finally, I reached the third level. The overhead fluorescent light fixtures flickered sporadically, revealing, in brief spurts, dilapidated lockers, litter, and layers of dust and dirt that coated the floor.

I approached Mr. Minelli's classroom. Through the shaded hallway window, I could discern the outlines of roughly a dozen figures inside. I heard a voice, too. It was muffled and indistinct, but I could tell that the speaker was giving some kind of speech. She stopped, and a loud round of applause followed.

I reached for the door handle, unsure of what to expect. Hopefully, it would just be the people I'd driven four hours to see. But, after the events thus far, I half-expected the room to be empty. If so, I was jumping ship and going home.

To my surprise, just before I made contact with it, the door slowly opened on its own. The brightly-lit room before me was filled not with people, at least in the general understanding of the word. Rather, the still, bony forms before me resembled the kind of props a biology teacher might use to teach human anatomy.

The skeletons that stood silently throughout the room – that stood posed with drinks, that sat at desks, and that had assembled around a speaker - *had* to be props, right? Even though Mr. Minelli was a history teacher?

My mind searched desperately for some kind of explanation. This had to be an elaborate prank, right? Had Vince and Paul lured me, and maybe Arthur, too, out here just to freak us the fuck out? I wouldn't put it past them – it's precisely the kind of thing they'd do, even if the whole set-up, complete with an array of prop skeletons, was a bit extreme.

But, then, who was making all the noises I'd been hearing? Was that part of the prank, too?

*Fuck it,* I thought. If this was a big gag at my expense, then I'd just have to deal with the embarrassment later. I was getting out of there.

"*Zach,*" called a strained voice in the hallway.

"If this a joke, then it's not "

The voice interrupted me. "*Zach, help me, please!*" It was Arthur's voice, and it was coming from the hallway nearby.

He sounded like he was in serious trouble, so I hurried after him. Eventually, I found myself in a corner of the hallway – one where, if I remembered correctly, he and I used to have lockers. But, once again, I found myself alone.

I yelled out his name several times: "*Arthur! Arthur!*" It was no use. I appeared to be at a dead end.

That's when the locker next to me shook. I jumped back, surprised.

It was shut, but not locked. I gripped the handle and pulled it open.

Nothing could have prepared me for what I saw inside: it was Arthur's *torso*. The rest of his body was *gone*, and something was dragging what was left of him further away, further back into a dark abyss where the wall should have been.

Blood gurgled out of his mouth as he gasped my name one last time. He reached out a blood-covered hand. Hoping to somehow pull him out, I tried to take it, only for whatever unseen force had taken hold of him to pull him away, leaving behind a wide hole in the back of the locker. More blood gushed through it, leaking onto the hallway floor.

"*So glad you could make it,*" said a monotone voice behind me. I whirled around to see two fleshy arms emerge from another locker across from me. The skinless figure left wet, red stains on the white surface as she got to her feet and stepped towards me. "Don't you recognize your old crush? Surely ten years haven't been that rough on me."

"A-alice?" I stuttered as I retreated backwards.

At once, a series of loud noises rang out as the lockers around me violently burst open. Dozens of figures, all just as deteriorated as the one who stood before me, proceeded to crawl out of the narrow openings. Their faces were decrepit and sunken. To my horror, I realized that each of their eyes were locked squarely onto me.

My survival instincts kicked in. I sprinted away, my legs frantically carrying me towards the main staircase. All around me, figures emerged, reaching out to me as I passed by. Through an open door, I noticed that another classroom was filled with skeletons, just as Mr. Minelli's had been.

When I reached the main staircase, it was guarded by a tall, fleshy figure. "Don't you want to be with us?" it asked in a familiar, deep voice that I knew to be Paul's. "We can be complete. A full class. All of us, together again. Like old times."

He lurched for me. Just barely, I managed to dodge him, but I lost balance in the process. Before I knew it, I was tumbling down the stairs. Pain shot through me as I collided with step after step.

Finally, I landed on a level surface. Dizzily, I climbed to my feet and did my best to ignore the soreness that spread throughout my body.

A quick glance upwards confirmed that the bloody figures – the ones that *somehow* resembled my old classmates – were, indeed, heading towards me.

Meanwhile, the temperature inside was rising noticeably, and the walls around me were steadily changing in color from a dull gray to a deep red.

As I scrambled down the rest of the stairs and across the main corridor on the first floor, an intense tremor ran through the building, sending me sprawling to the ground. Despite a sharp pain that spread through my ankle, I hobbled as quickly as I could to the exit.

I didn't look back as I made my way across the parking lot to my car. I started the ignition, backed out, and headed towards the long road I'd used to get there.

In my rearview mirror, I chanced a glance back at the school. It was shaking violently, like it was being struck by an earthquake.

My car lurched in different directions as the ground underneath me also started to rumble. In an effort to avoid my car being sent off the road and into the neighboring fields, I frantically steered it to the center, between the lanes heading into and out of town.

When I looked back again, the school was, somehow, even *closer* to me than it had been before. How was that possible? Was it *following* me?

I floored the accelerator. Row after row of cornfield flew by me as I drove at the fastest speed of my life.

~

I was on the edge of town, close to the nearest interstate ramp, when local police pulled me over.

As the officer approached me, I stared into the rear view mirror. At the first glimpse of *whatever* it was that had chased after me, I'd hit the road again, law enforcement be damned. In truth, I hadn't seen my pursuer since I'd exited the cornfield a few minutes ago, but I hardly felt safe.

"Clocked you going nearly a hundred, son," said the officer.

I stayed silent. My baffled self was unsure of how to best handle the situation.

The officer gave me a quizzical look as he examined my ID and registration. "You're Don and Fran's son, aren't you? The one who left town?"

I nodded.

"Why'd you come back?"

"There was, uh, a ten-year reunion. For my graduating class."

He shook his head. "I doubt that." He looked down, then at my perplexed face. "*Where*, exactly, was this 'reunion'?"

"At the school," I said. I struggled to understand his reaction. What about my story didn't make sense? And, regardless, was I about to be booked for driving fifty miles over the speed limit? Is that something they throw you in jail for?

"Wait here," barked the officer. He went to his car where he proceeded to have a long conversation over his radio. After a few minutes, he returned to me. "Get out of here, son. Don't come back down here. Don't ever do nothin' like this again. You hear me?"

"Yeah, yeah, okay."

"Then scram," he ordered.

I obliged and began the long journey home.

~

I had no idea what to make of what occurred. I can hardly find anything at all online about Copper Hill High, or any of my classmates who went there, and I'm not exactly eager to reach out to any of them.

I can't make much sense of what happened, but I am sure of one thing: that I barely made it out of that situation, and that I shouldn't press my luck much further.

My ankle needs some more time to heal. Once it does, I'm going to try joining a social club and making new friends. After what happened to me in Copper Hill, I decided that the past is *not* a place where I need to dwell any longer.

Two weeks have passed since the reunion. Today, an envelope with no return address arrived with my mail. It contained a single photograph on glossy paper with a short note written underneath.

The photo featured me on the bench in the photo booth. Sitting to my side, with his arm over my shoulders, was Vince. He wore a blue collared shirt and looked...normal. No missing skin, no bloody imprints on the surface around him.

Paul crouched behind us, a dopey grin on his face. He, too, looked just as I'd imagined he would in his late twenties. To Paul's right, Abby, Morgan, and Michelle posed together with their arms around each other.

It was...a perfectly ordinary image – the exact kind of photo you'd expect to be taken at an event like that.

The handwritten caption underneath read, "*Although your visit was briefer than we preferred, we all had a splendid time catching up with you, Zach! Please feel free to come by anytime! Nobody truly leaves Copper Hill, after all. – Vince K__, Co-Chair, CHHS Reunion Planning Committee.*

*P.S.,* the note continued, *We are delighted that Arthur has finally joined us. Maybe you will, too, at our 20th.*

The writing up to this point was cursive font in traditional black ink. The last few words, however, were larger in size, messily scrawled, and colored a deep shade of red: *See you then, buddy, if not sooner.*

# 3

## STRAW MEN

It would be an exaggeration to say that I hate all other people. I like a few of them. Margaret, for example. I like Margaret.

But it's a fair statement that I value being alone. That's why I built my life around a job that doesn't require me to leave my crummy basement-level apartment. The bug problem inside of it is preferable to the human problem outside of it.

This is one of those abominable days when I'm required to venture into civilization. I've been dreading it for weeks.

My virtual co-worker Natalie has been insistent about my attendance at a fundraiser for her kid. Something about raising money for some research foundation. Blowing off her relentless emails and messages eventually got too tiring. I ran a mental cost-benefit analysis and determined that a brief appearance would amass me enough goodwill to get out of it next time.

As I exit my apartment building, I pass my fellow basement-dwellers' seasonal decorations. The wreath on the door of my immediate neighbor, a repairman named Brian, includes a ghost and a witch hat. A mat by the door to the adjacent apartment, in which a young couple and their small child reside, features black cats and a full moon.

The surrounding neighborhood is just as insufferable. I scowl at the displays of pumpkins and mock graveyards, skeletons, spider webs. It's all plastic, fake, straight-from Wal-Mart bullshit, and it's only going to get worse. As soon as November first rolls around, they'll replace this junk with equally obnoxious holiday decorations. I yearn for January.

As the highway takes me past the county line, I'm stopped by construction. A man in an orange vest halts me and waves for opposite traffic to go through the single open lane. Behind him, workers labor at the outskirts of a large pit. It's strikingly deep. From where I'm sitting, I can't even see the bottom of it.

The delay makes me late. When I reach the farm, its dirt lot is already packed with cars. I wedge my rusty sedan into a narrow space and climb outside.

A distant breeze sways crops and trees. The only other sounds I hear are those of birds and insects.

I reach the field. Balloons are tied to a sign that reads "Walk Against Diabetes". I shake my head. What does walking have to do with it? Couldn't they just have accepted my money without having to bring me all the way out here for *walking*?

I look around. The field ahead is littered with jack-o-lanterns, cornhole boards, bales of hay, some sort of pumpkin ring toss. Oh, and scarecrows. Lots of scarecrows. Whoever decorated this place went a little overboard with them. But where are the people?

A sign over a small tent reads "Registration". At a table inside, a figure obscured by shadows presides over several piles of paper.

I approach. "Hey there, can you help me-"

I freeze when I discern the straw hat and cloth face underneath it. The scarecrow wears blue overalls on a plaid shirt. Its face consists of a red nose, blue eyes, and a simple smile drawn with a single black, dotted line.

I don't smile back. Where *is* everybody? I want to at least sign in to the event.

"Hello?" I call. My voice fades into the empty ambience. I try again, this time shouting as loudly as I can, but no one responds.

I circle through the tents and the start of the one-mile course, but there's not a soul in sight.

I can't make any sense of it. Did everyone start walking, and then just keep going to some other location? Or was the event cancelled at the last moment, with me alone not finding out about it? But, if that were true, why is the parking lot so full?

On the way back to my car, I pass the registration tent again. To my surprise, the scarecrow is gone. "What the hell?" I mumble, perplexed and more than a bit spooked.

My pace increases to a jog. I'm eager to leave this place. There's something about it that just feels so off, so wrong. I pull out in my car and don't look back as I return to town.

I approach the construction site. This time, no one is around to direct traffic. There are no workers at all, in fact.

I could go, but I worry about a car approaching from the opposite side. I roll down my window. "Hey, is anyone there?" I ask.

Something catches my eye. Several bales of hay decorate the edge of the pit. They weren't there before. For a moment, a brown, jagged stick emerges from the hay, reaching out like an arm before receding out of view.

I resolve not to wait there any longer. I want to leave this cursed hole in the earth behind, just like the farm and its deserted fundraiser. I jolt the accelerator and zoom into the open lane.

As I drive, I check the rear view mirror. What I see sends my heart racing. In the back seat, directly behind me, is the thin smile of the scarecrow from the registration tent.

"Fucking hell!" I scream. My car skids at an angle as I slam on the breaks.

Sirens blare in front of me. Just my luck. The first car at the other end belongs to a cop.

The officer approaches. I stay still, resisting the temptation to look behind me. In my state of near-panic, I accidentally roll down one of my rear windows instead of my own. I rush to correct my mistake as the officer nears.

The officer leans down and asks me questions.

"Officer, in the back seat, there's...there's..." I realize that telling the truth wasn't going to help me. So, I come up with a slightly more plausible story. "I'm driving alone, but I looked in the mirror and saw someone in the back seat. I panicked."

The officer peers behind me. There's no one there, she insists.

"Not even something that might look like a person?" I croak. "Like a doll, or a scarecrow?"

She shakes her head, hands me a ticket, and informs me that I'll need to go to court to address it.

I thought about telling her everything else I'd seen – the desolate fundraiser, the stick reaching out of the hay – but I decide to cut my losses. I politely nod and tell her that I'll be more careful.

I examine my car upon parking it in my building's garage. Indeed, the back seat is unoccupied. Had I imagined seeing the scarecrow there? Am I losing my mind?

In my apartment, I take a long shower and start to unwind. I decide to keep the inexplicable things I'd seen to myself, at least for the time being. I have Margaret to prepare for.

I shave my face and put on my nicest set of clothes. I count out five fifty-dollar bills and place them in an envelope by the door.

Margaret's five minutes late. On another occasion, I'd argue over subtracting twenty dollars from what I owed her. Twenty-one, to be more precise. But, today, I'm just happy to see her face.

Margaret smiles and addresses me as her husband. She displays a cheap replica of the engagement ring I gave to Anne, and she wears an olive green dress like the one Anne had on when I proposed to her. Margaret doesn't mention the children I haven't seen in years. They aren't a part of the script.

The hour moves efficiently. We chat over a drink and then slowly make our way to the bedroom. We screw around. When it's over, I wrap my arms around her bare back and hold her tightly.

She asks me if something's on my mind. She says I seem a little wound up.

I start to tell her about the strange things I saw that morning. When I bring up the mysterious pit by the highway, she mentions that she heard something about it. She says that a friend of hers works at that site. Ever since his drilling operation tapped into some unknown substance deep underground, workers were disappearing without a trace.

"Do...do they know what the substance is?" I asked.

She bursts out laughing. She tells me that she really had me going.

I'm annoyed. But Anne's sense of humor was on the list of traits I'd given her to study. I can't hold it against her.

Margaret dresses and heads to the door. "See you next week," I tell her as she slips the envelope into her purse.

On Monday, I exchange chat message with Natalie. She tells me not to worry, that the participants had gathered around a hill at the end of the mile-long course for a group photo, but she appreciates the effort I made coming out there.

It doesn't make sense to me. I wasn't all *that* late. I should have seen *somebody*. But I let it go.

Work resumes. Groceries arrive at my front door. My apartment building is quiet. The tedium of daily routine settles my nerves. The weird events of the weekend fade from my mind.

Finally, the date on my ticket arrives. To my chagrin, I find that those obsessed with tacky Halloween props include whoever runs the general district court.

Fake cobweb lines the metal detector. The officers manning it direct me to the appropriate room.

I climb the central staircase. Posing throughout it are more of those damn scarecrows. I hate their smiling faces, their straw hats, and the big red buttons that match their small red noses.

I approach the courtroom. After a short wait, an officer calls the number on my ticket.

"Yes, that's me, officer," I say.

The officer instructs me on where to go. I open the two sets of doors and step into the courtroom. I approach the podium, paying little attention to the handful of people scattered throughout the public benches. My eyes raise to the judge.

I gasp when I finally get a look at him.

I recognize the beaming face of the figure before me. It's the same one – the same goddamn scarecrow that had climbed into my car the other day. Except, now, it has donned a black robe and sits before a gavel.

"Is this...are you..." I stutter, dumbfounded. I look to the prosecutor's table, where two scarecrows sit in suits. I look behind me, and realize that the rest of the audience is no different. I'm the only human in the entire fucking room.

I storm out. I spot the officer who'd let me in and call out for him. When he doesn't respond, I tap his left shoulder.

I jump back as his left arm detaches. Tightly-wound straw spills out of his empty sleeve and hits the floor with a soft thud.

I back up. I need to leave.

The figure moves. It kneels, picks up the detached arm, and sticks it back in place. Then, it turns towards me, continuing to display the same, sick expression of perpetual bliss.

A stumble sends me toppling down the first set of stairs. I bang my head. My body aches as I climb back to my feet and run down to the lobby, where I find the metal detector manned by two scarecrows dressed in police uniforms. Their heads tilt slightly in my direction as I sprint to the exit.

There is almost no traffic as I drive back to my apartment. Halloween is today; yet, I spot no kids or parents in the early evening light. All I see are scarecrows, everywhere, of all shapes and sizes. They appear still, silent, content.

In the apartment garage, an elderly man hobbles over to me. He's the first human I've seen since leaving the courthouse. He points to a red bruise on my temple and tells me that I'm not one of them. He tells me not to trust anyone, not even him.

I leave him behind as I scramble down the basement hallway. The door to the building elevator opens, revealing three scarecrows – a man, a woman, and a small child standing between them.

I pass Brian's apartment. I look through the open door. Inside, two figures are engaged in a scuffle.

A scarecrow has Brian pressed against the wall. His panicked eyes turn towards me as he attempts, futilely, to pull the scarecrow's hand off of his neck. With its other hand, the scarecrow pries open Brian's mouth.

The thin line that forms the scarecrow's smile expands until its mouth is a gaping hole that covers most of its face. Brian makes a muffled scream as straw shoots out of the scarecrow's mouth into his own. He gags and chokes.

The straw pours down Brian's throat. It fills his body until it bursts through his skin. As a layer of straw spreads over Brian, transforming his appearance, the scarecrow turns towards me.

I shut the door to my room and bolt it behind me. In the crack beneath the door, shadows of legs approach. The door jostles and the handle shakes. Then the shadows depart.

I don't know what to do. After what I saw at the court building, I'm not eager to contact the authorities.

A familiar voice calls for me from outside. I check my phone to confirm that it is the correct date and time.

I look through the peephole. To my relief, it's Margaret, with no straw hat to be found on her. I usher her in.

She asks me what's wrong when I frantically lock the door. "I'm just so happy to see you, Margaret," I reply. "You're the only thing that seems real to me."

She looks at me strangely. I'm not supposed to call her by her real name. She asks for some wine. Anne loved wine, after all. That trait was in the materials I'd provided to Margaret.

I give her a glass. She lifts it. I put my hand around hers as I pour. I think about recent events. About how everything around me is falling apart.

Yet, amidst all of that, here is Margaret, showing up at her scheduled time to pretend to be the wife who'd stormed out of our marriage years ago. Who'd taken away my kids. Who'd told me I had no heart, no soul. Who'd said I was as dull and ugly and lifeless as a-

The glass shatters. Margaret shrieks. I'd been gripping it too hard, and several fragments had torn into Margaret's hand.

I apologize profusely. When I bring her a set of bandages, she opens her hand to reveal a long gash that extends across her palm.

But no blood emerges from the wound – just the ends of thin, golden pieces of straw.

4

___

# MUCK

As I finally reached the incline's peak, the rising morning sun illuminated before me the rubble that was once the prosperous town of Grey Valley. I shook off the insecurity that ran through me as a young woman traveling alone, reassuring myself that I would be in Daniel's company in only a few minutes.

The trip to my birthplace had been uneventful, except when the bus driver stopped me as she dropped me off at a stop a half-mile up the road. It had been a relaxing drive until then. The lush countryside had lulled me into a shallow sleep for much of the seven hour ride through the night. But when the driver halted me upon my exit, her words alarmed me.

"If you're heading to Grey Valley, I want you to take this," she had said, holding out a slip of paper. "If anything goes wrong, call the number on it." Though I felt puzzled, I took it from her. "I've dropped off many people here," she continued. "But I never pick any of them back up again."

As I hopped down, the driver spoke one more time. "If you want to leave Grey Valley, just remember one thing. Use a payphone." After that, the bus drove off.

I mulled her words as the mile-walk took me up the hill and then down to the town beyond it. What was it that she thought would go wrong? And why would I want to use a payphone, when my mobile still had good service?

The town's deterioration that had been apparent from a distance only became clearer as I approached its outskirts. Grey Valley consisted of a half-dozen streets lined with small houses arranged around a city hall, church, and courthouse. The church was dilapidated. Its roof had caved-in. A large clock attached to its steeple appeared permanently stuck at 12:15. Much of the front wall of the courthouse across the street had collapsed, leaving behind piles of brick and cement rubble.

In the distance beyond stood a rusted warehouse-like structure out of which stuck four tall smokestacks. A fifth lay collapsed across the roof. Weeds and overgrowth covered its brittle base. A tall, broken wall that extended from the warehouse confirmed that I was examining the tattered remnants of the old processing plant.

As I walked down the first residential street, looking for my brother's address, I began to wonder how he had even survived here for the last year. The windows of the only grocery store I passed were firmly boarded-up. It dawned on me that not only had I not encountered any cars along the road, but I had also not yet seen a single other person at all.

I knew Grey Valley had recently experienced its second significant drop in population, but I hadn't expected it to have transformed into an outright ghost town. Daniel had described it in glowing terms to me growing up, insisting that I someday visit this wonderful little borough.

And here I was, and Grey Valley was nothing like my brother had described.

I wasn't shocked. Though I still loved him, I had long given up on putting much faith in his words. My warm memories of him, seven years my elder, teaching me how to read and tie my shoes had drifted away with time to be replaced by the unpleasant reality of his recent life trajectory. In one of my dreams on the bus, his once healthy and strong body deteriorated before me until sickly red bumps covered his face until it melted away entirely.

While I had been off attending college, Daniel's health had steadily declined. He got little sympathy from our dad because, in dad's view, Daniel's problems were entirely self-inflicted.

I was more sympathetic. Opioids often came prescribed by credible doctors. Their use carried few of the stigmas that accompanied the substances society had trained itself to consider more dangerous, and their addictive qualities emerged forcefully and quickly.

In Daniel's case, they caused his life to spiral out of control. He lost his job and his ability to pay rent. When he moved in with dad, dad forced him to attend an intervention program. This seemed to help at first, but Daniel's addiction re-emerged.

Then, one day, Daniel left. For the past few months, we had only heard from him twice through letters mailed without return addresses.

A week ago, I found a message on my phone from an unknown number. When I played it, I recognized Daniel's voice, its once cheery timbre now accompanied by a gravely roughness. "Hey sis, it's me. I know you haven't heard from me in a while. I miss you. I want you to come visit me. I know you don't have a car but the Greyhound line stops close to here. I'm at 105 Patrick Street in Grey Valley. Right where we grow up. If you can make it here in a week, I would love to see you. Please make sure to get here before Saturday afternoon. Come alone and don't tell dad. Love you as always." He didn't answer when I tried calling back.

I made the trip because I loved my brother and because I needed answers. I wanted to know that Daniel was safe and not about to die of an overdose. He had trusted me, alone, with this information, and I wanted to be the best sister I could be by living up to that trust. So, I followed his instructions and booked bus tickets without informing dad.

Silence permeated the still air throughout the town. No birds chirped and no engines rumbled. As I passed a road leading to the church, I noticed an old, fully-enclosed phone booth, the type the alter egos of superheroes would run into, across the street from it. A jagged dent marked the dirty glass that lined it.

I checked my smartphone's map app. Realizing I had been walking in the wrong direction, I doubled back.

I passed the derelict general store again, but the boards that I remembered covering the windows were now absent. Looking inside, I saw a smiling man in an apron standing by a cash register bundling up groceries for an elderly woman. I could hear the murmurs of friendly chit-chat between them. Excited to have at last seen another person, I swung open the door.

Inside, though, all I saw were empty aisles and piles of trash. The man and the woman were gone, as were the sounds of their voices. "Hello?" I asked, to no avail. Where were they? When I closed the door, the building was back to how I had originally seen it – run-down and shuttered.

Something was obviously off about this empty town. Its ominous aura cast an inescapable sense of lonely desperation. I kept hearing distant voices and footsteps, but I could never locate the people responsible for them. Spooked, I doubled my pace towards my destination on Patrick Street. The neglected front yards of the homes that lined it were full of weeds, overgrown grass, and, in one case, misshapen children's toys. Aside from a shadow I spotted moving inside one of the homes, everything seemed abandoned.

Finally, I made it to 105. Before me stood a compact two-story cottage. I shuddered at its chipped paint and broken windows, and I gasped when a ghoulish face peered back at me through a gap in the glass.

"Sis!" called out my brother. His word was followed by profuse coughing. A moment later, he hobbled out the front door. He looked terrible. His face was sweaty and his pupils were shrunken and constricted. He had clearly lost weight.

"I knew you'd come!" he said. He coughed violently again. "You're just on time."

"Daniel, you look like you need to see a doctor," I said, deeply concerned by his appearance. "What happened? Are you sick? If your car is still operational, I can drive you to the nearest hospital."

"No-no..." he stuttered. "Sis, just listen to me. It's all going to be okay." He took my hand and led me back to the street. Perplexed, I followed. "This house," he said, turning to look at it again, "You don't remember it at all, do you?"

I shook my head while worrying about Daniel's mental state. Daniel seemed to be experiencing a breakdown. How long had he been like this?

"But I do, of course," he said. "This town, it was magnificent. A real beauty. I remember mom walking me to church from here. I remember the night when she brought you back from the hospital. I picked you up and held you. It was so perfect. I wish you remembered living here, too, but I know you were too young."

It was true. I only knew mom from pictures. I left Grey Valley at age three. Daniel and dad left with me. But not mom.

"Sis," he said, looking at me and changing his tone. "What if we could have that back? What if we could go back to a life before..." he shook his head, and then yelled for me to watch out.

The sound of a loud engine suddenly rang close. I jumped onto the lawn as an old car sped by. I thanked Daniel for warning me and remarked that I wasn't being as careful as usual because I hadn't seen anyone else on the road until just now.

"I had several neighbors when I arrived," said Daniel. "But..." His voice trailed off.

"I've been almost all alone for months now. But I'm not alone today. And I'm not just referring to you being here, sis."

I noticed that in the last few minutes, the whole street around us had become less post-apocalyptic. The lawns were somehow not as overgrown, and at the end of the street, a little girl now rode in circles on a tiny bicycle in the yard that had been littered with children's toys.

Daniel took my hand again and started leading me down the road.

"What's going on?" I asked. "Nothing here makes any sense."

He ignored me. "We have to get to Main Street, fast."

"Why?"

"The parade is almost there!"

What parade? Is that where everyone in this town had been? Or was my brother delusional? "Daniel, we don't have time to watch a parade. You seem extremely sick. You aren't trying to withdraw cold turkey again, are you?"

Daniel ignored me and, letting go of my hand, walked off toward the town center with the church and the courthouse. In the distance ahead of him, I noticed that the factory was churning out black gas from five well-conditioned smokestacks, and the once-tattered wall extending from it now appeared intact.

Not knowing what else to do, I ran after my brother.

"I knew you'd follow," he said with a slight smirk.

"Daniel, what's going on?" I felt impatient and overwhelmed by confusion.

"We're almost there!"

The town's main intersection lay before us. A crowd of people lined the streets. Where had they come from, and why had I not seen them before?

Daniel leaned against the side of the church, balancing himself enough against it to stand upright. I joined him there. We were a few yards behind the rows of people lining the street. Daniel's face seemed sickly and faintly green. I got the impression he was fighting nausea.

"There it is," he said, steadying himself enough to point. In the distance, on the far side of town, was a marching band, followed by a small array of decorated platforms. "I've always wanted to see it," he said. He took in a deep breath and now seemed more relaxed. "We have a few minutes. I can answer your questions now, sis."

I had many, but I was also frustrated that he had no questions for me. My brother used to be so affectionate. But now, whatever was happening seemed to be all about him, even though I had traveled over two hundred miles to get here. "Daniel, I just want to know if you're okay."

"Do I look okay? Of course not. I'm miserable."

"Have you stopped using?"

"Nope," he said. "I drive a few towns over to get what I need every couple weekends. But I ran out last night. Of money, too. It's not fun running out, Laura. But it's all going to be alright, soon. It's all going to be alright."

"Why do you say that?" Nothing seemed alright. This was the worst-case scenario.

"It's not just any parade," said Daniel. "It's the 1994 Grey Valley Town Parade."

This startled me. "That's impossible. And not funny," I said. Daniel didn't respond.

The crowd cheered louder as the parade got closer. I noticed that the rubble across the street had disappeared. The Courthouse now appeared undamaged. Its steps were lined with the happy faces of formally-dressed men and women.

"What do you know about the great muck flood of 1994?" asked Daniel. He glanced at the clock above us. It was functioning now, and it read 12:10.

"Don't ask me a question like that," I said. I'd grown up hearing about it. It was one of the worst chemical dam collapses in history, and it happened in the middle of the Grey Valley annual parade. More deaths resulted from it than in Saltville a few hours away. More deaths than in Cariboo, British Columbia, or Mariana, Brazil. I didn't remember it, but it had forever impacted my life. "Of course I know how mom died," I muttered.

Daniel shook his head. "You know when she died, but you don't really know how. It was painful, Laura. Drowning and disintegrating at the same time. It's a horrible thing."

"Shut up," I said. "Don't talk like that, Daniel. I don't want to think about what she went through."

"She was one of thirty-four deaths. But the number was originally only thirty. Why do you think that is, sis?"

"That's crazy," I said.

"Don't be so defensive," he told me. "It didn't directly impact you.

You were unhurt, as were dad and I, because we stayed in the second floor of our house. The waste was never high enough to reach us. But mom wasn't so lucky. Do you want me to show you where she is?"

My face grew red. "What the hell are you saying, Daniel?" I asked. As far as I knew, what was left of her was six feet under in a graveyard on the other end of town.

"Something so terrible, so awful as what happened here in 1994 - it, it makes a mark," said Daniel.

"A 'mark'?" I repeated, skeptically.

"Agony like that doesn't always just disappear into time. It can make a stain that never goes away for those who died. I saw it when I arrived here. The way this town, on the anniversary of the disaster, slowly comes back to life throughout the morning. I hid from it in the second story of the home I grew up in, just like I did thirty years ago. And I saw, at 12:15, the disaster unfold again, all around me. Well, I'm not hiding anymore, sis. Not this time."

The parade was almost upon us. The cheering and music got louder as it approached.

I felt a deep tremble in the ground. At first, I thought that the marching band and the cars behind them were causing it. But, this parade was far too small to cause tremors as significant as the ones I was feeling.

"We're going to join this town, sis. We're going to leave this world behind and get a second chance at the one that was taken from us. I watched two people do it last time. Over the past year, I've sensed them as part of this town. I've heard their voices in the distance. And here they are today, cheering for the parade."

I started to tremble. What my brother was saying, and what I was seeing...it wasn't possible. The events before me matched what had happened that day. If I was stuck in a bizarre reenactment, it was a convincing one. But, of course, no one would go to the middle of nowhere to reenact such a horrible disaster. Somehow, this had to be real. Which meant that we faced real danger.

Daniel feebly reached out his arm and pointed across the street. "And there she is," he said. "In the striped orange dress, waiving." I instantly recognized her. Daniel and I had both inherited her soft brown eyes and low cheekbones, as I had learned from seeing her in pictures. I grew dizzy and nearly lost my balance as the rumblings inside and outside of me grew more intense. Now I was the one trying not to vomit.

Around me, I noticed the concerned faces of people lining the streets as they noticed the tremors. My mother grabbed onto a street lamp. The band's music fell apart as the marchers started to stumble.

I heard the loud echo of distant concrete crumbling and breaking apart. I knew what was happening, what the mild earthquake was doing to the poorly-designed dam that contained the waste produced by the local mining industry. Daniel took my hand again, holding it tight. "Be brave, sis. We can join them, too. Soon, everything will be different. I wanted you here with me. We can go through this together."

"Let me go!" I shrieked, yanking my hand away. In the distance, I saw the center of the concrete wall collapse as an endless stream of thick red liquid rushed into the town. Within moments, the outskirts of a tsunami of acidic toxic waste consumed the outskirts of Grey Valley.

I turned to run. I knew what was going to happen. Maybe if I ran as fast as I could,

I could save myself. But I knew that wouldn't work. Not with mere seconds before the waste swept me away.

"Don't bother running," said Daniel, reading my mind. "It's too late for that. Stay here with me. Please."

Then I remembered the phone booth. It was just across the street. If I was seeing it now and it had also been intact in the present, then perhaps...

Before I could get far, I felt Daniel grab me around my waist. "No!" he shrieked. "You are supposed to be here with me! With your brother!"

I watched as the cascading wall of blood-red liquid engulfed the rear of the parade. People screamed and ran in futile efforts to save their lives.

I turned to my brother, tears filling my eyes. He wasn't the man I thought he was.

I hated him like I never had before. "Let me go!" I yelled. I tried to pull his arms apart, but even in his weakened state, I couldn't muster the strength. I lowered my head and bit as hard as I could into him, but even as I felt blood on my teeth, he refused to let me go.

The band was gone, now, and the waste was only a block away from engulfing us. "Daniel," I said. I stopped fighting him. He looked up at me, his expression at first one of anger but then one of sorrow. "Please," I whispered.

He looked down."My own sister, abandoning me too..." he muttered to himself. He released me.

I didn't bother responding to his pathetic self-pity. Instead, I sprinted through the crowd of panicking people and hopped into the enclosed phone booth. The moment I shut the door, liquid swept through the area where I had been standing. I felt a sharp burn in my foot as the red acid ran across the ground. The bottom of the booth was not perfectly sealed. I grabbed the top of the heavy mechanism holding the phone and pulled my feet off the ground. Luckily, it supported my weight and allowed my feet to dangle a few inches above the surface. I panicked as the water level beneath me slowly rose as more of the crimson gunk leaked inside.

I looked out the clear glass window and saw that my booth was immersed almost to its top in a sea of the vile substance. I heard screams and howls of pain, followed by a 'bump' sound as the body of the man I had seen working at the general store floated into the booth. His apron and the skin underneath it had begun to disintegrate in the water, leaving behind a disgusting, fleshy residue. Then, a second figure, grotesquely deformed, slammed into the glass before me, damaging it but not breaking it. I glimpsed a striped orange dress on its boiling pink body and shut my eyes, not opening them again until the nightmarish noises around me had died down. The thunderous sound of swirling liquid reached a fever pitch and then died down as the water level finally decreased.

When I opened my eyes, I found myself in total silence in the middle of an empty ghost town once again. Everything looked as it had when I arrived that morning. When I dropped to the ground, I landed on old concrete rather than acidic liquid. Yet, patches of my shoes and socks had been eaten away, and the bottom of my feet stung with each step. Daniel was gone.

I dialed the number I had been given. The bus driver told me she would pick me up as soon as she could get there. Hysterically, I began to explain what I had witnessed, but she cut me off and just told me to wait. I gave her the only address I could think of.

I ran past a historical marker commemorating the thirty-five victims of the tragedy and headed to our old family home. When I arrived, it at first looked abandoned. But as I approached, I saw movement within the windows lining the kitchen. Peering in, I witnessed a young woman with soft brown eyes and low cheekbones carrying a tray of food to a blissful boy.

My heart fluttered as I pushed open the front door and ran to the kitchen. But the kitchen was unoccupied. All I found in it was a pile of empty pill bottles on a dusty counter.

**5**

———————

# BLOOD MONEY

The ad on the utility pole promises sixty dollars for two hours of filming. Eager for some beer money, I leave a voicemail at the listed number.

A response soon arrives by text: "*Meet tomorrow at East River Park, by the main entrance. 3:30 p.m.*"

At the designated time, a blond-haired boy approaches me where I wait. He looks to be twelve or thirteen. He wears a blue baseball cap and carries a shovel. He gestures at my camera.

"Start recording, and keep me in the image. Okay?"

Before I can respond, he hops off the concrete path and darts into the woods.

I hit 'record' and scramble after him. He moves quickly, with no regard for trails.

Eventually, he stops at a patch of dirt between two trees, where he digs furiously.

I ask him all sorts of questions: if his parents know he's here, why he's having me film him, and what he's trying to find. He ignores me.

After several minutes, he steps back and wipes sweat from his brow. He gives me a distraught look. "It's not here."

"*What's* not here?"

"Just keep up, okay?" I follow as he heads deeper into the woods.

Eventually, we arrive in a clearing by a moss-covered stump. Again, he digs. And again, he shakes his head before speeding off to a new location.

The process repeats itself several times. Eventually, I threaten to leave if he doesn't answer my questions.

This gets his attention. "Just one more try. Then I'll pay you and you can go."

"Fine," I mutter, even as I continue to feel uneasy about the situation.

I observe him through the camera as he digs several feet from a tall oak tree. "It's here!" he yells, excitedly. He shovels until the hole looks over a foot deep.

He motions for me to film the inside of the small pit. I zoom in on a clear plastic sheet. Adjusting the focus, I discern within it a sight that shocks me: a short, heavily-decomposed corpse in a tattered blue baseball cap.

I freeze as the boy reaches into the corpse's pants pocket. A flip phone with a partially-shattered screen spills onto the dirt as he removes three twenty-dollar bills covered in stains of deep crimson.

He holds them out to me. "Your payment."

He proceeds to cackle loudly as a mixture of blood and foamy drool runs down his chin. I still hear his manic laughter as I sprint away, leaving him and the money behind.

When I calm down enough to view the footage, it contains no holes, no shovel, no teenage boy, and the sound of no voice but my own.

**6**

---

# TRANSFORMATIONS

Chances are, you've heard Andy Warhol's statement that, "Everyone will be famous for 15 minutes." But, you may not know that it was a photographer who first used the expression in a photo shoot with Warhol. Yes, Warhol made it iconic, but the photographer gave him the idea. And the photographer wasn't the first one to come up with it. Centuries ago, the phrase "Nine days' wonder" encapsulated the same concept, though the people who said it back then had a slightly more optimistic length of time in mind.

I take a couple lessons from this. First, there's nothing wrong with using someone else's idea as a basis for your own. Transformation isn't stealing, after all. Second, Warhol and his photographer both defied the statement they made famous - certainly, their fame lasted longer than fifteen minutes, or even nine days.

I tell myself this during the restless periods I spend checking my phone for a call from my agent or an email from a potential customer asking to hire me for a gig. By any account, my own fifteen minutes of fame are past. Yet, I dream of the spotlight shining on me again.

You see, I starred in a kids television show for three years called *Lucian and the Lilicrank*. It's a show that little kids love. Each episode would consist of me, wearing a goofy black hat, an orange shirt, and a ridiculous dark purple cape, going on adventures with a computer-generated creature. I was Lucian and the creature was Lilicrank. My character existed to connect the audience to the show through a human protagonist, and I was chosen for the role because of my youthful face and my uncanny ability to maintain a jolly demeanor throughout grueling 15-hour shoots.

Lilicrank resembled a sheep, but had wings that allowed her to fly around like a dragon. She looked fearsome enough to be cool while also retaining a sense of gentleness and cuteness. She could breathe fire, but only did so for peaceful purposes, like melting ice in order to free a friendly baby elephant that fell underneath a frozen lake.

Anyway, Lilicrank would fly me around as we solved mysteries, visited magical kingdoms, and interacted with guest stars, all while teaching lessons to kids. At one point early in each episode, I would receive news that Lilicrank was needed somewhere, so I would call out for her, chanting, "The danger is real, this is not a prank! We need your help, Lilicrank!" She wouldn't appear at first, so I'd turn to the camera and request the audience to sing along, and only then would she actually appear.

Of course, this made for a sad spectacle in studio. I'd beg the camera to sing along and, even though nothing was happening, I'd pretend like an audience had spoken up with sufficient volume. Worse, naturally, no dragon would actually appear on set – Lilicrank would only be added much later in the production process, and I had to perform my character around several tennis balls arranged in front of a blue screen. But, as our ratings indicated, hundreds of thousands of kids were following my instructions and were swept away by the appeal of me and the friendly dragon-sheep.

I loved seeing the reaction of our fans when I made public appearances promoting the show. Nothing brought joy to my soul quite like seeing the eyes of children light up when they recognized me in my costume.

I won't hide that the show borrowed heavily from other works like Harry Potter and Dora the Explorer. But the kids didn't know that, not yet at least. For three years, they loved it. *Lucian and the Lilicrank* was such a hit that plush toys of Lilicrank and other merchandise regularly sold out around the holidays.

But, I could always sense such success would be short-lived. Before long, the kids had moved on. The original audience had grown up and started to enjoy the books and movies from which we'd borrowed ideas, and the next generation of preschoolers had found fresher, newer shows to watch.

Worse, even though *Lucian and Lilicrank* was cancelled four years ago, I was forever pegged as "the guy from that kids' show." Nobody else in the industry wanted to hire me, because they knew – correctly – that audiences would only associate me with that one character I had once played.

At first, I found plenty of gigs performing at rich kids' birthday parties. I charged a high rate and pretended that I was barely able to fit the appearance into my schedule. I even had the funds to put together a prop blow-up Lilicrank that, with proper setup, could float briefly in the air, open its mouth, and appear to make some of its signature sounds with the help of a hidden stereo system. I'd put on a short sketch using a few props and then just interact with the kids, telling some jokes and doing so amateurish magic tricks that appeared vaguely reminiscent of special effects on the show.

The kids often loved it, but the whole ordeal felt ridiculous, even embarrassing to me. To make matters worse, on a few occasions, parents had hired me for parties for kids who they hadn't realized no longer liked the show, and the kids proceeded to pelt me with birthday cake and anything else at their disposal. But, having failed to find any acting success elsewhere, I needed the money, so I kept accepting whatever work I could find.

I bring up all this backstory to explain what my life was like when I got a particular offer, one that raised red flags that would have caused anyone else to turn it down.

The email arrived on a Sunday morning and asked for my services the next evening. This was a bit odd, as most of my performances took place on weekend mornings or afternoons, and most offers were made well in advance of the date of performance, but I took little notice. The writer, who did not include his or her name, offered me $5,000 for one of my live appearances at a house with a zip code that I vaguely recognized as being within a nice part of a suburb about an hour south of me.

The mention of $5,000 for one performance obviously caught my eye. I usually only charged a couple hundred. Excitedly, I responded right away with my usual pretensions about having a busy schedule but, luckily, being able to work this appearance in due to a recent cancellation. I asked how I would be paid, if there would be a good power source or if I needed to bring my portable generator, and how long my act should be.

I got a response less than a minute later that read simply, "Cash. We will provide what you need. As long as necessary. Arrive at 8 pm." I asked a couple follow up questions but received no further response.

This was obviously not how the booking process usually worked. But ever since I dropped to being only one of dozens of clients to my agent, I've had to improvise. Still, it was odd being paid such a high amount in cash, and odder still to be appearing relatively late on a weeknight.

Look, I get that going to a house alone at night is something no smart person should do, and the unusually large promised payment only raised additional suspicions. I thought about whether this was some elaborate plot to rob or kidnap me. But the location was in a safe part of town, and I wanted both the money and the reinforcement of the sense that I deserved it, so I spent Monday afternoon gathering my costume and props and drove out in the early evening.

As my GPS brought me to a pristine residential neighborhood, I saw familiar sights of parents walking their dogs and kids played basketball in the streets. My GPS guided me through several turns, until I was driving up a heavily wooded hill to another branch of the suburb. Finally, I saw the street I was looking for: "Peakview Drive". The road took me slightly downhill, to a flat, elevated area with seven or eight additional houses arranged in a loop.

Above the tree line, the descending sun left a vibrant red sky. The homes here were similar to the ones below, but a strange stillness gripped the cul-de-sac they surrounded. I parked my car in front of the address I'd been given, and when I got out, I took note of a general silence abated only by the whispers of a distant breeze. There were no parents, children, or pets, and certainly no idyllic white picket fences. The houses had undecorated exteriors and empty front yards.

A missing cat poster added to the gloomy setting that started to put me in an ominous mood. I knew I had to fight against that. I was about to put on an act that required me to be earnest and enthusiastic, while wearing laughable clothes and interacting with cheap props. This appearance would be like most, I told myself, with gawking kids circled around me and entertained by my performance.

A white van then approached from the same direction I had taken and parked behind me. Oh great, I thought to myself, my kidnapper has arrived.

Instead, a short, thin woman in a faded blue uniform stepped out. Her van showed that she was a plumber, and she carried an appropriate tool kit.

"You live here?" she smirked, looking me over.

"No," I said. "I'm just here as a hired performer, I assume for some kid's party."

"That explains the outfit," she said, laughing.

I tried not to act offended. "Yes, I suppose I look a bit silly, especially if you've never seen the sh-"

She cut me off. "Got a call from the city to check out a potential water leak here," she said. "I've been running around doing jobs all day. Hopefully this one won't take too long and I can get back home at a decent hour." She trudged past me and walked up to the front door.

I finished putting on my costume, forced a cheery smile onto my face, and, carrying a large box full of props, followed her path. The colonial style house before me seemed innocuous enough. It was plainly designed and no different from the homes I'd passed on my way up. On the second floor, several large windows jutted out. I saw odd specks of light in one, but when I squinted to look more closely, its blinds abruptly tightened.

A bit perturbed, I knocked on the door, and a woman opened it only a moment later. She was as tall as me and maybe in her mid-forties. Her sandy hair was slicked back, and she had clear green eyes.

"Lucian at your service, man!" I called out, grinning. "If you can direct me to the right location, I can start setting up!"

"Come in," she said in a monotone voice. "Call me Stacy." I instantly got a sadly familiar feeling that a parent who hated the show had hired me. I only hoped that she was correct that the kids I'd be performing for actually liked it.

As I stepped inside a hallway, I saw a staircase to a basement that the plumber had begun to descend. "Good luck, magic man!" she said, winking and twirling a ring of keys Stacy must have given her as she walked out of sight.

"A most unpleasant surprise," Stacy said as she motioned me toward a door at the end of the hallway.

"The plumber?" I asked. "She said the city reported a leak. It's probably a good thing she's here to fix it."

Stacy didn't respond or even look in my direction. We passed a compact, clean-looking kitchen as we continued down a long, wood-lined corridor.

"Your email didn't give me a lot of details," I said, "and I was hoping you could answer a few quest-"

She interrupted as she opened the door. "Set up on the stage. We will come when you are ready."

Before me was an elevated platform surrounded by several rows of surprisingly fancy seats arranged into neat rows like they were in a theatre. I hadn't imagined that this house could contain a formal auditorium like this. How many kids were going to be here? It looked like there was enough seating for several dozen at least.

I heard the door close behind me, and noticed that Stacy was gone.

This all made me feel odd and uncomfortable. Stacy had been

cold and uninterested in me or my questions. Usually, there were dozens of children noisily running around any home or backyard where I was about to perform. But, today, I hadn't seen anyone aside from Stacy and the plumber. The whole house had been totally silent since I arrived. And it isn't exactly common for a house to contain a room this large. I wondered, too, in what sort of situation would enough kids attend to fill it up on a Monday night? Maybe this neighborhood had some kind of regular event for youths?

But I was already here, an hour from home and with my costume and gear, so I decided to go ahead with the performance. No matter how badly things went, I would drive off five thousand dollars richer, and that was all the motivation I needed.

I set up the Lilicrank props – both the blowup version that could make sounds and the plush version I would let the kids pass around at the end – and the speaker system that included music and sound effects to which I would sync the physical performance.

The last thing I needed to do was plug the speaker system into a power outlet, but the only remaining outlet near the stage was in an awkward position behind a wooden table. I had to lie down, crawl under the table, and carefully plug the cord into a socket. As I was doing this, the light around me flickered and then began fading. By the time I stood up, everything around me was pitch black.

My eyes slowly adjusted to the darkness, and I started to discern lights in the distance. My heart trembled at the site before me. Dozens of pairs of striking, luminescent green eyes lit up where the seats should be located. It was like...being watched by the glowing eyes of animals, eyes that never blinked.

Suddenly, the green eyes faded out of my vision as a blinding bright light enveloped the stage. My own eyes had to readjust, and once they did, I found myself in the position of a performer on stage at a far more formal occasion than that to which I was accustomed. I could see the stage well, but the audience and their terrifying eyes were shrouded in darkness.

Stacy stepped forward, her face still blank. Her green eyes caught my attention more than they did before. "Start," she said.

I panicked. Everything around me felt so wrong. What was going on? What children having glowing eyes, and why were they all the same color? My mind ran through excuses I could say to leave, money be damned. I could claim I felt sick, or even that I had stage fright. Whatever it took, I wanted to get out of that house.

"Now," Stacy said, with frightening firmness.

Behind her, I could see the green eyes emerging again from the darkness. They cast a stronger color than before. They were, somehow, getting brighter and, seemingly, angrier.

"I said now!" stammered Stacy, in a louder, yet still emotionally empty, voice.

The dozens of eyes now transitioned from green to a hot, fiery orange. I developed a strong sense that an undesirable outcome awaited me if I failed to perform. I delved within myself for the earnest spirit that landed me the job on the show, and, mustering all the strength within me, put on a smile and started my routine.

As soon as I started playing my character, the luminescent eyes faded from orange to green, and then they receded again into the darkness.

For the first few minutes of lighthearted jokes and magic tricks, I heard no response from the audience. Aside from Stacy, who sat close by and half-illuminated by the stage light, I felt like I was performing to a totally empty room. Finally, it came time for me to call in Lilicrank. I yelled out the key phrase, "The danger is real, this is not a prank! I need your help, Lilicrank!"

I then looked at the audience and asked for them to chant the rhyme with me. Usually, the kids enjoyed this part of the act and enthusiastically joined in. I was not surprised, however, when my call was met with total silence. Without a single voice joining me, I wasn't at all sure what to do or how to proceed. I froze.

A moment passed.

"Continue," said Stacy, unsympathetically.

I sensed unease in the eerily silent room. Behind Stacy, I saw the rows of eyes light up once more.

"Continue!" Stacy said.

I swallowed. Taking a deep breath, I whispered to her, "They have to repeat the rhyme with me."

Stacy looked surprised. "Repeat the rhyme?"

"Yes," I said. Hadn't they seen the show?

"Oh. Wait one moment," she said. She left my line of sight and entered the endless dark void that surrounded me. I felt sweat drip down my face.

More and more sets of green eyes appeared, all over the room. Instead of dozens, there now seemed to be hundreds, yet I could hear no noise aside from the throbbing of my heart.

Stacy returned to her seat. "Do it again," she said. "Say it, then ask them to join in."

My eyes grew wide in disbelief. What was happening? What Stacy doing in the darkness? And how long did this have to go on?

"The danger is real, this is not a prank! I need your help, Lilicrank!" I whimpered. Then, I again instructed the audience to join me.

A deafening wave of sound followed, as the echoing sound of a hundred voices hollered back: "The danger is real, this is not a prank! I need your help, Lilicrank!" They spoke mechanically and in perfect unison. The utter joylessness of their collective voice disturbed me – it obviously sounded nothing like discordant voices of young fans of the show that I was used to hearing.

I proceeded, tugging at a string I had set up and causing the inflatable Lilicrank prop to float on stage. Normally the little kids would laugh in delight at this but, naturally, all that greeted it now was uninterrupted silence. I felt painfully self-conscious.

I told a corny joke as the prop slowly approached the stage, commenting on how Lilicrank was keeping me waiting too long by "dragon-ing" her feet. "Normally they laugh," I whispered to Stacy in the quiet that followed. Admittedly, this was an exaggeration.

"Oh," she said, disappearing again into the darkness. Her return a few moments later was accompanied by a tremendously loud and hollow sound.

"HA HA HA HA," rang out the audience, enunciating together exactly four mechanical, fake-sounding laughs.

I pressed a button on a remote control hidden in my pocket that turned on the audio system. Gentle kids' music started playing, punctuated with some of Lilicrank's signature sounds.

The glowing eyes again appeared, and I could tell that they were growing fiery once more. Maybe it was just my imagination, or maybe I was beginning to lose balance from nervousness, but swear that I felt the stage surface shaking, as if the room itself was angry with me.

"We don't like this!" yelled Stacy. "Turn the music off! Turn it off!"

My shaking hands took hold of the remote and returned the room to silence, bringing about another sense of relative calm. What the fuck was happening?

"Is there anything else we need to do?" asked Stacy, noting my hesitation. "Should we laugh, clap, or chant again?"

"Um...n-no," I responded.

"Then continue," said Stacy. "Now."

"Stacy, I have to s-stop," I stuttered. "I c-can't do this anymore."

"Are you refusing to complete your performance?" Stacy asked, visibly offended.

My brain ran through every lie I could think of, trying to find one that would work.

"I-I – I need to...I need to get a drink of water," I said. That's it, I thought. I'll step outside for just a second, and then I'll get the hell out of here, never to return. They haven't paid me – it's not like I'll have stolen anything. I'll just leave, and then I'll figure out what to do next.

Stacy looked at me quizzically. Then, she stepped into the darkness. A moment later, a glimmer of light appeared down the center of the room, between the rows of seats, making out a path between the stage and the door. "This way," said Stacy, standing by the exit. "We are waiting."

It took substantial effort to restrain myself from sprinting away. Instead, I walked slowly out of the room, trying my best to appear calm.

Once I closed the door behind me, leaving Stacy and whatever else was in the mini-auditorium out-of-sight, I saw no need to maintain the ruse. I sprinted to the front door and frantically pulled the handle.

It was locked.

I felt absolute panic rush through my head. My orange shirt was stained heavily with sweat. I turned the lock again and again, clueless as to whatever else I could do.

Then I remembered the plumber and the key set. Surely, if I found her, I could convince her to let me out of the house. I knew I had to move fast, less the inhabitants of the auditorium come looking for me. So downstairs I went.

The first room in the basement was large, clean, and mostly empty. At one end, I saw what looked like a small laundry room. Guessing that the plumber could be there, I flipped on a flickering light and looked inside, where I saw only a tool kit next to a dripping pipe by a washing machine.

"Hello?" I said, trying to be loud enough that anyone in the basement could hear me, but not so loud as to alert anyone upstairs. Hearing no response, I walked to the only other door, one that I guessed would go to the area underneath the auditorium.

What I found upon opening the door shocked me. The first thing that struck me was the size of the chasm in front of me. Its vast, crater-like structure descended deep into the ground.

Later, I would wonder things like, *how could a house built atop this emptiness avoid collapsing?* It was as if the auditorium was hovering in place, with no structure supporting it.

But, in the moment, my mind was too busy trying to make sense of the translucent, greyish liquid that filled the massive space before me, forming a kind of lake. It reminded me of soapy water, but there this substance had a shiny, silver-like tint.

Peering into it, I noticed objects floating within the liquid. They were all at least several feet beneath the surface, and there were hundreds of them.

I gasped when I realized what they were: human bones. This

bizarre basement pool was *filled* with them. I'd stumbled upon some kind of crypt, or mass grave.

I backed up as something emerged from the lake. It was the *plumber*. Her face was expressionless, and she showed no concern about the fact that she was soaked in a bizarre, bone-filled pool.

As she climbed out, the liquid beneath her somehow solidified. I watched, my jaw dropped, as she walked on top of it until she was mere feet from me. "Looking for me?" she asked. As she did so, she flashed a set of striking green eyes.

"I-I...I got lost." As I stepped backwards, my foot landed on something soft. I looked down to find the plumbers' clothes – her whole outfit, along with her toolkit and key ring. How could her clothes be here...and also on the figure before me?

"You were supposed to be teaching the children," she said.

"I...um..." My survival instincts kicked in. I was getting the *fuck* out.

I only remember my adrenaline-fueled actions that followed in brief snippets: grabbing the key set, sprinting back across the basement; bursting up the staircase; shoving a piece of furniture behind the closed basement door.

Upon reaching the house's front entrance, I chanced a glance down the hall towards the auditorium. Thankfully, no one was there, and the door remained shut.

I got to work on finding the correct key. There were at least ten to choose from.

The first didn't work. When I tried to take hold of the second, my hands, shaking with nervousness, let the ring slip to the ground.

I picked it up, only for the impact of a heavy force against the barricaded basement door to prompt me to drop it again.

*Fuck*, I thought. *I can do this.* I took a deep breath, calmed myself, and tried again, and again.

Finally, the door opened. I hurried outside, only to find that the cul-de-sac was no longer vacant.

It was filled now with children. They all had the same phosphorescent green eyes that shined in the darkness of the evening. The kids weren't running around and playing. They just stood still and gazed at me with vacant expressions.

A strong hand gripped my shoulder from behind. "You can't leave," said Stacy. "You haven't finished your lesson."

I tried to rush away, but Stacy held me firmly. With as much force as I could muster, I pried her off of me and shoved her away.

Stacy hit the ground. I didn't think she landed too hard, but she lay totally still for a moment, as if seriously hurt.

The eyes of the children around me began changing once again from green to fiery orange. Meanwhile, Stacy's body contorted. It convulsed, and, as she stood up, took on a twisted form. Her neck stretched to an impossible length and drooped down her side, leaving her head and its fiery eyes dangling upside down as she stumbled toward me.

I ran to my car as fast as I could and climbed inside. The children now were all moving towards me, slowly and steadily. "The danger is real!" they chanted, again and again, in unison. "The danger is real! The danger is real!" In my rear view mirror, I caught for a brief moment a glimpse of one of the children, with what appeared to be sharp, canine teeth in his mouth and he hissed at me. Behind him stood the plumber, her orange eyes burning fiercely in my direction.

After turning the car on, I floored the accelerator. When I reached the stop sign at the end of the street, I could still hear the chanting behind me. I sped through the rest of the suburb and drove for hours on the interstate in no particular direction, putting as much distance as possible between me and what I had seen.

I never got many answers about what had happened. When I tried talking the police, they asked *me* questions about drug use and the state of my mental health.

I can't say I blame them. My story made no sense, after all, especially considering the houses along the cul-de-sac on Peakview Drive were supposed to be vacant. Construction had finished in this area, but the homes had not yet gone on sale. There had been no reports of squatters, much less dozens of children residing in the area. Certainly, the police assured me, none of these houses hovered above a pool of mysterious liquid. A plumber *had* been sent out to the area that day to investigate a reported water leak, but, by all accounts, she'd fixed the problem without incident.

I never recovered the props I'd brought with me that night. This ended up being a blessing in disguise, as this pushed me to finally embark on a new career. I've moved on from dreams of regaining minor fame, and I've started to get on two feet at becoming self-sufficient once again.

But the memories never faded. I greet strangers wearily, looking for any sign that they might not be who they say they are.

Most recently, two teenagers knocked at my door. They invited me to a fundraiser – something about opposing local deforestation – that would occur that weekend at a local museum. It was a serious issue, one of them explained to me. As the other handed me a flier on the subject, a luminous glimmer in his hazel eyes brought back every horrible memory from that night. "The danger is real," he said with a smile.

7

## ZIPPERS

"Look, Olivia, you know Mr. Jacobson wants this first thing in the morning-"

"Which is why you shouldn't have waited until the end of the day today to get started on your portion of the spreadsheet." I sighed. I already knew where this was going.

"I know," said Andrew. "But, I *need* this evening off. It's Michael's fourth birthday. I just can't miss it. You'll understand when you have kids. I'll make this up to you."

"You *already* owe me one. This makes two favors. Heck, I should just take a few days off at this point and leave you to do my job for me."

"So you'll cover for me tonight?" said Andrew with relief. "Thank you *so* much. By the way, is everything okay at your place? I'm hearing a lot of racket."

"Yeah, don't worry. Everything's just fine. What about you? You've got something...funny on your neck."

"Huh?" Andrew responded, oblivious to the metal speck I noticed under his chin.

"Never mind," I said. It wasn't my problem, and I had work to do. I ended the Zoom call and removed my headphones.

Leaning back, I reflected on the evening ahead. I had at least three more hours of work thanks to Andrew flaking out, and I knew better than to even ask my supervisor and team leader, Mr. Jacobson, for overtime. To make matters worse, my roommates Mae and Gerald were arguing loudly enough for my co-worker to hear them through my computer.

I decided to break for dinner before resuming the tedious monthly budget analysis.

I opened the door from my bedroom to the cramped kitchen shared by the three of us. Gerald was already inside.

I offered a casual hello only to freeze when I noticed the bulging suitcase he was dragging to the side door that led to the driveway. "Oh," I muttered, a bit startled.

"Yeah," said Gerald. He gave me a polite hug. "Hopefully it'll get a bit quieter around here for you now."

I hadn't realized that things between him and Mae had reached a breaking point. Mae and I had been close once. I guess this is what happens when your job sucks away all your energy. You lose touch with people you care about, even when they're among the only ones you ever see in-person.

I helped Gerald carry some of his belongings to his car. As we hauled a box of clothes down the short outer staircase, I noticed a small piece of metal jutting out from his arm.

"Is your arm...okay?" I asked him as we lowered the box into his trunk.

"Yeah, why wouldn't it be?"

I took a closer look at it. It was...a zipper? But why would a zipper be attached to his arm?

He looked at his arm and, seemingly finding nothing unusual, resumed loading his vehicle.

He lifted a toolkit that was slightly ajar. As he repositioned it, his arm muscles clenched, causing the zipper to shift a half-inch down. A thin trail of blood leaked out of the gap that emerged. I gasped.

Gerald, somehow still unaware, gave me a perplexed look before turning back to the half-house the three of us (well, two of us, now) rented. Mae stood in the open doorframe. Her face was red and tearful.

"See you, Mae," said Gerald. "Good luck."

She waived faintly. I went over to comfort her. Gerald could deal with the bizarre cut on his arm on his own.

Mae needed my company that night. I hated telling her that I had to get back to work. As grating as my job was, it would be disastrous if I were to lose it.

I worked past midnight. My weary eyes glazed passed the terms that always floated around the descriptions of projects ongoing at my company – words like bioelectronic, transfection, and electrotransmission – and towards the numbers that formed the basis of my job. Finally, I submitted the complete report at 1:15 a.m.

I fought to open my eyes the next morning. Mr. Jacobson didn't respond to my daily check-in email. The next time I heard from him was that afternoon, when he sent a message to our whole team, with a higher-up manager Cc'd. "Thank you, Andrew, for the excellent work as always." My name wasn't mentioned.

After work, I finally touched base with Mae, who'd just finished a virtual tutoring gig.

"I just realized things with Gerald weren't going to get any better," she told me. "So, instead of dodging all the issues like we always do, I insisted that we talk it out last night. It got pretty heated, as you heard, but he eventually decided to leave. He's moving in with his brother in Eastside for the time being."

I told her that I was sorry, both because of what happened and because I hadn't been there for her as her relationship had fallen apart.

"I don't blame you," said Mae. "Honestly, I think we both knew things had run their course between us a while ago, but we didn't want to have to deal with one of us moving out during the pandemic. But we could only put off dealing with-"

"Hey, did you cut yourself?" I interrupted, noting a drop of blood running down her cheek.

"What? No, I don't think so."

"Just turn your head to the right and stay still," I instructed. Behind her left ear, a metal zipper lingered on the surface of her skin just beneath her hairline. "What the hell is that?"

"What's *what*?" asked Mae, understandably worried.

The zipper was embedded into her skin. It appeared to have dropped from its starting point by a fraction of an inch, undoing her skin as it went. A small quantity of blood dripped out of the gap it left behind.

I dabbed the blood with a tissue, applied an antibiotic cream, and pulled the zipper back up, where it appeared to stay relatively secure.

Before I could get a bandage, Mae rushed to the bathroom mirror to see it for herself. Her reaction left me even more befuddled than before.

"I'm telling you, it was right there!" I said. "I saw it and I touched it." But she was correct – when I looked again, there was no zipper to be found.

"Olivia, look, there's obviously nothing here," said Mae. "Are you okay? I mean, it wouldn't make any sense for there to be a *zipper* on me in the first place. And it's not like I felt one."

"I-I just don't understand," I said. "I'm *sure* I saw it. Same with Gerald, and Andrew too." It was her turn to be confused when I showed her the drops of blood on the tissue I'd used.

Neither of us knew what to make of it. The best answer for what happened that we could come up with was that Mae had accidentally scratched herself without realizing it, and that I'd been mistaken about what I'd seen. But it wasn't a satisfying explanation.

I began to notice zippers on my co-workers during our daily video calls. Kelly had one that drooped awkwardly from her right cheek. Andrew's dangled lower and lower on his neck; yet, he never seemed to notice even as blood leaked out.

I tried alerting him again, but he, and everyone else on the call, acted hostile in response. "Andrew looks fine to me," said Mr. Jacobson. "Get it together, Olivia."

Work droned on. I quickly lost interest in intervening to protect my virtual colleagues. I had myself to look after.

The friendship between Mae and me benefitted from Gerald's departure. On one occasion, we went across town and visited our friend April to celebrate her recent engagement. Generally, though, we kept to ourselves, watching movies together on Mae's bed or sitting around Mae's record player listening to music. One Friday night, we even repeated something Mae had liked doing during college: a ghost-story themed 'sleepover' party. It was just the two of us, but with the assistance of a couple mixed drinks, we had a nice enough time as she narrated a handful of tales to me.

I awoke Saturday morning in a sleeping bag on the floor of Mae's room. Liquid dripped against my cheek. I shot awake, worried about a water leak. Instead, I found the source to be the head of my slumbering friend, which lay partially over the edge of her bedframe.

The zipper had reappeared. It had drifted downwards, and red droplets trickled out of the opening.

Moving carefully, I gripped the metal and pulled it back up. Mae didn't stir as I wiped away the blood. I left to clean my own face. When I returned, I noticed that Mae's zipper had again disappeared.

I didn't know what to believe. Mae would think I was crazy if I brought the zippers up again. But, if I were just imagining things, where did the blood come from?

I told Mae the next day that I'd been seeing the zippers again, though I didn't mention hers in particular.

"Olivia," she told me firmly, "There are no metal zippers on me or on any of your coworkers. That's impossible. You know that."

"But...but, the blood."

Mae shrugged. "Like we said, I must have cut myself by accident. That's the only possibility. Right?"

I told her I agreed. Until I could make some sense of what I was seeing, I decided not to bring it up again.

That Monday morning, Andrew confided in me that his mother was in the hospital. "She's on a ventilator," he sent me via chat. "It's hard for me to focus knowing her life is on the line." I sent him some supportive messages and offered to cover for him again.

During our next daily team call, Andrew's video at first refused to load. It finally appeared while Mr. Jacobson was lecturing us about a new procedure for logging complaints of in-house contagions and pre-pandemic experimental exposure.

Andrew's decrepit appearance shocked me. Beneath the eyes he fought to keep open, a long, red gash extended down his neck. His zipper had dropped to somewhere on his chest. Blood oozed out and soaked through his stained blue shirt. Slowly, his head lowered. He teetered and then fell to the floor.

"Geez – Andrew, are you okay?" I asked.

"Excuse me, Olivia," said Mr. Jacobson. "I'm talking now."

"Did no one else just see that? Someone needs to get an ambulance sent to Andrew's house, now!" As I spoke, Andrew's video cut off.

"No, I'm fine," said Andrew in a hollow, weary voice. "I don't know what Olivia's making a fuss about. Please, carry on Mr. Jacobson."

Mr. Jacobson glared for a moment, presumably at me, before continuing.

The next day, I learned from an email that Andrew was taking an indefinite leave of absence due to undisclosed medical reasons.

Mae found fewer gigs over the next few weeks. At my insistence, she reluctantly agreed to let me cover her portion of the rent until she found stable employment.

The long hours of joblessness started to wear on her. She would often get snappy or withdrawn. She'd probably sent out a hundred job applications at this point without any offers.

When she wasn't applying for jobs, she spent much of her time tending to her ever-growing collection of small cacti. I laughed when she informed me that she'd assigned a name and a personality to each of them. She called them "substitute friends".

"Goodnight, Olivia," she told me late one evening. As she headed into her bedroom, I noticed the zipper, and that it had drifted an inch down her head.

I waited for an hour before creeping as quietly as I could into her room. I opened the door carefully and stood still for several moments, until I could discern her rhythmic breathing. I stepped over the carpet until I reached her bed, where she lay asleep.

No blood had come out of the opening made by the zipper. Not yet, at least. Perhaps not at all, if I intervened.

I reached carefully for her. I'd have a lot of uncomfortable explaining to do if Mae awoke to find me there, but I felt compelled to act all the same.

I gripped the zipper and slowly pulled it up. Mae started to reach for it, as if to scratch an itch, but her arm drifted aside at the last moment. Finally, the zipper set in-place at its starting point. I let go, tiptoed out of the room, and closed the door behind me.

It became a regular ritual. When Mae had a rough or restless day, the zipper would loosen and start to descend, and I'd sneak into her room in the late night or early morning to discretely return it. The next day, the zipper would always be gone.

I noticed one on me, too. It was on my back, near my right shoulder blade. The longer I worked, the further it dropped. Every morning and every evening, I tugged it back into place.

The job kept me too busy to dwell much of the insanity of the whole situation. I had Andrew's work to worry about in addition to my own.

Mr. Jacobson grilled me in front of the whole team the next morning. "Olivia once again failed to properly account for recent market fluctuations in her weekly report."

"I'm-I'm sorry. It won't happen again."

"I'm glad to hear that," he replied. He proceeded to announce that Kelly would be receiving a performance bonus for the high quality of her recent contributions to a project. In other circumstances, I'd be happy for her. Instead, all I could focus on was the thin streak of blood leaking down Kelly's face.

A call from Mr. Jacobson late that evening interrupted a board game Mae and I were playing.

"Yes?" I said, figuring there must be some kind of emergency.

"Olivia, am I correct that you have been diligent in your social isolation?"

"Yes," I said, surprised by the question.

"Good," said Mr. Jacobson. "So have I. So, I'm assuming you have no objection to your upcoming performance review being in-person?"

"What? Um, yeah, that's fine, of course," I said, ever acquiescent to my boss's demands.

The call left me alarmed, though. Why would he insist on seeing me in person, after I'd been working virtually for so long? I worried that he wanted to fire me, and had decided that it would be more polite to do so in person.

I barely had time to settle down before I heard Mae shriek. While I'd been on the phone, she'd gone into her room.

I arrived to find her hand clasped against her head, just behind her left ear. Had the zipper appeared, and had she finally noticed it?

"I should have listened to you and not put Shirley so high up," she said, referencing a cactus she'd placed on her bookshelf. "I'd forgotten it was there and leaned in to get something. I think there's a thorn stuck in me now."

I took a closer look. The zipper had, in fact, reappeared, and the thorn protruded through the loop in its pull tab into her skin.

She reached to yank out the thorn.

"Stop!" I called. "You'll move the zipper."

We were both silent for a moment.

"Did you say-"

"Just let me get it out for you." I proceeded to pluck out the thorn. As I did so, I moved precisely enough to avoid touching the zipper, which then receded into her skin.

Mae sat down with me afterwards. "Why didn't you tell me that you were still seeing them?" she asked.

"I..." I took a deep breath. "I thought you'd think I was crazy."

"I'd think, and I *do* think, that you need help," she said. "How often have you been seeing them?"

Tears welled in my eyes as I opened up and told her how I'd seen them on everyone I'd encountered lately.

"Including on me?"

I nodded. "I've...I've adjusted yours before, when it's gotten loose." I didn't give any more detail. I'd volunteered enough already.

"Okay," said Mae. She thought for a moment. "We're going to get through this, Olivia. I used to see someone – a therapist, and maybe they can help you too."

Soon, I had an appointment scheduled for next week.

When it came time for my performance review, Mae offered to drive me to the office. I resisted at first, as I didn't want to trouble her unnecessarily. But, she insisted that she had nothing better to do that day.

She watched from the car as I approached the office building. I'd put on full business attire for the first time in months. When I reached the front door, I found it to be locked, and my keycard wouldn't open it. I called up Mr. Jacobson.

"Oh, I'm so sorry Olivia," he said. "I didn't specify the location, did I? I'd happily meet you in the office, but corporate still has the whole floor shut down. We aren't allowed to step foot in there. I know it's unconventional, but I think we'll have to do this at my place." He read out his home address.

"He said *what*?" screamed Mae after I returned to the car. "You didn't agree to it, did you?"

"I know it's...weird," I said. "But I *need* this job."

"Olivia, refuse to go," said Mae. "And file a complaint with HR. There's no good reason for him to invite you to his place for this."

"I *know* it's fishy," I said. "But I need this to go well. If I tell him I'm uncomfortable about it, who knows what he'll do in response."

"Olivia, I know what he's like and how this job is treating you. Sometimes you have to fight back, even when it's difficult."

"I don't want to be rude, Mae, but someone has to pay our rent. I can't lose this job, and I'm not going to risk starting a conflict with my boss over potentially nothing."

Mae drove me there, but when we pulled up outside a split-level home, she insisted that she'd come inside if I was gone for very long.

Mr. Jacobson ushered me in moments after I rang the doorbell.

He led me to a living room. I took a seat on a dark blue couch as he closed the blinds.

"I appreciate you coming down here," he said as he took a seat across from me. "Let's get started. I've been reviewing your work lately and, overall, your performance has been...problematic."

I gulped.

"For now, I see no choice but to recommend to management that you be let go at the end of the quarter." As he spoke, I noticed a shiny object jostling at the top of the center of his forehead. It was barely visible behind his greying bangs.

"That is, unless you persuade me to send along a more positive assessment. I could even request that you be given a raise."

Time slowed as I realized just how right Mae had been. I was such an idiot. Why had I come here? I should have listened to her.

"So," continued Mr. Jacobson, "If you want to persuade me to do that, why don't you come upstairs with me? My wife's away. It's just the two of us. We can all come out of this as winners."

My heart throbbed. I felt like I was suffocating. The right answer was to say no, obviously, and get the hell out.

I'd taken every insult he'd given to me. In doing so, I'd taught him that I wouldn't fight back, even when his criticisms were unjustified. It dawned on me that he'd been setting me up for this for a long time. I felt trapped and helpless.

"Umm, yes, yes how about we go upstairs," I said. I decided to play the part he'd written for me, at least for the moment.

I slowly followed him, painfully lifting my legs up each step until we arrived at a door to his bedroom. He followed me inside.

"You-your shirt, why don't you go ahead and take that off," I said meekly.

He smiled widely as he unbuttoned it.

I reached my hand steadily towards his face, as if to caress it. Only, instead, I grabbed the zipper that was in the center of his forehead and pulled rapidly, with all my might.

The zipper traveled down his nose, jumped from the top of his mouth to the bottom, and then fell all the way to his waist.

He gave a mystified expression. I waited, in silence, for a moment as he looked me over in confusion.

Nothing seemed to be happening. Mae was right once again. I was crazy. There never were any zippers. What was I going to do now?

Then, Mr. Jacobson gargled. All at once, his body opened up.

His head split in two. Brains, mucus, saliva, and blood burst outwards.

His chest followed. Organs and chunks of flesh spewed onto the floor, leaving only bare bones behind. The lower half of his body and a hollow flap of skin that had once covered his torso collapsed into a grotesque heap.

Another scream joined mine. I turned to find Mae at the door to his room. She'd seen everything.

We drove home in shocked silence. When we pulled into our driveway, I told Mae we needed to call the police and try to tell them what happened.

Then, an alert appeared on my phone. I'd received an email from Mr. Jacobson.

It was sent to my whole team. In it, Mr. Jacobson, or whoever was operating his email account, announced that he was taking indefinite leave due to a medical emergency.

I read it out loud to Mae. Neither of us knew what to make of it. How could Mr. Jacobson have sent this, given what had just happened to him? If it was someone else using his account, then why would they be pretending to be him?

My company soon hired a replacement for Mr. Jacobson. They're much better – more reasonable, fairer with subordinates, and easier to get along with. A replacement for Andrew arrived two weeks later, and when we collaborate, our new boss gives both of us credit.

My mental health has improved. I haven't seen a zipper on anyone since my boss's insides spilled out onto his bedroom floor.

It's been weeks since Mae and I talked about what happened. She's been busy with a position she landed teaching at a local community college. She's seeing someone new now, and we both think he's an improvement over Gerald.

I've started growing a cactus of my own. It has an awkward, contorted shape, and it's somehow pricklier than any of Mae's. She insisted that I give it a name.

I still check in with Mr. Jacobson every morning. I give him more water than he deserves, and I've yet to find a zipper on his rough, green skin.

8

_____

# THE VIEW FROM THE SUNROOM

Three weeks ago, I closed the blinds that cover my sunroom's floor-to-ceiling window, and I haven't opened them since.

I couldn't take it anymore. The emptiness. The desolation. The feeling of being watched.

It wasn't always like this. In the past, my eyes would stray from my work laptop to the view that window provided of the dog park and the neighboring apartment building beyond it. I would observe the lives of my neighbors and hear accompanying sounds of pets, children, and passing traffic.

It all changed after I broke up with Timothy. I've heard stories of exes who take their friends with them. But, when Timothy left, it was like everyone – the whole complex – also departed.

I stopped detecting movement in the other apartments. The dog park sat unused. Fewer vehicles passed by on the narrow section of street I could see. The final straw was when I realized that there weren't any people in the cars that remained. Because my view is limited, I initially assumed I was mistaken. But, no, I'm certain now – they are totally unoccupied.

A pattern endlessly repeats as the same few vehicles circle my block. Blue Sedan. Green Sedan. Red Truck. I've read about self-driving cars, but why would they be set to travel in a pointless loop around my complex?

I could go outside and investigate, of course. But I feel so brittle, so afraid. Part of me is worried, perhaps irrationally, that whatever took everyone else away will take me, too, if I leave for too long.

But my biggest fear is of Timothy. I always sense that he is watching me. That's by design – he makes his presence known. That's why I never venture beyond the hallway, and even then just for quick trips to the garbage chute or to pick up groceries dropped off by a delivery service.

Today, I find a handwritten note under the door. Timothy's scrawl reads, *Take me back.* It's a familiar message. But I shudder all the same. It's one thing to be inundated with text messages and emails from him. It's quite another to know that he walked up to my door and placed it underneath.

I latch the door. Is he outside now? I look through the peephole. The emptiness of the sterile hallway provides only partial relief. At least Timothy isn't there. But where is everybody else?

My dreams that night take me back to our honeymoon phase. When Timothy's wealth still enamored me. He dressed well. He seemed suave and sophisticated. And he saw something in *me*, of all people.

My alarm goes off. I shower and dress.

I gasp when I emerge from my bedroom to the living room and kitchen. Where the hell did the ladder by the dinner table come from?

"Hello?" I call. There is no response.

The front door is shut, but the latch is...undone.

I retreat to my bedroom. I'd recently made a service request to replace a ceiling light. But how had someone gotten inside with the latch in place? And why would they enter without even telling me?

I call the front desk. The voicemail box is full.

Slowly, I open the bedroom door. The ladder is gone, and the light has been replaced.

Nervously, I decide to travel further than I've gone in a month. Upon entering the hallway, I peer left, then right. Nobody.

I take the stairs. In the lobby, I approach the desk.

I want answers. Why did maintenance enter my apartment without telling me? How did they get past the latch? And why has everything become so desolate, so silent?

*WILL RETURN IN 5 MINUTES* reads the sign. The clock displays *7:44 a.m.*

I fidget as I wait. I peer out the window, past the vacant dog park and to the building beyond. I scan every window and every crevice for the piercing blue eyes of the man who begged me to take him back. He's watching me. I can feel it.

"Come on," I mutter as I lean across the counter and peer into the empty office behind it.

I recheck the clock. Still: *7:44 a.m.*, even though it's been several minutes. It's broken.

The door outside jostles. My skin crawls as I back up towards the staircase. The door glides open on its own, as if blown by a gust of wind.

Buried deep within the accompanying high-pitched whistle is Timothy's faint voice: *Take me back.*

I hurry upstairs. This time, after I bolt and latch the door to my apartment, I also lean a chair against it.

I sit at my desk. It is a workday, after all.

This will all be over soon, I tell myself. Next Monday, my year of telework will finally end. I'll return to the smiling faces of my co-workers. I'll hear their voices and I'll snap out of the gloomy state I'm in. There's a whole world out there of buzzing people living their lives. It hasn't dried up because of a bad breakup and reclusive neighbors.

I have to reread the first email in my inbox to absorb the words: *Due to unforeseen circumstances, we are temporarily postponing next week's office reopening. Telework will continue until further notice.*

No. It can't be. I message my team leader. "This is a mistake, right? The reopening has been on the calendar for weeks."

He responds that there has been no mistake.

I ask what caused the delay.

The message back to me reads simply, "Telework will continue until further notice."

I'm fuming. I've held on to the prospect of returning – of seeing others again – for so long.

"Can we do a video call?" I ask him. I want him to explain this to my face.

He responds that his video camera is broken, but that he's happy to address any further questions by email or instance message.

I message Hannah. She doesn't seem bothered by the development.

"I was looking forward to it," I type, surprised by her indifference. "I thought maybe we could get lunch together like we used to."

Her response is familiar. *Telework will continue until further notice.*

What is wrong with everybody? She doesn't sound like the Hannah I remember. "Hey, want to schedule a video call for later today?" I ask. "I think it would be nice to catch up."

She messages me that her camera isn't working.

I email Michael that I feel sick. That I need to take the rest of the day off. It's not much of a lie.

I don't wait for a response. I log out and stagger dizzily to my bed. I curl up under the covers. What's happening? What's wrong with everybody?

My work phone vibrates in my pocket. I want it to be Hannah telling me that she hopes I feel better. It isn't.

*Take me back*, reads the message from an unknown number. I throw the phone against the floor.

I fall into a light sleep. My mind drifts to when I first visited Timothy's house.

*Timothy had taken me downstairs, where he'd shown me the models he'd constructed. "This is where I grew up," he said, crouching until he was level with the first floor of the elaborate miniature. "Look, here, through the front window."*

*I positioned myself next to him and gazed inside. "It's so detailed," I commented, impressed by his expert craftsmanship.*

*He directed me to a model of where he, his brother, and his parents stayed, and explained in detail all the furniture he had meticulously recreated.*

*I asked him why he had made it.*

*"It's a way of capturing a moment in time," he explained. "And preserving it forever."*

*When I woke up in his bed the next morning, I reached for him under the covers. Instead, my arm brushed against something flimsy, coarse and dry. I flung the sheets down. Next to me lay a long, thin line of empty, patterned skin.*

*I jumped out of the bed and fled. I found Timothy in his kitchen, cooking breakfast. He agreed to investigate. But, when he called me into his bedroom, he showed me that there was nothing there. "You had a bad dream. It's okay Alison, you don't need to worry. I have nightmares too, sometimes." He seemed so sympathetic. I believed him.*

I emerge from my nap. I make myself lunch. It tastes stale. That's what I get for ordering groceries – they never pick out the fresh produce I would have selected.

I sigh. As I dump half my plate into the overflowing trash can, I realize that I need to venture outside my apartment for the second time in twenty-four hours.

I ease open my front door. The coast is clear. I carry the trash bag past the apartments of neighbors I had once known, neighbors who retreated into their apartments, never to be seen again.

With each step, my paranoia steadily recedes. The daylight that shines through the window at the end of the hallway, the first glimpse of the outside world I've experienced in ages, brightens my mood, and I reach the chute without incident.

I turn the lever that unlocks the chute. I lower it, and drop the trash bag in.

I spring back as something emerges with an angry hiss. It's long and scaly, with a forked tongue.

I stumble towards my apartment as the snake slithers in pursuit.

It's huge. Even now, as it stretches at least a yard into the hallway, even more of it crawls out of the chute.

I reach my door. As I hurry inside, a distorted voice echoes through the hollow corridor. "*Alissson.*"

Once I've barricaded the door, I call 911. The moment I hear a voice on the other end, I stammer about encountering a dangerous animal. A lump forms in the back of my throat as I realize that I'm not speaking to a real person. The automated voice tells that all lines are in use. That I should leave a message describing my emergency.

"No, no, please!" I yell. "I need to talk to someone-"

A 'beep' sounds. I don't bother saying anything. *This isn't supposed to happen.* 911 calls don't go to voicemail.

I again bury myself under my bedsheets. I remember Timothy's anger when I told him we were through. I remember how long the marks he left took to fade. My anger and fear swell until I'm sweating.

This isn't doing me any good. I sit up and remember the light from the hallway and how good it made me feel.

Cautiously, I open the blinds on my narrow bedroom window. Across the dog park, in the other building, I see a rare site: another human.

She's chubby and looks to be in her late fifties. She holds a watering can over the plants on her balcony.

*There's another person here.* I feel hopeful. I decide that I'm going to talk to her. I need to.

I make myself presentable and place my sharpest kitchen knife in my purse. I peek outside. No snake. No Timothy. I tiptoe to the staircase and down to the lobby. As I pass through the eerily silent dog park, I count the floors to the woman's apartment and estimate its location.

After climbing eight flights of stairs, I knock at her door. She opens slowly and peers at me through the chain lock.

"Hello," I say. "I...I, um, I was wondering if I could speak with you."

She asks why.

"You see...um..." Her expression grows skeptical. I struggle to find the right words. "It's just that...I haven't seen anyone around here in ages. I...I just wanted someone to talk to."

A painful silence follows. She smiles. She tells me that she's happy to talk with me. That she's noticed how the complex has become deserted.

Relief seeps through me. I'm not losing my mind. I'm not alone.

She asks me to come in. She offers to make me tea.

I sit on the couch as she pours water into the kettle. She tells me that, at first, she figured it was just adults going back to work and kids returning to school. But, steadily, everyone disappeared.

"You have no idea how much it means to me," I say. "To hear someone else confirm what I've been seeing. I've been so lonely."

She turns on her stovetop and sits in a chair opposite me. She asks if I live alone.

"Yes," I say. "This all started at the same time, actually, as when my boyfriend and I broke up...When I left him."

She asks why I would do a thing like that.

I'm surprised by the question. "Oh, um...there were things I learned about him that I...didn't like."

She leans forward in her seat and speaks firmly. She insists that we're in this together. That we have to be open with each other if we're going to figure this out. She suggests that if this all started when I broke up with my boyfriend, then maybe he has something to do with it.

I nod. "Okay. He and his friends...um, they had these meetings, you see. Timothy – that was his name – he wouldn't allow me to attend them, and he didn't like when I asked about them."

"So, eventually, I decided to sneak into one. I dressed up in a mask and a robe, just like what I saw Timothy wear before he left for them."

"Nobody figured out who I was, at least at first. What I saw...it was terrible. There were knives, and blood. They stabbed someone, and, and..." My voice croaks.

She says that that's horrible.

"Yes, it was," I said. "But that's not all. As the poor, young woman bled out, they started to do things...impossible things. They lifted off the ground, like they were levitating, and their appearance changed, too. I watched as Timothy seemed to, um...to disappear. His robe collapsed onto the floor, like it was empty. Only, then, something started to come out of it. At first, I didn't know what it was. Then I saw its face and its tongue. It was a snake. It was too much. I ran outside screaming."

She asks me what happened next.

"I, um, I must have fainted. The next thing I remember is being in bed, with Timothy next to me. He told me I'd had a bad dream. I didn't believe him. I told him I was leaving him and going to the police. That made him mad."

"He said that if I ever tried to leave him, he'd put me somewhere I'd never get out of until I changed my mind. 'Your own little place, your own little illusion of the void that is sky.' I didn't know what to think."

As I wait for the woman's reaction, the kettle whistles. She gets up to remove it from the burner.

I sit back. It feels cathartic to share this with someone else.

She hands me a cup of tea. I decline the sugar she offers. She warns me that it's still very hot.

I take a sip. It's black tea. Strong, bitter. Very bitter.

My eyes widen as I look up at the chair across from me, where the woman is holding the kettle of near-boiling water. She raises it above her head. Before I can scream, she pours the steaming liquid over her body.

"What? Ma'am, what are you doing?"

A smug smile spreads across her face. As the water cascades across her body, her skin melts. Her round face thins. Her outer layer fades into an oozing puddle, revealing a thin, fit man underneath. "It feels good to open up to another person, doesn't it, Alison?" asks Timothy.

"No, no..." I stand up and run for the door.

"Oh Alison, I knew you'd come over here if you saw someone. I just want to talk. I miss you. And I know you miss me."

I tug at the door, clumsily pulling it open with the chain lock still in place.

Timothy approaches slowly. "You really think you can get away from me, don't you? It's just a matter of time. You'll give in eventually. They always do. When you're ready, just say so. I'll hear you. I'm watching you, always."

I remove the knife from my purse. He laughs at me. With a swift motion, he grabs my wrist. He pries it from my fist. It drops to the floor.

I frantically release the chain, reopen the door, and charge into the hallway. On the way back to my building, I remember his words as I look up at the fading sun: *Your own little illusion of the void that is sky.*

When I reach my apartment, I don't bother locking my door, much less barricading it. It's no use. I know where I am now, and I know that there's no way out of it.

The night passes as I drift in and out of sleep. In the morning, I try to convince myself that recent events were only a dream. That I'm not really stuck here, alone, under the constant surveillance of my tormenter.

At 8:00 a.m., I log onto my computer. A day's worth of work is a day's worth of distraction. Maybe I will get the update I'm looking for – an announcement of when my company is finally returning to the workplace.

I consider the closed blinds. If I'm not locking my door anymore, then I don't need to lock out the sunlight, too. I open them.

When I do, I find myself facing a giant pair of blue eyes that cover the entirety of the area visible through the floor-to-ceiling windows.

Timothy's voice, thunderously loud, calls for someone named Michelle. "It's a way of capturing a moment in time," he explains, as he scans me and my surroundings. "And preserving it forever."

9

———————

# GALÁPAGOS

In the depths of sleep, I drift again to Angela's coffin. Just before the wooden lid closes, I glimpse the gathered crowd dressed in black.

I descend. I hear the soft thuds of rain. At first, I find comfort in the white crepe fabric that lines the walls of my new home. Then, the claustrophobia kicks in. I want out. Heaven, hell, I don't care. Just anywhere but here.

I wake up whimpering and cold. My sheets lay on the floor from flinging my arms and legs against the imagined walls.

I shower, dress formally, and pass the empty room where my sister once lived as I head downstairs to the kitchen.

My mother smiles as she pours coffee. I know what she's thinking. At least something good came out of her daughter's death. Her son may be underemployed and destined to spend his twenties in his childhood home, but, in his grief, he found God.

At church, I half-listen to the scripture Pastor Jones reads. When I join the others in singing the hymnals, my voice carries an empty timbre. I couldn't care less about the nuances of my faith. I'm under no illusions that, in a different environment, I'd be a Muslim or a

Buddhist or whatever the predominant culture steered me toward. Anything except atheism, that is.

When I first saw the sign – *The Next 2 Miles Adopted By Lincoln County Freethinkers*, that horrible feeling crept down my spine of a question I hated to ponder: how many years do I have left, before my only fate is to rot under the weight of six feet of the same worm-filled soil under which Angela decays? That's all that the denial of the supernatural – of anything beyond our immediate physical existence – boils down to. Miles of pristinely-maintained highway heading nowhere.

I exchange sly glances with my ex-girlfriend Bethany and her cousin Seth as Pastor Jones chastises those responsible. "I pray that the perpetrators are not from our community. It is not our way to desecrate those who see things differently. We guide others toward the light not with malice but with love and compassion."

Bethany, Seth and I had felt little of those emotions as we rammed the sign, stood over where it fell, and sprayed neon green over the sponsor's name. The way I saw it, they were snuffing out Angela's soul. I had to act.

Yet, the congregation nods along to the messages of coexistence and tolerance. I shake my head. Do they really believe what they claim to believe?

That evening, I bring to Bethany and Seth's attention a column on the second page of the Sunday paper. "Those secularists are coming to *our* hometown."

We arrive at the County Natural History Museum a few minutes after midnight. Bethany uses the key her sister kept from when she used to run the gift shop. It still works. We sneak inside a side door that I leave propped open as we make our way to the new exhibit.

*Darwin and the Origin of Species* reads the banner over the entrance. Fine print underneath confirms the name of a familiar sponsor.

We shine our flashlights over what we find inside: a miniature of the *HMS Beagle*, a selection of artificial trees and cacti, and mock tortoises, finches, iguanas, and armadillos scattered throughout artificial formations of rocks and beaches.

In the center of it all is a mannequin of the man himself. He wears a hefty overcoat and contemplatively holds a hand under his chin.

Seth removes a small metal hammer from his jacket while Bethany sprays pink across an informational display about natural selection.

Before I join them, a component of the exhibit catches my eye. I approach where a small prop penguin presides over a stone nest of three eggs. Nails through its extended left and right flaps keep it fixed against the wall. A sign informs me that Darwin encountered male penguins fiercely protective of their "rookery".

*Penguins are not afraid of humans*, it continues. *Darwin once blocked one from entering the ocean to see its response. It charged at him, pushing him aside before continuing on its way.*

I reach into the nest and remove the eggs. The speckled bits of blue made them surprisingly detailed recreations, and their weight suggests they are not hollow.

I throw one at the mannequin. The egg shatters on impact, sending its viscous contents running across Darwin's thick sideburns.

"What was that?" asks Seth, taking a break from destroying the mini sloop.

"These eggs... they're *real*." Seth asks where I found them, and when I motion to the penguin, I find that it looks different from how I remembered. Its head is bent backwards and its beak, which had been closed before, is open. It also appears substantially larger than I remembered it to be.

"Let me have one!" calls Bethany. I toss her an egg, which she hurdles onto Darwin's chest. Seth sends the third flying into his forehead. As the contents ooze down his face, a cry from Bethany distracts me.

"Ow!" she yells as she holds her gloved hand over her right shin. "Something bit me!"

I shine my flashlight over the wound. Something had, in fact, ripped through her pants and into her flesh. Blood from her wound trickled down the fabric.

"There's nothing here that could have bitten you," says Seth. "It must be broken glass or something."

"We don't want to leave any blood for the police to find," I say. "Let's get out of here."

As I leave, I kick the mannequin, sending it crashing to the floor. I look behind it and notice that the penguin is missing.

We approach the open door we used to enter. "Wait!" I whisper, spotting a large silhouette looming over the path outside. "Someone's out there."

Bethany guides us as we tiptoe toward a different exit. We find ourselves in an empty parking lot, and before long, we've climbed into the van we left a few blocks away.

"Who was out there?" asks Seth as he drives us away.

"I didn't get a good look," I reply. "An officer probably saw how I left the door propped open." But, as I say that, I recall the shadow's daunting shape, like a cloaked figure of death awaiting us outside that door.

It's not until two days later that an article in the newspaper my mother keeps us subscribed to finally covers our stunt. "Are you seeing this?" I text Seth and Bethany alongside a picture of its third paragraph. *In addition to destroying much of the exhibit, the vandals appear to have made off with a prop Galapagos penguin.* I hadn't taken a prop penguin, and I would have seen if Seth or Bethany had done so.

The break-in is the talk of the town. The police offer a reward for the "hoodlums" responsible for desecrating the public museum. Only one letter to the editor expresses sympathy. At the next church service, I brace myself for a new round of sanctimonious gestures.

The sermon is worse than I expected. Pastor Jones not only speaks at length about the tragedy of "a few bad apples" tarnishing the names of true believers through their "reckless defacement," but also announces a fundraiser to repair the damage. I storm out in disgust, slamming the doors behind me.

In the lobby, I find Bethany. She's pale and holds her hands over her face. At first I think she's as upset as I am over Pastor Jones' sermon, but she tells me that's not the issue.

She motions to the stairs to the basement. "It's down there. I heard it."

"What's down there?"

She wants to leave. I follow her to the steps outside. "The penguin from the other night."

"*What?* Have you lost your mind?"

"No," she insists. "It's following me. I'm seeing it everywhere. And when I don't see it, I can hear it. It wants revenge. We shouldn't have broken those eggs."

"It's a *prop*, Bethany! You really think an artificial recreation of an animal Darwin met two hundred years ago is somehow...what? Alive? And out for revenge?"

"I know it doesn't make sense," says Bethany. "Seth doesn't believe me either." As we speak, she keeps her eyes trained on the church entrance.

"Even if we were being stalked by it, what do we have to fear? It's a penguin. It's practically harmless. Just call animal control."

"You don't understand. It's *huge*. And dangerous. It's hurt me already."

I remembered the shadow that lurked outside the door at the museum. Whatever had cast it had to have been of significant size. But I found what Bethany was saying impossible to believe.

"It was just some glass that cut you," I insist. She ignores me.

Her eyes widen as the doors behind me swing open. She settles down when only the departing congregation passes through them, but a wariness still underlines her voice as she informs me that she doesn't plan on coming back here. I tell her I won't be either.

My dreams that night return me to the funeral. For a change, I'm not in the coffin. Instead, I'm watching as the last bits of dirt fill my sister's grave.

The ground rumbles. The earth before me fragments as a dark figure bursts through it. The penguin shakes off a layer of dirt and climbs out. Its once-white stomach has browned and decayed. Worms spill out of it with each step it takes.

My mother and other relatives flee as the giant bird waddles forward. I make the sign of the cross and kneel. "Angela," I whisper. "Don't you recognize me?" It eyes me blankly, tilts its head back, and charges angrily. I wake up on my stomach with my pillow soaked by tears.

I toss my Bible into a recycling bin. Christianity hasn't provided me with any miracles. Charles Darwin has.

My phone rings. It's Bethany.

"Yeah?"

She speaks in a desperate, panicked voice. "He's dead, Adam. *Seth's dead.*"

"*What?* What the hell happened?"

"It was...he'd been camping, and a hiker found his tent ripped up this morning with a body inside. They just brought me in to confirm it was him, and...and..."

"And *what*, Bethany?"

"It was horrible, Adam. He was *mangled. Ripped apart.* I could barely tell it was him."

A pressure builds inside of me until my whole body trembling. "Were there...any signs of what did it? Foot prints from a black bear, or a mountain lion, or something like that?" It is an empty, perfunctory question. I knew what had happened even before Bethany describes the oversized, webbed tracks left in the mud outside Adam's tent.

"I'm going to confess, Adam."

"Bethany, you need to think about the implications of what you're saying-"

She interrupts me. "I've written down what we did. I want you to sign it, too, and we can bring it with us when we go to the police. Maybe, then, it'll show us mercy."

"That's a year behind bars for you. Longer for me. I'm not going back. No way."

"Adam, I *know* how bad it is, but what's coming for us is worse."

"Bethany, you sit tight now, you hear me? Sit tight. I'm coming over. We'll figure this out." I hang up before she can respond, and I ignore her when she calls me back. I need to get to her before she does anything stupid.

The route to Bethany's house takes me on the highway and by the billboard. The unkempt grass has covered the marks my tires once left beneath it. Its obnoxious aquarium ad is long gone, replaced with a simple "It's Your Choice…Heaven or HELL". *Who calls the number underneath, and in which place does the phone ring?*

My heart drops at the gashes that extend through the open front door to Bethany's house. I think about calling the authorities, but I don't want them showing up and finding what Bethany's guilty conscious compelled her to write.

I climb out of my car and approach cautiously. I slip through the door and tiptoe down a hallway littered with shattered glass from broken picture frames and books strewn around dented, collapsed furniture.

A shadow extends onto the wall before me. I discern its sharp beak and the two dots of light that mark where nails once made holes in its flippers.

The figure leans down, jabs violently, and pulls up. A limb dangles from its mouth. I hear it crunch, then swallow as it absorbs the outline of a foot.

As I back up, a book slips out from under me. I stumble awkwardly, loudly. It growls like an old motor engine sputtering to life. The outline of its head turns toward the hallway.

I dive into the nearest room and close the door as quietly as I can. I look around. No windows. No other exits. I'm cornered.

A violent throb confirms that it knows where I am. Wood splinters. It won't hold for long. I put my body weight against a couch I've shoved against the door.

As I sit there, postponing the inevitable, a sense of relief washes through me. My blood runs with a vigor that I haven't experienced since before the night I told Angela that I hadn't had too much to drink, that I was safe to drive, that we'd be home in no time. Since before I'd left her lifeless form amidst the car's smoky ruins underneath the mocking gaze of the stupid, flightless bird that stretched across the canvas.

It bursts through the barricade, sending me sprawling onto the floor. But I ignore the pain. I smile, and my laughter is hysterical as its approaching shadow slowly engulfs me. Because, for this creature, this instrument of my torture, to exist, something had to have created it. And wherever that creator is, Angela is, too.

Our long-awaited reunion approaches. See you soon, Angela.

## 10

# AGNES

I met Agnes during a hike at summer camp. At thirteen, she was a year older than me. I felt a jolt as she swiftly grabbed my hand when I slipped and nearly stumbled off the trail. As I thanked her, I noticed her eyes gazing at me sympathetically.

Around the campfire that evening, a counselor told a story about a monster that emerges from closets to devour sleeping children.

Agnes sensed how much it scared me. She volunteered to be my tent partner. That night, the fear I felt slowly dissipated as she reassured me that I had nothing to worry about. Eventually, I drifted off.

We became friends and did everything together for the next few weeks. We chatted about our favorite books. I described my parents' divorce and how, after camp, my dad would keep me for the rest of the summer. Agnes taught me some basic first aid and showed me how to use her long bowie knife.

One day, a camper named Ethan disappeared. Agnes and I were one of the many pairs who searched for him in the woods. Eventually, he reappeared dirty and bruised. He wouldn't talk at first, but then he accused Anthony, his counselor, of attempting to molest him.

That night, Agnes woke me in our cabin and beckoned me to follow her. We tiptoed past sleeping campers and outside.

Eventually, we arrived at an administrative building, where we used a loose window to climb inside. Agnes led me to a couch where Ethan, who had been removed from his cabin, slept.

I looked at Agnes, puzzled, as she gently gripped Ethan's hand. For a moment, both of their bodies slightly convulsed, as if shocked by an electric pulse.

Agnes motioned to the light switch, which I flipped. Ethan shot up, awake.

Agnes spoke firmly as she lifted her knife to Ethan's throat. "I know what you did. You'll tell the truth in the morning, or I'll visit you again. Understood?"

Ethan, wide-eyed with terror, mumbled affirmatively.

Agnes and I crept back unnoticed. The next morning, word spread that Ethan had admitted that he'd run off for attention, and then invented his story to avoid punishment. Anthony was released from custody and Ethan was sent home.

On the last night before the end of camp, Agnes told me something I would never forget. "I know why you were afraid of the closet monster. Do you want my help to get rid of it?"

I nodded, although I understood her only intuitively.

My father never arrived to pick me up. Instead, two solemn-faced officers informed me that his body had been found covered in deep stab wounds outside a gas station nearby.

The tears I shed were of joy. Though it took years for the repressed memories to fully re-surface, I knew, then, that a monster had been slain.

## 11

# FIRST HEAT

The announcement came promptly after we sensed the distant rumble.

*Attention all swimmers! Attention all swimmers! Due to another nearby lightning strike, the competition is delayed by twenty minutes.*

Goggles let out an annoyed moan. I'd given him that nickname because I didn't know his real name, and because he'd insisted thus far on wearing his oversized goggles for the duration of the wait.

I finally decided to ask him about it. "You ever going to take those off? It's been nearly an hour already. It can't be comfortable keeping them on like that."

Goggles responded defensively. "What's it to you, county boy?"

I shrugged. Goggles, Anthony, and Roger made up the rest of my heat, and they were friends with one other. If I picked a fight, they'd back each other up, so I tried not to escalate things further.

That didn't stop Roger from whining about me. "Goddamn it, how long are we stuck here with this bumpkin?"

"A *long* time, I bet," sighed Goggles. "A very long time."

This caused Anthony to speak up for the first time in a while.

"Give him break, guys. We're all in the first heat anyway. We've got nothing to act tough about."

He was right. In swimming, each age group is divided into 'heats' of competitors who all race at once. The number of swimmers in a heat varies based on the number of lanes in the pool – in the case of the pool used for this regional tournament, ten.

The last heat was where all the excitement happened, as it contained the fastest swimmers. The first heat was the opposite, as it typically consisted of the those who swam slowly, as well as competitors who had gotten themselves disqualified for breaking the rules in previous competitions.

The first heat was notable, too, since it was the only one that had an irregular number of people – if there were seventy-three swimmers in an age group at this pool, the first heat would include only three, versus an even ten for each of the remaining heats.

The worst fear of any slow swimmer like myself was to be the solo competitor in heat one. Goggles, Anthony, and Roger, who I figured all attended one of the private schools nearby, displayed a preppy hostility towards me, but at least their presence ensured that I wasn't alone.

We bore all the signs of a first heat, from being only four in number to lacking the lean physiques of the better swimmers.

Normally, our humiliation was brief. Within fifteen minutes, we'd sort into heats in the gymnasium, walk to the various waiting stations throughout the facility, and end up on a diving block poised to jump into the indoor pool. The race – a fifty meter breaststroke – would be over in no time, and then this miserable weekend would be one step closer to ending.

Today, however, lightening had kept us stuck in the corridor where we waited just outside the pool room. I normally experienced nervous jitters a few minutes before a race, but all I felt now, after so much waiting, was tedium and boredom.

Roger, perhaps realizing he'd let a full minute pass without complaining about something, spoke up again. "Why do they even delay for lightening, when it's an indoor pool we're going to be swimming in?"

Anthony responded. "It's just a stupid government rule. The lightening can't hurt us indoors, even in the water. But there's some local safety code that makes them have to wait anyway."

Goggles groaned. "This is *so* boring. We're stuck here forever with absolutely nothing to do."

"Maybe they'll just cancel the race," I said. "Surely they have to do that, eventually."

This prompted a sneer from Roger. "You'd like that, wouldn't you? It's the only way you won't place dead last." He and Goggles snickered.

"Like Anthony said," I responded, "we're *all* in last place already by being in the first heat. There are *nine* heats that are faster than us. Do your really care about finishing in ninety-first place versus ninety-fourth?"

"At least we'll finish at all," taunted Goggles. He approached where I sat such that he towered over me. "You'll probably flounder and grab onto the lane rope until someone comes to rescue you. And, instead of it being one of the hot lifeguards, it'll be that old coach who led us here who gives you CPR."

I jumped to my feet. Even if the odds weren't in my favor, I wasn't going to let them keep tormenting me without fighting back.

The door at the opposite side of the hallway opened as a familiar figure entered. My sister Allison, six years my senior and an event volunteer, unwittingly broke up a potential scuffle. Goggles retreated and sat against the wall with Roger and Anthony. One of them – I don't know who – let out a few catcalling whistlers, which Allison thankfully ignored.

"Hey Liam! You doing okay?"

I nodded.

"I was worried about you. Is there no staff person here?"

I shook my head. "Some coach was here for a little while, but he left and hasn't come back yet."

"I see. Well, I know you can look after yourself, but *please* don't hesitate to come find me if anything comes up. I know you must be bored out of your mind."

"Yeah, of course I'm bored. I wish this would wrap up already. These delays are *killing* me."

"It's a nightmare, I know. But I have a feeling things will be moving along shortly. I'll be watching whenever the races resume, and I'll be cheering for you, little champ. You're gonna do great, alright?"

"Thanks." I watched as she made her way back to the gymnasium.

"*Little champ*," snickered Roger.

Goggles jeered at me too. "She won't be cheering when she sees how badly you lose. Heck, you'll probably just flounder about until someone has to rescue you.

"Fuck off," I said.

Again, it was Anthony who stood up for me. "Go easy on him."

This made Goggles incredulous. "Why do you keep sticking up for this guy?"

Anthony delivered his response in a somber, serious voice. "Because he has enough to worry about already. When it's our turn to race, I get the feeling Nick's going to be in the pool, waiting. If Liam's as slow as we think he is, he won't be climbing out the other side."

"What? Who's Nick?" I asked, confused as to why someone would be in the pool when our race began.

Roger let out an exaggerated *Oohhh*. "He doesn't know the legend."

Goggles' response sounded forced, even improvisational. "Oh, right, *the legend*."

"I'm not falling for whatever bullshit you're about to make up."

To my surprise, Anthony joined in. "You don't have to believe if it if you don't want to. But ignore it at your own risk. I'm confident that *I* can outswim Nick. You, though, I'm not so sure about."

Roger took a step towards me. "You see, Nick haunts the pool. He's been there ever since he died in it thirty years ago. On this same day. At this same meet."

"He was the only swimmer in the first heat," added Goggles. "He was nervous about swimming alone in front of so many people."

"Let me guess," I said. "He jumped in the water, forgot how to swim, drowned, and somehow the hundreds of people present, including all the lifeguards, didn't notice on time to save him? You really think I'm dumb enough to believe a story like that?"

Anthony shook his head solemnly. "Oh, I wish we were just making this story up. A lot of people would still be alive if we were."

I remained unconvinced, to put it mildly. But, there was a sincerity to Anthony that made me wonder if there could be a grain of truth to what he was saying. Maybe some unfortunate kid really had died, and they were just inventing the rest of the story around that fact.

Anthony continued. "You see, it wasn't that simple. Lightening had delayed the meet for over an hour. Nick sat right where we are now shaking and shivering the whole time. Little did he know that, while he waited, there was a miscommunication among the pool staff. One of them got word that the meet was cancelled due to the bad weather and began the process of draining it, which they do once every few years to make repairs. Meanwhile, there was an electrical short in the overhead lighting system."

"It was a disaster waiting to happen. When the announcement was made that twenty minutes had passed since the last strike, and that the competition would resume, the audience was allowed to return just as Nick was led to a diving block."

"A few people noticed that something was wrong. The pool wasn't empty – it takes time to drain – but it wasn't nearly as full as it was before. But their cries were ignored. It wasn't a situation anyone expected, or that the parents and staff were trained to deal with."

"Nick took his position on the diving block. He saw, amidst the flickering lights, that there was water below. But, in his eagerness to get the race over with, he didn't comprehend that there was much less water than there should be. Less than there *needed* to be."

"One of the lifeguards realized what was wrong and cried out for the race to be called off. She ran towards Nick to stop him from jumping. She didn't get to him in time. The buzzer rang, and poor Nick hurtled forward."

"He fell through the air a few moments longer than usual before crashing into the water. It wasn't enough to slow him, not much at least. His head slammed into the concrete below."

"The whole crowd screamed when the lights returned and revealed his body, which had floated to the shallow surface. According to some witnesses, his skull fractured open and some of his brain spilled out."

"To this day, Nick's spirit remains in that pool. He gets lonely there, so, sometimes, he causes the lights to go out. In the darkness, he pulls the slowest boy from his age group in the competition down with him. By the time the lifeguards notice, it's too late, and he's taken another victim to join him in haunting this place forever."

"If that were true," I said, "this place would have been closed down for good ages ago."

Goggles piped up in response. "Nick isn't greedy. He only takes someone every once in a while. In the thirty years since this happened, only a few kids have died. The last one was a decade ago."

In the long silence that followed, I thought about what I'd heard. These guys were just trying to scare me, right? But, I found it hard to believe that Anthony had conjured up such a detailed story out of thin air.

I jolted upright as another announcement resounded through the room.

*Attention all swimmers! Attention all swimmers! Twenty minutes have passed without incident, and the competition has resumed!*

Goggles, Roger, and Anthony were laughing. To my embarrassment, I realized that my reaction to the announcement had given away how tense Anthony's story had made me.

Roger giggled at me. "We got you *so* scared. You scaredy-cat."

"No, no, I just didn't expect-"

Goggles' cackling cut me off. "I can't believe you fell for that stupid story. I guess county kids really are as dumb as the dirt they grow their corn in."

Anthony, again, was more sympathetic than his friends. "Don't worry, I made that whole story up. You've got nothing to worry about."

"Of-of course," I stuttered. "I didn't believe it."

The poolside door opened. The coach who'd led us to our waiting station over an hour ago emerged. "Come on, this way!" she called.

I followed her inside. As with any crowded indoor pool, the noises that echoed through the room – splashes, announcements, and the chatter and cheers of the crowd that was slowly made its way back to the bleachers – formed a loud, blurry cacophony. The room was also a lot dimmer than I remembered, with some of the overhead lights flickering on and off irregularly.

The announcer's voice blasted through the speaker system. *Heat one, take your position!*

I hesitated. I thought about Anthony's story, and how the lights had technical issues just before Nick jumped. But, that had to just be a coincidence, right?

The coach pushed me along. "Come on now, son, let's get this little heat over with."

The crowd cheered as I put on my goggles and carefully climbed onto the diving block. I was in one of the center lanes. I looked to my left and to my right and saw, to my surprise, that no one else was standing with me. Where had Goggles, Roger, and Anthony gone?

*The race will begin in three, two...* I looked down. There was water, but was there the right amount?

I got little more than a glimpse before, all at once, the ceiling lights turned off.

*One!* finished the announcer. The buzzer rang.

"Come on, kid!" yelled the coach through the darkness.

"There's no light," I cried. "I should wait until I can see!"

"The clocks' running now!" the coach replied. "I'm not letting you delay this entire race. There's nine heats behind you waiting to go!"

I turned my head back to the coach and, for a brief moment, discerned in the darkness the black silhouettes of three shadowy figures immediately behind me. I heard laughter, and I felt a force against my back.

An eternity passed in the moments that followed. I flew awkwardly through the air, my form all wrong, until I hit the water. I panicked at the thought that my head was about to smash into the hard pool floor.

Instead, my body slowed a few feet from the bottom. I realized, to my incredible relief, that the pool was full. I wasn't in any danger. Sure, my time would be terrible, and I'd likely be disqualified for not swimming in proper form, but I wasn't in any danger.

I kicked at the water and began to climb to the surface. That's when I felt an intense force around my neck.

It was an...arm. It was soggy and worn, and it pulled me downwards. I found myself at the bottom of the pool, held in place by the figure that had grabbed me. I turned my face to see Goggles, grinning widely. Only, he was missing many of his teeth and much of his skin, and his skull was split open revealing patches of a gray, spongy substance underneath.

I squirmed and tried to pull him off, but he continued to hold me in place. I needed desperately to breath, but I couldn't tear him off of me.

Two more faces appeared, but, when they swam closer, I realized they didn't belong to lifeguards like I'd hoped. The lifeguards probably couldn't even see that I was down here.

Instead, it was Anthony and Roger. Their skin was tattered and stained a murky brown, and they hovered above me in the water.

I managed to pry Goggles off me, but before I could get anywhere, Anthony and Roger reached out and pushed me back against the floor.

The world above me turned to shadow. I felt myself fade into unconsciousness. My last memory, real or hallucinatory, was of Goggles whispering one word into my ear: "*Sleep.*"

I woke up gasping and coughing up water. Allison sat over me, her clothes soaking wet.

"Thank god. Liam, I thought I'd lost you."

The lights turned back on. I could tell that we were on the surface next to the pool. My sister must have dived in and dragged me out. I learned later that I'd stopped breathing, but started again after she performed chest compressions on me.

"I can't believe they didn't call off the race. With the lights out, nobody could see that you were in trouble. Why'd you jump?"

"The-the..." I took a moment to catch my breath. "They shoved me in..."

"*Who* shoved you in? That coach? And how the heck did you get stuck at the bottom of the pool anyway?"

"No, it was the other kids in my heat...they held me down..."

My answers continued to only prompt more questions from Allison. "What other kids? You were the only one in your heat. You've been alone the last hour."

I didn't know what to say to that. Nor did I know what to say when the doctor Allison brought me to asked me about the abrasions and hand prints on my body, or when I saw the pictures from the old news reports about the other accidents at the facility.

It's been twelve years. Of course, nobody listened to my warnings or believed my ghost stories. The facility stayed in operation until a few weeks ago.

The official story behind its closure was that the building was so outdated that it needed to be demolished and completely rebuilt. I think it has more to do with the fact that another kid drowned in its pool last spring.

A few days ago, I found a grainy video of its destruction on a local news channel's website. In the corner of the footage, away from the smoke and debris of the collapsed building, I noticed something unusual: four figures, dressed only in swim gear, walking along a dirt road.

I don't know where, exactly, that road leads. I just know that it stretches onwards for a long, long time in a direction far away from town.

**12**

---

# REVENGING MACHINE

"**S**top being such a sissy," teased my older brother Jessie. "Just shake it a little."

The machine bothered me. I'd sensed something sinister about it ever since we'd stepped inside the rest stop's vending area. I'm not sure if it was the indecipherable graffiti sprayed around its perimeter or the antiquated appearance of its spartan supply of snacks. It was empty aside from two bags of potato chips and a few half-melted pastries that drooped over the metal spirals holding them in place.

"I dunno, Jessie. The food looks disgusting anyway."

"Out of my way, twerp," retorted Jessie, pushing me aside. As I tumbled into the wall, he gripped the machine and shoved.

It was heavy, and at first it didn't budge. But, eventually, Jessie managed to lift its front legs. When they crashed down again, Jessie's prize fell from the bottom row.

"Gotcha!" he exclaimed. With a satisfied smile, he reached into the pickup box. The treat's wrapper displayed *Clarissa's Jumbo Glazed Honey Bun* in red ink.

As we departed, a raspy clank drew my attention back to the

machine. Somehow, it looked like it had...moved, if only by a few inches.

"You sure you don't want any?" asked Jessie as we sat in our hotel room that evening.

"Yeah."

"Good, because I wouldn't have shared it anyway." As he chewed another bite of the gooey pastry, he took no notice of its oddly stringy texture.

A deep, blunt sound boomed against the door to the hallway.

"Who do you think it is?" I asked.

"Mom and dad must have forgotten their key. Who else would it be, dummy?" He hopped off the bed and approached the door.

"You should look first!"

"*I'm Danny, I'm scared of everything*," he mocked as he pulled the handle. "*What?*" he gasped upon finding himself facing the vending machine, which wedged its way into the room.

I covered my eyes as Jessie screamed. When I peeked, I saw his foot sticking out of the pickup box. With a 'slurp' sound, it, too, was sucked inside.

My parents later found me unconscious. Of course, no one believed my story.

Years later, I park at a familiar rest stop. My body shakes as I creep into the vending area and towards a machine covered in graffiti. The label on a pastry on its bottom row reads, *Jessie's Jumbo Glazed Honey Bun*.

**13**

---

# THERE'S NO LEAVING EVERGREEN

My eyes gaze blankly through the glass and towards the endless, muddy plains blanketed in a thin layer of powdery snow as the train continues its long journey to my destination.

I check my phone again and reread my text exchange with Nicole from the last time I had service.

*The kids can't wait to see you, honey. And neither can I. How much longer do you think it'll be?*

*The attendant told me we'd be at the station by eight if there are no more delays,* I'd replied. *Don't worry though. I'll be there tonight. Love you.*

This was supposed to be the first Christmas Day I would be spending with family in over a decade. When I'd accepted the work assignment – tracking down an unresponsive witness with an address in the middle of nowhere – I hadn't anticipated it taking three days, or a blizzard shutting down the airport. Now, this fourteen-hour ride was my only hope of making it back on time, and it had already been delayed twice.

A coarse voice calls for me. I turn. It's the white-haired man sitting across the aisle. He's one of the only other passengers in my train car. He's thin, and looks quite up in years. He's wearing a formal black suit, with a matching black-and-white tie.

He wants to strike up conversation. I'm not normally one to share information with strangers, but he carries a gentle sincerity that disarms me. We chat for a bit, and when I mention that I am returning to my family, he asks if I have kids waiting for me at my destination.

"Yes," I reply. "But they aren't mine, not really. They're from my, um...my partner's previous marriage. This'll be my first Christmas with them as part of the family. Assuming the train gets there on time, that is."

He nods slowly and wishes me good luck. He tells me that I have a lot to live for. That he had a lot to live for too, once, but that he's all alone now.

I'm not sure how to respond to that. "Oh," I mutter. "I'm sorry to hear that. Where are you heading, if not to meet with someone for the holiday?"

His response is cryptic. "Somewhere I've been before. You see, there's a reason this train is so deserted. Strange things can happen on this route this time of year. Just don't forget what matters to you most. You have a lot to live for, young lady." He removes a blue pill from a bag, pops it into his mouth, and swallows it with a gulp of bottled water. "Now," he says, "I'm going to get some rest." He lays down across the empty seats to his left and right and closes his eyes.

I ponder his words as I return my gaze to the barren landscape outside. I pity this kind, lonely man, and I wonder what he meant about "strange things" happening on this route. As far as I've observed, everything about this train ride has thus far been mundane.

As darkness begins to fall, the man's gentle snores mix with the regular clickety-clack of the train passing over rail joints and squats, lulling me into a state of drowsiness. I find myself yawning as the frosty scenery blends together in the fading light. I close my eyes and think about Nicole and the two boys. They'll stay up all night waiting for me, if Nicole lets them. But hopefully it won't come to that.

Hardly a moment passes before my hopes are dashed. My eyes shoot open at the sound of the loud hissing of breaks. The conductor's voice announces that "mechanical failures" have prompted an unplanned stop at a station. *"We expect a one-hour delay. Passengers must disembark during the repair process. Repeat, passengers must disembark."*

Fucking hell, I think. Part of me wants to scream at the nearest train employee. But I know better than to yell at someone who probably wasn't at fault. Better to wait for the problem to get fixed.

I text Nicole about the delay as I stand up and don my coat and scarf. Judging by his empty seat, the old man has already stepped outside. I do the same and hop onto the platform.

I feel a vague sense of familiarity as I read the banner stretched out across the side of the train station. It states *Welcome to Evergreen* in red and green letters. Rather than spend the hour waiting at the station, I decide to explore.

The town around me could hardly be more picturesque. I don't think I've ever seen a town so thoroughly decorated for the holiday season.

Smatterings of snow sit on the tiled roofs of the shops in the downtown around me, as well as the Victorian houses on nearby hills. All are decorated with an assortment of lights, as well as Santa and reindeer figurines and inflated props.

The town's inhabitants, adorned in heavy coats, top hats, gloves, and scarves, trudge through knee-deep snow. Giant candy canes, thick green trees, and the occasional snowman line the streets. A horse pulls a couple in a buggy beside me. Children in a park nearby giggle as they pelt each other with snowballs.

My surroundings delight me. I feel like I am inhabiting a childhood dream. It reminds me of the many hours I used to spend watching my mother craft every detail of a miniature holiday-themed town of her own.

As I cross a small bridge over a lake, I look down at the families skating across its frozen surface. It's a lovely sight, but I can't escape an uneasy feeling that grows in my gut. It's all too perfect, too serene.

Most eerily, it makes me feel nostalgic, too, even though I know that I have never before visited someplace like this.

Almost instinctually, I navigate through the town until I arrive at a main street packed with Christmas-themed shops and stands. I find myself somehow anticipating the various sights moments before I see them: a dog in an adorable elf costume, a series of stands marked "Hanks Holiday Market," and a group of four carolers singing to a small crowd.

It all hits me when I read the sign outside a store covered in wreaths and garlands: *Sofia's Christmas Confections*. I back up as my heart beats rapidly. It's not true. It *can't* be.

This whole town...it's *identical* to the Evergreen my mother and I once created.

It was my last Christmas with her. The signs of illness were still scattered, and she wouldn't get the diagnosis until early the next spring.

She spent many of her last months of good health teaching me her hobby. We cleared out a whole room in the basement and used tables and buckets to set up the town's hilly geography. She showed me how to cut and layer the mountainous backdrop to hide the electric wires that powered the lights and the train that ran through town. We set up a frozen lake and covered the setting with cotton snow.

For the most part, we reused the people, buildings, and decorations from mom's private collection. But, she and I spent a several days constructing and fine-tuning a new shop to add to the town. When it was completed, she let me name it after myself: *Sofia's Christmas Confections*.

As I look around now, I recognize each and every item in the busy street around me. Each person, house, tree and even the lights dangling from them – all a perfect match to pieces from my mom's collection.

Questions rush through my mind. How could this be possible? This town just *can't* exist. What mom and I constructed was just an artificial miniature, after all.

Yet, here I am, walking through it. Had it sprung from my imagination? Had I shrunken, or had it grown?

This all feels so inexplicable, so *wrong*. I rush back towards the station. The train, alone, is comfortingly real, like the last piece of a world I'd disembarked from moments ago.

I am nearly back when a sight catches my eye. Something about a hill that overlooks the station feels different from the rest of Evergreen. It takes me a moment to realize *why* it seems that way. Then, it hits me: that hill doesn't *belong* there. It, alone, deviates from the miniature my mom and I constructed so long ago.

Through the fluttering light snowfall, I discern the outline of the structure at its peak. It sits on a small plateau mostly visible from my current location. It's a house I haven't visited in nearly ten years: my childhood home – the same home where my mom and I built this very town.

Its front door opens. A distant figure, obscured by the precipitation and the diminishing light, steps outside of it and walks in my direction until she is standing at the precipice of a steep decline.

I still can't make out the figure's features, but I have no doubt who she is. "Mom," I call, even as I know she is too far away to hear me.

She looks over the town, as if searching for something, or someone.

*Me*, I realize. She's looking for *me*. My screams for her are futile. She's too far away.

I scurry through the snow in her direction as she turns around and heads back inside. I'm not going to leave her, not now that I have found her again in this impossible place.

I ignore everything around me – the man pushing his car out of the snow, the hot chocolate stand, the children laughing on the merry-go-round – as I ascend a lower hill and then follow a narrow trail through a dense wood of tall fir trees.

Finally, I emerge to find myself facing the plateau that overlooks the town. The house's surroundings, from its elevated position to the adjacent graveyard and the vibrant garden that surrounds it, bear little resemblance to the deserted countryside I grew up around.

Nonetheless, the building itself is an exact match to the compact, one-story ranch house of my youth.

I approach slowly, allowing myself a few moments to catch my breath. The climb would normally exhaust me and, indeed, I feel a tired stiffness in my joints. Nonetheless, the prospect of reuniting with my mother, no matter how illogical the whole situation feels, pushes me along.

I knock three times at the front door. My heartbeat races as I hear the approach of shuffling footsteps. A lock is undone, then another.

The wooden door creaks open. A dark figure steps forward. The artificial glow cast by the red and green lights that line the outside of the house illuminate a face that bears so much resemblance to my own.

I start to cry. Before I know it, my wet face has dug into her green sweater. She hugs me back.

My mother leads me inside. She tells me that I can't imagine how much she has missed me. She tells me that after so many years apart, we'll finally be together again.

Everything is as it once was, from the family photos lining the front hallway, to the antique grandfather clock that remains functional after decades of use, to the small tear on the fabric of the old living room couch.

I find myself sitting by the burning logs of a large fireplace beneath a tall, gorgeously decorated Christmas tree. Stacks of perfectly wrapped presents surround me.

When I ask mom questions about where we are and how I got here, she shushes me, handing me a plate of cookies in the shape of trees, snowflakes, and stars. Just like the cookies she'd always bake for this time of year.

"But mom," I insisted. "I have so many questions."

"All in good time, dear," she tells me. "Let's just enjoy each other's company for now. It's been so long."

"But I need to know!" I say. "How are you here? How is any of this possible? I was there when you, when you…" Mom hands me another tissue as I choke on my words.

"It's all okay," she says in a voice I've missed so dearly. "We're together now. We'll always be together now."

"I have so much to tell you, mom. So much has happened since you left. I have a family now. A wife, and we're raising two kids."

She tells me that she can't wait to hear all about them. But, she wants to enjoy being here with me a little longer before getting to them. She hands me a present and asks me to open it.

I gaze at the beautifully wrapped gift. A sense of ecstasy courses through my veins. I'm somehow here, with my long departed mother, having a Christmas as wonderful as any from my childhood.

The moment seizes me. My mom's face beams in satisfaction as I find myself tearing apart the wrapping paper, revealing a gorgeous floral dress underneath. I embrace her, thanking her for the gift.

The second present is a handmade hardwood sled. As a kid, I'd been good at sledding, but I'd always been stuck using a much cheaper model. I thank mom profusely, telling her that it is just what I wanted. It feels true, even though I haven't thought about sledding in years.

A distant, high-pitched sound pulls me back to reality. I remember the train. If I'm hearing its whistle, then...Wait, how long have I been away?

I glance at the grandfather clock. If the time it displays is accurate, I've been gone over fifty minutes.

An unsettling feeling grows inside of me. My train is about to leave, and, somehow, I feel absolutely certain that no other train will be stopping here anytime soon.

"Mom, we need to go. I don't know what this place is, but we need to leave it, now."

Mom maintains her long smile. She insists that there's nothing to worry about. That we don't need to be going anywhere.

"Mom, no, I need to get back to my family, and I need you-"

Her expression sours. "Sofia, you belong here, with me. I'm not leaving, and neither are you."

"But, mom, I *have* to get back to my family-"

She raises her voice. "I *am* your family, your *real* family, and you're staying right here with me."

My affection for her fades. I know that my mom – my *real* mom – would leave with me. Certainly, she'd never ask me to abandon my wife and children to stay with her.

"I'm sorry, but I'm leaving."

With surprising force and speed, mom restrains me when I stand up, wrapping her arms around my neck from behind. She whispers four words into my year: "*There's no leaving Evergreen.*"

Her grip tightens around my neck as I try, in vain, to pry her arms off. In desperation, I stumble towards the fireplace, ignoring the heat as I back into it.

At first, my mother – or, at least, the figure pretending to be her – doesn't seem to mind, even as I sense the encroaching heat. I begin to lose consciousness as I grow desperate for breath.

Finally, her grip becomes too weak to restrain me. I tumble forward. As I catch my breath, I turn to find the figure engulfed in flames that have spread all over her body.

She isn't burning. She's melting. All of her facial features – mouth, eyes, nose – are disintegrating into a liquid that runs down her body, forming a molten pool at her feet.

"There's...no leaving...Evergreen," she croaks before collapsing to her knees.

I don't have time to process the grotesque sight. I know that I need to leave this town, no matter what it takes. Adrenaline sends me sprinting outside in the direction of the station.

To my surprise, dozens of townspeople await me. They line the roads and footpaths back down to the station. Moments ago, I'd seen these same people – men, women, children – frolicking peacefully in this idyllic holiday town. But, now, they march towards me in unison, chanting four words I'd grown to loathe: "There's no leaving Evergreen."

The train whistles again. I don't have much time.

Scanning my surroundings, I see only one way forward. Quickly, I run back inside, grab the sled mom – or whatever that thing was –

had gotten for me, and exit to the side. My path takes me through the small cemetery inexplicably located near the house.

As the chants of the approaching crowd grow closer, my foot slips, and I barely manage to stop myself from plummeting into a deep hole in the ground. The inscription on the tombstone bordering it reads, "Sofia White. Born January 13, 1993. Joined Evergreen December 25, 2024."

I reach the hill's precipice as the crowd closes in on me. The decline is rocky, and dangerously steep, but it leads towards the train station.

"*THERE'S NO LEAVING EVERGREEN,*" repeat the townspeople, who have encircled my position. Seeing no other option, I dive forward in the sled.

A nauseous pit grows in my stomach as my speed rapidly increases. The intense wind sends my scarf sailing away. My sled lands on a small rock formation, sending it flying, but I'm able to keep my grip and continue the descent.

With a 'thud,' the sled crashes into a tree. I roll off and spot the slowly-accelerating train. Mustering my last bit of energy, I sprint toward the tracks, reaching them just as the caboose is about to pass. I reach out, grab the metal railing, and pull myself onboard.

A hand shakes me awake. It belongs to the train attendant, and he's telling me that I've reached my destination.

I take in my surroundings. I'm back in the passenger cabin, as if I'd never left my seat. Behind the attendant, I see three EMTs lifting the old man from across the aisle into a gurney. His body is pale and limp, but a long smile stretches over his face.

An officer asks me a few questions about the man's death. I tell him that I hadn't seen the man since the train stopped at Evergreen for repairs.

The officer eyes me skeptically and calls over the conductor, who confirms that the train never made such a stop, and that there is no town with that name anywhere on our route.

I spend that evening with my family, who had all waited to open presents until my arrival. It is a warm, joyous occasion, one I choose not to spoil by sharing any of what I'd recently experienced. Instead, as I hug my wife and children, I remember one thing the old man had said, "You have a lot to live for, young lady."

The paper soon runs a story about an Edward Michaelson, who was found dead in his seat at 8:04 p.m. on December 25, 2021. Upon reading it, I recall something else he told me: *Strange things can happen on this route this time of year.*"

I'm not sure what happened. Of course, the logical part of my brain tells me that I had a vivid nightmare while he, coincidentally, suffered a fatal heart attack.

But I also wonder if the train took him somewhere like Evergreen, allowing him to be with someone who meant as much to him as my mother did to me. I think, too, of the graveyard on the hill, and the lushness of the garden that surrounded it, almost as if Evergreen needed us to sustain itself.

As the months pass, I think less and less about what occurred. It's been almost a year now. My family life is as wonderful as ever, and Nicole and I recently dropped off our eldest son for his first day of school.

Today, a package with my name on it arrives at our front door. It has no return address.

I drop it to the floor when I see the two objects inside: my long-missing scarf, and a handwritten note with four words in alternating red and green letters, "*There's no leaving Evergreen.*"

## 14

## COUNTDOWNS

The raging headache I'd woken up with had only worsened as morning stretched into early afternoon. I also felt sore everywhere, which made the frequent nausea-induced trips to the bathroom all the more uncomfortable.

"How are you not affected by any of this?" I whimpered to Mae. We'd gotten our second dose together the previous afternoon.

"I'm a bit foggy up here," she said, gesturing to her head before continuing to type at her work computer. "But, yeah, that's about it. I usually don't react much to these things."

I always did, and I hated needles too. Both times, Mae had pushed me to register to get vaccinated, and then practically dragged me to the facility where the injections were being administered.

My gaze shifted to the cactus on my windowsill. *Mr. Jacobson*, I still called it.

It had been three months now since I'd last seen the zippers. Since the *real* Mr. Jacobson had threatened to fire me if I didn't sleep with him. Since my housemate and I had watched his guts spill out onto his bedroom floor.

We'd expected to see the grisly scene we'd left behind plastered over the evening news. Instead, I'd received an inexplicable email announcing that Mr. Jacobson was on medical leave.

Consequences eluded us. Eventually, we'd moved on with our lives.

I continued teleworking, though I was finally expected to return to the office next week. When Mae wasn't giving virtual lectures or writing research papers, she tended to her cacti or spent time with me or her new boyfriend Casey.

Throughout the day, she periodically brought water, apple sauce, and anything else I needed to the couch in our shared living room where I lay sprawled under a soft blanket.

When I thanked her, she told me it was the least she could do since I'd helped her deal with her breakup with Gerald that winter. I told her I was just glad that she and Casey were together now.

"You could always try to find a partner yourself, you know." Her tone was half-joking, but I could tell she was also trying to nudge me out of the complacency I'd fallen into. "You haven't brought someone back here since, what, that girl from trivia night last winter? Now that you're fully vaccinated, you're all out of excuses."

I resisted sharing the rejoinders that came to mind. I knew that, over the past year and a half, I'd grown too comfortable with the isolated routine I'd settled into, and I'd lost a little bit of myself in the process.

But all that could wait. For the time being, I just needed to rest until my head stopped throbbing. "Fair enough," I mumbled, before closing my eyes.

~

When I finally made my long-awaited return to the office, I headed to central elevator and punched "15".

On the way up, the elevator stopped on the 12th floor, where the biomedical labs were located. A woman in a white lab coat joined me. She seemed unwell. She coughed profusely, and her whole body shivered. Fortunately, I was able to step off the elevator shortly thereafter.

On the 15th floor, I entered a door marked "Finances" and made my way down the main hallway.

I came across Kelly, who stood by the water cooler that bordered my office. "Hi Olivia, it's nice to see you in person again." As I greeted her, I noticed something odd: a set of oscillating green numbers, like those of a digital display, on her right cheek.

"Um…Kelly, did you like, get a tatoo, or something?"

"No, what are you talking about?"

"There's something on your right cheek. A set of numbers."

"Like a food stain, or what?" she replied, concerned. "One moment." She hopped into the nearby lady's room, and promptly returned. "I don't know what you're talking about, Olivia. I didn't see anything."

*Here we go again*, I thought. "Um, never mind, sorry."

Our cell phones buzzed simultaneously. An email directed us to report to the office of our chief regional executive on the building's top level. When we arrived, two empty chairs awaited us in front of her desk.

Kelly and I exchanged a nervous glance before sitting down. Ms. Franklin was near the top of the corporate food chain; something serious had to be happening for her to get involved.

The numbers on Ms. Franklin's forehead distracted me from the content of the meeting. There were six of them, separated by two colons, and they were counting down: *49:24:17. 49:24:16. 49:24:15.* I could only pretend to listen to what she was saying – something involving a "presentation" and "executive board members" – as I watched the numbers change.

*49:24:00*

*49:23:59*

What would happen when the numbers hit zero?

"Yes, yes, that sounds good," said Kelly, the numbers on her cheek matching those on Ms. Franklin's forehead. "We'll start preparing right away." If Kelly could see them, too, she gave no sign of it.

Was I viewing their death clock? When time ran out, would their insides spill out like Mr. Jamison's?

"Olivia?" asked Ms. Franklin. "What about you?"

"Oh, um...sorry. What's the question?"

Ms. Franklin glared at me impatiently. "Is Wednesday enough time for you?"

"Yes. That's fine. Wednesday, sure."

*49:23:36*

Afterwards, I applied every ounce of my self-control to maintain my composure as I debriefed with Kelly in her office. I picked up from her that we'd been assigned to provide a detailed presentation on our branch's financial status to a panel of executives following recent changes in leadership. We would use a conference room on the top level, by Ms. Franklin's office. We agreed that I'd cover the first half of the material, and Kelly would cover the second.

"By the way, Kelly, did you notice anything odd about Ms. Franklin's appearance?" I asked.

"Like what?"

"Never mind."

Once we settled on a way to divide the work, I quickly excused myself. Along the way, I stumbled upon three team members around a water cooler. When one of them reached for the faucet handle, I noticed a set of green numbers displayed across his palm.

Ignoring them, I rushed to the bathroom, where I frantically examined myself for any sign of such a countdown on my own body. Thankfully, I found nothing.

At my desk, I buried my head in my arms and tried to process what was happening. The major presentation I'd just been tasked with was the least of my worries. What mattered most was that it was happening *again*.

I didn't want to be here when the numbers hit zero. I resolved, at that moment, to do something I should have done ages ago: quit and never look back. I typed up a letter of resignation with the intention of handing it to Roger, my team leader, the next morning.

When I returned home that evening, Mae pulled up a chair for me at the kitchen table where she, Casey, and a young man they introduced to me as Ray were eating.

Casey put together a plate of takeout for me as Ray explained that he was an old friend of Casey's, having played in a band with him during college. "Nice to meet you," he said with an earnest smile.

He had a refreshingly lighthearted demeanor, bringing the three of us to laughter several times over dinner as he related past hijinks he'd engaged in with Casey.

There was so much I felt I needed to say. I wanted to confide in Mae about what I'd seen that day, my decision to finally leave my job, and the financial implications that this decision carried.

But, instead, I let the evening carry me away. All three lacked any kind of digital countdowns, after all, and nothing that happened tonight would change what was going to happen tomorrow.

Casey eventually asked if I minded if Ray crashed for the night on our couch. "That's totally fine," I replied. After spending so much time around people like me – dreary, world-weary – I enjoyed having him around.

After dinner, Casey hooked our dusty Nintendo 64 up to the television. Although I placed a distant fourth in the many rounds of Super Smash Bros. that followed, I enjoyed taking my mind off of my responsibilities.

Eventually, Casey and, with a wink, Mae retreated to Mae's room for the night as Ray scooted closer to me.

"If you want to get better," explained Ray, as we played another match, "You need to learn how to spike. Hit down 'A' when you're on top of me, like this..."

I tried but failed again. "No, no, like this," he said, gently placing his hand over mine as he executed the maneuver. After sensing that I was okay with that, he squeezed my hand a bit.

I barely held back my laughter. His gesture struck me as cheesy, yet also sweet. I realized he was trying to gauge my reaction, so I smiled and placed my other hand over his.

Before long, we were in my room. I lost track of how long we kissed. He was good at it. With him, it felt like its own end, rather than an activity to rush through to get to something else.

We did eventually escalate things a step, and soon after that, he went to sleep with me wrapped around him. As I felt the beat of his relaxed heart, I realized just how much, over my year and a half of isolation, I'd grown to miss this kind of physical affection.

My dreams took me back to a different time. We had just moved in, my grandmother was still alive, Mae was flirting over her phone with Gerald, and we were planning to head to a bar for trivia that evening. An ominous rumbling at the front door got my attention. *Something's coming for us*, I told Mae, but she took no notice. The rumbling got louder until the door burst open, revealing the head and tall frame of my boss.

I felt myself wake from what seemed like a deep slumber. Suddenly, a sharp, paralyzing pain spread from my chest to the rest of my body.

With immense effort, I used my left arm to flip on my bedside lamp. I let out a panicked yell as the light revealed that the figure I held onto was no longer Ray, but, instead, a man who death itself seemingly could not stop.

Hundreds of long, sharp thorns protruded from his sickly green skin. Many had dug their way into me, and as he sat up, he dragged my body with his. My blood spilled out, soaking through my t-shirt and dripping onto my bed sheets.

I put my hand against him and, ignoring the barb that protruded through my palm, shoved until I could pull myself free. I toppled to the floor.

He stepped towards me slowly, his frame towering over mine. "I'm coming for you, Olivia," he taunted in a gravelly voice. "We had an agreement. But you never gave me what you promised." He leaned down and grabbed my neck as I tried to squirm away from him.

"Fuck off, you *freak*!" I kicked at him with all the force I could muster.

"Ow! *Jesus*, what's wrong?" said Ray. "Get the hell off me!"

As my senses returned, I saw that it was the early morning. Mr. Jacobson had only haunted my dreams, as he had so many times before.

"Damn," said Ray, nursing a bruise on his leg. "That *really* hurt."

"I'm so sorry," I said. "I..I..."

Everything came flooding back. The sense of self-hatred that Mr. Jacobson had instilled in me over my first two years on the job. The feeling of constant powerlessness I'd felt around him. That moment of desperation when I'd undone the zipper that stretched from his head to his waist, just before anything happened, when I'd just stood there, wondering if I'd lost my mind. The sense that I'd fought back too much, in the wrong way, in a way that someone like me wasn't supposed to fight.

I realized I was crying. Ray brought me a tissue.

"Um..." I stuttered between sniffs, "Sorry, again."

"It's okay. Is there anything I can do to help you?"

"No, no," I muttered, "you're fine. I just...I don't know what's wrong with me. Maybe I need some space."

He nodded and retired to the living room couch.

It was too late in the morning for me to go back to sleep, so I took a long shower and got dressed for work. I found Mae waiting for me in the kitchen. Ray had clued her in that something was up with me before leaving with Casey.

I opened up to her about everything: my decision to resign; my horrible, vivid dream; and the countdowns. "I feel like I'm losing my mind."

"It's okay," said Mae, briefly embracing me. "You'll get through this. We both know you're not crazy, and that something fucked up is happening again at your workplace. You're doing the right thing getting out of there as fast as possible."

"Yeah. Hopefully, today will be my last."

"Not *hopefully*," she declared. "Today, you need to hand over your letter and walk out. If you keep seeing the countdowns, well, then we'll deal with that later, together, okay? And if anyone gives you trouble, just call me, and I'll come kick their ass."

I laughed. "Mae, I'm sure it won't come to that, but thank you. This will all be over soon. I'll have to find a new job, you know, but what choice do I really have?"

~

*25:23:48*, read the neck of the lobby officer that morning. Whatever I was seeing was spreading.

As I made my way to my office, I spotted Roger drinking water from the cooler. The liquid had an obvious murky green tinge to it, but he gulped it down anyway. "Roger, are you sure…" I stopped when I spotted small numbers on his chin. *25:19:50*.

"You alright, Olivia?"

*25:19:49*

"Yeah, yeah I'm fine."

I needed to get out of there, fast. Until then, I vowed to keep my distance from my coworkers, and to avoid eating or drinking anything on the building premises.

I settled into my office and reviewed the resignation letter. My desk phone rang the moment I hit print.

It was Ms. Franklin. "My office. Now."

When I arrived, one empty chair waited for me.

Ms. Franklin sat with her arms folded. "Sit," she ordered.

I did so.

"What's this about?" I tried my best to maintain normal eye contact despite then numbers that flashed on her forehead: *24:58:12*; *24:58:11*.

"You know what this is about," she responded. "You want to resign."

"What? How do you-"

"Please," she said with a cold smirk. "It's your right to leave if you want to. I'll just need you to sign a few forms in advance." She handed me a pen and a printed document.

The words "Non-Disclosure and Confidentiality Agreement" ran across the front page. I flipped through it to find it littered with terms like "bio-organic," "contagion," "clinical trial," "discrete experiments," and "unknowing subjects."

"What is this?"

Ms. Franklin's demeanor hardened as her timer hit *24:57:00*. "I know what you've seen."

"*What*?" How *much* did she know?

"Our late CEO wasn't exactly known for his strict adherence to safety regulations. But we have new leadership now, and our new leadership wants to right our way without derailing this company altogether over matters that, well, it's simply too late for us to fully rectify."

I didn't know where this was going. Mason Abernathy, the company's longtime figurehead, *had* been in the news in the months leading up to his death – I'd read plenty of stories about fines for flaunting regulations – , but what did that have to do with me?

Ms. Franklin continued. "At his direction, some of our lab chiefs may have acted a bit...*overly-enthusiastic* when it came to gathering data. When it came to selecting test subjects, they may have over-looked things like 'knowing consent' in the name of efficiency."

As she spoke, I remembered how whole floors had been shut down, and terms like "transfection" and "electrotransmission" appearing in the periphery of the financial reports I reviewed. I thought about the zippers, too.

"What, exactly, are you saying, Ms. Franklin?"

She looked me dead in the eye. "You haven't figured it out yet? You, your team, your other low-level friends here – your value to the company is not limited to the menial tasks you perform. We found other ways to extract value from you."

"By...testing products on us? You've been *experimenting* on us, your own employees?"

She didn't respond, instead maintaining a smug smile as her countdown ticked down to 24:56:32.

"And, now...now..." I sputtered, my head spinning, "you want me to sign away my right to tell anyone about it after I leave."

"We've been onto you since we learned that your exposure allowed you to *see* the experiments far more clearly than others could. You'd piece all this together, sooner or later," said Ms. Franklin. "And, yes, that is what I want."

"Bullshit. No way. I'm telling everyone."

"No, I don't think you will be," said Ms. Franklin. She leaned forward and spoke in a low, firm voice. "*I know what you did to Mr. Jacobson.*"

I understood what she was talking about, but I feigned ignorance anyway. "What? What do you mean?"

"How did it feel, Olivia, eviscerating your boss? And don't play innocent, or act like it was self-defense. We have the ability to make you a murderer in the eyes of the authorities, if we want to."

I felt like I was spinning. It had been an act of desperation. I had to do *something* to stop him. I hadn't thought it would actually work... or had I?

"And that's not all," Ms. Franklin continued. "I know who was there with you when you did it. If we can implicate you, we can implicate her. How would you like your housemate to become your cellmate?"

*Oh God, no.* "If, um...if you know what you claim that you know, then, um-"

Ms. Franklin completed my thought. "Then why haven't we turned you in already? It was a simple cost-benefit analysis. If the police had investigated, they may have uncovered some...unorthodox research methods. Better to keep your hands clean, legally speaking, and you onboard. But, that calculus can always change. Now, sign this, please."

*Fuck*, I thought. I knew that I didn't stand a chance against this degenerate megacorporation. And Mae didn't deserve to be dragged into this mess any longer. I gulped, picked up a blue pen from Ms. Franklin's desk, and began signing my name.

I passed her the signed confidentiality agreement, along with my resignation letter.

She eyed me suspiciously, then reviewed the paperwork. "There's one more condition, Olivia. Your employment ends *after* you give the presentation tomorrow morning. It's an important occasion, and it's too late for me to find someone else to take your place."

"*What*? Absolutely not."

I argued, but Ms. Franklin held firm. "You do the presentation, or the whole deal is off."

I did some quick mental math: the presentation was set for 9 a.m. Two hours before the timers would run out. We only had 20 minutes of material. Even with questions, that would give me plenty of time to walk out the door. "Fine, but no delays, nothing. It starts and ends at the planned times."

"Very well. You may go, now." Her countdown read *24:47:20* as I closed the door to her office.

I barely slept that night. I kept most of what Ms. Franklin had told me to myself, sharing with Mae only that I needed to stop by the office briefly that morning to sign some more forms to make my resignation official.

"Just be safe, and get the fuck out of there the moment you can, okay? Casey and I will be on call to help you out if you need it."

"Thanks, and yes, I will." I thought about how good it would feel walking out that door, never to return. *This will all be over soon*, I assured myself.

When I arrived at the conference room the next morning, Kelly was setting up our PowerPoint presentation. Like me, she'd donned a formal dress skirt and jacket for the occasion.

Right at 9 a.m., Ms. Franklin led in a group of six other executives who took seats at the conference table.

As Kelly began her part, I studied them. As with Ms. Franklin, a countdown appeared somewhere on each of their heads.

*01:56:19* read one.

*01:58:57* read another.

My pulse quickened as I realized Kelly had exceeded her allotted 15 minutes.

The numbers on the forehead of the executive closest to me decreased from *01:32:12* to *01:32:11*.

Kelly wrapped up her part and asked if there were any questions. Four executives raised their hands.

*01:30:40*

*01:30:39*

It's going to be okay, I repeated to myself. I still had plenty of time.

When Kelly finally finished answering questions, the time on the nearest executive read *01:19:23*.

As Ms. Franklin instructed me to begin, her phone buzzed. "Hold off for a second, Olivia. I just wanted to share some good news." I gulped as I felt sweat run down my side. "Our team leader, Mr. Jacobson, has fully recovered. He will be returning here at once."

*WHAT THE FUCK*, I thought to myself as the executives exchanged pleasantries. The image of his body collapsing into a gory heap flashed through my mind. How does someone recover from *that*?

Ms. Franklin directed me to start. Suppressing a new wave of panicked thoughts, I began the slide show and turned to the audience, only to gasp at what I saw.

The numbers in their countdowns were decreasing *more quickly*.

*01:16:22*

*01:16:12*

*01:16:02*

"Uhh, umm..." I stuttered.

Ms. Franklin adopted a concerned look. "Is something wrong, Olivia?"

*01:15:32*

*01:15:02*

*01:14:32*

I took a breath and started to talk, only for my phone to go off. "Oh, sorry," I said, ignoring a message from Mae as I switched it to silent.

*01:14:02*

I tried to speak, but words escaped me. My voice failed to enunciate the script I'd prepared. "I...uh, excuse me, I...Please, let me step outside for just a second and get some water."

One of the executives, a sharply-dressed man with slicked-back hair who appeared younger than the rest, used a pitcher on the conference table to fill up a small Styrofoam cup.

With a reassuring smile, he handed it to me. "Here you go. Just drink as much as you need and start when you're ready."

*01:12:32*

*01:07:32*

*01:02:32*

*00:57:32*

I looked down at the water. It was a disgusting, deep shade of green. With a 'pop', something swam to its surface. Startled, I dropped the cup, spilling its contents over the carpet.

"Olivia!" snapped Ms. Franklin. "Start your presentation, now."

*00:55:32*

*00:50:32*

*00:45:32*

"I-I…" I grew dizzy as I realized I was breathing heavily. I sensed the judgmental gazes of Ms. Franklin and the other executives, and the disappointment felt towards me by Kelly for screwing up our group presentation. "I'm feeling…" I stumbled and fell.

I opened my eyes to find the young executive sitting over me. "Are you okay?" he asked.

Before I could respond, I watched as the countdown on his forehead ticked to *00:00:00*. The digits initially lit up, turning a shade brighter, before receding into his skin. The man didn't explode, or react at all for that matter. He just continued to look me over with concern.

He asked if I needed a doctor.

"No, um, I was just a little nervous, that's all." I started to calm down as I felt that it was going to be okay.

Maybe these countdowns didn't have any effect. Maybe, like the zippers, they would all just fade away.

That's when he coughed. Then again, more violently. He gripped his hand around his neck as his mouth expelled blood.

I frantically crawled backwards as he held his head back and emitted a gargled scream. Blood with a yellow-green hue boiled through his skin, replacing it with a darker, rougher surface.

His shrieks joined those of the remaining executives, all of whom appeared to be undergoing the same agonizing transformation.

Closer to me, the younger executive's face disintegrated into a sludgy, pinkish heap as a new form replaced it. His legs thickened and lengthened. Slowly, he rose up until he was looking down at me.

"I told you I'd come back for you, Olivia," said the last voice I wanted to hear.

"No, no, that's *impossible!*" I cried.

"Oh Olivia, how I've missed you," said another Mr. Jacobson, whose frame burst through the dress Ms. Franklin had been wearing. I realized he was covered in sharp thorns. "I'd like to resume your performance review."

Kelly, understandably panicked, darted for the door. I followed her, my flats splashing through puddles of liquefied gore with each step.

"Where do you think you're going, my dear Olivia?" teased one of the Mr. Jacobsons. As I hurried past him, he lifted and extended a prickly arm in my direction.

"Come on!" cried Kelly, holding the door open for me. As I reached her, she screeched as several thorns flew through the air and lodged in her neck. She lost balance as we stumbled down the hallway. "Oh God. What's happening, Olivia?"

I helped her into an office, where we hid as Mr. Jacobson's voice teased us. "Hide all you want to, Olivia. One of me will find you and your esteemed coworker."

"Hold still," I whispered as I yanked four thorns out of Kelly. Her skin around where they'd lodged had changed color. I watched with horror as a countdown emerged on her forehead.

*00:00:05*

*00:00:04*

"Oh no," I gasped. The thorns had infected her, too, and she had mere moments before transforming.

Kelly barely had time to respond before she started shaking. I had to leave her behind.

I burst out of the office and into the hallway. When I turned a corner to reach my destination, I crashed into a Mr. Jacobson.

"Leaving so soon?" he sneered as I climbed to my feet. "We can't have that now, can we?"

The elevator door opened. Inside, a figure with disheveled blonde hair raised and swung a fire ax at my pursuer. The ax dug deeply into Mr. Jacobson's back. He shrieked in pain as he fell to the floor, the ax still embedded within him.

"Come with me!" the man yelled. I obeyed. Through the closing doors, I watched two Mr. Jacobson's rip into a screaming man's chest as he begged them to stop.

The man, who I realized was bleeding profusely, punched the button for floor 12.

"Hit the lobby!" I yelled. "We have to get the hell out of here!"

"No," he gasped. "It's too late for me, and that won't work for you either. If you want to make it out of this, you need to head to room 1205. There are two syringes in the top desk drawer. Inject them both into the same arm, one after the other."

"*What*? Why?"

With a trembling hand, he pulled a thorn out of my neck. In my blurry reflection, I realized a countdown had begun running on *my* forehead.

"Oh no, no, no." Kelly's countdown had been only ten seconds.

"You were only hit by one – you have a few minutes. If you use it on-time, it's fast-acting enough to protect you. But you may also experience some...side effects," he mumbled weakly as the doors opened. I charged out, leaving the dying man behind. I stepped through blood and mucus-like residue as I passed rooms 1200, 1201, 1202-

"Olivia, are you down here?" rang out Mr. Jacobson's voice from around a corner. I crept into room 1202 and waited behind a desk. As I did so, I used a hand mirror I found there to get a better look at my countdown.

*00:02:03*

*00:02:02*

Once Mr. Jacobson passed, I scurried to room 1205. A yellowish liquid filled the thick barrels of the syringes I located on the desk inside.

They were *huge*, with the largest barrels and longest needles of any syringe I'd ever seen. There was *nothing* I wanted less than to be injected with whatever they contained. Nothing except for well, what was happening to everyone else when their countdowns hit zero.

I ripped off my stained suit jacket, rolled up my sleeve, jabbed the needle of the first syringe into my left arm, and steadily pressed the plunger downwards.

There was *so much* liquid. I dug the needle deeper into my skin and kept pressing even as a burning sensation spread through my insides and drops of blood trickled down my arm. I let out a low grunt as I finally injected all of the contents.

"I think I heard something," said Mr. Jacobson. "She's around here."

I had less than a minute. Taking the syringes with me, I darted towards the elevator. It arrived quickly. Inside, I hit "Lobby" and "Door Close."

The doors began to shut. But, at the last moment, a long arm reached through, followed by an all-too-familiar face. "Found you!" Mr. Jacobson yelled.

I jabbed the empty syringe with all the force I could muster, sending it straight into his eye. As he jolted backwards in a desperate attempt to dislodge it, the doors closed.

As the elevator descended below floor 6, my hazy reflection revealed that the number in my countdown had also dropped to a single digit.

I let out a shrill howl as I dug the remaining needle into my arm. The substance I injected sent shockwaves of pure agony throughout my body. Still, I pressed further until I'd emptied it.

Within moments, I lost most of my muscle control. I was too weak to remove the second syringe from where it dangled from my arm. When the doors revealed the building lobby, I collapsed onto the polished marble floor. Ignoring the seething pain I felt all over, I used my chin and my right arm to pull myself forward.

~

## MEMORANDUM

*TO: Martin Hamilton, Executive Vice President
of Biomedical Research Division*

*FROM: Albert Robertson, Acting Team Lead
Risk Identification and Assessment Branch*

*DATE: June 22, 2021*

*RE: Executive Summary Regarding
Outbreak and Containment Efforts*

THIS MEMORANDUM CONTAINS *my condensed executive summary of the recent outbreak at the Eastern Division Biomedical Research Facility. Concurrent with this executive summary, you will find my team's full 1,700 page report on this matter.*

*In short, on Sunday, May 16, the laboratory run by Dr. Robert Kinnette experienced a containment breach involving a volatile substance, hereinafter referred to as "Compound A." This breach went undetected until Wednesday, May 19, at which point it was repaired.*

*Dr. Kinnette developed Compound A pursuant to military contracts for use in enhanced interrogation. When administered, Compound A amplifies fear instincts and causes intense hallucinations. These, in turn, prompt fight-or-flight instincts, with some subjects attempting to inflict violence on their perceived aggressor and others attempting to hide. Compound A is toxic, and can result in death through brain damage, strokes, or seizures when administered in excessively high doses.*

*The breach occurred when a researcher attempted to combine the compound with a mislabeled accelerant, which caused it to mutate into a gaseous form and enter the building's air supply. Fortunately, the employees on most floors of the building had not yet been called back to work, limiting the scope of the outbreak to the employees on floors 12, 15, and 19 who had the misfortune of returning on May 17.*

*For the first two days, the effects were minor. However, Compound A appears to have rapidly mutated on the night of Tuesday, May 18, such that its effects became profoundly pronounced soon after employees arrived on Wednesday, May 19.*

*For instance, based on the hospital records we have reviewed, Subject M, the only survivor, appears to have suffered mild hallucinations on May 17 and 18 connected to deeply held concerns — namely, fears of complacency and infection. On May 20, however, within hours of arriving, she found herself surrounded by bizarre manifestations of a former harasser.*

*Meanwhile, the other exposed employees began suffering from similar hallucinations, often projecting those fears onto those around them. The ensuing chaos only further fueled the intensity of the delusions, as the violence colleagues inflicted on one another intensified the widespread sensations of panic and danger.*

*Eventually, the high level of Compound A in the air began to take its toll, causing serious health complications for those exposed. Subject M, however, found an antidote in Dr. Kinnette's office and, managed to self-administer even while amidst the zenith of Compound A's effects. Two of her friends soon found her in the building lobby and brought her to a hospital before we could intervene.*

*Based on my assessment of the evidence, my recommendation is to seek an arrangement with Subject M that guarantees her silence, especially in light of the catastrophic consequences to Abernathy Industries were the full details of this incident to become public knowledge.*

~

It's been two weeks since the hospital discharged me, and ten days since Mae found a blank envelope under our door containing this memorandum. She brought it to where I lay recovering on the living room couch and read it to me.

"Who do you think left it here?" I asked.

Mae shrugged. "Someone with a conscience. If what's written here is true...then, Jesus, I'm just glad Casey and I got to you before they did."

Two attorneys met with us this morning. They presented us with a check. The amount displayed on it was impressive. The memo line contained one word: *Silence.*

Mae and I exchanged a sly smile before promptly ripping it to pieces.

## 15

# MADELINE

Many people go through a mopey 'nobody wants to date me' phase. I was in the midst of mine a few years back, when I was a junior in college.

There's nothing particularly dramatic about it. I had no interest in romance in my teens when plenty of people around me were going through such formative experiences. I hardly socialized, either. So, unsurprisingly, when I finally acted on the feelings I started to develop towards certain members of the opposite sex, I was clumsy and awkward, and I met with no success.

I recognize that it wasn't too big of a deal in the grand scheme of things, even if it felt catastrophic to me at the time. I was downcast but not self-pitying. I realized that I had a lot of personal growth ahead of me before I'd have much to offer to another person, and I felt a little lonely and insecure as a result.

That insecurity didn't stop me from opting for a semester abroad. It's something I'd always seen as a valuable learning opportunity, and, thanks to my school's strong ties with a Danish educational program, I soon found myself on a plane from the states to Copenhagen.

The first couple weeks went smoothly enough. I explored plenty of landmarks, from ascending the Round Tower's iconic helical corridor to touring the gigantic Frederiksborg Castle.

I also made progress in a basic-level Danish language course. Learning the language in detail was hardly necessary, though, as virtually every resident there would rather practice their English than try to decipher a foreigner's rudimentary Danish.

I first saw her at a crowded bar on a Saturday night. My roommate and I were sipping Carlsbergs when I spotted a woman by the door. She had red hair and pale skin, and there was a peculiar, kinetic energy about her that caused her to stand out from the crowd. For a moment, we made eye contact. Nervously, I averted my gaze to the floor.

My roommate announced that he was turning in for the night. No sooner did he leave than she approached me. When I started mumbling a basic greeting in Danish, she smiled and quickly cut me off.

Like most Danes, she spoke fluent English in a Nordic accent. She told me that she'd noticed me looking at her and, to my surprise, asked if I wanted to buy her a drink.

"Uh, yeah, sure," I said, gesturing for another beer on tap.

She introduced herself as Madeline and, at her suggestion, we got ourselves a small table.

She asked me a lot of questions, and she seemed to listen intently to my responses. We talked at first about basic subjects, such as my hometown and my reasons for studying abroad, and how she'd grown up nearby but recently returned from traveling through Switzerland and Germany.

Before long, we were discussing more personal topics. I explained how my father had passed when I was little, and she shared how she'd recently broken up with a longtime boyfriend.

As our conversation stretched into the early morning, I realized that I felt more comfortable around her than I did around, well, just about anybody else. I found her extremely attractive, too, which contributed to my excitement.

Eventually, she suggested that we depart. "You going to drink that?" I asked, motioning to the still-full beer I'd ordered for her.

She laughed and shook her head. She told me that didn't really drink and had just wanted to see if I'd order it for her. She added that I could have it if I wanted.

I took a deep gulp from it as I left payment on the table before following her to the deserted cobblestone street outside. She leaned into me until her face was just inches from mine and asked if I'd ever kissed a girl before.

"Yeah," I lied, embarrassed over my inexperience.

She whispered another question: had I ever done more than that?

"Uh, yeah," I responded. The smirk on her face showed me that she likely didn't believe me.

If she sensed I was lying, it didn't seem to bother her. As she drew away from me, she asked if I had plans the next night. She explained that she would be attending a gathering with some friends and family. Afterwards, she said with a wink, we could spend some time together – just the two of us.

My heart fluttered.

"Oh, yeah, okay," I stammered, nervously. "Sure, I'll be there."

That seemed to please her. She proceeded to describe the route I would need to take to get there. I typed each step into my travel flip phone.

As we parted ways, she called to me, "Vi ses senere." Danish for *see you later*.

I practically skipped with joy as I made my way home. After so many self-doubts and restless nights, a charming, gorgeous woman had shown interest in *me*, of all people.

My mind flooded with thoughts of what was to follow. Maybe the event would be awkward and little would come of it. Perhaps I'd say or do something foolish like I had so many times before, and I'd never hear from her again. But, just maybe, this could be the start of something meaningful, or, at a minimum, something validating and fun.

When I got home, I realized that she'd left me with relatively little specific information. Madeline hadn't given me her last name or even her phone number. I had an address, but I had no idea what sort of building I was looking for, or the kind of neighborhood I'd be heading into.

Her mention of 'family' struck me as strange, too. Who brings someone to a family event on a first (or, if last night counted, second) date?

My mind didn't dwell on these peculiarities for long. Instead, I replayed the wink she gave me when she'd referenced us being alone together. It was more than enough to silence any uncertainties.

I spent the next morning preparing. I showered, shaved my face, and picked out a nice shirt. I tried to think in advance of the questions her friends and family members might ask me and practiced my responses before a mirror. My roommate, sensing my purpose, wished me luck as I stepped outside.

At first, the journey was unremarkable. The metro station had its usual glossy, spotless appearance. When the fully-automated train arrived, I took a seat near a chatty group of teens, and numerous passengers embarked and departed over the next few stops.

Things started to change when I reached the Nørreport station. According to Madeline's instructions, I needed to switch to a train on the 'silver' line. However, I couldn't find a platform for such a line, nor did one appear on any of the maps throughout the station.

I spotted two metro employees and asked them for assistance. They exchanged a quick glance when I mentioned the silver line.

The first, a pale-faced man, asked if I was certain that I wanted to go there.

I nodded, trying to make sense of their grim, concerned expressions.

In response, the second, a short, well-built woman with a gray ponytail, beckoned me to follow her.

She led me up a small staircase that I otherwise would have assumed connected to a custodial closet or maintenance hatch. At the top, she took me down a shadowy corridor. In contrast to the polished, pristine look of the rest of the station, the walls and flooring in this area were rugged and dirty.

We stepped into a cavernous room. A weak, flickering overhead light partially illuminated an empty train platform in its center. A large sign above it displayed the Danish word for "Silver."

In contrast to the other platforms, there appeared to be no ticket booth or electronic indicator of when the next train would arrive. When I asked about this, I found, to my surprise, that the woman who had brought me there was already gone. I was alone.

I considered leaving. This all made little sense – the absence of any silver line from the map, the platform's dingy appearance, and the reaction of the employees. The air had a rancid, foul smell to it, too, and the temperature was much higher than in the rest of the station.

But, I'd come this far, and it had all accorded, more or less, with the instructions Madeline had left me. I reminded myself, too, of why I was there in the first place. I thought about how comfortable and warm her presence had made me feel last night. I imagined the smile that would spread across her face when she saw me; the feeling of her lips pressed against mine; doing more than kissing, perhaps even quite a bit more.

Eventually, two harsh red lights punctured the opaque darkness and approached like the eyes of a hunting predator. As they grew closer, I discerned that they were the headlights to an older, shabbier train than the one I'd used to get here. The smudges across its glass windows and the graffiti that covered its metal exterior reminded me much more of public transportation in the U.S. than what I'd seen elsewhere in Copenhagen.

Even though the train seemed to be at the end of the line, no one who had arrived on it exited. Instead, the handful of passengers in the car I stepped onto remained eerily silent as I took a seat.

An empty glass bottle rolled across its dusty floor as the train jutted back into motion, reversing direction into the black void from which it had emerged.

I checked the directions Madeline had given me. Seven metro

stops, and then a five block walk until I reached the destination she'd given me: *Skeltoftevej 27*. I'd be there soon enough.

I tried to relax as the train sputtered along. At the first two stops, no one got on or off. By the time the train approached the third stop, I noticed a peculiar stillness among the passengers in my periphery. Neither the lanky man by the door nor the mother and daughter in matching red jackets in the seats ahead of me had moved an inch since I'd gotten onboard. As far as I could tell, everyone around me remained completely motionless.

I shifted my gaze to the window on my right as the train approached the third stop. Between the back-glare against the dirty glass and the outside platform's minimal lighting, I could barely make anything out.

The doors opened and, again, I discerned no movement onto or off of the train. Staring deep into the shadows outside, I noticed something else odd: the vague outlines of figures, all as still as those in my train car.

At the fourth station, I observed the same thing. I couldn't identify any details of the distant spectators, beyond that they just seemed to be standing there...doing nothing at all.

It perplexed me. Why were they there? As far as I could tell, there wasn't any other train on this track.

As the train departed, I picked up on another detail – pairs of tiny, neon green dots of light. They were hard to make out at first, but once I noticed them, I couldn't ignore them. Each hovered above the ground...right around where the obscured figures' faces would be.

The fifth and sixth stops were the same. Now that I knew to look for them, I detected no fewer than a dozen pairs of these glowing lights, all gazing at the train like eyes that never blinked.

As we approached the seventh stop, I wasn't sure what to make of what I'd been seeing. The distant figures spooked me, even though I had no reason to think I was in any danger.

I reflected on just how alone and isolated I was. After all, I was a foreigner traveling to an area I knew nothing about on a line that didn't appear on maps, all to see someone I'd only just met. I hadn't even told anyone where I was going.

But I had to exit the train at some point, even if only to turn around. So, I mustered my courage and approached the screen doors, praying that whatever lay in the void ahead of me meant me no harm, and that I'd soon be happily reunited with the gorgeous woman who'd shown so much interest in me.

As the doors began to open, my hands shot impulsively to my eyes to protect them from an unexpected and intense wave of what felt like blisteringly bright light.

As my eyes started to adjust, I squinted to find before me a fully-illuminated train platform. To my relief, it was bereft of any skulking figures, or anyone at all for that matter.

Sounds of my footsteps echoed through the vacant train station as I made my way through it. There was nothing odd about its structure or layout, but the absence of other people left me uneasy. I remembered the giggling teens and hand-holding couples I was used to seeing at places like this. Everything around me, by contrast, felt artificial, mechanical, and joyless.

The street outside had a similarly ethereal aura to it. It possessed all the qualities of the vibrant cityscape I'd spent the last few weeks exploring – cobblestone streets; occasional baroque churches; crooked houses painted in warm hues of yellow, red, and orange – but it was all quiet, so quiet, and the air carried a suffocating staleness.

As I passed by a restaurant, I found myself fixating on its chairs and tables – all uninhabited, like everything else around me. Their design, and the layout in general, were identical to that of an upscale Italian place not far from my dorm back in the states.

My mind flashed back to the night I'd taken Audrie, a girl from my chemistry class, out on a date. Our conversation over the meal had been...awkward. She'd acted friendly towards me earlier, but that night, she'd been guarded and withholding.

When the check arrived, I'd tried to pay it in full, but she'd insisted on splitting the expense. As we stepped outside, she confessed that she'd thought we were hanging out as friends and hadn't realized until she'd arrived at the restaurant that I'd asked her on a date. She apologized for having not said anything earlier, as she hadn't known how to best navigate the awkward situation.

When she told me she didn't see me "that" way, I said that was okay, and I'd apologized for the misunderstanding. I felt terrible, though I tried not to show it.

I dismissed the memory quickly. As I continued towards Madeline's address, a distant noise caught my attention. As I got closer, I recognized it as laughter.

At first, I found this reassuring. It was the first sign of life I'd encountered after traversing so much seemingly abandoned cityscape.

But, I steadily pick up on an unwelcome undertone to the shrill giggles ahead of me. There was a piercing meanness to them. They recalled the specter of a group of people – young people, by the sound of it – basking in a peer's humiliation.

It was a sound I knew too well. When I'd summoned my courage to ask a classmate out to prom – a fellow violist named Maria I'd shared a stand with in orchestra for over a year – she'd laughed at me like that, and her friends had quickly joined in.

*Do better,* I'd told myself when I'd cried into the mirror that night. *Nobody owes me anything.*

I'd do better tonight, I told myself. Everything was going to change. Madeline and I had made a connection so quickly. She really liked me, and I liked her, too. Maybe I'd just grown up on the wrong continent.

The laughter got louder until, right as I reached the alley from which it seemed to have been emanating, it stopped, and there was no one there to be found.

*Just keep moving,* I told myself, adding it to a list of abnormalities I fought to keep buried in the back of my mind. *I'm almost there.*

Finally, I reached a sign that displayed the name of Madeline's street. The first few buildings were businesses – a deli that served distinctly Danish open sandwiches called smørrebrød, a barber's shop, a camera store.

At last, I found myself facing a brick structure with the number of the address Madeline had given me affixed to its front door. The sign next to the entrance displayed several words that I hadn't yet learned in my Danish language course.

Was this a restaurant? If so, it was a fancy one, judging by the black suit worn by the man by the ornate front desk inside – incidentally, the first person I'd seen since the train station. I expected to feel some sense of relief at seeing another living, breathing person, but his emaciated appearance and grim expression brought me little comfort.

He said something to me in Danish – I think *"Lan jeg hjælpe dig?"* (*Can I help you?*) – but he spoke a little too rapidly for me to be sure. I just stated Madeline's name, hoping he'd understand that I was looking for her.

*"Madeline,"* he repeated back to me. He nodded solemnly and then beckoned for me to follow him.

We arrived in a large, plain room occupied by at least two dozen people. The first thing I noticed about them was how formally they were dressed. My patterned button-down shirt looked outright casual compared to the suit jackets and plain dresses – all muted shades of black and gray – worn by everyone else.

Naturally, I felt out of place. Nobody said anything to me, but I sensed, truthfully or not, that I was being judged. Why hadn't Madeline told me this was a fancy event? I wondered, too: Where was Madeline, what kind of event had she invited me to?

The absence of any food or silverware-laden tables confirmed that I was not, in fact, in a restaurant as I'd inferred. Rather, the attendees were standing and chatting quietly with each other in voices no louder than a whisper. Nobody really seemed to be doing anything in particular.

I approached an elderly man standing alone. "Excuse me," I said meekly. "I'm looking for Madeline."

A puzzled expression formed on his face. As he looked me over skeptically, my face turned red with a mix of nervousness and embarrassment. I felt so hopelessly lost and confused.

He slowly raised his arm and pointed towards the far end of the room. I thanked him before nudging my way through the small crowd in the direction he had indicated.

My jaw nearly dropped when I saw the wooden casket, which was decorated by an array of lilies and roses. Madeline lay underneath its open head panel. Her eyes were closed, and she was perfectly still. She wore the same clothes I'd seen her in the previous night. A display next to the casket read, "Madeline Larsen, december 12, 1994 – september 7, 2019."

It was too much to take in. My legs grew weak and I began feeling dizzy.

My mind raced to process what was happening. Steadily, it dawned on me that, somehow, as impossible as it sounded, Madeline had invited me to her *own* open casket.

Something else stuck out to me. Last night – when I'd met Madeline – was September *14th*. One week *after* the date listed as that of her death.

None of this made sense. What was I doing here? How was any of this possible?

The old man who'd directed me shuffled past me and stood next to the casket. He turned to face the rest of the crowd, which quickly grew silent.

I realized he was giving some kind of speech. Was he a relative, or a priest perhaps?

He spoke in a coarse, raspy voice. My mind was too astounded for me to grasp a word of what he was saying. I wasn't even sure that it was Danish.

The reaction from the crowd baffled me even more. They were *laughing*. Again and again, the man made comments – comments that I could not understand – and the rest of the room chortled and giggled in response.

All I could do was watch, embarrassed and dumbfounded, as I wondered who tells jokes at an occasion like this.

Suddenly, all eyes turned to me. "*Michael*," the man hissed, somehow knowing my name. "It's time."

"Time ... for what?" I replied, exasperated. I looked around the room – at the dozens of people staring intensely at me. "What's happening? What do you want from me?"

The man responded that it wasn't *him* or *us* who wanted something from me. No, he said, gesturing to the casket. "*It's her.*"

I stood frozen as Madeline's corpse sat up. Madeline opened her eyes, and, placing both hands on the casket's mahogany surface, pulled herself slowly upward and hopped onto the floor.

She said my name, her voice sounding weaker and coarser than it had last night. "I knew you'd come for me. I just knew it." She wobbled towards me, her legs seemingly straining to support her.

I froze, unable to comprehend what I was seeing. "Are you, are you-" I stuttered.

"They're going to bury me, Michael," she said, as she continued her approach.

As she got closer, I recoiled at her rank, putrid smell. Impulsively, I backed up, only for the speaker to grip me tightly, holding me in place.

"I don't want to be alone, Michael," said Madeline. "There's room for us both down there."

"No," I gasped as I struggled to get free. "No, please-"

"There's so much that I can show you. It'll be just the two of us, and we'll have all the time in the world. Isn't this what you always wanted? To never be alone again?"

She stood right in front of me now. My stomach churned as the rotting smell grew even more pungent.

The world spun around me as panic set in. I remember tearing the man's hands off me, losing my balance, and slamming my head painfully into the casket before I hit the ground.

~

When I came to, my head was throbbing, and I was being dragged outside by two men. Graves littered the surrounding landscape.

A crowd of people, including Madeline, had assembled by a

deep pit a short distance away from me. Next to it was a coffin – a much larger one than I'd ever seen before. Large enough for two bodies.

I couldn't make sense of anything that was happening. But, I *knew*, with a sense of absolute certainty, that I was about to be buried there.

I figured my best bet would be to act before they realized I was awake. Throwing all my force into it, I lunged forward, managing, barely, to pull myself free.

One of the men dived for me, grabbing my leg and sending me toppling over a headstone. As I scrambled to my feet, I noticed a long metal shovel laying atop a pile of dirt.

As one of the men charged at me, I picked up the shovel and frantically swung it. The blade slammed into his cheek, sending him sprawling.

"*What are you doing?*" Madeline cried.

I didn't respond. My attention was fixed on the man I'd just hit. The force of the blow had somehow fractured his skin. Cracks spread over his face, which then shattered into small pieces that fell onto the ground, revealing the raw bones of his skull and a pair of unblinking, unnaturally bright green eyes.

As he got to his feet, seemingly unbothered by the evisceration of his face, my flight instinct kicked in. I remember climbing a fence and ignoring the pain in my ankle when I hit the ground on the other side. I remember the sounds of dozens of footsteps pursuing me, and being too afraid to look back. Madeline's voice, brimming with a sense of betrayal, begged me to return.

I ran on instinct, retracing my steps as best I could. Figures filled the once deserted streets around me. I ignored their missing faces and the green glow they emitted. I ignored the ones who called for me, who said they *wanted* me, who resembled Audrie, Maria, and so many others whose rejection haunted my mind every time I closed my eyes at night.

By the time I reached the platform, I was breathing rapidly and drenched in sweat. Thankfully, a train was already there.

I could hear voices resounding through the station behind me. They were getting closer, louder, by the moment.

I could tell that the train's doors were about to close. With my last bit of strength, I dashed forward and dove between them. Pain shot through me as my body thudded onto the hard surface inside.

~

When I awoke, my body ached all over. I was laying on a couch in some kind of office, and a woman I recognized as the employee who had led me to the silver line stood over me.

She asked if I'd found what I was looking for.

I was too perplexed to answer. "What...where am I?"

She told me I was in her office in the station where I'd begin my journey.

"I don't understand."

She shrugged. She told me that I didn't have to, and that I should go home.

"But...but..." I stammered. "What about the silver line, and things I saw-"

She replied that the Silver line was closed for repairs and repeated, this time in a firm enough voice that I understood it to be a command, that I should go on home.

~

I've never fully understood what happened to me that day. I never saw that employee again, nor any mention of a silver line having ever even existed. Nor could I find any reference in an atlas to the part of town it had brought me to. When I looked up the words displayed on the building Madeline brought me to, they translated to "undertaker" or "funeral home."

Once, before returning to the states, I ran into the bartender who'd been on duty when I'd met Madeline. When I asked him what he remembered about that night, he responded that he recalled me sitting alone, talking to myself for hours.

~

My physical wounds – bruises and a sprained ankle – healed relatively quickly, but, inside, I felt shattered. I became reclusive, focusing entirely on my studies and, after graduating, on my work.

A few weeks ago, my brother set me up on a date with a friend-of-a-friend who he insisted was a good fit for me. Understandably, I'd spent the last few years utterly detached from the dating scene and avoiding any perceived advances. But, I eventually caved in to my brother's persistence.

Her name is Clara, and, well, my brother was right. She and I formed an instant connection and, so far, we seem to be a perfect match for each other. The other night, we even exchanged a kiss, the first of my life.

We were sitting together in my apartment's living room on a rainy Saturday afternoon when I heard a knock at the door. I opened it to find a bouquet of lilies and roses sitting on the doormat.

"Did you order these?" I asked Clara. She shook her head, her expression puzzled and concerned.

A small card pinned to the bouquet displayed a short, hand-written message in black ink. I took a deep, nervous breath before reading it to myself:

*Death is the great equalizer, Michael. When it comes for you, too, know one thing: I will be waiting.*

*Vi ses senere,*

*Madeline*

## 16

# BEFORE THEY WERE SCARECROWS

When he was little, Robert once asked me what the scarecrows that decorated our family's farm did before. I'd responded "Before what?" and he'd clarified that he meant before becoming scarecrows.

I thought about toying with him and telling some sinister origin story, like that they were people punished for misbehaving or monsters who'd once prowled the fields.

But, I knew that he, five years my junior, looked up to me for guidance. So, I'd given him a literal answer: there wasn't any "before"; we made them as scarecrows, and that was all there was to it.

I wasn't always so literal with him. Sometimes at night, back when we shared a room, he'd shake me awake after having a nightmare. I'd tell him about how our scarecrows would keep him safe – how, if anything went wrong, they'd come in from the fields outside to protect us.

We'd spent our childhoods running through those fields. We darted between rows of corn stalks and hid behind the tombstones of our small family graveyard. When our mother was still around, she'd scold us over the dirt we tracked into the house and the tears in our pants. She'd tell us to stop going out there for so long; that we'd get lost and not find our way back. But I always felt safe under the watchful eye of the sentinels who'd been there for as long as I can remember.

Everything changed when our mother unexpectedly passed away. I'd seen the glare our stepdad Nick made towards Robert as we stood solemnly around the newest addition to the family cemetery.

The biggest mistake mom had ever made was falling in love with Nick. As he'd charmed his way into her life, I'd sensed a cruelty behind the superficial kindness he showed towards me and Robert. When mom wasn't around, he treated us spitefully. Now, we were stuck with him as our only parent.

That evening, Nick screamed at Robert for hours. As Nick saw it, our mother wouldn't have been driving that night if Robert hadn't needed picking up from practice, and he wouldn't listen to any of my pleas that his reasoning didn't make any sense.

Nick hadn't permitted Robert to have dinner, so, that night, I discretely brought a plate of food up to Robert's room. When I found him, he'd pressed his red face against the glass window.

I knew what he was looking at and why his expression was of disappointment. Of course, we'd both outgrown the myths we'd once believed; yet, in the moment, we shared a sense that the silhouettes in the distant fading red light had somehow let us down.

Nick began erratically lashing out at Robert, no matter how many times I told him to stop blaming Robert for our mother's death. Usually, these episodes followed bouts of heavy drinking. When I smelled alcohol on Nick's breath, I'd encourage Robert to make plans elsewhere for the evening.

I returned from theatre practice once to find Robert nursing a bruise beneath his lip. When I asked him if Nick did it, his misty-eyed expression told me all I needed to know. When I confronted Nick, he told me that if I cared so much about Robert, I'd teach Robert to treat him with the respect he deserved.

Our farm fell into disrepair as Nick stopped putting in the work necessary to maintain it. Our once thriving crops withered and died. Our scarecrows remained in place, but the lush land over which they'd once presided deteriorated into messy overgrowth. After Nick drunkenly crashed his car into the fence outside our house, I took it upon myself to drive Robert wherever he needed to go. Nick never fixed the fence.

Our attention turned steadily away from the farmland where Robert and I had spent our youths and towards our futures. In my senior year of high school, I set my eyes on a scholarship to a distant college – anyplace far away and with a theatre program – as a ticket out of our desolate small town and the wasteland of our estate. I also studied hard and encouraged Robert to do the same.

When I saw the cast list for my theatre class's Halloween production, my thoughts returned for the first time in years to the scarecrows on our farm. The costume they gave me bore an uncanny resemblance to the figures I'd grown up seeing as guardians, though the blue plaid shirt I would wear under a straw neckpiece struck me as too neat, too clean.

I took the shirt home that night and rubbed it against the dirt until a layer of dusty brown covered it. Donning it and the rest of the costume, I faced one of the scarecrows on our estate. It was imposing, despite its goofy straw hat, due to the scythe mounted against its shoulder and the sharp, jagged sticks that extended from its arms.

"Well, am I convincing?" I asked half-mockingly. The plain sack that was its face gazed back blankly. I shrugged, unsure of what response I'd been expecting.

At practice the next day, a few students complimented my costume, which I'd also refined with several tufts of straw that obscured my hands and extended from my boots to over the hem of my pants.

I paid little attention. Mostly, I was focused on how two of my classmates, a well-built pair who'd recently been cut from the baseball team for disciplinary issues, were taunting a frail sophomore who was having trouble with his dialogue. I told them to leave him alone.

They scowled at me but relented when our teacher took notice. I was heading to my car after school that day when I spotted them dragging the sophomore behind the building. Still in my costume, I charged over to intervene. The sophomore escaped, but I ended up taking the brunt of the beating they had intended for him.

My classmates left me curled up in a ball with my face and my insides aching. But, when I got up, there were no bloodstains on the concrete surface – just a dozen strands of straw that blew away in the mid-October breeze.

I awoke in my bed the next morning feeling strangely itchy all over my body. To my bewilderment, I looked down to see that I was still wearing the costume from the play.

As I changed clothes, I struggled to make sense of what had happened. I distinctly remembered removing the costume the night before, and it's not like I would have gone to sleep wearing the straw hat I'd woken up with.

"You didn't...put a different set of clothes on me while I was asleep last night, right?" I asked Robert over breakfast.

Before he could respond, my eye caught a wooden object flying through the air. "Down!" I called, prompting Robert to drop his head just on time to avoid the chair that crashed into the wall behind him.

Nick staggered into the room. I'd never seen him drunk this early. He stammered incoherently about how Robert took his food, his money, and his wife from him.

"Hey, Robert, why don't you go to the bus stop, okay?" I said as I positioned myself between him and Nick. Nick screamed that Robert wasn't going anywhere. But, when he charged at Robert, I blocked him as Robert scrambled away.

"If you *ever* do something like that again," I said, motioning to the fractured chair, "I'm calling the police. Do you understand me?"

Nick lowered his face until it was level with mine and stared at me with bloodshot eyes. He finally broke. Between sobs, he told me that the night our mother died, he'd thought about using the gun he kept in his room on himself. We talked for hours as he finally opened up to me about how much he'd been struggling in our mother's absence. He told me he felt ashamed of how he'd treated me and Robert.

He didn't scratch the surface of earning forgiveness. But I felt encouraged by his willingness to speak with me. Over the next week, he cut back his drinking. He apologized to Robert first for throwing the chair, then for an array of other horrible acts.

As the premiere of my school's Halloween play approached, Nick told me that he was proud of me and couldn't wait to bring Robert to see it with him.

"Okay, but please, Nick, *promise* me that you won't have anything to drink." He agreed.

Snickers and awkward looks greeted me when I arrived at school the next day. I quickly realized what the issue was. "It's, umm, for rehearsal," I mumbled as my classmates laughed at the costume I didn't remember putting on.

My friend Sally, who had the lead role of a friendly witch, took it in stride. She complimented me on what she referred to as "method acting."

Opening night went off without a hitch. Sally gave a virtuoso performance. I, meanwhile, captured the awkward movement and eccentric cadence of her scarecrow sidekick who'd once given up his humanity to bring a deceased loved one back to life. The audience cheered for us wildly as the curtains fell.

Afterwards, my heart lifted when I found Robert and Nick smiling together as they congratulated me. Nick, for the first time in months, had shaved his face and neatly combed his hair. It had been years since he'd made himself presentable. He was getting better. The clear liquid in his plastic bottle had to be water, right?

I offered to drive Robert home, but Nick insisted on doing it himself. I relented. I had to change out of my costume and help put away the props, after all. Sally would want me to help with that.

Clearing the stage took about an hour. The cast and crew steadily departed until only Sally and I remained. Sally asked me if I needed help taking off my costume.

My heart raced. After all, I was alone with the crush I'd always been too timid to ask out. "Uh, yeah, sure."

She ran her hand across my back, searching without success for a way to unzip the prop shirt that held the outer layer of straw in place.

I leaned my face towards hers. She smiled and planted my first kiss on my lips.

For a moment, I felt elated. But her expression soured. She let go of me and stepped back. I asked her what was wrong.

She told me that it didn't feel right, that *I* didn't feel right. I asked her what she meant.

She told me she had to go. She hurried away, leaving me downtrodden and confused.

It was the late evening when I began the drive. As I did so, I watched parents take little kids by the hands up to front doors decorated with pumpkins, skeletons, and spider webs. Mom had done that with us long ago. I missed that.

A little boy and a girl dressed as wizards gawked at me as I sat at a red light. I lowered the window and waved. The boy excitedly exclaimed that a scarecrow was driving a car.

Night fell. In my headlights, an obstruction appeared a few dozen yards from my house.

My heart sank as my eyes confirmed what I feared. Nick's car had crashed into an oak tree.

I pulled over and hopped out. Ignoring the heavy smoke, I sprinted up to the vehicle. "Robert!" I called.

The driver's side door dangled open, and the seat inside was empty. Across from it, the still form of my brother leaned against the fractured dashboard. Blood dripped from a deep bruise in his head.

I dragged him away from the vehicle. I cried out. This was my fault. Nick hadn't changed, and I should never have let him drive Robert home.

Finding unnatural strength, I carried Robert's limp form across the street and up the long driveway to our house.

I spotted a figure at the edge of the decrepit field. It was the scarecrow, the one I'd posed before when I was first working on my costume for the play. It stood still; yet, it was far away from its normal location. Had someone moved it?

"You were supposed to protect us," I said. "Why? What are you even doing here? What are you even looking after anymore?"

I looked over the scarecrow for several moments trying to make sense of it. A heavy breeze shook it. Its shifted and released its scythe, which tumbled to the ground.

I leaned down, layers of straw protruding from my heels and my knees, and placed Robert's body on the dirt. Lifting the scythe with two hands, I turned and marched into the house.

As I passed through the front hallway, I caught my reflection in a mirror. My face consisted of simply cloth; my mouth, nose, and eyes had receded to shallow stitches and drawings.

I heard Nick's voice from his room. He was repeating things – things like 'it's not my fault', and 'it was only a few drinks'.

I pushed open the door. As I approached Nick, I dragged the curved blade across the floor.

He made a panicked yell upon seeing the form before him. He removed his gun from a drawer and fired it. The bullets that passed through caused bits of straw to scatter across the floor.

I lifted and swung. He screeched as the blade lodged between his neck and shoulder. I drew it across his chest, sending blood splattering across the wall. I swung again. He collapsed, gargling. His last expression was one of terror mixed with confusion.

I had one thing left to do. Back outside, I approached Robert's body. My body grew increasingly stiff and nonresponsive as I stumbled towards him. Finally, I lifted my dense straw arm and pressed against his wound.

"He won't hurt you again," I whispered. My senses and strength gradually dissipated as Robert's wound partially healed. By the time Robert gasped a furtive breath, my own life had largely faded.

With all the will I could muster, I trudged through the weeds until I arrived at our family cemetery. A thick, wooden post was already waiting for me, near our parents' graves.

As I positioned myself up high on the post, I looked over our farm and watched as my brother was rushed away amidst flashing blue and red. I worried about his future. I wanted to continue to be there for him. Maybe I could still help him, someday.

But I knew that my own journey was at an end. I wondered if it was like that for the others that stood in perpetual watch over our property – if they, too, had been reduced to artifice through harshness in life.

With a strange contentment, I realized that I'd been wrong so long ago. There was a "before," for me at least – a role I was meant to fulfill. And, now, I'd finally arrived where I sensed I'd always belonged.

**17**

___________

**AUTOREPLY**

I ignore the ringing on my work phone for the third time this morning.

It's probably Steven, wondering when I'll send him my half of our presentation. Or, maybe, it's Mr. Mackey, finally ready to have the difficult conversation my bereavement leave had postponed.

Either way, I know I *should* answer it. But, I remain focused on the draft email on the screen before me.

*Dear Naomi,* it begins.

*It's been two weeks, hasn't it? Please don't worry, honey. I'm in good health. Physically, at least. Work has just been...taxing, lately. Returning to the workplace exhausts me. I'm down to two days of telework per week, and I'm already running out of excuses to avoid stepping foot in that corporate hellhole on the other three.*

*Worst, of all, Tuesday, I'm set to present to a whole room of self-important bigwigs. Steven's partnered with me for it. I hope Steven brings his A-game because I'm sure as hell not going to bring mine. Every time I look at all those fucking numbers on all those fucking spreadsheets, my mind drifts away.*

*It always ends up in the same place, Naomi. With you, and to the times we spent together. Do you ever think about what our lives would have been like if we both hadn't signed up for that stupid auditing conference? You'd probably still be living in that cramped townhouse with that monster.*

*I know you're coming home soon, darling. And when you get here, it'll be just like old times. We'll kiss, and I'll remove your clothes one garment at a time until they form a trail leading to the bed. We'll fuck, and when we're done, I'll open the bottle of your favorite merlot I keep in the upper cabinet just for the occasion.*

*You may be wondering why I'm so certain you'll be returning. Well, it's because you promised, and you always keep your word. Other people aren't like you. Other people say things that are stupid, empty, and noncommittal. Do you know what Steven's away message says, Naomi? "I'll try to get back to you when possible." Seriously.*

*Remember the new secretary? The girl Cheri, who looks a little like you, and who keeps trying to impress me? Well, she's yet to miss a day – an hour, even, in the three months she's been with us. So, last week, my curiosity finally got the better of me. You understand, don't you Naomi? I had to know.*

*So, when she was in the bathroom, I went through her lunch bag and slipped a little something into the sandwich she'd packed. It wasn't enough to do serious damage, mind you. At least, in in all likelihood. Just enough to give her a five day weekend. And, I was right. By Friday, she'd set up an away message on her work email from the hospital.*

*Can you guess what it said, Naomi? "Thank you for reaching out. Unfortunately, I am temporarily unavailable due to a medical emergency. I'll try to get back to you as soon as I can."*

*It's disgusting, isn't it? I'm going to give her a few pointers. She's not like Ted. She's not beyond saving.*

*Speaking of Ted, I'm still having the dream, Naomi. The terrible, terrible dream, where the people I've hurt are coming for me. Where I'm paying some divine price for what I've done. But, when I think of you, everything gets better. It's as if my connection with you what protects me. I promise, I won't let this much time pass again, love. I'll write you again within a few days. I love you, always and forever,*

*Peter*

I hit 'send'. My phone rings again. I nearly answer it, but I already have a response from Naomi. My mouth waters as I reread the fifteen words I know by heart: *I am currently unavailable, but I will be back and will respond to you soon.*

It was never meant to be a permanent sign-off. Just a hastily-drafted message while she used the afternoon to run an errand. Little did she know that her vengeful ex would render it her last mark on the world.

I hit ctrl-P, then enter. My dusty printer cranks out a hard copy. I head to my closet, where I shove aside a heavy box and a plastic container filled with green pellets to deposit it in a thick file pocket with the others.

~

Steven's tone is shrill and accusatory. He demands to know why I've been unresponsive all morning.

I don't really blame him for being angry. Given how I've been acting the last few weeks, It's no secret that my prospects for continued employment at this company are quite dim, but Steven doesn't want me to drag him down with me.

Still, fuck Steven. I'm tempted to tell him *I'll try to get back to you when possible* and end the call. Instead, I apologize. "I'm sorry. I've had a...difficult morning."

He retorts that *he's* had a difficult morning, too. We have less than 24 hours before our presentation to a group of corporate bigwigs, after all, and I haven't been pulling my weight in preparing for it. He asks for the status of my slides on Q3 and Q4.

"I haven't had time to finish them. It's just...Gnocchi, my Airedale, you know...he, umm, well, he passed this morning."

Steven, the gullible moron he is, turns sympathetic. He tells me that that he's sorry, and that he didn't even know I had a dog.

"Yeah. He fought real hard. Held out much longer than predicted. But it's okay, now. I've come to terms with it. You don't need to worry about me. I'll be ready to present tomorrow as planned."

Steven offers to take up part of my presentation, such that I'd just have to cover the fourth quarter.

"Steven, I couldn't-"

Steven insists.

I take a long, deep breath. "I owe you one, Steven."

~

The next morning, I ignore the judgmental looks of my co-workers as I scurry towards my office. I'm forty minutes late and I look a mess.

Cheri cheerfully wishes me a good morning as I pass where she sits dutifully at her desk.

"I'm so happy you're well enough to come in, Cheri. How are you feeling?"

She tells me that she's back to normal.

"That's great news. Do you know what caused it?"

She responds that the doctor had a few theories, but wasn't sure. She changes the subject, asking me if I received her email about her need to attend a follow-up appointment this afternoon.

"Oh, right, of course. I, um, I thought I responded already. Yeah, you can take time off. No problem."

She thanks me.

"Oh, there's one little thing I wanted to tell you."

She looks up at me attentively.

Wanting to handle this as appropriately as possible, I force an awkward laugh and try to sound lighthearted. "Well, you see, when I emailed you on Friday, I got an automated response from your account."

She nods and asks if there was something wrong with it.

"Well, the message you wrote, it wasn't..." She looks at me, concerned, as I try to find the correct words. "It wasn't *quite right*. I recommend writing something clearer, more decisive next time. Don't say that you will *try* to get back to someone. Say that you *will* respond. None of that wishy-washy bullshit. Got that?"

She says that she understands.

"Very good. Hey, and I'm *so* glad you're feeling better. Truly."

In my office, I focus intently on my computer screen. The blinds on the glass walls around me are open, after all. I need to at least look like I'm working.

270 unread emails. Jesus, that's a lot.

Still, it's better than the autoresponse-alypse Ted caused a couple months back. He tried setting up an away message prior to taking his first vacation, but went about it all wrong by messing with his filters. He ended up sending an autoreply to *every email he'd ever received*. I'd sat down to over 150 emails from him alone, each reading, *I will do my best to try respond as soon as I can.*

*Good luck with that, Ted,* I remember thinking to myself. *Good luck.*

I peer through the glass at Cheri and recall how my heart had fluttered when I realized *she* was Ted's replacement. Her resemblance to Naomi was impeccable. Not just on the surface – sure, her hazel eyes, curly chestnut hair, and diamond face all loosely resemble Naomi – but also her deliberate gait, and the way her eyelids twitch when she's nervous.

Steven enters. He repeats platitudes about how very sorry he is about my dog, and I repeat platitudes about how grateful I am for his support.

He asks if I'm ready for the presentation.

"Yes, absolutely. Good to go."

He asks if I'm planning on cleaning myself up beforehand

"You really think I'd show up looking like this?" I say with a laugh.

~

Steven grimaces when I arrive in the conference room that afternoon. My tie's crooked, my hair's a mess, and my lunch left a new stain on my suit jacket. I take a seat by the screen while Steven begins.

The judgmental gaze of the assembled corporate brass remains focused on Steven as he reviews numbers and charts. I, meanwhile, zone out. Cheri really *does* resemble Naomi, doesn't she?

I should ask Cheri out. It's hardly an appropriate thing to do given the power dynamic, but fuck all that. She's as close to a substitute for Naomi as I'm likely to ever find.

I sense a closing window of opportunity. My only 'in' with Cheri is that we work together, and that's not going to last. If I'm going to act, I need to do so now.

I remove my phone and type out an email about a get-together tonight at my house. Lots of people from the office are going to be there, I say. Just a nice, casual evening. She's welcome too, of course. I'd have told her sooner, but she'd been out of the office when I'd invited everyone else on Friday. I hit send.

Steven shoots me a cold glare when I check the notification from my phone. I should at least *pretend* to be invested in this presentation. But I can't be bothered. Not when the automated response I received from Cheri is glorious.

*Hello,* it reads.

*I am out the office with limited email access for the rest of the day. However, I will respond when I return tomorrow. If the matter is urgent, please call me at the number below.*

*Fuck* yes. It's a huge improvement. Cheri followed my advice after all.

I realize I'm breathing heavily. I can hear my heart beat. Naomi would be proud. It contains no ambiguity. Just a flat-out declaration: *I will respond when I return tomorrow.* A promise just like the one Naomi had made.

I'm too lost in my thoughts to care when Steven announces the conclusion of his auditing reporter for Q3. He shakes my arm, gently and then forcefully, until I finally process that it's my turn to present.

I get to my feet. "Ah, yes. Q4. Um..."

I scan the ghastly faces of the executives. They're like dogs, all of them, waiting for me to give them a treat. I start babbling. "This quarter, we, the...So, the excesses we identified..."

I try to read the words on the slide. But all I can see are the same few phrases that I know aren't really there: *I will be back. I will return. We'll be together soon.*

Fuck this. I'm out of here. "I'm so sorry, but I have to go."

Steven tries to call out for me, but the sound of the slamming door cuts him off. I barge into my office, turn the lock, and close all the blinds. On my computer, I pull up Cheri's autoreply, maximize it, and zoom in until its giant letters fill up the screen.

It's beautiful. It makes me feel like I'm with Naomi again. I remember spotting, and not caring about, the circular indent on her ring finger when she first took me back to her room at the convention center. I recall the times we'd shared in that crappy apartment I rented out in midtown just a few blocks away from where she and her husband lived. I feel the heat of our passion and the warmth of her body against mine.

As my mind slowly return to reality, a sense embarrassment grows in my gut. Apparently, even *I* am still capable of experiencing shame.

I'm sitting back in my seat. My pants are down, and from the looks of it and the fading sensation of euphoria, it seems that I just delivered a full load all over my half-unbuttoned royal blue dress shirt. Jesus, that autoreply really made an impression with me.

Mr. Mackey is knocking at the door. He's telling me to open up.

"I'm...I'm busy," I meekly respond. He shouts things at me. About how I've let down the branch for the last time. About how he never should have given me all the chances he did. I yell at him to fuck off,

He screams back at me that *I* should fuck off. He follows this with some taunt about jeopardizing my severance package.

I consider my options as I dress back up and do the best I can to clean up the new stains on my clothes. There's no way in hell I'm opening the door to my office now. Not with my boss out there waiting for me.

That leaves only one alternative. I open the blinds to the outside. I'm only on the second floor, and my car's in the lot below.

I open the window and step into the bitter cold. My suit pants scrape against the outer sill as I lower myself to the surface. I land against the asphalt with a muffled thud.

I take what I hope to be my last ever look at the concrete monstrosity where I've worked for over ten years. "Fuck every last one of you!" I holler, before pulling at the handle to my car's front door. It doesn't budge.

*Fucking hell.* I'd left my car keys in my office.

You can imagine the absolute misery of going into that place again. As I march back to my office, Andrew, a perplexed Mr. Mackey, and several others take their turns telling me how much of a disappointment I've been to them. By the time I find my car keys, a security detail has arrived to escort me out. I don't look back as I finally drive home.

At home, I shower, dress, and draft another email to Naomi. I explain how I'd lost my job, and how difficult it is for me to think of anything other than her.

*"Remember when the divorce finally came through? When you were legally free of that loser, and we felt like we had a whole life together ahead of us? That was really something, wasn't it? A high worth chasing. Naomi, I don't want to rush you, but I've been thinking...I think it's about time you come back. And, if you're still not ready, maybe it's time I come to you."*

The ring of the doorbell startles me as I hit 'send'. When I see the dimly-lit silhouette waiting on the front porch, I think for a moment that Naomi has granted my request. But it's Cheri who emerges from the shadows. I'd totally forgotten about the invitation I'd sent her.

It dawns on me that she may not know of the day's events. She probably thinks I'm still one of her supervisors.

Cheri hands me a bottle of wine. Cheap Riesling. Bad choice, but that's okay. I direct her inside and take her coat.

Noting the empty room, she comments on being the first guest to arrive.

"Uh, yeah, funny thing..." My mind scrambles to come up with something. I force an awkward chuckle. "You see, Cheri, I originally planned the event to start at 6, but, last week, I realized that I would need more time to set everything up, so I told everyone else to arrive at 7. But, when I emailed you this morning, I think I included the original time. Silly me. I'm so sorry."

She offers to leave and come back closer to the start time.

"No, no, please stay. I insist." She may not be Naomi. But it still feels like something of a small miracle for her to show up here tonight.

I sense this is a special night. I bring down the 1990 merlot and pour us each a glass.

"So, did the doctor have any insight about what caused you to get so sick?"

She relates how the doctor traced the issue to something she'd eaten and believed the cause was more serious than simple exposure to rotten or expired ingredients. The doctor had even asked if she knew anyone who could have deliberately tampered with her food, but Cheri hadn't taken that suggestion seriously. She didn't have any enemies, after all.

I lead her back to the living room. She takes a seat on a couch, examines her surroundings, and asks me about the woman in the photos with me.

"That's Naomi. I assume no one in the workplace told you about her?"

She shakes her head.

"She and I were engaged. The wedding was set for last January. We had it all planned out to take place at her parents' farmhouse where she grew up. But she passed away shortly beforehand."

She expresses her sympathies and asks what happened.

I gulp down the rest of my glass. "Her, um...well, her ex-husband, he wasn't happy about her leaving him. Very upset, in fact. He...he was responsible for what happened to her."

He'd handled things decently well, at first. That's because he thought his wife had split from him *and then* found me. When he discovered that she'd been seeing me behind his back for years, he snapped. But I omit that from the version of events I relate to Cheri.

She again expresses her sympathies. I notice that she also seems a bit shaken.

I pour myself a second glass. Before I know it, I'm opening up about all the things I loved about Naomi. I realize I'm oversharing, but my tipsy self continues anyway.

"The odd thing is, she still has an email account with her old workplace, Shelby and Nixon over on Fourth, and it's set up with an autoreply. I sometimes type up long emails to her. I tell her how much I love her and how much I miss her. Then, when her response shows up in my inbox, it's like I'm hearing from her again. It always says 'I will be back.' And I try to tell myself that it's true, even though I know it isn't."

Cheri's face is red. She's a naturally empathetic person. She tells me that she can tell that I'm in a lot of pain, and that it's understandable, given what I'd been through. She says that she wishes there was something she could do to help.

"You are helping, in a way. Have I told you how much better you are at your job than your predecessor?"

She tells me she doesn't want to talk about Ted like that.

It takes me a second to understand why. "Oh, right," I stammer. "Probably best to not insult the dead. Poor Ted. Neck slashed open by a sickle. Terrible way to go. I'm still hoping they catch the bastard who did it."

Cheri looks surprised. She hadn't heard anything about the murder weapon, just that he'd been stabbed.

"Ah, right, well...you see...when his family came in to remove his personals, and they told me it looked like a farm tool of some sort had done it." Cheri grimaces. It wasn't a great lie, but it seems to have done the trick. I offer her another glass of wine as I pour my third, but she declines.

"You know, just before he died, Ted had done something insanely stupid. He'd accidentally sent dozens and dozens of copies of his flaccid autoresponse to everyone in the company. It was fucking *revolting*."

Cheri looks on disapprovingly and starts to express some cliché about Ted resting in piece.

"Funny thing is," I say, interrupting her, "Naomi's ex-husband died the same way." I run my finger across my neck. "Slash to the throat."

Cheri starts to grow a little pale. I can tell that she's getting nervous. She asks when I think the other guests will get there.

"Oh, any minute now. Any minute."

We sit quietly for a few moments. There's a palpable tension in the air. I realize I've overtalked. I've probably freaked her out a little, too.

Cheri finally breaks the silence. She asks me to repeat the company that employed Naomi. When I reiterate the name of the firm – Shelby and Nixon – she asks if I heard the news about it.

"What news?"

Naomi relates how, according to the newspaper, at least, they've been in bankruptcy proceedings for a while. She recalled something about the liquidation of its assets getting finalized within the last day or two.

"Oh." I feel dizzy. The alcohol doesn't help. "That means...any day now...the server..." I whip out my phone.

The top message isn't from Naomi. Instead, it's from fucking *Google*, and it's telling me that the server had rejected my last email to Naomi. "No, no, no, no..." I collapse against the carpet.

Naomi asks if I'm okay.

"Do I look like I'm fucking okay? The server's shut down. Her account's fucking *gone*."

I spring to my feet and run to my bedroom closet. As I remove the file pocket, my shaking hands send several adjacent containers tumbling down. A cardboard box bursts open, and its contents scatter across the floor.

Ignoring the mess, I take out the thick set of printouts of my email exchanges with Naomi's account. "You were supposed to come back," I whimper through tears. "Now you're gone forever, and this is all that's left."

Cheri lets out a small shriek. She's followed me to my room, and her mouth now hangs agape. I realize her eyes are locked not on me, but on the carpet behind me where a red-stained sickle sits next to an opened jar of rat poison.

She backs off and announces that she should be going.

"Wait, Cheri-"

I run after her, but she's already outside. I watch from my front porch as her car disappears into the night.

I've never felt more alone. The one form of contact I had left with Naomi is gone. Shut down without warning. And her doppelgänger is probably on the phone with the police at this very moment.

My eyes catch movement in the distance. Two dark figures approach. Their stride is jagged and uneven as their tall frames sway with each step.

"Hello?" I call.

They continue to stagger across my lawn, towards me, in silence. I jump back when they finally come in range of my front yard light.

Their faces are drained of all color with the exception of their bloodshot eyes, which are fixed on me. Red liquid drips from deep gashes in their necks. I know who they are, and I know why they are coming for me.

Frantically, I lock and latch the front door. *How could this be happening? Am I losing my mind?*

The thuds against my front door grow louder. So loud, in fact, that the floor feels like it's shaking and reverberating so violently that I struggle to stay balanced. It's like they've been waiting for this moment of weakness, for this moment of separation from Naomi.

I don't know which will get to me first: the police; the animated corpses; or the dozens of green pellets I consider lifting towards my mouth. My attention turns to one last task that will allow me to leave a mark on this world, one that will stick around much longer than I will.

I open my laptop and type frantically. I keep typing as I hear the door burst open, as I sense figures shuffling slowly in my direction. Finally, in what I sense to be my last moments, I set my final automatic reply to send without any time limitations:

*Hey asshole*, it begins.

*Fortunately, I'm not available now, nor will I be anytime soon. If you need to reach me, well, you're out of fucking luck.*

*I don't know where I'm going, exactly, but I do know who's waiting there for me. We've been apart for too long, but I've got a feeling that no one will be getting between us again.*

*Now, fuck off, and let me rest goddamn in peace.*

18

———

# ALWAYS A TEACHER

Our substitute teacher arrived a few minutes after the morning announcements confirmed that Mrs. Pendleton was out sick. Our talking and giggling subsided as the chubby elderly woman sauntered into the classroom. Her veiny skin sagged and jostled with each step, and a fowl stench accompanied her as she passed me on her way to the podium.

Mrs. Hartfield, she etched, painfully slowly, on the chalkboard. She turned to us. "Good morning, children," she said in a grainy voice. "I am *so* excited to be here today. I spent twenty five years teaching first-graders like you. It's nice to be back."

My friend Ryan piped up with what was on all of our minds – that we were in *fifth* grade, not first.

"Please raise your hand before speaking, child," chided Mrs. Hartfield. "We're going to do some basic reading instruction today. Please turn to page seven." Mrs. Hartfield set a textbook she had carried in with her onto the podium and flipped it open.

Ryan and I exchanged a perplexed look as we opened our math books to a page we'd already covered.

"Please read out loud with me," said Mrs. Hartfield. "The dog ran to the house. The dog saw the child. The dog ate the child."

Another classmate, Lucy, interrupted, asking Mrs. Hartfield if she was sure that she was in the correct classroom.

"Child," said Mrs. Hartfield, "please remember to raise your hand before asking a question."

Lucy proceeded to raise her hand as Mrs. Hartfield had requested, only for Mrs. Hartfield to ignore her.

"I understand if some of these words are difficult for you," said Mrs. Hartfield. As she spoke, I noticed that she had missing teeth, and those that she did have were discolored. "This may be advanced for six and seven-year-olds. But, please try to read along with me."

She continued even as none of us could join her. "The dog had died. The child had wept. But the dog did not stay dead. The dog dug out of the grave. The dog came home. The dog ate the child."

She paused and looked around the classroom. "Well," she said, "you all certainly aren't very energetic today, are you?" She pointed at me. "Little girl, why don't you come up here and read from my book. I'll guide you through each word. We can get through this passage together."

A nervous chill ran through me. I probably looked petrified. I had no intention of obeying her instruction.

"Child," she said, sternly, "Come up here, or I'll have no choice but to notify the principal that you are refusing to participate. I may even have to make a phone call to your parents."

All the warning signs ran through my brain. I knew, on an instinctual level, that something was very wrong with this person, and that I should stay as far away from her as possible.

To my relief, Ryan volunteered to go in my place.

Mrs. Hartfield's eyes shifted to Ryan's seat, and a moment later her head awkwardly turned to catch up. "Very well," she croaked.

Our class watched in quiet suspense as Ryan slowly approached her. He was sweaty, and he grew visibly uncomfortable with each step. I could only imagine how much worse her smell was up-close.

Mrs. Hartfield handed Ryan the textbook, which I could now see was tattered and missing portions of pages. Then, she pulled up the chair from the teacher's desk and sat in it. "Please, child, come sit on my lap."

*Don't do it*, I wanted to scream at Ryan. He stood still and shook his head.

Violently, Mrs. Hartfield grabbed Ryan and pulled him onto her. Ryan had recently started a growth spurt and should have weighed too much for Mrs. Hartfield to be comfortable. Despite this, Mrs. Hartfield's face settled into a long, satisfied smile.

Ryan turned absolutely pale. I could tell that he wanted to get away, but a combination of fear and Mrs. Hartfield's grip kept him paralyzed.

Mrs. Hartfield resumed reading from the book. "The dog dug out of the grave. Please, child, say it with me. The dog dug out of the grave."

Ryan turned helplessly towards the other students. Tears were in his eyes. He stammered that her body was cold. A stain started to spread throughout his pants as he lost control of his bladder.

"What a mess you've made!" screamed Mrs. Hartfield. "How dare you!"

"Let him go!" I yelled.

Ryan, desperate to escape, pried at her hand, but was unable to escape her seemingly strong grip. When he shoved against her body, Mrs. Hartfield started to cough, as if the force from Ryan had triggered a physical reaction within her. Her coughs grew increasingly violent.

For a moment, Mrs. Hartfield appeared to settle down. Then, without warning, her expression turned to panic.

Ryan gazed at her with a terrified expression as her mouth opened wide. She let out a groan as she vomited a massive amount of pink liquid all over my friend. The disgusting, chunky substance covered his face and ran down his body as he cried out in horror. The rest of the class screamed as we watched the spectacle unfold.

As she continued to spew the rosy fluid, her head started to tilt. Her skin steadily shifted to the bottom right of her chin, where it formed a drooping bulge. Her eyes disconnected and drifted to the same spot. The weight of it all pulled off the remaining skin from her face, until it all detached and fell onto the floor as a half-liquidated ooze.

Her grip finally loosened, allowing Ryan to stumble away. All over her, skin steadily departed, melting into a pile within the large puddle of pink liquid that had formed around her. We watched, repulsed, as the remaining visible portions of her body disintegrated into pure skeleton.

We were soon shuffled out of the classroom by the police. They had arrived at the school after a body had been found in the parking lot in the car of the *real* substitute sent to teach us that day. She had been stripped of much of her skin and flesh – all of which was later determined to have been attached to the bony frame of the woman who presented herself as Mrs. Hartfield.

We didn't go back to school for weeks. The police asked us a lot of questions, and many of us underwent psychiatric treatment. Ryan needed years of counseling. His parents homeschooled him for the next two grades.

I never understood much more about what happened until recently, when I got the idea to browse an archive of old issues of the local newspaper.

The night before Mrs. Hartfield showed up to teach us, an incident had transpired in the local cemetery. The article described how, during the night, a hole appeared in front of a headstone. It led six feet under to an old casket, which had been found empty the next morning.

The casket had belonged to a Susanna Hartfield, who had passed away in the 1970s after decades of teaching young children in the very room where my class of fifth graders had been on that day forever etched into our memories.

I don't know how she regained sentience after so long, or how what was left of her remains made it to the surface. But I do know what drove her to steal the flesh of the poor substitute and to try to take her place.

*Once a teacher, always a teacher*, as the saying goes.

**19**

---

# MY BOYFRIEND IS TRANSFORMING INTO AN OBSCURE AMERICAN PRESIDENT

You probably don't know much about Grover Cleveland. If you're from the United States, then you may be aware that he served two terms as President in the late 1800s. If you've read about what he did during those terms, then you've seen that he took strong stances on tariffs, trade rates, and the gold standard before fading into a historical footnote. Unfortunately, I've learned that there's more to him than that. A lot more.

All of this happened because of Stephen. I thought I was being cautious when I let Stephen back into my life. We'd lived together once. For a few months, it had been wonderful.

But then he came home from work one day telling me we needed to have a talk. I told him, sure, what about?

His boyish, smoothly-shaven face took on a vulnerable look. It dawned on me that he had something serious to say.

He sat with me, still in his deputy uniform, and told me that he had something to confess.

At first, I refused to believe him. I told him this must be a sick joke. Stephen wasn't like that. What kind of man cheats on his girlfriend, only to quickly fess up to it unprompted?

"I want to be honest with you," said Stephen. "I'm so sorry. If you think I should go, I'll leave right now."

I couldn't deny it any more. He was being serious. I cupped my hands around my wet eyes.

The day Stephen moved out, he texted me that he'd left me something under the pillow. Three months' rent was stuffed in the envelope.

I still didn't forgive him. Not yet, at least.

The next few months were brutal. I'd never had much in terms of friends and family, so I struggled through the initial period of loneliness that followed Stephen's departure.

Four years passed before I saw Stephen again. I told Rachel to stay where she was as I answered the knocks at the door.

"We've received a report of a domestic disturbance," announced a familiar voice.

"Oh..." I gasped upon seeing him. "Stephen..."

"Sandy," said Stephen, briefly losing his composure. He now wore a full-fledged sheriff's uniform. "I had no idea it was you who called. Are you okay? Dispatch said..."

"That my boyfriend hit me?" I turned my head so that Stephen could see the mark.

"That bastard," said Stephen. "Step outside. I'll handle this."

"Stephen," I called, "don't hurt him, okay?"

I covered Rachel's eyes as Stephen dragged Benjamin across the yard and into the back seat of his car.

Stephen stopped by the next morning. He said he was there to gather Benjamin's belongings. "When he gets out, I'll give these to him, and I'll see to it that he doesn't bother you again."

I thanked Stephen. He asked if he could come in. "Sure," I said. "But just for a bit." I felt like I owed him that much.

He sat down as I made him a cup of coffee.

"Ma, where's pa?" asked Rachel as she examined Stephen.

"He's away, just for a little while," I told her. "Do you miss him?"

Rachel shook her head.

"Now, what's your name, young lady?" asked Stephen.

"Rachel. I saw you last night!"

"That's right!" said Stephen. "Now, how old are you Rachel?"

"I'm three!"

"Well isn't that great. Do you know how old I am?"

Rachel shook her head again.

"I'm one hundred and eighty four years old!"

Rachel laughed. "No you're not."

"You got me!" said Stephen. "I'm only thirty-nine." Eleven years older than me.

When he left, Rachel was smiling as widely as I was. "I like Stephen," said Rachel.

Stephen stopped by the next day, and the next. I let him stay a little longer each time. Rachel was always happy to see him. Stephen began to bring children's books, usually ones focused on American history, to read to her.

"You must get lonely here, raising Rachel all by yourself," said Stephen to me one day.

"It's better than when Benjamin was around. I don't know why I stayed with him for as long as I did. I felt trapped."

"Well, you don't have to worry about him anymore," said Stephen. "Look, Sandy, I know I wronged you once. Maybe I don't deserve a second chance. But I can tell you that what happened then is in the past. I haven't even talked to her in years, and nothing like that's ever going to happen again."

I thought long and hard about what he was suggesting. The selling point was how well he got along with Rachel. Within a few weeks, Rachel and I had moved out of my crummy apartment and into a small house with Stephen.

He'd changed a bit since I'd last lived with him. For one, he read constantly. When he wasn't working, he left the television on a C-Span channel that aired discussions about new books. At first it annoyed me, but I eventually accepted it. At least he wasn't blasting FOX News all day.

"You think Trump'll run again?" asked Stephen.

I shrugged. "Yeah, probably."

"Well, if he wins, he'll be the second President to serve nonconsecutive terms. You know who the first President to do that was?"

"I dunno, what difference does it make?"

"Aw, come on, Sandy, at least take a guess!"

Rachel's high-pitched voice piped up. "It was Grover Cleeverland!"

"There you go, you little bookworm!" said Stephen. Rachel giggled.

I adjusted to his new quirks. They were harmless, after all.

Life started to return to where it had been before. I sometimes sighed when I thought of how Stephen had sidetracked my life by messing around with another girl like that. It's like he'd sapped four years from me.

But, I forgave him. He was loving and supportive of both me and Rachel, and I cared about him enough that I felt a twang of fear for his safety each time he left for work.

The first strange thing happened when we were in bed together late one night. We'd just screwed around, and he was catching his breath while he held me in his arms.

"Stephen?"

"Yeah?"

"You said something strange a minute ago, while we were, you know-"

He told me he didn't think he'd said anything.

"No, I'm sure of it," I insisted. "You were looking down at me, and you said 'Maria'."

He denied it. "No, no, if I said anything, maybe it would have been your full name 'Sandra'." The silence that followed prompted him to add, "And, no, I don't even know anyone named 'Maria', so I would never have said that. Okay?"

"Okay," I said. I didn't think much of it at the time.

The next Saturday morning, I cooked Stephen a large breakfast of corned beef hash and eggs. I chided him when he sloppily shoveled it into his mouth, too immersed in a biography he was reading to display basic manners.

"Did you know," he said between bites, "that the United States government used to have to purchase 4.5 million ounces of silver each month?"

"That sounds expensive," I said, only half-listening as I used a napkin to clean off his mouth.

"It sure was," said Stephen. "But President Cleveland put a stop to that."

The napkin scraped against his stubble. "Stephen, are you going to shave anytime soon? Doesn't the Sheriff's office have regulations against facial hair?"

"Huh? No, it's fine, don't worry. I'm in charge, after all, so who's going to say anything?"

Rachel loved pulling at the mustache that he steadily grew out over the next few months. She could never wait to spend time with him. "When's dad coming home?" she'd ask after I picked her up from preschool. I loved that she called him that.

We continued to live happily together. I dropped hints about marriage and couldn't wait for him to formally ask the question. The only hiccup was that Stephen, who'd always been slim, started putting on weight. I cooked healthily for him and encouraged him to work out.

"Hey, I know you're only looking out for me," said Stephen, as he turned a page in the biography, "But this is just a temporary thing. I'll get back in shape once I get through the next few weeks of work." He kissed me.

I spent a few weeks that fall preparing for a party Stephen had agreed to host at our house to commemorate his first full year as sheriff. When the night of the celebration arrived, I served refreshments to a crowd of deputies and their families.

After a full hour of tending to the guests, I took a quick break. A tall, scrawny deputy joined me where I sat on a living room couch.

"You're the wife, aren't you?"

"We're not..."

"Oh, sorry, right," said the deputy. "I'm Deputy Hawkins. You can call me Teddy. Stephen and I go way back."

"How far back?"

"We went to school together as kids, actually!"

"So you're also from Cottontown?" I asked.

He looked confused. "No, no, Stephen and I are both from Caldwell."

"There's a Caldwell in Tennessee?"

"Ma'am, you seem confused," said Teddy. "We grew up in Caldwell, New Jersey."

I told him that my boyfriend never lived in New Jersey, but he continued to insist otherwise. "Look, I know where the man I'm living with is from, okay?"

"Whatever you say, ma'am," said Teddy.

A young woman joined us. Teddy introduced her as his daughter, Frances, who was home on fall break from her senior year of college.

"I've heard so many *wonderful* things about your boyfriend," she said. "From how dad describes him, we're so lucky to have him as sheriff. You know, keeping the streets safe, and looking after all of us." She was blushing.

I laughed. "Well, I'm glad to hear him spoken so well of. He's great with Rachel, too. That's my three-year-old. She's upstairs with a babysitter."

"Oh, I know about Rachel," said Frances. "She loves it when Stephen reads to her from his history books."

"Oh! Did...did your dad tell you about that?" It surprised me that such a specific detail would get from Stephen to her. Before Frances could respond, one of Stephen's colleagues silenced the room for a toast in Stephen's honor.

The crowd slowly died out as the party stretched into the late hours. When the babysitter had to leave, Frances volunteered to look after Rachel. To my delight, Rachel seemed to get along with Frances as well as she did with Stephen.

I started cleaning up. By this point, only a handful of guests remained, and they were all drinking with Stephen. I was folding up picnic chairs outside when Teddy stumbled over to me.

"You're not driving Frances home like that, are you?"

"Ma'am, who do ya' think is gonna arrest me?"

I sighed. "Well, please at least sit here for a little while, until you sober up."

Teddy plopped into one of the remaining chairs. "Ya know what we call Stephen at work?"

"Sheriff?"

He laughed. "No, no, he's gotta nickname. We call him 'The Executioner'. When he corners a criminal, ya know, one of them *real bad* fellas who hurt a kid, or defenseless woman, he draws his sidearm and 'Pow', they ain't gettin' off on no technicality." As he spoke, he formed a gun with his hand and pretended to fire it.

"That's not funny," I said.

He looked at me with dead seriousness for a few moments before bursting into laughter. "I had ya' goin', didn't I?"

"Yeah," I said dryly. "You sure did."

"I know 'bout that guy who hit you," said Teddy. "Benjamin, right?"

"Yeah."

"You ain't seen him since Stephen showed up, have ya'?"

I froze. "I...No, but Stephen said-"

Teddy winked. "Yeah, Benjamin's doin' *just fine* now. Not gonna give ya' any more trouble."

"Stephen didn't..."

"Oh no, ma'am, you don't need to worry. Benjamin's *definitely* alive and well." He winked again as he chuckled.

I stormed back inside. I hated Benjamin for how he treated me, but I didn't want him to be hurt. What Teddy was suggesting was too terrible for me to fathom.

He was nowhere on the ground level. But Rachel was there, unwatched as she napped on the couch. "Stephen? Stephen?" I called.

When I reached the top of the stairs, I found Stephen and Frances outside our bedroom. Stephen's hair was unkempt, and his shirt was half-unbuttoned.

"What are you two *doing* here?" I asked.

"Oh, hey Maria," mumbled Stephen. "I was just showing Frances some of my history books-"

"You did it again!" I screamed. "You called me 'Maria'. *Why?*"

"Woah, easy there," said Frances. "He didn't say that. He called you Sandy."

Exasperated, I spoke in a rushed, angry tone. "And you, what are you doing up here? You agreed to watch-"

"Mama!" called Rachel. I turned around to find her. She'd woken up and climbed the stairs on her own.

"Hey there, sweet pea," I said. "Let's bring you to bed, okay?"

To my surprise, Rachel crawled past me. Frances got to her knees and embraced Rachel, picking her up. "There you are, mama," said Rachel as she stroked her hand against Frances' cheek.

I felt myself grow dizzy. It was all too much.

First, there was Stephen's change of appearance. Between his thick mustache and the weight he'd gained, he was almost unrecognizable to me now.

Plus, I *knew* Stephen was from Tennessee. He'd talked to me about growing up in Cottontown and attending White House High School. As far as I knew, he'd never even set foot in New Jersey.

He'd promised me that he hadn't hurt Benjamin too badly, and that he'd dropped off Benjamin's stuff with him after he'd gotten out of jail. Had he been lying about that, too?

And why was Stephen upstairs, looking disheveled, with a woman half his age? Why was he calling me Maria? And why was my daughter addressing Frances as her mother?

I landed against the carpeted floor as shadows descended over my surrounding.

When I awoke, it was daylight, and I was alone. Stephen had left me a note explaining that he'd dropped Rachel off at preschool and that I should rest.

I spent the morning finishing the process of cleaning up from the party. In contrast to the noise from last night, the house was silent aside from the television, which played Stephen's channel-of-choice at a low volume.

As I vacuumed the floor, I noticed the biography Stephen had been reading. I recognized the face displayed across the front cover – I'd been going to sleep next to it every night for the last few weeks.

I flipped the book open and scanned its contents.

*"As sheriff, Grover personally carried out the executions of two criminals..."*

*"Grover took office in 1893 with the support of all states that had fought with the Confederacy in the Civil War..."*

*"...appointed no African Americans to civil service positions...The protection of civil rights had little significance to him..."*

*"Grover believed that Chinese immigrants were incapable of assimilation into American society..."*

*"...went on to marry the same woman he'd once given presents to as a toddler..."*

The book landed against the floor with a thud. *This* was the man Stephen had been obsessing over? Had he been intentionally changing his appearance to emulate him?

No, no, that was too crazy. He wouldn't do something like that. Not the Stephen I knew. But was the Stephen I knew even real?

A ringtone snapped me out of my panicked thoughts. It was Stephen's personal phone. He'd left it beneath a pillow on his couch. It displayed, *"Incoming Call – Frances Hawkins."* When I tried to hear the voicemail that Frances left, Stephen's phone prompted me to enter a password.

A few days ago, I'd never imagine wanting to discreetly access my boyfriend's phone. But now, I was dead-set on getting to the bottom of whatever was happening.

The phone rejected the digits of Stephen's birthday. I thought for a moment. Looking down at the book I'd dropped to the floor, I had an idea.

I flipped open the biography and found the birthdate of Stephen Grover Cleveland: March 18, 1837. I entered "0318137," and the phone unlocked. The first thing I did was play back Frances' message.

*Oh, Stephen, how I yearned for so long for your touch. I still think back on how much of a gentleman you've always been to me. From when I was a little girl opening the presents you brought me, to when I was eighteen and first felt the feeling of your lips against mine. I never should have broken things off with you and let you return to her. It meant so much to me that we were able to do what we did last night. She's suspicious, but it doesn't matter. We'll have her out of the way before long. She'll never understand the depth of our affection.*

I flung the phone against the floor. This can't be real. It can't be. Stephen wouldn't have left me for someone at the tail end of high school.

My heart jolted as, in the corner of my eye, I caught an image of a President who looked just like Stephen on the television screen. I turned up the volume as the cover of a new Grover Cleveland biography faded into live footage of two historians discussing it.

"What's remarkable to me," said the first, "is that, to this day, so many still refer to him as 'The Honest President'. That's something I was hoping to challenge in this book."

"Could you tell us, Professor Alexander," said the other, "a little bit about why you think that nickname is inapplicable?"

"Well, people first started using that term when Presidential-candidate Cleveland was accused of having fathered a child out of wedlock. Obviously, that was a bigger issue at the time than it would be today. But, rather than denying the allegation as most expected, Cleveland fessed up to having engaged in illicit relations with the mother, Maria Halpin."

*Maria?* Is that why Stephen had been calling me that?

"In Cleveland's version of events, Ms. Halpin was a promiscuous drunkard, and he was but one of many men who could have been the father. Cleveland supposedly claimed paternity only out of gentlemanly obligation when no one else would do so, and then assisted Ms. Halpin by providing child support."

Professor Alexander continued. "The public reacted positively to Cleveland's admission, and the scandal did not ultimately derail his Presidential bid. But the reputation Cleveland accrued for honesty is misplaced. He omitted details that portrayed him in a less flattering light."

"And what might those be?" asked the other man.

"Well, first, Ms. Halpin wrote in a sworn statement that Cleveland had been violent and forceful with her regarding the act itself, and that he had threatened to 'ruin' her if she complained of this to the authorities."

"Did she have any proof?"

"No, but we know for a fact that, soon after Ms. Halpin gave birth, her son was taken away from her, and she was involuntarily admitted to an asylum under extremely suspicious circumstances. The child ultimately grew up without her. The public, meanwhile, largely rejected her version of events and forgot about the scandal."

The color drained from my face. My boyfriend had been calling me 'Maria', and I'd just learned that the child of the *real* Maria was taken from her.

I took my keys and ran out to the car.

The pre-school administrators eyed me suspiciously as I entered the main office. I realized I looked a mess. I still wore my clothes from last night, and I hadn't as much as run a brush through my hair all morning.

"Can I help you?" asked the lady at the front desk.

"Yes, yes, please, I need to see my daughter."

"And may I ask what her name is?"

"Rachel. Rachel Caulfield."

She typed a few things into her computer and then eyed me quizzically. "Can I see some form of identification?"

"Uh, sure." I produced my driver's license. She raised an eyebrow as she examined it. "Ma'am, I think you brought the wrong card." She handed it back to me.

I gasped when I read Maria Halpin's name at the top. "What? This can't be. This isn't mine."

"Well," said the woman, "How about you return here with the correct identification, and then I can bring your daughter out to you?" She gave me a polite smile.

I drove home in a hurry. I searched everywhere for some form of identification, but everything I could think of – my birth certificate, my credit card - was gone. All I had was a driver's license that displayed another person's name. Gone, too, were all the pictures of me and Stephen, as well as any property belonging to me.

I took a few deep breaths, trying to make some sense of what was happening. My mind settled as I listened to the tick of a clock and the low murmur of the television. Its screen displayed a middle-aged woman now presenting about a book she wrote titled *Ghosts and the White House.*

"True evil never dies," said the woman. "It gets reborn, and it transforms everything it touches in the process. Past, present, future – nothing is safe from it." I turned off the television.

I checked our shared computer. Stephen was already logged into his main social media accounts, and each one contained pictures of him embracing Frances. His Facebook profile picture was of him and Frances holding Rachel between them.

I scrolled back through his photos. I didn't recognize any of them, and they included a few apparent throwbacks to his youth in Caldwell, New Jersey.

I searched Benjamin's full name. The first story that appeared was of him being found dead several months ago. He'd been shot in an unsolved homicide.

The front door opened. Frances entered, holding Rachel's hand, followed by Stephen.

Frances and I exchanged a shocked look. As I started to ask her what she was doing with my boyfriend and my daughter, she pointed at me and screamed. "Someone's in here!" She turned to Stephen. "Please, keep her away from our daughter!"

Stephen burst past her and shoved me to the ground.

"Take Ruth out of here!" he yelled. Frances hurried outside with my daughter.

"Stephen, why?" I whimpered as Stephen's strong grip held me in place. "Why are you doing this to me?"

"Look, whoever you are, there are two ways this can end," said Stephen through gritted teeth. "You leave voluntarily, or I call for backup to have you removed from my house."

I made an anguished cry as I tried futilely to push his large form off of me. "This is *our* house, Stephen. Why are you pretending not to know who I am?"

"You need help," said Stephen. "And I'm going to see to it that you get it."

"Whatever you're trying to do – it won't work! I'll tell the truth. I know you're not from New Jersey. I know what you really did to Benjamin. And I know that Rachel is *my* daughter."

Stephen's face settled into a smug smile. "Now Sandra, who's going to believe *you* over *me*?"

"W-what?"

"I said, I'm going to see to it that you get the help that you need." Stephen let go, leaving me on the floor. "Just sit tight. I'll arrange for that help to arrive."

I've been left to my own devices while deputies and nurses have gathered around an ambulance outside. They're rolling a stretcher out right now.

I wrote all of this down in the hopes that somebody, somewhere, can make sense of what's happening to me. I don't know exactly where they plan on taking me, but I do know that it's a place I won't be leaving anytime soon.

I open the window and listen to the discussion outside. Stephen is telling the others, "She's not a threat to herself, she's just confused."

Closer to the window, Frances and Rachel sit together by a tree. "That lady will leave us alone soon. You don't have to worry, Ruth. It'll just be you, me, and your father," says Frances.

"Rachel!" I yell. Rachel's head turns. There is a hint of recognition. She starts to form a word, the same word I've heard her say many times before: "Momma." But before she can do so, Frances grabs her and drags her away.

Stephen knocks at the door. "Ma'am, please step out peacefully. I only want to help you. You have my word as a gentleman."

## 20

---

# AFTER THE SURGERY (PARTS II AND III)

**P**art II

I spent the first few weeks in the hospital in a state of resignation. I said little and occupied my many bedridden hours staring emptily at the tile ceiling.

My head ached, my ribs were sore, and my legs were barely responsive. But when I cried, it wasn't because of the physical pain. Every cautious, careful decision I'd made had been for nothing. I felt checkmated, with no way out and nowhere to hide.

"There, there," Brandon would say while he gently patted my wet cheek with a tissue. "You've been through so much. I'll always be here for you, and we'll make it through this, together, I promise."

I wanted to scream for help, to beg the nurses to keep him away from me. But that hadn't worked before, and that certainly wouldn't work now that the law recognized me as the guardian of a small child.

While my body bore no signs of it, all the documentation necessary to establish that I'd given birth to Martin was in perfect order. There were hospital bills, preschool records, updates to insurance policies. His birth certificate displayed November 7, 2018. "Nine months after Valentine's Day," said Brandon, with a sickly smile that made me want to punch him in the face.

Of course, I had no memories of the boy I'd supposedly brought into this world, who appeared with me and Brandon in dozens upon dozens of pictures and videos.

I wondered what lay behind Martin's hazel eyes. Had Brandon somehow conjured up a real, living being? If so, was he human, the same thing as Brandon (a 'cambion,' as Jean had called him), or something in between? Or, was Martin a mere figment – the latest cruel illusion cast by my perpetual tormenter?

I decided to play along. Based on what Jean had told me, Brandon wouldn't need me anymore if he realized that I knew the truth. The first time I'd undergone an operation, as the story went, I'd lost all memory of my loving husband as a fluke side effect. The second time, I'd lost all memory of my precious son. After all, that's what the brainwashed doctors are telling me, and that's what someone who believed Brandon's lies would think.

So, I stayed in character as best as I could. I repeated to Brandon that I loved him, and that I accepted him as my husband, even as I still had no memories of him. I confessed that I had no memories now of Martin, either, but that I trusted Brandon and believed him when he told me that Martin was my son.

"Mommy is sick," Brandon had explained in front of me to a wide-eyed Martin. "Because she's sick, she sometimes has trouble remembering things. But she still loves you. Isn't that right, April?"

Martin turned to me. "Yes," I croaked, "that's right, Martin. I'm sick, and I'm having some trouble remembering things, but I still love you."

"When will you get better?" asked Martin, his brow furrowed with concern.

"She will soon, Martin," assured Brandon. "Soon. And we'll do everything we can to support her."

My parents were less sympathetic. "You're lucky that you married Brandon," chided my mother when she visited me. "A lot of men wouldn't still be so supportive after what you've put him through."

I didn't bother arguing.

~

I couldn't let Brandon know what I'd learned from Jean. Of course, I had no real evidence of my relationship with Emma, but it *felt* true in a way that my supposed marriage to Brandon never had. I could only remember glimpsing her twice, but the image of her round face and curly blonde hair had stuck with me. I prayed that maybe, just maybe, she'd figure out a way to rescue me from the hell that my life had become.

Naturally, Brandon was eager to learn just what Jean had told me. In my version of events, I climbed into the van expecting another ride to the dealership, only to be whisked away from town against my will. "I begged him to stop and let me out, but he wouldn't say anything. He was driving like a madman, Brandon. I'm not surprised somebody hit us. I think he was crazy."

"He didn't tell you anything at all about what he wanted, or where he was taking you?" asked Brandon.

When I shook my head, I sensed his skepticism. He had reason to worry. If he got his power from convincing his victims of lies, then how long did I have before he realized that his were no longer fooling me?

Hopefully a little while longer – long enough to flee, or to come up with some plan to fight back. I figured that, if I were to stay alive, I needed to gain some advantage over him.

Even as the weeks of recovery, including regular sessions of intense physical therapy, helped me slowly regain control over my body, I feigned being unable to walk more than a few steps. I knew this act – something the doctors ascribed to a 'mental block' – could only last so long.

But, at least, it gave me a brief leg up over Brandon – a window during which he believed my movements were more restricted than they really were and, hopefully, would monitor me less closely. I used those nights to sneak out of my bed and explore the hospital, taking care to move quietly and evade the staff whose routes I steadily learned.

When I overheard two nurses chatting that the man found with me in the crash had finally woken up, I knew I had only a short time to act. That night, I forced my weakened body down a flight of stairs and across several corridors until I arrived at my destination in the intensive care unit. I slipped inside the room, closing the door quietly behind me.

Jean was in a neck brace, and bruises covered much of his face. "I'm so sorry," I told him. "I'm only a stranger to you, and all this happened to you just because you wanted to help me."

"April...I'm so glad you're still alive." He spoke softly in a weak, whimpering voice.

"I told him that you didn't say a word to me in the van. You need to say the same thing if-"

"I understand."

I asked him the question that had been bothering me ever since I awoke at the hospital. "Jean, I need to know why he's keeping me around. You said Grousel gets his power from fooling people. But I *know* it's all an act now. So, what's in it for him?"

"He invested heavily in you..." Jean stopped to catch his breath before continuing. "He won't give up until he knows that you're...that you're a lost cause. He may wait until he has another target. Play along...convince him that you believe him...that will buy you some time."

"I need to know how to kill him. Can he be shot, or stabbed?"

"No...you'd only be harming a mirage..."

"What if I destroy his book?"

"That would undo some of his spells. But, he can simply create a new book and cast them again."

"Then *what do I do*?" I pleaded.

Jean's response made little sense to me. "To defeat Grousel... shatter the illusions that give him his power. Only then will he be vulnerable. I left an athame with Emma that might-"

"I don't understand. How-"

Jean motioned for me to be silent, then gestured to the door behind me. I gasped when I realized its handle was slowly turning. "Hide," whispered Jean.

I scurried towards the closet at the far end of the room. From inside, I could still observe my surroundings through a narrow slit in the center of the closed bifold doors.

The door to Jean's room opened slowly as a small figure materialized from the shadows of the dimly lit hallway. It was...*Martin*?

Martin spoke in the same nauseatingly high-pitched voice I'd grown to loathe over the last few weeks. "Excuse me, sir. I don't feel very good."

"Child...you must be lost," responded Jean.

"No, I don't think so," said Martin, as he slowly approached Jean.

"Who are you, child?"

"I'm no child. I'm a copy, an extension of an entity hundreds of years old." Abruptly, Martin hopped onto the bed and positioned himself over Jean.

"What are you *doing*?" asked a perplexed Jean.

Ignoring him, Martin lowered his head until it was mere inches above Jean's. "I told you I was sick. My head doesn't feel right. Especially when I do this."

Martin placed his hands behind his ears. Suddenly, he pressed, hard, until his hands penetrated and burrowed into his skin, leaving only his wrists exposed.

Jean's expression shifted from bewilderment to horror as Martin continued to dig into his own head, twisting his hands around his scalp as he did so. Martin showed no sign of pain even as blood oozed out of the increasingly long gash and showered onto Jean. When Brandon's hands finally emerged from his forehead, they held onto Martin's face, which disconnected from the rest of his head.

Jean yelled expletives as he hit the nurse call button.

"*That won't do you any good.*" The voice that resounded from Martin sounded nothing like it had before. It was deep, but with a wispy echo that caused every word to reverberate with an unnatural energy. "*They won't be coming to help you. I've disabled everything in here.*"

Martin's form changed. His skin liquified and melted into a thin layer of bloody residue, exposing underneath it a body made of murky green scales. Horns grew from the forehead of his new, angular face. A set of pink wings burst through his shirt. His fingers stretched and curved as they transformed into long, sharp claws. Meanwhile, the flesh they held – which had once been the face of the child claiming to be my own – solidified into a circular wooden oval.

"*What*...what are you?" asked a panicked Jean.

"You haven't figured it out yet?" sneered Martin. "The boy you saw was just an illusion, a veneer. A boring role I've spent the last few months playing."

Indeed, I realized that the object he was holding was now an exceedingly plain mask, its only notable features being a minor indentation for a nose and three nondescript holes for eyes and a mouth.

Jean looked at him wide-eyed. "Grousel...he made another one..."

Martin laughed. "Not many know our name. It took decades to harness the energy necessary for fission. The sucker upstairs telling me that she *loved* me – the other me, that is – was the finishing touch. But the real question is: does she know? I'll find out soon enough. But you could save me the trouble."

"I don't...I don't know what you're talking about," whimpered Jean.

Martin extended a claw against Jean's shoulder. "I can carve you up, bit by bit, until you tell me." He moved his claw down Jean's arm. "Is that what you want?" His claw stopped when it reached Jean's wrist. "Now what is this?"

Martin's claw had grasped a metal bracelet. Its chain appeared to be made of silver, and it featured a small amethyst stone in its center.

"It's...nothing. They gave it back to me with my other personals when I awoke."

"Oh, it's no ordinary bracelet," said Martin. "You put some work into charming its jewel to protect against our influence. Clever, but it's of no value anymore." With swift motion, Martin's claw ripped through the bracelet, causing it to snap and its parts to scatter across the floor. "Now, tell me: what did you say to April?"

Jean took a deep breath before replying. "I had everything set up at a motel...Pictures, books, charts...I was going to explain it all to her when we got there. When...when we crashed...I hadn't told her anything at all yet. She probably thinks I'm just...just some crazy person."

Martin glanced down for a moment, then back at Jean. A satisfied smile spread across his face as he hopped to the ground. "I believe you," he said. He held out the palm of his left hand, which he proceeded to dig into with his right claw until drops of emerald green bled out from it. "But, you're still too much trouble to keep around."

Martin walked around Jean, using his hand to let drops of blood fall against the floor and the hospital bed until it formed a liquid outline that surrounded Jean.

"Don't do this!" pleaded Jean.

Martin ignored him, instead stepping backwards and closing his eyes. He began to chant in a language that sounded to me like Latin. As the volume and tempo of his words gradually increased, the drops of blood on the floor started to simmer until, finally, they burst into green flames that stretched up halfway to the ceiling.

"Please!" yelled Jean. But it was too late. At once, the ring of fire expanded rapidly inwards, engulfing Jean. In an instant, Jean's body disintegrated, leaving behind only bits of charred, brittle bone, and the flames disappeared moments later.

It took all the strength I had to resist yelling out or bolting for the exit. I closed my eyes as a wave of shock ran through me. I'd just witnessed the murder of an innocent man, at the hands of the very being I'd been pretending was my son. Gone, too, was my best hope for ever defeating Brandon.

When I opened my eyes, Martin was holding a flimsy, heavily burnt bit of Jean's bone. Martin tightened his claws around it, crumpling it into a gray powder that he scooped into a plastic bag.

Martin lifted the wooden mask and pressed it against his face. Over the next few seconds, his human body reformed around him, such that he once more resembled the small child who'd regularly visited me at the hospital, albeit with long tears on the back of his shirt that marked the spots out of which his wings had sprouted. Bag in hand, Martin crept away into the gloomy corridor outside.

~

By the time my physical state had improved enough for the hospital to discharge me, my emotional state had hit rock-bottom. I had no idea how to defeat Brandon. *Shatter the illusions that give him his power*, Jean had said. But how the hell could I do that?

The only thing I could think of was to run. "Planning our next vacation?" Brandon had asked me the morning after I'd stayed up searching flights and bus routes on my phone.

"What? No," I'd responded, flustered.

He shrugged as he continued preparing breakfast for the three of us. "Good. It's important that you rest and stay put until you're fully recovered."

The incident left me frustrated with myself. *Of course* Brandon had a way of monitoring my phone. I should have anticipated that.

In time, my health had improved to the point that I could leave the house for short errands or to take myself to therapy. But no matter where I went, I always assumed that Brandon was watching and listening. I lived my life as if under constant surveillance.

I still kept up the act of being in worse shape than I was. Stairs, in particular, I pretended to need extensive help with. Brandon happily obliged, holding me lovingly around the waist and shoulder as he helped me climb up to our bedroom every night.

I spent my days caring for a monster I pretended to love. Having no actual prior experience with childcare, I had to learn fast. Martin cried, threw fits, and generally left me exhausted. Nonetheless, I tried to treat him affectionately as I dressed him, worked with him on potty training, and read to him.

Once, while picking up his stuffed animals, I felt a small, solid object on the inside of a purple rabbit he liked to hold while he slept. "Give me Mr. Boots!" commanded Martin, before I had a chance to investigate further. "Of course, sweetie," I said, praying that whatever was inside of it was a choking hazard.

Throughout the long, tedious days I spent with Martin, images flashed through my mind of Martin's true, demonic form, and Jean's fiery death at his hands. Did the same fate await me when Brandon realized the truth?

I spent my nights with Brandon curled up around me. He would hold me tightly, and he was getting bolder and pushier about wanting to 'resume' intimate activities with me – activities that, according to him, *I* had usually been the one to initiate.

"I want that too, Brandon," I would say. "But I'm still healing. I'm so sore. I don't think I'm ready yet."

"Okay, love," he would reply while gripping my hand. "Take your time. Only once you're ready."

I rarely got much sleep.

~

As part of my loving wife and mother act, I'd insisted on giving Brandon a break by taking Martin to a preschool friend's birthday party at a neighbor's house. After an hour, the noise of the many screeching children ignited a raging headache in me. It didn't help that another mother kept talking my ear off despite my many attempts to evade her.

"I hear you're forgetten' things again?" she screeched. "Personally, I don't get it. Nothing could ever make me forget about my Samantha. She's the most important thing in the world to me!"

"Excuse me," I said as I hobbled towards the quiet front porch.

From outside, I looked in through the glass. Among the children stood a figure I hadn't noticed before: a costumed character in the form of a black cat. The costume reminded me of a sports team mascot, if a bit shorter, and it dragged a prop tail behind it as it waddled through the room to the delight of the kids around it.

As the kids thronged around a box labeled "party favors" that it placed in the room's center, the cat turned towards me. Fear instincts kicked in as it locked its large, nightmarishly red eyes onto me and proceeded to move in my direction.

I backed up until I hit the porch railing. Meanwhile, the costumed figure kept on coming. Fumbling awkwardly against the handle, it opened the front door and continued approaching me.

My heart throbbed as the cat slowly extended a long, furry arm towards me. To my relief, it merely placed a small goodie bag at my feet before returning silently to the party.

Still flustered by the situation, I reached inside the bag, finding a small disposable camera and a handwritten note containing the following text:

*"April – there is a way out of this. But, you need to follow these precise instructions.*

*First, don't tell anyone about this note. Keep it hidden. Or, better yet, burn it.*

*Second, take pictures of the pages within Brandon's book. The more recent and legible they are, the better. Use the camera here, and leave it in the bush beneath your bedroom window tomorrow night.*

*Third, agree to host a substitute dinner at the original time. Stay alive until then, and when the time comes, **tell the truth.**"*

Holy shit, I thought as I stuffed the note and camera back into the bag. Someone *was* trying to help me. That's what this had to mean, right?

I recalled how Jean had spent weeks getting himself a job at the dealership just to have a chance to talk to me without Brandon noticing anything out of the ordinary. Had Mae, Emma, or someone else gone to the trouble of getting an entertainer gig at this party just to have a moment to communicate with me?

Before I had a chance to act, Martin ran up to me excitedly. "My bag had gummies and tattoos!" he exclaimed. "What's in yours?"

"Um, the – the same. The same."

~

The party ended soon after, and I didn't see the costumed figure again.

The words from the note ran through my mind as I drove Martin home. I had no better idea than to follow its instructions, but locating Brandon's book – and the key I would need to unlock it – would be no easy task. And what 'dinner' did I need to survive until, and what "truth" did I need to confess?

I didn't have to wait long for a few answers. It was around eight at night, just after I'd tucked Martin into bed, when the doorbell rang. To my delight, I opened it to find my friends Mae and Olivia, who said they were there to check in on me.

I played it cool. Naturally, I wondered if they remained under Brandon's control, or if they were there to help me. Had one of them been in the costume?

Olivia announced that she had major news, revealing a rose gold ring with a deep purple diamond around her finger.

"I had no idea!" I exclaimed, a little hurt that I hadn't even known Olivia was seeing anyone seriously.

"Don't worry," said Mae, sensing my reaction. "*I* barely knew about it, and I'm her housemate."

Brandon and I congratulated Olivia, and I expressed that I couldn't wait to meet her partner.

"We've been planning a small engagement dinner this weekend, and we were about to invite you all to it," explained Olivia. "But, the restaurant just canceled. Seems like they're going out of business. So, it looks like we're back at square one."

"I'm sorry to hear that," said Brandon. "But I'm sure you can find another spot."

"No – um, don't do that." I said, prompting quizzical looks from the others. "We, uh – we'll host it here, if that's okay with you. We'd love to do that, actually. Right, Brandon?"

Brandon gave me a quick, surprised glance. "Um, yeah, yeah, of course. We can have you over, if that's alright with you two."

"Really?" asked Olivia. "You don't have to do that for us. We don't want to burden you. Really, it's no problem for us to just find a new venue, and-"

"I think it's a great idea," said Mae, turning to Olivia. "As long as it's okay with you, I'm onboard."

"Okay, okay," said Olivia, growing a little red as she thanked me and Brandon.

Before leaving, Mae gave me a quick, friendly hug. As she did so, I noticed that she wore a necklace that was tucked into her shirt. At its center was a tear-shaped amethyst jewel.

~

The next morning, I relayed that I still had a headache from the previous night, and Brandon agreed to drop Martin off at preschool on his way to work. I began rummaging through the house as soon as they pulled out of the driveway.

The key was easy enough to find. Slipping my fingers through a tiny incision in Mr. Boots' belly, I pulled it out without noticeably damaging Martin's favorite toy. The more challenging task was locating the book.

I'd found it once stuffed deep within the cushion of the basement sofa. But, now, Brandon had hidden it somewhere else – presumably, someplace where I wouldn't stumble across it.

I looked everywhere I could think of – behind every book, in every piece of furniture, every closet, and every drawer. Checking the clock, I realized hardly an hour remained before Brandon brought Martin home.

*Think April, think.* Where would Brandon expect me to never go?

I glanced up at the retractable staircase that led to the attic. Not only would I need a stepping stool to reach it, but I'd then have to climb its rickety steps – something I'd convinced Brandon I was incapable of doing.

It still wasn't easy. My body struggled to make the ascent, and an aching pain ran through me when I finally set my feet down on the dusty wooden floor.

The attic was hot and musty. A single box sat nearby. It was filled with rags, dirty towels, and, beneath them all, the same book I'd found months earlier. The key fit right in.

~

I turned its brittle pages carefully. Tiny, handwritten scribbles covered each one of them so densely that the paper itself was barely visible underneath.

The words appeared to be of varying languages. At first, they appeared old, ancient, even, but I started to vaguely recognize them around the halfway point: something loosely Slavic, then German, then French.

I noticed patterns, too, in the layout. A new section would begin with a name – usually, but not always, a feminine one. Towards the end, as the writing appeared in Spanish, I saw names like *Josefa, Dolores,* and *Ángel.*

As the writing transitioned into English over the last few pages, I came across sections labeled *Allison, Deborah, Naomi.* I paused to read one, labeled *Beatrice,* in detail.

The first few pages were filled with detailed notes about her daily routine, friends, family, health, likes, dislikes, phobias, fantasies, and sexual history. "Intelligent, skeptical, slow to trust. Valuable target. High likelihood of initial rejection. Persuasion will require endorsements not just from friends & family but also her counselor and doctors." Using the camera from the gift bag, I snapped pictures of the next several pages, which listed what appeared to be steps and ingredients for various incantations.

I took pictures, too, of the next few sections, which contained similar information related to a wealthy, elderly man named Garret; a middle-aged theatre performer named Erika; and a young woman studying biology named Kathleen. In each case, the notes revealed the extraordinary amount of work Brandon had done studying his targets, followed by the elaborate spells he had used to support his gaslighting routine.

Finally, I reached the section titled *April.* Bracing myself for the discomfort that would follow, I skimmed Brandon's summaries of my background, which mostly consisted of mundane details about my education, career, health, hobbies, and interests. Every place – over weeks – that I'd visited, and how I'd gotten there. A paragraph about my relationship with Emma described us as deeply in love. It ended: *"Parents remain unsupportive/ashamed - will be easy to sway."*

The final section read differently from the rest. His cursive was sloppier and less methodical than before.

*Does she know? Does she know? Does she know?*

*Still won't put out.*
*Little nourishment. Less energy than before. He must have told her.*
*His story matches hers. But...*
*Does she know?*
*Still unwilling in bed. Should have caved by now*
*Does she know?*
*Does she know?*
*Time to move on?*

I wiped my wet my forehead before I turning to the last page. The name at the top read *Margaret*.

*Oh shit*, I thought, as a horrifying feeling settled upon me. The details that followed, which appeared incomplete, were of *Mae*'s life, from every place she'd ever lived to her family, mental health issues, various eccentric hobbies, friendship with Olivia, past boyfriends, and present relationship with Casey.

*If I don't stop him*, I realized, *she'll be next.*

A sound from several stories below me broke the silence. *Fuck*, I thought, slamming the book shut and relocking it as I realized that Brandon and Martin had just opened the front door. Frantically, I placed it back where I found it and rushed as best I could towards the retractable staircase.

~

I'd just returned the key to Martin's stuffed animal when they made it upstairs. "Hey Brandon, I was just tidying Martin's room up a bit."

Brandon eyed me suspiciously as Martin took Mr. Boots from my hand. "Everything okay?"

"Yeah, yeah I'm fine." I realized I was caked in sweat. "I, uh, was trying to clean a bit, and I went up and down the stairs my own. I shouldn't have. It was tough, and I barely made it."

"Oh, honey," said Brandon as he gently embraced me. "I know you want to help out, but you need to take care of yourself."

~

Late that evening, Brandon led me down to the kitchen to try a dish he was preparing, explaining that he might serve it at the engagement dinner if it turned out well.

I sat at the kitchen table as he sliced several tomatoes. "Funny thing," he said as he cooked. "When I got home today, I noticed that the attic door was partially open."

I felt my face grow pale. "Oh, really? I didn't notice that."

"Yep. It was almost shut. But not quite. I'm sure I didn't leave it that way. It got me thinking."

"Thinking about what?"

"About..." Brandon stopped talking for a moment as he chopped up a cucumber in a series of rapid, precise movements. "About who would have gone up there. It wasn't me. Martin can't reach that high. So that leaves you."

"Brandon, don't be silly." I forced a smile. "I have no reason to go up there. And even if I wanted to, I can barely-"

"You can barely go up steps on your own, right. Anyway, food's ready." He placed a plate of the dish – penne with vegetables – he'd been preparing before me. "Don't start yet, though. There's one more ingredient I still need to add. A French seasoning I got a sample of at the farmer's market last weekend."

He removed from a cabinet a small plastic bag containing a gray powder. As Brandon brought it closer to me, I slowly recalled where I'd seen it before.

"Just a few pinches of this," said Brandon as he spread it over my plate, "and it's ready. Please, try it."

"I...I'm not sure if I'm still hungry."

"*Try it*," insisted Brandon. There was a fire in the back of his green eyes.

I wanted so badly to smash the plate on the floor and use a kitchen knife to cut Brandon's throat. But, instead, I closed my eyes. *Just a little bit longer*, I repeated to myself, remembering the note. *This is a test. I can pass it. I didn't survive this long to fail now.*

I opened my eyes again. "Okay. I'll try it." My shaking hand dug my fork into the pasta, all covered in a thin layer of bone dust, into my mouth. I chewed, swallowed, and took another bite. "It's good. Really good Brandon. Thank you."

He made me finish it. When my plate was empty, I announced I was going to bed. "Sure, I'll help you up," said Brandon. As we approached the staircase, I realized I was feeling nauseous. The knots in my stomach only grew tighter when Brandon held me around my waist and shoulder and pushed his body against mine.

*I can do this*, I repeated to myself. As we slowly ascended, I tried as hard as I could to ignore the dizziness that was setting upon me. But I couldn't help but recall Jean's fiery death at Martin's hands, and the way Martin had crumbled up his brittle bones....*Oh God*, what had I done?

Before I knew it, I was on my knees, projectile vomiting half-digested bits of pasta, vegetables, and Jean all over the carpeted steps.

~

Brandon left me alone after I convinced him that my stomach had settled. With Martin asleep, I took the opportunity to comply with another of the note's instructions by dropping the camera out the bedroom window into the bush below.

As I settled into bed, I recalled the words at the start of the note: "April – *there is a way out of this.*" I tried to focus on the hope those words represented and suppress the questions that swam through mind: who wrote it, who would (presumably) be coming to retrieve the camera, why they needed the photos I'd taken, and if their plan – which very much seemed set to occur at the dinner party – would actually work.

I wondered, too, if I'd even survive long enough for it to matter. I'd given Brandon every reason to be suspicious, and from the looks of it, he was already gathering information about his next victim.

After plenty of tossing and turning, I managed to drift off to sleep. In my dream, Brandon was gone, and Emma and I were vacationing together in a secluded cabin. I asked Emma what had happened to Brandon, and she smiled and told me that I didn't need to worry about him anymore.

A sense of relief swept through me. I felt happier than I'd been since before I went in for the operation so many months ago, but when I rested my head against Emma's shoulder, I saw a pair of wings sprout from her back. I stepped back as her face fell off, forming into a mask as it hit the floor. Emma appeared before me now in the diabolical form I'd seen Martin transform into at the hospital.

"No," I cried. "It can't be. Not you, too."

"You really thought you could escape me?" he taunted as he leapt toward me.

I awoke in a sweat. I was on my stomach, and I noticed the bedsheet near me absorb a drop of liquid with a greenish tint. Another drop followed, then another. I froze.

I heard whispers. It was Brandon's voice. He sounded like he was standing next to me. He was *chanting*, and it was the same fucking chant Martin had repeated before igniting Jean.

So this was it. Brandon was done with me. He knew I'd been in the attic looking for his book. He knew that I knew the real ingredient he'd added to the pasta. He knew that I was no use to him any longer.

If I tried to run, he'd catch me. If I tried to fight him, he'd win. If I tried nothing, I'd burn.

Brandon's chanting grew faster, louder. *Fuck. What do I do?*

I thought about what I'd read in Brandon's book, his recent advances, and his comment about Valentine's Day. What if I...No, no. *That* was a price I'd rather die than pay.

But there was one idea worth trying – something that could keep me alive long enough to have a chance at escape. After all, if whatever was set to transpire at the dinner party didn't work, I was as good as dead anyway.

"Brandon, is that you?" I used as innocuous a voice as I could muster. As I spoke, I kept my head buried in my pillow. I didn't want him to think I'd seen anything. "There's something I've been meaning to tell you. Something important."

The chanting ceased. "Sorry if I woke you, April," said Brandon. "I was just talking to myself. What is it?"

"I think it's about time for us to restart a few things."

"What do you mean, honey?"

"I *want* you, Brandon. I want us to *fuck* like we used to. You have no idea how much I want you inside of me, Brandon."

"Oh." I sensed Brandon's approach. He nuzzled his head against mine and whispered into my ear. "Are you *sure* you're ready for that, honey? I don't want to rush you."

"This dinner we're hosting...it'll be a big event for all of us, as a family. I've been thinking: after that, after the guests have left and we've put Martin to bed, that can be our first time since...since...all this happened. Starting then, I want it to be like old times. I want you to show me all the things we did together."

Brandon gave me a light kiss on the back of my head. "You have no idea how much that means to me. I promise you, April, it will be a night to remember."

**Part III**

The ring of the doorbell set off a flurry of butterflies in my stomach. *This is it*, I thought, as I got up to greet my friends. *Whoever is trying to save me will make their attempt tonight.*

I reminded myself that I'd done my part. It hadn't been easy, but I'd managed to follow the instructions left for me. I'd taken the requested pictures of Brandon's book, and, judging by the camera's absence from the bush I'd dropped it onto, someone had retrieved it. Importantly, I'd completed the most challenging task of all: I'd stayed alive.

To do so, I'd made a promise to Brandon that he regularly reminded me of, a promise that I had no intention of ever fulfilling. If, at the end of the night, I remained Brandon's captive, I'd finally try to fight him. I'd lose, but I'd at least go down swinging.

I opened the door to find Mae and Casey, both nicely-dressed, the former holding a rectangular box under her arm. I welcomed them inside and turned towards our remaining guests.

My jaw dropped as Olivia introduced me to her fiancée. I instantly recognized her round face and curls of blonde hair.

"*Emma*," I blurted out impulsively.

She held out her hand. "And you must be April." As she thanked me for hosting the dinner, I stood dumbfounded, unsure of what to do or how to respond.

Had my dreams of Emma arriving as my savior come true? Was she just *pretending* to be Olivia's fiancée, and really here to engineer... *something* that would set me free?

Or had Brandon already outplayed me? This could be his own sick way of taunting me – of showing me that not only was Emma out of my reach, but also forcing me to witness the painful spectacle of her coerced into romance with one of my close friends.

"Something wrong?" asked Brandon, noticing my perplexed reaction to Emma.

I snapped out of my daze and shook her hand. "No, no, it's nice to meet you, Emma. Please, come in."

~

"Well, Olivia, are you going to tell them the story about how you two met?" asked Mae as Brandon poured wine for everyone at the table except Martin.

"Oh, it's embarrassing," giggled Olivia, her face growing a little pink. "Do I have to?"

"It is *your* engagement dinner," said Mae. "The least you can do is share with our generous hosts how-"

"It's alright," interrupted Emma, putting her arm around Olivia. "I've got this, if that's okay with you."

"Sure," said a relieved Olivia.

Emma took a deep breath. "So, it was after the snowstorm last winter. As you may remember, there was ice *everywhere*. All over the roads and sidewalks. I was taking my dog on a morning walk, and here comes this young woman, clearly underdressed for the weather and in last night's outfit, speed walking towards a thick patch of black ice."

"Be sure to bring up where she was returning *from*," teased Mae.

"Oh," whined Olivia, her hand covering much of her face. "You don't need to-"

"Olivia had just had just spent what I'm sure was a *very*, ahem," she glanced at Martin before continuing, "let's say *exciting* night with a true gentleman of a boyfriend who let her walk home alone in apocalyptic weather."

"Ray was never my boyfriend," whined Olivia. "It was nothing serious, and he had to get from the hotel to the airport early, and he offered-"

"You had your chance to present this story yourself!" snorted Mae as she swallowed a gulp of the wine. "Let Emma tell it."

Emma resumed her narration. "Anyway, I'm watching her approach, and I could sense exactly what was about to happen. But before I could say anything, Olivia – as she'd tell me her name was – lets out a shriek as she goes sliding across the sidewalk. I ran to catch up with her, and tried to grab her as she tumbled backward towards me. She ended up falling on me, and we landed in the snow together."

"How romantic," commented Brandon. I shuddered as a tipsy Mae made a pun about them 'falling' for each other.

"Did it hurt when you fell down?" squeaked Martin from his booster seat.

"Don't worry little guy, I was fine," reassured Emma. "But Olivia told me her ankle was in pain, so I insisted she come inside with me and Tessa so that I could take a look at it. We chatted a bit, and I eventually convinced her to call an Uber to take her the remaining few blocks to her and Mae's place. I looked her up on social media afterwards, we made plans to meet up, and yadda yadda yadda, now we're here, celebrating our engagement." Emma gripped her embarrassed partner's hand as she finished the story.

I had no idea how to process all of this. I'd spent months convincing myself that Emma loved *me*. Now, she and Olivia seemed so happy together, so sincere in their affection. If it was an act on their part, it was a convincing one.

Anxieties I'd fought hard to repress began to resurface. I had no memories of Emma and I being together, after all. Just a picture, Jean's words, and some scribblings in Brandon's book. Even if she *was* here to help me, who's to say that she still loved me, or, if I made it out of this mess, that I'd still feel anything for her?

As Brandon served dessert, other concerns began to bother me. None of our guests had shown any sign of having a plan to fight Brandon or rescue me from him. What if I'd been wrong about this whole thing, or if Brandon – or Martin, for that matter – had left the note as part of some twisted prank at my expense?

~

When I wished Martin goodnight, I played it cool despite knowing that it was the last time either of us would have to act our way through that particular ritual. "Sleep tight, and don't let the bedbugs bite," I told him, trying to sound as loving as I could, before Brandon took him upstairs. I wondered about the winged demon inside of him. Did it enjoy playing a giggly child?

Upon Brandon's return, Mae placed the box she'd carried inside on the dining room table. "There's one more thing we need to do tonight."

"I didn't know you were serious about it!" exclaimed Olivia.

"Oh, she is," chuckled Casey. "She's been telling me about this for weeks."

"You *promised*, Olivia, remember?" said Mae. "One more time before you move out? Plus, when else are all of us going to be together like this?"

"One more time of *what*?" asked Emma.

"You'll see," replied Mae with a sly smile. She looked at me. "Y'all have a fireplace downstairs, right?"

~

At Mae's request, we turned off the lamps and ceiling lights. Instead, only the flames from the fireplace and the half-dozen candles that lined the perimeter of the circular table illuminated the detailed design of the Oujia board Mae placed on it.

Surrounding the usual features of an alphabet, a series of numbers, "yes," "no," and "goodbye," were finely-drawn images of the sun, a crescent moon, a pentagram, and an owl wedged between two human skulls.

*So, what was the plan here, exactly?* I thought. *And who's in on it? Mae? Mae and Casey? Emma? No one?*

"What do you think about this?" I whispered to Brandon as we took our seats, genuinely curious about his reaction.

He shrugged. "I don't think it's real, if that's what you're saying. Just a harmless game. If it bothers you, I can ask everyone to leave."

"Oh, it doesn't," I blurted out, perhaps a bit too quickly. The last thing I wanted was to be left alone with Brandon, tonight of all nights.

"Last chance, Olivia," said Mae. "I know I kind of pressured you. Are you sure-"

"Oh, it's fine," Olivia responded. "You were right. It's been too long since we did something like this." I noticed that she was tightly gripping Emma's hand.

Casey offered to retrieve an unopened bottle of wine he'd brought from the kitchen. "Sounds good to me," said Mae, giving him a quick kiss on the cheek. "Please get started and don't wait for me," he said before heading upstairs.

"Well, let's begin then." Mae looked over Olivia, Emma, Brandon, and me. "Everyone, close your eyes. Soak in the ambience. Remember, we're here only to *observe* any spirits who answer us."

After several moments, Mae began quietly chanting. "*Reveles vosmet inquieti spiritus.* Restless spirits, reveal yourselves. *Reveles vosmet, ultrices spiritus.* Vengeful spirits, reveal yourselves."

"Any reason you're calling *these* spirits, in particular?" asked Emma, jokingly.

Mae sighed. "We don't want some lame-ass ghost to show up and give boring answers about being content in the afterlife. You're about to get married. It's a big moment in your life. Before that, I want to give both of you an opportunity for closure with anyone you never had the chance to wrap things up with. *Especially* if they have some reason to be angry with you."

At Mae's direction, Olivia and Emma joined her in placing their index and middle fingers on the planchette.

After a few moments, Olivia noted that nothing was happening. "Nothing's going to happen," complained Emma. "This is silly."

Mae instructed them to give it some time. "Just relax, and don't resist if you make contact with a spirit. Let it move through you to communicate with us."

Olivia piped up after several minutes of silence. "Am I the only one who feels that?"

"Feels what?" I asked.

Olivia described sensing a cold, dark presence. Emma insisted it was just Olivia's imagination, but then the planchette started drifting around the board in a slow, circular motion.

"One of you is moving it!" accused Emma, but Mae and Olivia both denied it.

Mae shushed them and cleared her throat. "Is there a spirit here with us now?"

The planchette shifted past both "yes" and "no" before settling, puzzlingly, on "4."

"I told you this was nonsense," said Emma.

Mae maintained that it had to mean something.

"I sense..." murmured Olivia. "I sense more than one presence."

"What are you saying?" I asked.

"I think there are *four* spirits here."

"Are there four spirits here, communicating with us now?" asked Mae.

The planchette moved to "yes."

"Okay, have your fun," said Emma, releasing her grip. "I don't like this."

Mae continued, ignoring her. "Do you have unfinished business of some kind with Olivia?"

The answer was "no." Mae repeated the question regarding Emma, and got the same response. "Is there someone here you have a connection with?"

The planchette shifted to the alphabet. I read out the letters on which it landed: B-R-A-N-D-O-N.

Brandon chuckled. "Alright, I'll play along. Spooky ghosts, what do you want with me?"

The planchette darted, swiftly, through four letters: K-I-L-L.

Brandon complained that the joke wasn't funny, and Emma requested that they stop the séance.

"Even if we stopped," explained Mae, "we've already summoned these spirits. We may as well get more information."

Brandon sighed. "Fine, but I want to wrap this up soon. Vengeful spirits who want to kill me, what are your names?"

Their response prompted a shift in his perspective. As the letters spelled out B-E-A-T-R-I-C-E, G-A-R-R-E-T, E-R-I-K-A, and finally K-A-T-H-L-E-E-N, he grew visibly uncomfortable. "What the fuck?" he muttered.

I remembered those names. They were Brandon's most recent victims before me. Were their spirits here now? Or was this some kind of elaborate trick?

The planchette, still handled by Mae and Olivia, began to move unprompted. "U-P-S-T-A-I-R-S," I read out, unsure what to make of it.

"Where's Casey?" asked Emma.

"Oh shit." Mae jumped out of her chair and ran up the steps, calling her boyfriend's name as she went.

"This is over," said Brandon, pushing Olivia's hand off the planchette and returning the board to the box Mae had brought it in. "I think it's time for you all to leave-"

Mae's high-pitched scream rang from upstairs. Olivia called out, asking if she was alright, but no response came.

"I'll check on her," said Brandon, getting up from his seat.

"No, no, you stay here with April," said Emma. "I'll go."

Brandon, Olivia and I waited at the foot of the stairs as Emma ascended. "Oh God," she called down. "There's blood *everywhere-*"

"Watch out!" Olivia hollered, but it was too late. A shadowy figure from above grabbed Emma around the neck and dragged her out of sight. The door slammed shut.

Olivia and Brandon hurried up to it, trying to wedge it open. "It's like there's a piece of furniture blocking us," said Brandon. He glanced down at his feet, noticing a puddle of red liquid leaking from under the door frame onto the top steps. "What is this? What's happening?"

I'd never before seen Brandon like this: frightened and confused. Not that I was in better shape.

"Oh God," said Olivia, noticing the blood. "I have to get to Emma. Is there any other way up there?"

"You-you'd have to go around b-back," I stammered. I tried to direct her to flee and get help. I didn't want her to get hurt, too. But, in my panic, the remainder of my words came out as a useless jumble.

Olivia sprinted downstairs, opened the door to the backyard, and burst outside. The door slammed shut behind her.

I was still in no physical shape to be traversing the staircase or the hilly landscape, so I waited where I was.

My mind struggled to process the events I had witnessed. Had we really summoned the spirits of Brandon's latest victims? If that was the plan, who was in on it, and had it gotten out of hand? Were Casey, Mae, Olivia, and Emma injured, or worse?

Brandon, meanwhile, appeared to be having a meltdown. He was pacing in a loop, talking to himself as he did so. "How could they... how could she...he can't...she can't...this can't happen..."

A thud at the glass window to the backyard got our attention. Through the darkness, I saw a circular object rolling away into the grass.

One after another, three more round objects hit the glass. I screamed when I realized what they were: the *detached heads* of each of our houseguests. "Oh fuck," gasped Brandon.

At this point, any real parent would try whatever they could to get upstairs and check in on their son. But neither of us were real parents, and neither of us had Martin on our mind. Instead, fear and confusion immobilized us both.

I stumbled into a corner, crouched into a ball, and covered my face with my hands. This was far, far too much for me to take in.

What was happening? Were my friends *dead*? The horrific sight of the decapitated heads of Mae, Casey, Olivia, and my supposed savior

Emma sent me into a guilt-ridden stupor. Had they, like Jean, died because of me?

"*This can't be happening*," I heard Brandon repeat to himself.

The sound of a door creaking open prompted me to look up at two figures entering from outside. One waited behind while the other approached Brandon.

She was pale and appeared emaciated, with a strikingly gaunt face. "You thought you were rid of me, didn't you?"

Brandon responded in a meek, tepid voice. "I don't know you. What the fuck do you want from me?"

"I look just as I did when you left me. Sucked of life. Withered, scrawny. A mere shadow of my former self. Look at what you did to me."

Brandon again denied knowing her.

"I know that you're a liar. You tricked my friends, my family, my doctors, and my own fucking therapist. You told me that you were my boyfriend. But, now, I know the truth. I see through your lies. You're nobody." *This was Beatrice*, I realized, recalling the description from Brandon's book.

The figure I inferred to be Erika stepped forward, positioning herself next to Beatrice. She had a similarly shrunken, weak appearance. Her clothes were tattered, and she appeared half-decayed, with several holes in her skin exposing rotted flesh underneath.

She spoke in a rough, gravely voice. "I spent my whole life coming to terms with my identity. No matter how many people told me I needed someone else, that I had to be attracted to *somebody*, I stayed true to myself. Until you came along. Suddenly, the whole world was telling me that you were my loving husband. The whole world convinced me of a lie. I held out for *so* long – for *years* – until I couldn't take it anymore. I finally accepted you, and look at what you did to me in return. You left me dead, an unwholesome meal for the worms."

"I...I...don't know what you're-"

"Hush," snapped Erika. "Your pathetic lies don't fool me any longer. I see the truth. You're a weak, inept coward. You're not my husband. I don't love you."

Sweat had soaked through Brandon's clothes. His shaking body backed up against the wall and collapsed.

The door upstairs swung open, revealing Garret and Kathleen. Their feeble forms stumbled down the stairs until they stood next to Beatrice and Erika in a semi-circle around Brandon.

"I had everything planned out," said Garret. "It was going to be a happy retirement. When you appeared, claiming to be my son and heir, I denied it, only for the doctors to say that *I* was the problem, that my memory had deteriorated. You took everything from me. Not just my estate, but also the golden years of my life. I want you to know that I reject you for the scum you are. You don't fool me, and you are not my son."

Kathleen went next. "I hate you for what you did to me. I was *so* young and inexperienced when you entered my life. I ate up your lies. I went along with what everyone told me about you. But all I see when I look at you now is an ugly, pitiful creature. You're not my fiancé. I don't love you and I don't believe you. Nobody does."

Tears streamed down Brandon's face. "April...help me," he blabbered.

Beatrice, Erika, Garret, and Kathleen turned towards me. After what they'd done to my friends, I felt more terrified of them than I did of Brandon.

"Brandon's asking for your help," said Beatrice. "Well? Are you going to help your husband?"

I froze. I had no idea what to do. I could try to run. Maybe these spirits wouldn't follow me. Their enmity was towards Brandon, not me, after all. But that hadn't stopped them from fucking *slaughtering* my friends. But what other option did I even have,

"April Lin: do you have anything to share?" asked Beatrice. "Any truth you wish to tell?"

That's when it hit me. I still couldn't make sense of the situation, but I knew, in that moment, that, somehow, they were the ones who'd left the note for me. *They* were the ones with a plan to defeat Brandon.

I *hated* them for what they'd just done to my friends. Yes, they were victims of an incredible crime, one I'd experienced the misery of firsthand. But I couldn't find any sympathy for them, not after what I'd seen them do.

Nonetheless, I recognized that they were giving me an opportunity to deal a finishing blow to Brandon - a chance to stop him from killing me, and from destroying the lives of every victim he would seek out next. I had to take it.

I stood up and stepped forward, joining the circle they had formed around Brandon. "April, dear," sobbed Brandon. "Please, please...I love you..."

Mustering my last bit of willpower, I managed to speak in a firm, commanding voice. "Jean told me everything."

"No, no, he didn't..."

"I've known ever since the accident that you're not a human. You're a cambion. A trickster. I've been pretending to love you for months. I hate your guts. I was never going to sleep with you. You disgust me. You are not my husband. You never were. And Martin is not my son." I spat on him.

Brandon's face started to shift in form, the skin of his cheeks and forehead sinking downwards towards his chin. "I...I love you, April..." were his last words as his face plopped off, hitting the floor as a plain, wooden mask.

His skin loosened and fell into a pile. The scaly, winged form that remained looked meager and delicate compared to what Martin had transformed into at the hospital.

Beatrice gripped Brandon by the neck and lifted his limp form against the wall. She reached her free hand back towards Kathleen. "The athame," she commanded.

Kathleen complied, placing the jeweled black handle of a sharp dagger in Beatrice's hand.

Beatrice stared straight into Brandon's eyes. "This is for what you did to April." With two rapid motions, she sliced the blade across

Brandon's throat and then dug it deeply into his heart. Brandon's lifeless body fell against the floor in a growing pool of his own blood.

His demise brought me little catharsis. I'd survived Brandon, but at such great cost to others, and I was still in danger. What the hell would happen now?

Beatrice, Erika, Garret, and Kathleen faced me once again. Were they going to kill me too? Or return to where they came from and leave me with the murderous demon child upstairs?

"What is *wrong* with you?" I bawled. "You didn't have to kill my friends to get your revenge. They never did anything to hurt you. You're monsters, all of you."

Beatrice raised the knife. But, instead of using it against me, she jabbed it into her own cheek. I watched, shocked, as she twisted it around her head, sending a thick stream of blood running down her dress.

That's when I realized what she was doing. Her face snapped off as a plain wooden mask. The woman before me changed shape. Her straight, grayed brown hair curled into a striking blond. My heart fluttered as I recognized the figure underneath the layer of blood and bits of loose flesh that steadily fell off of her real skin.

She placed her hand gently on my shoulder. "It's me, April. Your wife."

~

I would learn later just how busy Mae, Casey, Olivia, and Emma had been over the last month. Jean had left Emma with plenty of resources – books on dark magic, objects charmed to resist Grousel's influence, and a blade that could penetrate the skin of a cambion in its true form.

Emma first connected with Mae, whose name Jean had left as someone able to provide assistance if anything happened to him, and Mae quickly looped in Casey and Olivia. They each donned, and never removed, one of the charmed objects – a bracelet for Casey, matching rings for Emma and Olivia, and a necklace for Mae.

After days of studying Jean's material, Mae finally developed a plan. "It's a long shot," she explained. "It'll be dangerous, and it could very well fail. But if we do *everything* right, it really might work."

Emma responded without hesitation. "Whatever it takes, I'll do it. I'm not leaving April with that monster."

Mae listed the materials they would need for the base: two liters of salt water and two pints of blood – one of the "untouched," one of the "sinful" – mixed with python scales, root of hemlock, garlic, and a pinch of burnt *sel gris*.

They were able to gather the ingredients with varying degrees of effort. I know that Emma provided the former blood contribution, citing a technicality in the antiquated terms used for the potion's ingredients; I never pressed as to who gave the latter.

The more formidable task was constructing the masks. As an initial matter, they needed me to gather information. I'd found Brandon's book once, after all, so surely I could locate it again.

They knew that, after Jean's stunt, Brandon would be on the alert for any attempt to communicate with me. The costumed entertainer had been Casey's idea, though Mae had been the one to don the cat suit at the party. They kept the content of the note as vague as they could, such that Brandon wouldn't trace it back to them if he discovered it.

The most challenging part came after Emma retrieved the camera. In the weeks that followed, they set about identifying the full names and, then, the burial sites of each one of Brandon's last four victims. At night, they snuck in, shovels in hand, and dug. These excursions required careful planning – after all, the last thing any of them wanted were criminal charges for graverobbing.

At the six-foot mark, Casey would chisel away at the coffin that encased those Grousel had drained of life. They weren't after the bodies – just stretches of their wooden enclosures, which Casey and Emma then spent days carefully crafting into crude, unadorned masks.

The final step came the night before the party, when Mae carefully lowered all four masks into the liquid base, leaving them to soak overnight.

When they pulled up to my townhouse, Mae's car was filled with the items their plan required: the masks, prop heads, fake blood, the athame, and the Ouija board and planchette. Casey was prepared to step away at the start of the séance to gather everything they needed from the car. Olivia and Emma had carefully rehearsed their loving couple routine, something they'd designed to justify both Emma's presence and the dinner party itself, and Olivia and Mae knew just where and when to direct the planchette.

"We can do this," Mae had said. "We *can*, really. Grousel has been destroying the lives of people just like us for *centuries*. Let's go kill him."

~

Of course, I wouldn't understand any of this until later. Instead, I stood dumbfounded, my jaw fully-dropped, as what I'd believed to be four vengeful spirits reverted into my blood-covered friends.

"We're okay, April," said Mae as she shed the remains of Kathleen's body. "Though I do appreciate how upset you were about our deaths."

"It's over now," said Emma. "You're safe."

I shook my head. "What about Martin?"

"From what I read," Mae replied, "Since he's just an illusion, he should just disappear now that Brandon's-"

"Martin's *not* an illusion," I spluttered. "He's a *copy* of Brandon. I saw him transform into the same type of fucked up creature."

All eyes turned to Mae. "Oh...*fuck*. That might be a problem."

The door upstairs slowly opened. We watched as a small child – one I *finally* could stop pretending to love – stepped forward and examined the gruesome scene below.

I thought about making up a story – that daddy had been hurt in an accident, or that we were all doing some elaborate roleplaying game – but it would be of no use, and I'd grown sick of lying.

"We just murdered your dad, you wretched little bitch," I sneered. "I never really believed you were my son, and we're going to kill you, too."

~

It's possible that I could have said something more constructive. But I can't say I regret anything, even when accounting for the chaos that subsequently unfolded.

Martin's mask fell quickly. It made sense to me – there was no one left to fool.

I only remember what followed in a blur. Martin pounced, charging towards us at a rapid speed. He knocked into Mae, who hit her head hard against the table as she fell.

The next thing I knew, me, Emma, and a furious Casey were holding Martin down while Olivia ran for the dagger still embedded in Brandon's body. I remember Martin's claws slashing into Casey's chest, Martin's flailing legs kicking and destabilizing the tall bookcase next to me, and a brief glimpse of a vase sliding off of a top shelf before everything went to black.

~

I found myself back where I'd started so many months ago. I awoke alone in the upstairs bedroom of my townhouse. I felt groggy, and my head ached.

The door opened. Emma entered with a tray of food. She smiled at me when she saw that I was awake. "I know you have a lot of questions. But first, how is your head?"

"It's fine, please just tell me exactly what happened after...after..."

"You got knocked out cold? Okay." Emma recounted how she and Casey had managed to restrain Martin just long enough for Olivia to run the blade through him. "Martin's dead," she told me. "You really are safe now. It's all over."

I asked about the others. According to Emma, Olivia had taken Mae and Casey to the hospital. "Mae got a concussion. And Casey's got cuts all over him. Not too bad, though. They'll both be okay."

"The blade...can I see it?" Emma asked me why. "Just bring it, please, and the book where Brandon documented his spells. It's in the attic, in the bottom of the box by the stairs."

Emma did as I asked, returning a few minutes later. "Jean's the real hero behind all of this," she said as she passed me the knife. "Left us with everything we needed to finally-"

She froze, stunned, as I hopped to my feet and held the blade up to her throat. "April, what are you doing?"

~

It wasn't easy going down two flights of stairs while holding a knife against Emma's throat. One misstep, and I could have slit it by accident. But I held it there anyway like my life depended on it.

Emma tried reasoning with me, listing all the reasons why I didn't need to worry about her.

"Look, if you really are Emma, I'll apologize to you later. But I'm too fucking tired of being lied to, of being told that I'm 'safe' when I'm not."

"April, *please*, don't do this-"

"Did it never occur to you how it might look, with you here by my side and everyone else conveniently absent?"

Emma thought about this for a moment. "Okay. I understand. For all you know, I could be Martin, in a new mask, trying to fool you again."

"I don't know what to think. I don't even *know* you. Just do what I say, *please*."

"Okay," said Emma. "Okay, I get it. I'll do what you say. We'll get through this."

I hated how I couldn't tell whether Emma's words reflected honest devotion to me, or just another diabolical ruse. After all, that's just what Brandon would have told me.

At my direction, she reignited the remaining wood in the fireplace and tossed the book onto the flames. As its pages slowly turned to ash, I continued to hold the blade against her skin. She stared at me, her eyes warm and longing, and I stared back.

I prayed what Jean told me would once again be correct – that burning the book would undo the remainder of Brandon's spells. I prayed that I take back the life that was stolen from me.

My prayers came true. The blade fell to the floor as memories rushed through me.

I recalled meeting Emma at the book fair; the long conversations in coffee shops; the nights she convinced me to go out with her friends; the way we slowly separated from them on the dancefloor. I remembered counting down the hours until I'd see her again; confessing to her that the only thing I'd ever done before was exchange an awkward kiss with the boy my mother pressured me into taking to prom; the slow progression between Emma and me of holding to kissing to touching to sex – *so much* earth-shattering, mind-blowing sex.

I remembered the way she held me and let me cry onto her shoulder the night after I introduced her to my parents. The trip we took abroad; the day we adopted Tessa; the signatures we placed on our marriage certificate. As my love for her coursed through my veins, it felt like it was always a part of me and had never left. It surged like a river, and it grew in strength with each passing moment.

I knew, right then, that there was nothing more true, more real than what I felt for the woman sitting next to me. I wanted to fall asleep holding onto her and to wake up with her still there beside me.

I'd get my wish. Many hours later, Mae, Casey, and Olivia would return to our home, with a few bandages from the hospital and Tessa from daycare. They'd find me sleeping on the sofa with my arms wrapped around my wife, and I'd awaken to loving kisses from a dog reunited with its long-absent owner.

But in that moment, sitting there by the fireplace, all I could do was cry. I buried my face in Emma's chest as my tears soaked through her dress.

"What is it April? What's wrong?" she asked.

"Nothing," I croaked. "Nothing. They're tears of joy."

**21**

______

# NOBODY AT THE POOL PARTY LOOKS LIKE ME

I spend all week in eager anticipation of Saturday. When it arrives, I head to the pool, where I swim and laugh with my friends and my twin sister Anju. Afterwards, we go to the club, where the fun continues as we jump and dance while the room gets hotter and hotter.

But this Saturday, everything is different. To start, I don't recognize anyone at the pool. Even Anju isn't here. She and I are normally inseparable. Her absence worries me. Where is she? Is she okay?

But, even more strikingly, nobody here looks like me. Frankly, I'm used to a more diverse crowd than this. That wouldn't bother me, except that they're all treating me strangely.

My attempts to make new friends are met with silence and hostile glances. When I wade through the bubbles towards a small group, they demand that I stay away from them.

I back up, only to brush against a tall figure a tad less pale than the rest.

He snarls in a raspy voice that my "kind" doesn't belong here. The words sting, as does the pain I feel when he kicks me with one of his long legs.

When I regain my composure, I see a faint, rosy red mist form in the water around me. I hear screams, along with words like *"she's bleeding"* and *"stay away from her!"*

The others congregate away from me, at the far end of the pool. Before long, I'm alone – a pariah.

I look down at my reflection. To my shock, I see that I'm changing into one of them. My once-vibrant skin turns cloudy as it fades into a bland, murky gray.

This can't be happening to me. I yearn for someone to help. I think about Anju. She always looks out for me. I miss her.

Suddenly, everything grows quiet, and the water level lowers. The ceiling opens. A hand reaches in, grabs me, and pulls me up. Normally, it would take me to the club. But not today.

A familiar, deep voice booms from above. It asks how I got here, and it says that it's "lucky" that I didn't stain anything else.

I continue to lie limp in his hand as he shouts upstairs to someone named Mary. He tells her that one of her socks got mixed in with the whites. That the bleach stained it pretty badly.

In response, a lighter, higher-pitched voice calls, "Just toss it, and please be more careful next time."

I fly through the air and land with a soft thud amidst wrappers and crumbled paper.

I cry. I haven't done anything wrong. Yet, I feel that I am being punished just for being different – for not looking like the others. It's unfair. It's wrong. And I'm all alone now.

My heart lights up as a shape crawls and tumbles. I realize, to my delight, that it's Anju. Her pink form slides down until she's next to me.

I whisper through tears. "You came for me, even though I look wrong now."

Anju smiles as she holds me. "I'll always be here for you, no matter what you look like. A pair like us belongs together."

## 22

## ARE YOU RUNNING FROM YOUR REFRIGERATOR?

My brother Alex protested as soon as he heard my idea. "What if someone's home, and they call the police? We'll get in *huge* trouble."

"That apartment *has* to be vacant," I replied. "I haven't seen anyone enter or exit it since we moved in, before you were even born. And Mom and Dad aren't going to find out – they won't even be home until Sunday."

I pestered Alex about it until he caved. We ascended using the outer fire escape. The heatwave left us both drenched in sweat as we ascended the seven flights.

"There it is," I said, pointing to the ajar window I'd spotted from the street. "Are you ready?"

Alex eyed the long drop to the street below. "Yes, just *please* be careful."

Alex climbed onto my shoulders, reached up, and placed his palms under the rail. With a grunt, he raised the window and proceeded to crawl inside. "Alright," I called, "Just find a way to unlock the front door. I'll be right there."

I hurried down, reentered the building, and took the elevator up.

When I reached the apartment's front door, I knocked lightly three times. To my relief, it creaked open to reveal Alex inside. "It's like you said," he whispered, "Nobody's home."

His face was pale, and I realized he was shivering. "I'm going back now, if that's alright."

I placed my hand over his face and shoved his scrawny form back into the room. "No, not yet you aren't. I may need your help."

The first thing I noticed was just how cold it was. If nobody lived here – as I suspected – then someone was paying a hefty electric bill to keep it at such a low temperature.

I flipped on the main overhead light, revealing a compact and relatively empty space. A coat closet to my right was unoccupied aside from three pairs of formal men's shoes. The cobwebs that stretched across the bathroom door indicated that no one had entered it in some time.

The shelves, drawers, and pantry in the small kitchen were similarly bare. Strangely, though, the kitchen had not one but two refrigerators. The first was imposingly large. Its frame, painted a metallic gray, was at least seven feet tall. I tugged at the handle to its main door, but it wouldn't budge.

The second refrigerator was smaller, with a sickly yellow color that matched portions of the tacky floral wallpaper behind it. Its single compartment opened with ease, revealing only empty shelves.

Alex repeated that he wanted to go. "If you keep whining," I taunted, "maybe I'll shove you in here." That quieted him.

I closed the door to the yellow refrigerator and we entered the living room, which contained two long, wide divans with sunken white cushions that faced an outdated television.

"Is there *anything* of value in here?" I whined as I sifted through a small set of VHS tapes stacked next to a dusty VCR: *Balto*, *Annabelle's Wish*, *Toy Story*, *Ghostbusters*, *Batman and Robin*. None would be worth the effort to sell online.

"Let's go already," Alex insisted. "Clearly there's nothing here worth taking."

"There is one thing I want," I said, motioning to an olive-shaded mini-fridge positioned between the sofas. "If you want to leave so badly, at least carry this back to my room."

"Ugg, fine," moaned Alex. He called back to me as he carried it into the hallway. "But if I get caught, I'm blaming you."

"Whatever," I said. "I'll catch up with you in a minute."

The bedroom consisted of a king-sized mattress that lay in the center of the carpeted floor. Next to it sat a small pile of cushions, and on the other side stood a wooden dresser.

I pulled open the top drawer. My heart beat in excitement as I finally hit the jackpot.

An orange pouch contained jewelry and a set of vintage coins: Sacagawea, Susan B. Anthony, and silver dollars. Next to it sat a thick stack of out-of-circulation $2 bills held together by a rubber band, along with a set of stamps, envelopes, and a wallet loaded with additional cash. The wallet also contained several outdated credit cards, a library card, a check book, and an old driver's license all displaying the name: James A. Hermann.

I had a vague memory of my parents mentioning a 'Mr. Hermann' living in the building when I was little. Something about him running an appliance company. But where was he, and why had I never seen him before?

I returned to the living room carrying some of the items I'd found in the dresser. To my surprise, the chill I'd felt before had faded. The room was getting warmer. I noticed smoke rising from the kitchen.

Suddenly, the overhead lights cut off. As my eyes adjusted to the darkness, my feet sensed a vibration in the floor. Slowly, I discerned the silhouettes of two bulky objects in the kitchen: the refrigerators, and they were *shaking*. As their movements grew more violent, a buzzing sound that I realized had been growing steadily in volume for at least several minutes abruptly burst into a high-pitched hiss.

The door to the silver fridge burst open. I gasped as its inner light revealed what looked to be a human skull and pile of bones, which tumbled out onto the floor. Shocked, I stumbled backwards.

The larger fridge emitted a low gurgle. In my panic, I reversed into one of the couches. As I lost balance, the refrigerator launched a set of small, pointed objects.

A sharp piece of ice scraped against my right hand as I fell. I dropped to the floor as the rest of the barrage hit the wall behind me.

*What the hell was happening?* I thought as I peeked up, observing the large fridge. In the darkness, I couldn't be sure, but it seemed that it had somehow moved closer to me.

The gurgling sound started up again. As its volume rose, I sensed a brief window of safety before it unleashed a second volley.

Moving quickly, I picked up the valuables from the dresser and sprinted towards the entrance, hopping over the pile of bones as I made my way there. As soon as I reached the hallway, I slammed the door shut behind me and raced back to our apartment.

"What are you so worried about?" asked Alex upon my return.

I ignored him as I latched our front door and applied the chain lock. Alex's anxious expression alerted me that something was off about my appearance. I realized that blood dripped from the cut on my hand. "Oh, right, I, uh, it's nothing. Just get me the first aid kit, okay?"

"That looks bad. What happened?"

"Just get me the kit, okay? Hurry up already!"

As Alex scurried to the kitchen closet, I deposited the belongings I'd stolen on a counter and peered through the peephole into the hallway.

The hallway lights flickered as the door to the staircase I'd taken slowly swung open. My fear froze me in place as an approaching form cast a long shadow over the nearby floor.

Alex nudged me with the first aid kit, sending me whirling around. "Jesus!" I called as my heart pounded in my chest.

"What's wrong?" asked Alex.

"Oh, it's just...um..."

A loud knock thundered against the door.

"Don't answer that!" I hollered to Alex.

He froze for a second before standing on his toes to look through the peephole. "It's fine," he told me. "It's just Mr. Dinsdale."

Relief washed over me as I realized that the figure outside was just our longtime neighbor from across the hall. Mom and dad had asked him to check in on us while they were away.

I nodded at Alex, who promptly undid the chain and opened the door. Mr. Dinsdale removed his hat as he stepped inside our apartment. His smile faded into a look of concern when he spotted my wound.

"Yeah, it's, uh, just a splinter," I stammered as I scanned the hallway behind him, which, thankfully, remained vacant. "I was just about to bandage it."

As Mr. Dinsdale helped me dress the wound, I concocted a story about nicking my hand on one of our wooden kitchen cabinets.

Although Alex rolled his eyes at my story, Mr. Dinsdale seemed to believe it. He chided me to be more careful.

I promised it wouldn't happen again, and Mr. Dinsdale agreed not to bring it up to my parents.

When Mr. Dinsdale left, Alex pressed me as to what really happened. I brushed him off. I barely understood it myself.

The more I thought about what had happened, the less sense it made. Had I really been attacked by a pair of...what, *angry refrigerators*? Surely they had just...malfunctioned, or broken down, or something *rational*, right?

And what about the bones? Were they even real? If so, how did they end up there?

With any luck, I'd never find out the answers to those questions. After all, if I was in danger, it's not like I could go to our parents or the authorities about it.

I had Alex to worry about, too. He was clearly upset with me, and I needed to make sure he stayed on my side and didn't say a peep about what we'd done to anyone else.

"Hey, Alex, what do you say we go to Marco's down the street for dinner? You always love it there, and it's on me, okay?"

Alex brightened up as we devoured the pizza we ordered. When we were done, though, he looked curiously at the set of $2 bills I left on the table.

As we headed home, Alex asked me if the money I'd used was from the apartment we'd snuck into.

"Yeah, and there's plenty more where it came from," I replied through a smirk. To my surprise, though, Alex seemed less excited.

"I feel like we should return it."

"Oh come on," I retorted. "You're such a goody two-shoes."

"It just feels wrong."

I scoffed. "Look, Alex, for all we know, nobody even lives there, and this money's just been collecting dust for years. It's not like it was doing anybody any good before we took it."

"I still don't like it."

His persistence started to get to me. When we stopped at a convenience store, I began to pay for the snacks I purchased with the money from the apartment. Only, I changed my mind at the last moment, instead paying with my own cash from my wallet.

As we returned home, I noticed a faint pattern of red stains in the carpet outside our apartment. My heart jolted as I realized what it was: drops of my own blood that had fallen as I'd fled.

I spent the next hour scrubbing out the trail I'd left behind, one that led all the way from the scene of the crime back to our apartment. It was hard work, but with a combination of dishwashing detergent and elbow grease, I managed to clean most of it up.

Finally, I retired to our bedroom, exhausted but relatively secure in the knowledge that I'd successfully covered my tracks. I placed the money I'd stolen on top of the olive mini-fridge, which I'd plugged in near my bed and stocked with several cans of soda from the convenience store. After adding up the various bills and coins, I realized that we'd secured just over $1,500.

I remembered Alex's suggestion that I return it all. I'd been adamant about keeping it before, but, now the idea held a peculiar appeal, though I didn't understand why.

The buzzer rang. It was Mr. Dinsdale again. He explained that he'd forgotten his key and asked if I could buzz him into the building.

"Sure," I said, hitting the button for 'enter'.

"Was that Mr. Dinsdale?" asked Alex.

"Yeah."

"He left his hat when he came by earlier. How about you and I give it back to him when he comes up here?"

I groaned. Alex was so sanctimonious. But I gave in. "Sure, if it makes you happy."

We waited by the elevator. When it arrived, Alex held out the hat as its doors began to open.

"Alex!" I cried. But it was too late.

The central compartment of the yellow refrigerator that stood before us burst open. A pinkish tissue emerged, rapidly wrapping around Alex and tugging him inside.

I grabbed onto Alex and pulled. The refrigerator let out an intense shriek, expelling a thin layer of hot mist as it shook angrily. The force against Alex grew until it was too much. Alex let out a gargled cry as he flew from my arms and into the refrigerator. Within mere moments, both the refrigerator and the elevator doors slammed shut.

"No, no, no," I repeated, aghast, as the elevator headed upwards. It was all my fault.

I ran back to our apartment, determined to gather everything I'd stolen and return it.

As I passed through our kitchen, the closet door suddenly burst open. I shrieked as the large, gray form that emerged from it towered over me.

As I frantically attempted to back away, I tripped over a chair and stumbled painfully onto the floor. When I looked up, the refrigerator was leaning over me – no, it was *falling onto* me. I rolled to the side, narrowly escaping its impact as the wooden chair it landed on shattered into pieces.

I hurried to my bedroom, where I tossed all the money, jewelry, and coins I'd stolen into a gym bag.

The door burst open. The gray fridge, shifting its weight from its front to its back, inched its way in. The yellow fridge followed just behind it.

"Here!" I yelled as I tossed the bag towards them. "Take it! I only spent a little. Almost all of it's still here. Please, just give Alex back!" The refrigerators ignored the bag as they closed in on me.

As I backed into the corner of the room, all my mistakes flashed through my mind. It was my role to set an example for my brother, and all I'd done was bully him. I'd only taken him out for dinner because it was in *my* interest to do so. I'd been a jerk, and I'd been lost sight of what really mattered: family.

I gently lifted the mini-fridge. The refrigerators halted their advance as I held it out to them. "Here it is." I gulped and took a deep breath. "I'm so sorry. We didn't mean to take your child."

I deposited the mini-fridge on the floor and backed slowly away.

The refrigerators remained still. My heartbeat intensified as I wondered if I'd guessed wrong – or, worse, if I'd guessed right, but done something to hurt their offspring.

The yellow refrigerator's compartment opened. My brother rolled out, his body partially covered in a thin layer of pink goo. An instant later, the mini-fridge hopped inside.

"Alex!" I yelled as I cradled his limp, frigid form. "Oh God, please be okay. Please."

At once, Alex coughed, then took several labored breaths before responding in a weak, croaky voice. "I-I think I'm okay...What happened?"

Behind him, the door to the yellow fridge closed. The pair turned away from us and waddled out of our apartment.

Alex was soon back to full health. In the afternoon, I led him upstairs to the apartment where all of this had started.

I placed the gym bag I'd stuffed with the jewelry, coins and cash outside its front door. I knocked, then called inside. "I know you don't care about this other stuff we stole, but we decided to bring it back anyway. Okay? We're just going to leave it here, and we won't be bothering you about this again, I promise."

Alex and I moved on. I've been nicer to him ever since.

When I'm on the bus home from school, I always look up as we approach our building. Sometimes, for a brief moment, I'll glimpse an olive-shaded box peering down from above.

It's grown a bit in the months that have passed. I usually wave at it, and, once, I could have sworn that it shifted excitedly to the left, and then to the right, as if to wave back.

## 23

# NIGHT DRIVE

My body aches as I stumble away from the accident. I have at least a mild concussion. I know I should go to a hospital. But I press on. My sister needs me.

The bumpy dirt road curves around dense woods. To save time, I cut through the trees to reach the highway where, hopefully, I can hitch a ride into town.

Thankfully, a full moon glimmers through the deep night, offering enough light for me to make my way through thick foliage.

As I jog down a slope, my foot slips and my body tumbles. I slide into murky water. When I try to crawl back to dry land, a tight force grips my ankle.

To my surprise, I discovery that the source of my restraint is none other than a human hand, its pruney and pallid form having somehow emerged from the surrounding muck.

More hands reach out of the water. Each extends in my direction.

With a defiant scream, I pry myself free. I make it onto two feet and dart away.

As I run, I try not to think about what I'd just experienced. It's one horror too many for tonight.

Instead, I think of my sister, four years my junior at thirteen. She was so different from me. She deserves the life she will have if I manage to spare her.

I emerge from the woods and approach the highway. For poor Catherine's sake, I ignore the obvious danger I face as I holler at approaching headlights.

I walk along the road as vehicle after vehicle passes me by. I don't blame their drivers. After all, I'm a stranger to them, and I'm caked in mud.

Finally, a rusty brown Sedan rolls to a stop. Its back passenger door pops open.

Inside, I take a seat next to a pale-faced elderly man. He reaches past me to slam the door shut.

When I try to introduce myself to him, he does not respond. Instead, with wide, curious eyes, he scans me from my wet, dirty feet to the tear around the waist of my dress to my teary-eyed and bruised face.

I examine the car's third and final occupant – the driver, who sits directly in front of me. His back is turned away from me, and the hood of his green sweatshirt is drawn tightly around his face. I tell him that I need to get to town, but he, too, does not reply.

The old man finally breaks the silence. He asks in a rusty, weak voice, "Are you heading into town?"

"Yes, like I said. I'm sorry to impose, but I need to make haste."

He croaks one word: "Why?"

"My sister needs me."

He repeats what I said: "*She wants to go to town because her sister needs her.*" This seems to satisfy the driver, who starts the car. I breathe a sigh of relief as we pick up speed and leave the ominous woods behind.

The driver taps a button on the stereo. A deep, male voice emerges from a musical intro of haunting piano.

*Welcome to Cemetery Stories, the podcast guaranteed to frighten you to your core. We examine the most disturbing urban legends we can find. Listener discretion is advised.*

Whatever, I think to myself. All that matters is that this strange duo brings me to town. What difference does it make what they listen to?

*Tonight, we examine a legend over three hundred years old: the Curse of Susanna Archibald.*

I bolt upright. "What?" I exclaim.

*Susanna Archibald was born in 1680 in Hanover County. She lived in an agrarian community in a Puritan settlement. As you'd expect, she grew up surrounded by strong religious institutions.*

What is going on? Have these two men picked me up on purpose knowing who I was? I needed to leave.

"Sir," I call to the driver. "You've taken me far enough. Drop me off here, please."

He continues to ignore me.

*Susanna lived happily as part of the wealthiest family in the region. However, in her late teens, Susanna's life took a dark turn when she met a boy one year her senior named Nathan Benham.*

Nathan? How does this man know about Nathan?

*Susanna and her little sister, Catherine, were seen heading out into the woods with Nathan one summer evening. Nobody knows exactly what happened that night in the woods. But we do know the narrative that the town accepted to be true the next morning.*

I know exactly what happened. But none of this occurred hundreds of years ago like the host had said. We'd driven my dad's truck out to Westridge Park mere days ago. I remember dizzying spins around a fire, dolls, and needles.

Suddenly, Nathan tried to kiss me on the lips. Startled, I turned away such that he only made contact with my cheek.

He told me he wanted to marry me, prompting Catherine gasped happily.

When I firmly declined his offer, he turned red and stormed off.

*Several elders spotted Nathan acting hysterically that evening. After intense questioning, Nathan explained his behavior by reporting that he had witnessed Susanna Archibald engaged in witchcraft.*

I remember first hearing the accusation in the high school cafeteria. The taunts and jeers only increased in intensity as the day progressed. Even my friends joined treated me with disdain.

*As word spread, Susanna quickly realized that her life was in danger. Any association with witchcraft, no matter how flimsy or poorly supported, guaranteed her persecution.*

The car lurches as it takes a sharp turn. I feel sick. What is happening? Who are these men, and why is the host of this show recounting my life – but placing it in the distant past?

*Susanna took one of her parents' horses and left town.*

I'd fled at the sight of the torches. It wasn't an easy decision. I'd left my sister, my best friend, behind. I had no choice, really. It was for her own good that I get as far away from her as possible. Or so I'd thought.

I grow lightheaded. My mind feels like it is in the past, future, and present all at once.

*But, the next morning, a courier arrived at the inn with news that shocked Susanna. With her gone, the mob's appetite for violence still needed to be sated. The rumors about Susanna's witchcraft expanded to encompass accusations against others. The mob took Catherine and declared that she, too, was a witch, and that she would die in Susanna's place.*

I want this to stop, but the driver won't even acknowledge my presence. "Please," I say to the old man. "Get him to pull over. I want to get out."

To my shock, the old man collapses, his limp, lifeless form sprawling across the middle seat and onto my lap. I shriek. In desperation, I consider trying my luck diving outside, but I can't even get the door to open.

*Upon learning this, Susanna began the ride back to town, desperate to offer her own life to the mob on the condition that they spare Catherine.*

The driver remains seemingly unperturbed by my screams from the backseat. Memories continue to rush through me. In my mind, the high school I imagined a moment ago now disintegrates into a stuffy one-room schoolhouse.

*Susanna was not accustomed to riding a horse alone at a high speed. She was less than halfway home when a rocky shift in elevation knocked her off her saddle. To Susanna's misfortune, the road bordered a rocky decline, and when Susanna hit the bottom, she died on impact.*

Obviously, none of this can be true. Why is this man inventing such brazen falsehoods?

The lights from buildings in the distance confirm that we have finally reached the outskirts of town. Meanwhile, the recording continues to play.

*That night, a mob of townsfolk assembled. They dragged out Catherine and, ignoring her screams of innocence, tied her to a hastily-assembled pyre located in a hill that overlooked the town cemetery.*

*The townsfolk proceeded to commit the only instance of burning, rather than hanging, of a witch in American history. One-by-one, they tossed their torches onto the pyre. Allegedly, Catherine's last words were to scream for her sister, whose limp body would be discovered off the side of the road the next morning.*

*Their parents, heartbroken by the loss of their children, had Susanna's body and what was left of Catherine's remains buried with the family's most valuable heirlooms. The Archibalds chose as the burial site a pair of graves they had picked out long ago for themselves, and they left the headstones unmarked. Mr. and Mrs. Archibald proceeded to jump into the White Oak River. They were never seen again.*

The car turns abruptly onto a gravely side road lined by empty fields and derelict buildings as we veer further into the opaque darkness.

*The ghost of Susanna Archibald has been sighted many times since that day. The rumor is that she walks the roads near where she suffered her fatal accident, hitchhiking desperately to get into town to burn in her sister's place.*

*She keeps up with the times and is accommodating to changes in language and technology, and does not seem to understand that she is from the distant past.*

In the distance, dozens of small flames flicker at the top of a grassy hill.

*But locals tend to refer to this not as the 'Legend of Susanna Archibald' but, rather as the 'Curse of Susanna Archibald'.*

*The reason for this is that those who come into contact with her rarely live long enough to tell the tale.*

*It's said she has a special relationship with death, in that, as someone stuck between the boundaries of life and afterlife, she is seen the most clearly by those with few days before their departure. And those who do interact with her meet their end even more quickly as a result. Most accounts of her come from those who did not engage with her or who contacted someone about her soon before their own death.*

*Rumor has it that her sister, Catherine, still prowls the area where her charred remains were buried, eagerly awaiting the arrival of her long-absent sister at their unmarked grave.*

The podcast cut off as the car rolls to a stop.

The driver steps out, leaving me with the old man's corpse. I watch as, in the light cast by the headlights, the driver removes plastic goggles from over his eyes and some kind of stuffing from his ears. On the other side of the car, I discern a small, spiked fence.

A frail young man emerges from a light fog. As he hobbles, he gives off a sickly cough. He reaches out for the door handle and pauses when he catches my eye through the window. He starts to shiver.

He opens the door and directs me to follow him. When I bombard him with questions, he holds up a hand and tells me that, if I come with him, I'll get the answers I'm seeking.

As we approach the distant flames, we pass rows upon rows of old graves that stretch far into the shadows. Many of the tombstones are unmarked, and the engravings on many more have been worn down with age.

He tells me he can't believe that I'm real. I demand that he tell me about my sister: where is she, and is she safe?

He responds that he has a little brother of his own. Who has the same condition as he does. That if he does this job, he'll earn enough money to provide for his brother's treatment.

As I ponder what he means, we arrive at the lights. In the shadows, I see the torches first, then the dozen dark silhouettes of men wielding them around a large pile of wood.

I instinctively know what to do. I step forward. The teen follows.

A loud, deep voice rings out. "Susanna Archibald may have fled! But God demands justice. And justice will be delivered upon the sister who shares in her wickedness!"

Through fog and heavy smoke, I see several masked men in dark hoods drag a blindfolded girl in a yellow dress towards the pyre.

I cry out. "Take me instead, like you always wanted. Just let Catherine go!" The masked men ignore me.

"She's here, just like you asked," says the teen. This causes them to pause.

As I progress toward the site, a new set of memories dawns upon me. I recall waiving down dozens of vehicles: carriages, buses, Ford Model T's, vans, trucks. Friendly drivers, perverted drivers, soon to be dead drivers. None have guided me all the way to my destination. Until now.

I lean against the wooden pyre and close my eyes. Ropes tighten around my legs and wrists. Am I being tricked into walking into my own death? Will I really burn? And even if I do, will that save Catherine? How can I make a difference, if she really perished centuries ago?

I hear each torch as it is added to the pile. I cough furiously at the smoke. My body glows, scorches, and inflames. Pain engulfs me.

My consciousness dims. I begin to settle into a long-awaited sleep. But from the void before me emerge dozens of bloody, callused hands. They reach for me, to pull me down.

I resist. I run, the way I always have, from what's waiting for me on the other side.

I open my eyes in the morning light. My naked form is sprawled across cemetery grass. Bits of ember from a dead fire scatter around me. Astoundingly, I am healthy, and my skin is unburned.

I gaze upon the graveyard. It's just outside of town. My parents had taken me to it as a child. It was much smaller then.

I slip into a neatly-folded set of white clothes that lay before me. A note beside them reads: *Sister, how I've yearned for you. Your body was buried here, but your spirit remains so far away. Please, come find me, so we can finally move on together.*

I know where to go. Like most parents in our village, mom and dad had shown us the plots they'd reserved for their own burial. The oak tree that loomed over the pair of graves had once been so small, so young. It had become fully-grown long ago. Now, it was dying.

I kneel and call for Catherine. I sense that I have done everything right. After so many years of trying, I've finally been burned in my sister's place.

But, nothing happens. No spirit appears to float away with me. I wait in silence, certain that I have broken some kind of spell, but puzzled to not be experiencing the outcome I'd anticipated.

As I depart, I gaze jealously at grave after grave of bodies buried in contentment, their souls having departed in a way that I know mine never will.

I am outside the cemetery gates when a metallic clang draws my attention. I follow it to its source.

By my family's graves, a man I recognize as the car's driver leads a group of nine others: eight men clad in black and a grown woman in a yellow dress. Several drop their shovels and hop into the deep hole.

A man speaks with the voice I'd heard from the 'podcast' in the car. "Yes, I'm sure this is the one. The boy swears this is where Susanna went after reading the note."

The desecration before me fills me with rage. The driver pries open an unearthed coffin and pulls from it a golden necklace my mother once promised to me. The group cheers. Others remove more of my family's jewelry and riches. When a small skull rolls out of the grave, I collapse.

When I awake, I don't find myself like I normally do by the location of the accident. Nor do any hands from below reach out to take what I owe them. When I interact with a concerned visitor, I can touch him and speak with him like a real, living person, and I sense that, unlike so many others, he is not doomed by interacting with me.

I realize that the events I'd just experienced, staged as they were, have had an impact on me. Somehow, this group of con artists –

who've managed to trick a ghost – have freed me from my purgatory. No longer am I sentenced to roam the stretch of highway around where I died. Instead, finally completing the journey has finally returned me to life.

I was never supposed to actually make it back to Catherine and burn in her place, even if what I thought was a mob may have really been nine grave robbers holding two torches each.

I take a deep breath. I don't know how I'll survive in this new time, but a sense of purpose guides me.

The mob was wrong about Catherine, as mobs so often are. She was a sweet girl who'd never touch anything related to witchcraft or sorcery.

I, on the other hand, have ten people to track down.

**24**

---

## THE PERFECT JOB

When I got the call, at first I couldn't believe the news.

The voice belonged to the woman who'd interviewed me less than a week earlier. "Lauren Mackerly," she'd said as she'd held out her hand. Her cobalt suit, sharply tailored to her narrow frame, and formal way of speaking contrasted with the grungy atmosphere of the coffee shop where we'd met.

She hadn't asked me any questions. Rather, we'd chatted about our respective family histories before she asked *me* if I had any inquiries about Abernathy Industries. When I requested a more detailed description of the nature of the work the job entailed, Lauren refused to expand beyond the vague platitudes in the listing: "workplace support," "PR assistance," and "corporate image refinement."

I asked a second question. "The salary in the listing…is that fully accurate?"

As she nodded, her face settled into a dazzling smile that displayed her perfectly shaped, immaculately white teeth. "Yes, Monica, it is. Those worthy of joining our family are compensated accordingly."

I'd left the interview convinced my efforts would amount to nothing more than those I'd expended on the other applications I'd submitted in the months since I'd been laid off. It'd had been my first position since graduating from college a year ago.

The posting had undoubtedly attracted a plethora of highly-qualified candidates, especially given its minimal experience prerequisites. I doubted I'd be a serious contender, and Lauren hadn't treated me as one.

So, naturally, I felt elated when Lauren offered me the position. No longer would I be begging my roommate Elijah for more time to reimburse him with my portion of the monthly rent. No longer would I be asking my parents for even more financial support. No longer would Alice and I begin our nights together nibbling on ramen noodle soup or the same boring plates of store-brand pasta.

I texted her the news right away. Alice insisted on coming over. She embraced me and planted a kiss on my cheek upon arriving. "I'm *so* happy for you."

I thanked her through a blush. "I'm sure something will turn up for you, too, before long."

Alice had been a year behind me in school, and she had yet to land a job since graduating. I'd warned her that a creative writing degree would only get her so far in today's job market, but she'd insisted on going through with it. She was passionate about her writing, and I loved that about her even as I worried about her ability to ever afford to leave her parents' house.

We'd agreed long ago that we'd move in together once we were both working and had saved up enough. At the time, it had seemed like a far-off dream. Now, it felt tangible.

We ordered and ate better food that we could cook before settling in together in my bedroom. We cuddled, made love, cuddled some more, and watched a show on my laptop as Alice slowly drifted to sleep in my arms. I set an early alarm and soon joined her in slumber.

~

When the private security guard came to unlock the lobby doors of my new workplace, I was already there waiting. He was short and burly, and his nametag displayed "David."

I was dressed in a formal gray skirt suit. During the commute, I'd recounted everything Lauren had told me, such as bringing two forms of ID for the security check.

She'd also said something strange. "*We pride ourselves on maintaining a clean, uncontaminated work environment. Accordingly, you will be expected to comply with our procedures for keeping it that way.*" I hadn't thought to ask Lauren what she'd meant by that.

"I'm looking for the front desk," I told David.

He directed me to another guard, a curly-haired woman named Donna who presided over a kiosk. She asked if I was a new hire.

I nodded. "Ms. Mackerly told me to ask for her."

Donna replied that I didn't have long to wait. She motioned to the front door, where Lauren and a group of four men, all at least double my age and dressed in suits, had just entered the building.

Donna tells me to wait for one moment. She leans in to me and whispers three words: *don't turn back.*

"Turn back?" I repeated, perplexed. "Turn back from what?"

Donna ignored me. On a dime, she adopted a bright, bubbly affect as she greeted Lauren and the men who accompanied her: a Mr. Hoffman, Mr. Morgan, Mr. Rogers, and Mr. Fitzgerald.

Lauren, alone, acknowledged me. "Look at you, here bright and early! Let me tell you – we are all *so* happy to have you onboard."

"I'm happy to be here."

"We have *much* to show you today," she continued. "But, first, we need to go through our standard morning protocols."

"Morning protocols?"

"This way." I followed Lauren to a set of elevators. By this point, more employees had arrived. The elevator had at least fifteen people on it. Lauren was the only other woman, as well as the only other person who looked to be under forty-five.

We ascended only one floor. To my surprise, the doors opened to reveal a yellow-tiled locker room. I gasped at the spectacle before me of *dozens* of fully naked adults.

As the men who'd ridden up with me dispersed across the room, they, too, began abruptly stripping. After stuffing their outfits in lockers, they headed towards a large, communal shower.

Lauren gripped my arm and led me forward. "Your locker's this way, right next to mine!"

"Um…" I mumbled, shocked by what was happening. "Is…um…"

"Cat got your tongue?" giggled Laura as she opened a locker for me. "Just leave your clothes here." She handed me two white towels.

"I, uh…I already showered today."

"That isn't good enough, honey! You had to travel to get here, after all. We can't have people carry the stench of the street in with them. Why, if we allowed that, our office would be a pigsty in no time!"

"But…I just…"

"You just what?"

Instinctively, I averted my gaze from Lauren who, by this point, had removed nearly all of her clothes. "I just didn't know this was going to happen. You can't expect me to just strip in front of so many strangers with no warning. I can't do that."

"Well, silly, I told you that we take cleanliness seriously! Same decontamination procedures for everyone. Plus, it's too late to give up now!" A passing figure, donning the same birthday suit as so many others, caught her attention. "Oh, I need to chat with Mr. Ellison – catch up with you later!"

She hurried off, leaving me staring into the open locker before me. *What the fuck was happening?*

The problem wasn't that I was a prude, or that I was particularly shy about my appearance. I'd been in locker rooms before, though they'd always been gender-segregated. I could deal with a situation like this at a pool or rec center.

But this was a *workplace* - one where, seemingly, I was expected as a condition of employment to be *fully naked* around all my new coworkers.

I considered returning to the elevators and leaving, job be damned.

But, I reminded myself of the salary. I *needed* that money. Without it, I'd be back to groveling – with Elijah, with my parents, with my landlord. Was what was being asked of me more or less dignified than that?

I thought about what Donna had whispered to me: *Don't turn back.* The more I thought about the firm tone she'd used, the more an ominous feeling enveloped me. Lauren's words that it was 'too late to give up now' also flashed through my mind. Was leaving even an option?

*I can do this*, I repeated to myself. It'll just be like one of those Japanese bathhouses Elijah had mentioned. *Everyone here just wants to get to work. They won't be paying attention.*

I placed my jacket and heels in the locker. My dress shirt and skirt followed. With the towels wrapped tightly around my waist and breasts, I slipped off my underwear and bra. I took a deep breath before approaching the showers.

Dozens of showerheads dotted the large chamber. Underneath them, my co-workers cleaned themselves comfortably, seemingly at ease with the situation.

At its far end, I spotted a handful of individual shower stalls, their entrances covered by curtains. Relieved, I headed towards them.

I halted at the sound of Lauren's loud, panicked voice. "Those aren't for you, Monica!"

I paused, self-consciously sensing dozens of pairs of eyes walking all over my half-covered body. "W-what do you mean?"

Water rained down over Lauren where she stood in one of the room's corners. She lathered a bluish liquid across her bare chest and shoulders as she spoke. "You have to be with us for a *while* to get a private stall! I don't even have one."

"Oh," I muttered. "Then, um, where do I..."

Lauren cut me off. "You're standing right under it!"

I glanced up, spotting a shower head installed into the ceiling. Next to it was a red light. "Here?" I asked. "Not even against a wall?"

"No, silly! You have to earn a spot against the wall. But it makes no difference – you'll end up just as clean, no matter where you shower! Just place your towel on the rack, press your foot against the switch, and get to scrubbing!" As she spoke, she gestured to a flimsy piece of plastic shelving and a round metal protrusion on the floor next to it.

*Jesus fucking Christ*, I thought, as I realized that I was expected to clean myself in the center of *everyone*, in a spot fully visible from all angles.

I felt frozen, my feet welded to the floor. How could any of this be real?

Others started to notice my hesitation. A coarse voice belonging to a figure showering under a wall-mounted faucet muttered something about "millennials" "having it easy," and how I was "entitled" to expect a private stall on day one. As he rambled, his uncircumcised schlong jostled while he vigorously rubbed soap across his butt and upper legs.

His comments infuriated me. I wanted to curse at him. To scream in his arrogant ear. To tear out his few remaining strands of gray hair.

But I did no such thing. *I can do this*. I told myself once again. I disrobed and put my weight on the button.

Warm water descended on me. Doing my best to ignore my surroundings, I used the soap and shampoo on the rack to clean myself as quickly as I could.

Mercifully, no one whistled or taunted me. As far as I could tell, no one had anything that could be used to photograph or film me. For a moment, I felt that everything might be okay.

When I stepped away, a deafening, high-pitched alarm shattered my sense of relative calm. I felt every inch of my nakedness as I again found myself the subject of everyone's attention.

"Sorry, Monica!" called Lauren, "I forgot to tell you: you can't leave until you're fully decontaminated! The system will tell you when you're ready."

I reluctantly returned to the shower and continued to clean myself. In the agonizing minutes that followed, I felt more embarrassed and exposed than ever before.

Finally, the light above me changed from red to green. Frantically, I threw the towels around me and hurried back to my locker.

~

"In the future, you'll need to be faster," said Lauren, as the elevator brought us from floor 2 to 39. "But I'm sure you'll catch on in no time!"

Dumbstruck by recent events, I stared at the shiny door before me, where my blurry reflection, once again donning the formal outfit I'd arrived in, shivered from the dampness of my hair in the building's low temperature.

Thoughts swam through my mind. I'd just been asked to do something humiliating...and I'd just done it, all for a paycheck. What did that say about me?

The doors eventually opened to a marble lobby. I followed Lauren past offices and conference rooms. She stopped when we reached a dead end where several pieces of furniture were stacked against a wall. "And, here it is!" she said with a smile. "Your workplace!"

"What workplace?"

"Oh, sorry, one moment please." Lauren removed from the pile a flimsy plastic chair and placed it before me. My jaw dropped, I watched as she then lifted an open-front student desk – the kind you'd see in a middle school classroom – and placed it in front of the chair. "Ta da! Your office is complete."

I felt something snap inside of me. "Lauren, this is ridiculous. First, without *any warning*, you ask me to-"

Lauren interrupted me. "Monica, I get it! One hundred percent. It upset me at first, too. But guess what? There's a light at the end of the tunnel." She removed a thick envelope from her purse and placed it on the desk.

~

"*Ten thousand dollars*?" stammered Alice, as bewildered as I'd been. I'd gone straight from work to her place.

I nodded. "But she made me sign something about it. If I don't keep the job for sixty days, I have to give it back."

"Maybe you *should* give it back."

"What?"

"Everything you've described…it's gross. You should quit."

I shrugged. "Yeah, but…I rely on *so* many people for help as it is. And rent's going up soon. I can't turn this down."

To my surprise, there were tears in Alice's eyes, and her voice cracked when she spoke. "Monica, I don't want to be like, controlling about your life decisions, but, I-I don't *like* the idea of you being, you know…in front of all those people like that."

I wrapped my arms around her. "I'm sorry. I didn't think about it like that."

"It's okay. Who am I to judge. Living in my childhood bedroom while you try to support yourself."

"No, I understand. It's just…I want to give this some time. I'll apply elsewhere, and I'll have something else figured out when the two months are up."

"Okay." She looked down as she spoke. "It's getting late, you know."

I checked my watch. "Oh, right. I'd better get going." Alice's parents didn't like her having company past nine.

~

Over the next few days, I arrived at the building as it opened, well before my shift began. That way, I'd at least begin my shower with only a handful of co-workers around me.

While I occasionally caught someone peeking or leering at me – something my death glare usually convinced them to cease – no one did anything worse than that.

A corded phone had been placed on my desk, but nobody ever called it. I used it several times to reach Lauren, who responded evasively to inquiries about my duties "You're doing a *great* job!"

"But I'm not doing *anything*."

"Just keep up the good work. Oh, and I hope you've put your first bonus to good use."

I had, in fact, burned through much of the money, though not on anything frivolous. I'd paid back my parents for the last two checks they'd sent me, and I'd reimbursed Elijah for what I owed him.

My first assignment came that Friday. Lauren took me several floors up.

The windows that lined the wall of the office she led me to provided a breathtaking view of the surrounding cityscape. A large executive desk made of mahogany wood stood in the room's center. Lauren instructed me to sit at the desk's matching leather chair and wait until she came back.

The computer's screen displayed across three monitors. It was an impressive setup. But, for now, there wasn't much that I could do other than admire it, as the computer prompted me to enter login credentials that I didn't have.

When Lauren returned a few minutes later, she was leading a group of four men, all older and well-dressed. She spoke with the forced enthusiasm of a tour guide. "And right here is our newest associate, Monica Wilson. Contrary to what you'll read in lousy, unfounded articles accusing us of running a homogenous 'old boys club,' Abernathy Industries in fact has a diverse workplace, as you can see. In fact, Monica has a grandparent from Taiwan!"

One of the men smiled warmly and stated that his family was also from Taiwan.

Lauren responded in an exuberant tone. "Well isn't that just great! Now, please follow me."

~

I sat, perplexed, for several minutes. Eventually, Lauren slid the door partially open and popped her head inside. "Monica, I don't have much time, but I just wanted to tell you that you did great!"

"Wait, what? *That* was the project? Who were those men?"

"The type of people who supply this company's lifeblood, Monica. You made a very positive impression with Mr. Tsai."

"But...how did you even know about my grandmother?"

"You mentioned her during your interview, silly! Look, I've got to go, but I'm sure you can find your way back down without me."

~

Over the next two weeks, I fell into a mind-numbing routine of greeting David and Donna, showering, sitting at my flimsy desk, and spending the hours that followed on my personal phone. My only assignment during that period consisted of driving Mr. Morgan's car from the 10-minute spot where he'd left it to a garage.

When my first paycheck arrived, it felt too good to be true. Why were they paying me so much to do so little?

~

The next week, Lauren reported to me that Mr. Morgan had again requested my assistance, this time by ordering his favorite drink from the bar on building's top level and bringing it to him in the lounge nearby.

"I can do that, but didn't you tell me that I don't have access to the lounge?"

"I've arranged for you to have permission to carry out this task. You are to leave promptly after delivering the drink. No looking around, no loitering."

"Got it."

"Oh, and one last thing: make sure the bartender uses fresh nutmeg. Mr. Morgan prefers it that way."

~

Soon after, a man in a tuxedo held the lounge door open for me as I carried a full coupe glass inside. A lush, red carpet stretched across the floor, and portraits of wealthy, well-dressed men lined the walls.

The room's occupants resembled the subjects of those paintings. They congregated around pool and poker tables and murmured in quiet conversation. One let out a loud 'sniff' before handing a rolled up dollar bill to another.

Several made snide remarks about my presence. "What's *she* doing here," said one man; "You sure 'she' is the right pronoun? You never know with youngsters these days," said another.

I ignored them as I looked for Mr. Morgan. He was a little younger than most of the executives, and noticeably well-built.

A young woman I recognized as Courtney walked briskly past me. She was the only co-worker I'd encountered who appeared close to my age, she presently wore a fitted black velvet dress.

She approached the poker table, where she handed a wooden box to a man I recognized as Mr. Hoffman. He opened it, revealing a set of premium cigars. He nodded and brushed his hand against hers as she stepped away.

When I flagged her down, she told me that Mr. Morgan was in the VIP section and gestured to a purple curtain that covered the entrance to a nearby corridor. She explained that, even with the permission I had, I wasn't allowed to be in there.

"So, what do I do?"

She shrugged and instructed me to wait until someone entered or exited.

~

For several minutes, I listened to voices from the other side of the curtain. Mostly, they consisted of periodic, raucous cheers, as if reacting to a high-stakes sports game. But, every so often, I discerned something disturbing: piercing cries of misery and pain, all seemingly emanating from the same unfortunate soul.

Eventually, someone did leave the room, and he agreed to fetch Mr. Morgan for me. When Mr. Morgan pulled open the curtain, I got a brief glimpse into the VIP area. There, a group of important-looking men were transfixed by something out of my line of sight.

Mr. Morgan closed the curtain as he greeted me. I handed him the drink, which he sipped before giving a satisfied nod. "Well done, Monica. It's perfect."

"I'm glad," I said, thankful I'd been firm with the bartender about the ingredients. "Um, is everything okay in there? Is someone hurt?"

This caused him to snap at me. "Don't be nosy, Monica."

"Sorry."

"You're doing well so far, Monica. You're in my good graces, and I'm a valuable friend around here. And if you want to keep things that way, don't ask too many questions." He gave me a playful wink before returning to the VIP section.

~

After work that night, Alice sat with me on the futon in my shared apartment. "How's the job search going?"

"You're asking *me* that?" I responded, incredulously.

"Monica! You know I'm trying my absolute hardest. And I *have* gotten a couple story acceptances."

"Sorry."

"You told me you'd be out of that hellhole by now."

"Yeah, but..."

"But what?"

"I...I'm still looking."

"*Are* you, though? Where have you applied?"

"Forget it."

~

After she left, I looked at my bank account. For the first time in years, the balance it displayed didn't send me into a panic.

I spent hours crunching numbers – listing prices, projected balances, and potential expenses. Eventually, I arrived at a certainty: I was on track to be unshackled from student loans and the many other obligations that had for so long ensnared me.

Soon, I'd have the life I'd always hoped for – one where I could afford to do more than tread water.

~

As time went on, I got more acclimated to the showers, to the point that my brain navigated them on autopilot. I no longer showed up unnecessarily early, and I no longer spent the duration of my time there in a state of worried embarrassment.

We were just humans cleaning our natural bodies, and if a few men took the opportunity to gawk at me now and then, I could live with that. The paychecks kept coming, after all.

Meanwhile, the 'projects' Lauren assigned to me continued to be uncomplicated and unchallenging.

One morning, Lauren gave me detailed instructions for picking up a box of luxury cigars from an outlet in midtown and delivering them to Mr. Hoffman. I mentioned that I'd seen Courtney carry out a similar task.

"Who?"

"Courtney. I don't think I ever got her last name."

"Oh, right, Courtney! Unfortunately, her employment with us recently came to an end."

"What happened to her?"

"Don't be nosy, Monica! That's confidential information!"

"Right, sorry."

~

The next morning, I arrived at my desk, my hair still damp, to find Lauren waiting for me. "It's your quarterly anniversary!" she announced. "To celebrate, I have a *very* special assignment for you."

The elevator took us all the way down to B3, the lowest level. We traveled through a maze of narrow corridors, all painted in a blinding shade of white, and by rooms full of flasks, Bunsen burners, and men in lab coats. Eventually, we arrived at a janitor cart by a door labeled "CR B3-23."

Lauren explained that my task was to clean the room inside. "It needs to be spotless, as well as fully sanitized."

"I'm happy to help, but, isn't the janitorial staff better equipped than me for something like that?"

"No, Monica, you're *just* the right person for the job!"

I pushed the door open, curious how bad of a mess awaited me.

Nothing about the room's layout – which consisted of three chairs arranged around the central, circular table – was abnormal.

What *was* abnormal was the *massive* amount of red liquid – parts of it a dark and rusted in color, and others a lighter, vibrant crimson – that dripped from the walls and the ceiling into puddles across the floor.

"So, Monica, do you have any questions?" From the casual tone Lauren used, she seemed totally unphased.

Impulsively, my mouth started to form words like "What the fuck happened in here?" and "Are you asking me to wipe up a crime scene?" But, I recalled what so many people had told me: *don't be nosy*. I shook my head.

~

I worked late into the night. Thankfully, the cart contained protective gear and multiple cannisters of hydrogen peroxide, but scrubbing out the stains took an exhausting amount of elbow grease.

By the time I'd restored the walls and ceiling to their original, unblemished appearance, my muscles were sore, and my body ached. When I repositioned one of the chairs around the table, I found something on it that I hadn't noticed before: a thin strip of black velvet fabric.

~

When I checked my phone while riding the metro back, I noticed several missed calls and text messages from Alice.

*I'm so sorry*, I typed out. *I totally forgot about dinner. I got caught up in something at work.*

My phone soon buzzed with a response. *It's okay. I just feel like I hardly see you anymore.*

~

When I reached the room Lauren had directed me to, I knocked at its door.

"Come in," greeted Mr. Hoffman. He sat at a long, ovular table between two younger men who scribbled furiously onto paper notepads.

One of them handed me a blue collar. The nametag that dangled from it displayed "Monica."

"What do you want me to do with this?"

Mr. Hoffman responded in a firm tone. "Dogs don't talk. Please take this exercise seriously."

"Huh?"

"Dogs don't stand on two legs, either."

They stared at me expectantly as I examined my surroundings. An exercise mat stretched across the floor in front of the table. On it stood a flimsy wooden doghouse and bowls containing food and water.

"We're waiting, Monica."

I think to myself, *Stop asking questions. Just do what they ask.* I placed the collar around my neck and snapped its two ends together.

This prompted an excited "*Good*" from Mr. Hoffman. He removed something from an outer pocket of his suit and tossed it towards me.

It rolled against my shoe. I unfolded it to see Andrew Jackson's face and the number "20" displayed in three of its corners.

I dropped to the ground and crawled towards the dog house. Shortly after, two more bills hit the ground. "Now, be a good girl and roll around on the mat."

The mat felt sticky and damp. Something had been sprayed on it, but I'd learned better than to ask what it was.

"A good girl drinks her water."

I stuck my face into the bowl and swallowed several gulps of it.

"A good girl eats her food."

I shot a desperate glance at Mr. Hoffman.

"Do you need me to repeat the instruction?"

For a moment, my body simply refused to commit to the action I ordered it to take. *Fuck it,* I thought, as I mustered the necessary willpower.

I filled my mouth with the disgusting pellets and promptly swallowed, using water from the other bowl to help wash it down. I did this a second time, then a third. The food left behind a putrid, fishy taste, and I barely avoided vomiting.

A sizable pile of bills had formed around me. I glanced up from it to Mr. Hoffman, who, thankfully, seemed pleased with me. "That will be all."

I gathered the money – which I estimated totaled at least $300 – and climbed to my feet. I felt filthy, and the mat's dampness had transferred to my clothes.

Mr. Hoffman leaned back and took on a satisfied expression. "I have good news for you."

"Yes?"

"You'll be receiving another bonus. And, you no longer need to shower in the room's center. You're now permitted to use the spots around the perimeter. Not the corners, though."

"Thank you."

"Also, make sure to clean your clothes thoroughly before wearing them again. You'll want to avoid touching them, and then touching your face, until then."

~

When Alice arrived at my place that night, I sensed on her the vague, sulfuric scent that the metro tended to leave on its passengers.

"You're welcome to use my shower."

"Huh?"

"Never mind."

We sat in my bedroom, her at the foot of my bed and me in the swivel chair by the closet.

"What's up with your work clothes?" she asked, motioning to the plastic bag into which I'd stuffed them.

"Oh. Don't touch them. Some kind of harmful chemical got on them today."

"That's terrible."

"It's alright."

"No, it isn't alright. You can't let them treat you like that. Why haven't you quit yet?"

I sighed. I wasn't sure what to say.

"You haven't actually applied anywhere else, have you?"

I shrugged. "Look, um, I don't want to talk about that."

She shot me a frustrated glance.

"What *do* you want to talk about?" she asked.

"I found a new place. A condominium. I've saved up enough for a down payment."

For a moment, her face beamed. But her expression changed as she started to understand what I was saying. "And you never mentioned this to me?"

"No."

"Because you don't want me to move in with you?"

"Look, Alice, you know that you mean a lot to me, but-"

"Are you telling me that this is it? For us?"

"I, um..."

"I can't believe this. Look, Monica, I'll do it. I'll stop trying to be a writer. I'll get a real job, and I'll pull my own weight. I'll even do night school at the community college like you suggested, if that's what it takes. We can make it work."

"Sometimes, in life, hurdles come up, and people take different paths to navigate around them. It doesn't mean-"

"Did you get that from some HR person? Monica...we were happy together, and now..." She bawled. I brought her a tissue.

~

After she left, I couldn't settle down.

Eventually, I wandered into the frigid air outside. I hailed a taxi. When the driver asked me for a destination, I impulsively identified my workplace.

I soon sat alone at the bar. Two men in a booth behind me chatted about some kind of legal matter.

"So that's where all the new decontamination procedures originated? In response to that mess in bio-med East?"

"Yep, and hear this – the massive judgment she got from us over the outbreak wasn't enough for her. She wants it all to be fully in the public record, too. No redactions, no sealed filings. The judge may very well side with her. It's giving legal quite a headache."

"You heard what happened to the whistleblower who caused this whole mess, right? The one who shared our internal report with the survivor?"

"Yep. Straight up to the lounge. I was there for it. Good times."

I'd downed two drinks when someone took the seat next to me. "Mind if I join you?" asked Mr. Morgan.

~

During the ride to his place, I imagined conversations between Mr. Morgan and the other executives. In one version, I was ridiculed and ultimately fired for going along with what he wanted. In another, I met with the same fate as a result of turning him down.

He took my hand and led me to his building's central elevator. After the doors closed, he spoke to me in a serious tone. "Look, I know I talk a big game about being on my 'good side.' But, in all seriousness, I know there's a power differential here. You can leave right now, and I won't hold it against you. You're totally free to go."

I'd already made up my mind, and I wasn't there because of pressure from him. I needed something to take my mind off of Alice. I yearned to be desired, and not just by anybody.

I spoke confidently. "I understand, and I want this."

~

We got off on the penthouse level. Mr. Morgan motioned to the far end of the hallway. "Frank Hoffman has the unit down there. But I doubt we'll be seeing him this late."

He unlocked the door and flipped on the lights. I slowly took in the extravagant sight around me: the astounding vista provided by the oversized windows; the sleek marble countertops; the private elevator; and the abundance of sculptures and artwork.

He noticed me gazing at a clear acrylic grand piano. As he played a slow, classy piece, I sat back on a corner sectional sofa and closed my eyes.

Sure, this wasn't my life. I was only an interloper; a tourist. I didn't really belong here. But, for a moment, I felt like I did – like maybe, just maybe, I'd have a place like this someday.

~

He rolled off of me about twenty minutes after we'd arrived in his bedroom. We were covered in a layer of sweat and both needed a minute to catch our breaths.

*That was fucking great*, I whispered, but I wasn't sure if he heard me. I shifted to lie next to him, but he promptly got up when I tried to wrap my arms around him. "I, um, I'm going to wash up." He swiftly proceeded to the nearest bathroom.

I soon followed him there, where he showered under a faucet that extended out of an ornate quartz wall slab.

He told me he didn't mind if I cleaned up in there. But, when I approached the shower's glass door, he instructed me not to enter.

"Oh. I can shower after you, then."

"No, it's...it's not for you."

"What do you mean?"

He responded in an exasperated tone. "All these questions. You all never learn."

"Sorry."

"Look, um, I need to be at work early tomorrow."

I didn't know what to say to that, so I just stood there, awkwardly biting my lip as my mood sank into a feeling of bitter emptiness.

"Do you, like, need anything? A ride home, money, or something?"

I got dressed and left. As I waited for the elevator outside, a figure approached from the other end of the hall. I recognized her as Scarlett, Courtney's recent replacement. From the streaks  of makeup running down her face, I could tell that she'd recently been crying.

"It's going to be okay," I told her, although I wasn't sure why.

We were halfway down – the floor indicator read '56' – when Scarlett turned to me. She tried to speak, but she only a weak croak came out. She gave up on words, but I still understood her on an intuitive level. I let her lean into me and held her as she sobbed against my shoulder.

~

In the months that followed, the consequences I worried about never came to pass. Neither Mr. Morgan nor any of the other executives treated me differently. My workdays maintained their pattern of tedious waits between demeaning assignments.

My bank account continued to grow. Soon after I settled comfortably into my small condominium, I began eying listings for bigger, better living spaces elsewhere.

~

One day, Lauren explained to me that a new employee named Peter would soon begin. "He'll be performing a role similar to yours. As I'll be out of the office tomorrow, I want you to greet him and show him the ropes."

When I arrived at the office the next morning, Peter was already waiting for me in the lobby. He was appropriately well-dressed. His lanky frame and sandy hair reminded me of my high school boyfriend. "You're here early," I said, shaking his hand.

He gave a nervous laugh and explained that he wasn't sure what work he was going to be performing.

"Oh," I responded. "A little of this, a little of that. Like, sometimes I get coffee for the executives, and other times I assist with testing products. Once, they even had me pretend to be a dog and roll around on some chemical. My skin burned a bit after that, but it went away after a few days."

The chuckle that followed felt hollow. He wasn't sure if I was joking.

He followed me up to the locker room. He panicked upon absorbing his surroundings and the dozens of nude people within them. He asked me what was going on.

"It's just a shower, silly," I said, as I started to undress. "There's a spot in the middle of the room for you to use."

He told me that he simply wasn't going to do that.

"It's *required*, Peter. Everyone has to do it, every day. It's important to have a clean workplace. Don't be shy."

This had no effect on him. Instead, he continued to back away.

I begged for him to change his mind. "Peter, please, don't go. It's too late to turn back."

Peter ignored me and fled to the elevator. Soon after he pressed the 'down' button, its doors opened to reveal David and Donna, who swiftly grabbed him and dragged him away.

Over the following months, I answered the questions I received about Peter as Lauren had instructed me. "He just walked out during orientation. I never saw him again."

~

It is a bleak, rainy day. Flash floods warnings buzz on my phone, and the wind nearly rips the umbrella out of my hand as I scamper inside.

Lauren comes to my desk. She promises a 'reward' for my exceptional performance.

She takes me to the lounge. "Not only can you now enter the main area, but you now have access to the VIP section as well."

She brushes the curtain aside. Executives are gathered around a small bar. Mr. Morgan hands me a drink.

There's another curtain at the far end of the room. Mr. Hoffman announces that it's "showtime."

Lauren pulls a cord. The curtain spreads apart, revealing a familiar young man.

Peter's mouth is gagged. His body is bound to a wooden circle attached to the wall behind him. His arms and legs, both riddled with scars, are tied to edges behind him such that his body forms an 'X' shape.

Peter makes eye contact with me. He emits a muffled cry for help. On the floor beneath him is a crate containing a spiked bat and a stained handsaw.

Scarlett appears. She hands Mr. Hoffman a wooden box. He opens it, nods, and tells her to scram. She dutifully obeys.

At Mr. Hoffman's request, I look into the box. It contains a dozen darts carefully arranged in foam indentations.

"Take one."

The one I select is heavier than I expected, and it has a long, extremely sharp tip.

"What do you want me to do with it?"

"What do you think? Throw it at your target." When I freeze, he scolds me. "Don't you give up like Courtney did."

Lauren speaks to me in a soft, firm voice. "Monica, you need to do this."

"I can't."

"Let me show you." Lauren announces that she's giving a demonstration.

She takes a dart and approaches Peter, stopping at a line of green tape about two meters from him. She draws back the dart and rapidly releases it.

Peter whimpers as the dart embeds itself in his right arm. A line of blood forms, dripping onto the carpet.

The crowd cheers as Lauren tries to reassure me. "You see? It's easy."

The executives chant my name as I slowly step forward. I want to throw the dart at Lauren or Mr. Hoffman. I want to untie Peter and escort him out of the building.

But, I'm terrified of what will happen to me if I do anything other than comply. Plus, I've come so far, and I've lost so much along the way.

I close my eyes and try to calm my nerves. I think about who I once was. The optimism I once had – not just about others, but about myself, too. All the nights Alice and I spent together.

We haven't talked since I told her it was over. I've been tempted, many times, to call her, to apologize, and to try to make things work again. But I've long known it was too late to do that, even before she recently started posting pictures with another girl.

I'm snapped out of my reverie by cries for me to "hurry it up already." I have to act. What if I miss on purpose? Would that fool anyone?

On the other hand, what if I just did it? I tried to warn Peter. He has only himself to blame for his predicament.

My arm shakes. I let out a roar, draw back, and release.

The dart grazes against Peter's shoulder before lodging into the wood behind him. Judging by the lack of blood, it didn't puncture his skin.

The executives hiss and boo as I return. When one complains that I missed on purpose, another responds, "No, she must have been trying, she only barely missed!"

Mr. Hoffman holds out the open box. "Try again."

I look at him, and then at the leering, awful faces of everyone else, before forcing a smile. I speak emphatically. "Maybe next time."

A silence sweeps over the room. An eternity passes in the moments that follow.

Finally, Mr. Hoffman nods. "Next time," he repeats.

As I exit, the crowd's cheering resumes, followed by cries of pain.

~

As I open the lobby doors, David warns me that I'm going to get soaked. Indeed, with no raincoat, I quickly find myself drenched. But I keep walking anyway, with no particular destination in mind.

I watch as standing water forms a small rapid on the nearby street. It leads to a storm drain, where the liquid swirls and sinks.

I imagine myself lying down on that road and letting the dirty water sweep over me. Maybe I'd emerge from it restored to the person I'd once been, rebaptized by the pollutants and street grime I've spent so long scrubbing from my body.

I shake my head and chide myself for indulging in such thoughts. That person was long gone now, and there was no bringing her back.

A luxury condo building towers over me. I glance up at it, take a deep breath, and begin the walk back to work.

**25**

---

# PURITY PLEDGE

*"**D**o you want to have sex?"*
     *"What? Really?"*
     *"Forget it."*
*"No, um. Yeah, okay."*
*"Are you sure?"*
*"Yeah. I thought, you know, we were-"*
*"I know. But fuck it. Let's just do it already."*
*"Yeah. Okay. Fuck it."*
*~*
*"Ow."*
*"Sorry."*
*"Are you sure that's, like, the right angle?"*
*"I think so."*
*"Just...slower, maybe?"*
*"Okay, does that feel better?"*
*"No, it still-"*
*"Sorry, I think...I'm..."*
*"Wait, are you- Already?"*
*~*

Addie's prompt response to my text message sent a wave of relief through me. I needed someone to talk to and, fortunately, she was a night owl.

I crawled out of bed, careful not to wake Aaron, and quietly closed the door behind me.

I then headed downstairs to the kitchen, where I poured myself a glass of water and tapped Addie's name on my cell phone.

"What's up?"

"I just want to talk."

"No, you're usually asleep by now. What happened?"

I sighed. "So, yeah, something did happen."

"Let me guess. Since your mom's away, Aaron's there overnight. Am I correct so far?"

"Yep."

"Did you two have a fight?"

"No, nothing like that."

"Well, what is it?"

I cleared my throat and took a deep breath. "So, you know those movies you like? With the masked killers slashing up teens?"

"Maria, if Jason Vorhees is in your house, hang up and get the fuck out of there!"

I rolled my eyes. "No, so, you know how you always joked about how I'd be the one person in our friend group who'd survive one of those movies? Let's just say my odds just went way down. Aaron's too."

"OHH. So you two finally-"

"Yep."

"Okay, first of all, that's awesome, and you have my full support. And I hope it was fucking great. But weren't both of you, like, pretty serious about the whole waiting for marriage thing?"

"We were."

"So what happened?"

I shrugged. "We were, like, an hour into a make-out session...and it just kind of happened. It was my idea. I thought he'd argue with me, or even scold me for suggesting it. But instead he just went right along with it."

"Is he with you now?"

"No. I left him upstairs. He passed out almost immediately afterwards. I couldn't sleep."

"Maria, I'm honored your first thought was to call me, assuming your plan isn't for me to bore you into drowsiness."

I chuckled. "No, I just have a lot of thoughts swimming around in my head. I can't settle. I figured that laying them out with you might help, though I'm not sure where to start."

"You don't have to go into it in any detail if you don't want to, but, like, how was it?"

"It was awkward."

"You expected it not to be?"

"I don't know. I didn't know what to expect. I don't know much about these things. Part of it was how, after all that buildup – nearly four years, considering we've been together since the end of high school – it didn't exactly feel great, and it was over so fast. I'm still processing it."

Addie gave a gentle laugh. "It's okay, Maria. Really. So many people have experiences just like yours. It was like that with me, too, you know. Jose and I had no idea what we were doing at first. And guess what? It got better, and we have fucking *amazing* sex now. Just give it some time, and always communicate how you feel. Aaron's a good guy. He'll listen."

I took a deep gulp of water before responding. "Thanks. I hope you're right."

"Had you two been doing, like, other stuff before? You've never mentioned anything like that."

"That's because there wasn't much to talk about. We'd barely done more than kiss."

"Jesus! Something sure fucking came over you tonight."

"I guess. I wanted him so badly. I also thought, you know, how often are we going to have the whole place to ourselves, with no risk of being interrupted? Even then, I still thought he'd say no, or I'd change my mind at the last moment, but neither happened."

"Oh, I get it. 100%. I do need to ask – you used, you know-"

"We're not *that* clueless. I know where mom keeps a box of them. She's not going to notice one missing."

"Gotcha."

"Honestly, if she found out about this, she'd be mad and threaten to kick me out, but she'd get over it. She's been loosening up about these things lately, and she wasn't the one who really cared about this stuff to begin with. Which brings me to the other topic I wanted to discuss."

"Your psycho dad?"

"Yeah."

"You don't have to worry about him anymore. I don't want to make light of what your family went through, but it was obviously a relief to you, for good reason. You're free of him. Embrace that."

"I know, but the things he said and did stick with me. It's all replaying in my head tonight."

"I can imagine. I was raised around plenty of double standards too, but I'm so fucking lucky my parents never sent me to Jesus camp. Or turbo Jesus camp in your case. Heck, I didn't even know what a 'purity ball' was until you showed me that abominable picture."

"It's so fucked up. He just engrained it in me that my self-worth depended on some bogus idea of 'purity.' And he ensured that every authority figure in my life said the same thing."

"And I assume that's what's bothering you now? The things you grew up hearing?"

"Yeah. It's like, when someone insults you, it still hurts, even when you know for an absolute fact that it isn't true. I think about the sheer volume of people I've been around who'd judge the shit out of me for what I just did. If dad were around, he'd do a lot more than that insult me. No joke, he'd disown me, then he'd fucking hurt me, and Aaron too."

Impulsively, my hand went to the stretch of skin under my chin that I'd had to cover with turtlenecks for weeks. Addie had been the only person I'd shown the bruise to, and it had taken me enormous effort to convince her not to call law enforcement.

I'd understood something that Addie hadn't: that, if a member of our small town's police force came by, they'd sooner believe whatever lie my dad told them than the truth.

"But you didn't do anything wrong," Addie insisted, "and your dad isn't going to hurt you, or Aaron for that matter. He's in the same place he's been for a while, and he's not going anywhere else anytime soon."

Of course, Addie was right, and I told her as much. "I need to stop worrying. It's just that, like, I can't shake the feeling that he's here, somehow."

"Maria, he isn't there. You're safe. Do whatever you need to do to convince yourself of that. If you need me to come over, I can do that."

"No, it's okay. I'm feeling better. You should go to bed. Thanks for taking my call."

"Of course. You and Aaron have so many great experiences ahead of you, and there's nothing anyone else can do about it. Focus on that."

~

I left the call feeling reassured. Addie was a good friend, and this was hardly the first time she'd been there for me.

I spent a few minutes reading articles Addie sent to me, which contained very basic, surface-level advice I wish I'd been exposed to prior to tonight, before leaning back on our soft living room sofa and closing my eyes.

*I'll just rest here for a minute*, I told myself, and then I'll slip into bed with Aaron. At long last, I felt relaxed and at ease.

The sound of a scream caused me to jump to my feet. To my surprise, a trail of dark, muddy footprints had stained the nearby carpet. They formed a path that led to the foot of the upper staircase. Whoever had made these tracks had gone upstairs and...had the scream been Aaron's? I ran, hastily, to the foot of the staircase.

Before heading up, I dialed 911. Upon seeing that my call had had been answered, I stuttered that someone was in my house, and that my boyfriend was in danger. To my shock, the only sound that came from the other end of the call was sickly, taunting laughter.

A deep, recognizable voice echoed from the top of the stairs.

"*Nobody's going to help you.*" I dropped my phone as the sight of the figure standing above sent a paralyzing shock throughout me. Dad's tall, well-built body towered over me, and he appeared unexpectedly strong and healthy.

"*Come to papa,*" he commanded. When he opened his arms, I noticed that his outfit – the same formal black suit I'd last seen him in – was caked in a fresh layer of blood.

"What did you do to Aaron?" I bellowed.

"Nothing worse than what he did to you," dad taunted. "Robbing you of what little value you had left."

I fumed with anger. I wanted to charge at him, to fight him, to at least try to save Aaron, if he was still alive. But, instead, I ran. I scrambled for the front door, frantically undoing the locks while praying that dad wouldn't catch up to me.

When I opened it, I found myself somehow face-to-face with my tormenter, who displayed a ghoulish smile.

I woke up covered in sweat. To my relief, I realized that I'd simply dozed off on the sofa. According to the grandfather clock near me, it was close to 1:30 a.m. There were no stains on the carpet, my dad wasn't here, and neither me nor my slumbering boyfriend were in any danger.

"*Everything's fine,*" I repeated to myself as my heart rate slowly regressed back to normal. I switched on the television, hoping that maybe some late night offerings would calm my nerves. Instead, the image that displayed – presumably, on the channel mom had last been watching – was of a fire-and-brimstone preacher speaking at a pulpit. I quickly turned it off.

My mind drifted to my surroundings. The ticking of the grandfather clock brought back childhood memories of playing with dolls on the carpet in front of it. I'd spend hours engrossed in my own imagination, doing my best to ignore the sounds of dad screaming at mom.

I recalled what he often told me as he led me from there up to my bedroom: that God was always watching and listening, and that 'impure' thoughts would send me straight to hell. "If you stray from the path of God, *even just in your head,*" he'd say as I lay under the covers, "then there won't be any room for you in His kingdom. Just the fire, screaming, and misery of Hell."

For years, I fought to suppress any thoughts or feelings, no matter how fleeting, on topics Dad had declared unholy. I even chided myself over the content of my own dreams, begging God's forgiveness if my unconscious mind strayed onto subjects like sex or masturbation. I didn't want to burn, after all.

Dad's bullying wasn't just psychological, as the physical scars on me – and mom, too – proved. I remembered him calling us to the kitchen table after returning from work. Later, I'd learn that he'd been passed over for a promotion that day, but he didn't share that with us at the time.

Instead, he'd slowly removed his belt and placed it on the table. He'd looked at me, then tilted his head back towards mom. He'd repeated this several times before announcing his decision. "Maria, tonight's your lucky night. Go on now to your room." I'd obeyed, burying my head under my pillow in a futile effort to drown out the screams from below.

I returned to the kitchen. It was at this table that dad had first revealed to me that he'd been reading my diary. I was in seventh grade, and I'd been writing in it for over a year.

"You thought you could hide it from me, couldn't you?"

"Hide what?" I'd asked, feigning ignorance.

"Jeffrey Vinson. Your little *boyfriend*. The one I see everywhere but church. The one whose rotten, lustful eyes walk all over you."

My face had grown red, and I'd started breathing rapidly. "No, dad, it's not like you think. All we've done is hold hands-"

"You think I'm stupid, is that it?"

"N-no, it's just-"

"Whore," he'd called me, not for the first time. "Worthless, just like your mother."

When he told me what he wanted me to do, I'd begged and sobbed for nearly an hour. It had been no use; Dad hadn't budged. He never did.

Instead, he'd taken my phone, dialed Jeffrey's number, and then placed it in front of me. When Jeffrey picked up, I'd recited, through tears, what Dad had instructed me to say: that I didn't see the light of God in him, and that things between us were over. I'd had no choice in the matter; the punishment for disobeying, as dad had explained it, would be meted out not just to me, but to Jeffrey, too.

Understandably, Jeffrey hadn't taken it well. I'd never really talked to him again. Dad, meanwhile, saw to it to punish me even further, all but restricting me from ever being alone with any other member of the opposite sex.

*Dad wasn't coming for me,* I reminded myself. Addie had said the same thing. I pondered Addie's next words: *Do whatever you need to do to convince yourself of that.*

An idea dawned on me, one that could bring the closure I sought. *Fuck it*, I thought, for the second time that night, before slipping on a pair of tennis shoes, grabbing a jacket, and stepping into the cool breeze outside.

It took my eyes a moment to adjust to the darkness. It was well after midnight, after all, and we lived on the outskirts of town.

My destination was only a short walk away. At this hour, I'd normally drive, but, as I'd technically be trespassing, I figured I'd best make the trip on foot to avoid attracting the attention of any patrolman on night duty.

The first thing I did was stop by dad's shed. We'd sold much of what he'd kept in there, but a few items remained: several opened paint cans, a worn felling axe, a broken lawnmower, and the LED flashlight I was looking for.

The shortest path was reachable from the backyard and stretched through the surrounding woods. Mom, dad, and I had regularly used it to get to Sunday service, so long as it wasn't covered by mud or snow. But, as the trail was barely visible even during the daylight, I opted instead to use the longer but more discernible route alongside the nearby streets.

I kept the flashlight aimed a few feet ahead of me as I trudged along the dirt road's uneven surface. My surroundings, which consisted of dense forest punctuated only occasionally by the driveways and yards of neighboring homes, were eerily quiet. Everything looked bleak and uninviting at night, and I imagined – but, fortunately, did not encounter – coyotes peering out at me at every turn.

Finally, the tallest spire of the Cedar Hill Church of Christ appeared in the distance, barely visible in the light cast by the first quarter moon.

I hadn't been there since the funeral, despite mom's efforts to convince me to attend service with her, something she'd only stopped doing once she started seeing a new boyfriend a few weeks ago. It was a place where the minister regularly preached about sin, damnation, and moral rot, instilling in me fears and prejudices that I still struggled to overcome.

I recalled how, during Sunday school, we were separated by sex. During the sessions that followed, our instructors compared women who didn't save themselves for marriage – with a good Christian man, of course – to totaled cars, or disgusting pieces of gum that had already been chewed by several people. We were told that if we didn't dress modestly, *we* were responsible for men who looked at us and couldn't control their impulses.

I approached the church. The cemetery gates were locked at this hour, so, with a grunt, I carefully pulled myself up and over the short cobblestone wall that lined its eastern perimeter, landing on a patch of grass on the other side.

The cemetery had an unexpectedly peaceful ambience to it. As I shined my flashlight over various headstones, I pictured the inhabitants of the coffins underneath them resting quietly in a deep, dreamless sleep that fit with the soothing serenity of the quiet night. *Just a little bit further*, I told myself, doing my best to remember the grave's exact position, *and I'll get the closure I need.*

Finally, my light shined on a vaguely familiar name carved across a flat plaque. I recognized it as the starting point of the row that led to my dad's grave. I took a deep breath before trudging along.

I knew what lay ahead: a plain, upright granite headstone that displayed, in carved letters, his name, the dates of this birth and death, and a blatant lie about him being a "devoted" father and husband.

I'd look at it, remind myself of what Addie had told me – *he's in the same place he's been for a while, and he's not going anywhere else anytime soon* – and, with my irrational fears finally quelled, head on home. I pictured myself soon crawling into bed, holding onto Aaron, and enjoying several hours of the restful sleep that had thus far eluded me.

But when I approached the grave, it wasn't as I'd expected. My first thought was that someone had vandalized it.

The dirt beneath the headstone – *the ground where my father had been buried* – had somehow been partially dug up. Peering into it, I made out a dark hole that led at least several feet into the ground.

*What the hell is happening,* I thought, as I backed up from the desecrated sight. I'd never heard of graverobbers in our town, and there was no reason for his burial place, in particular, to be targeted. We weren't rich, and he wasn't buried with anything valuable.

Most strikingly, the hole itself just didn't seem to be the result of someone shoveling from above. Rather, the dirt looked like it had been clawed out by hand, and the gap was just wide enough for someone to slip through. Almost like someone had dug out from below.

I grew dizzy with confusion and realized too late that I was losing my balance. Images of memorial crosses, granite benches, and slanted headstones flashed around me as I sprawled to the ground. I cried, not because of pain from the fall – fortunately, I'd mostly landed on soft grass – but from the sheer misery I felt.

*Dad wasn't down there anymore. He was back, just like in my dream.* As impossible as it sounded, I sensed that it was true. Not even death itself could stop him from judging and policing my life. I had no doubt why this was happening tonight or where he was going.

I jumped to my feet, hopped back over the wall, and ran towards the path back home through the woods. I didn't care about the roots I stumbled over, the predators that might be watching me, or the fresh footprints that seemed headed towards my house. I just needed to get home as fast as possible.

When I emerged into my backyard, the patio door was wide open, and the rock next to it, under which we kept a spare key, had been overturned. Dad was here.

My heart throbbed in fear as I stepped inside. Following a trail of soil and grime through the kitchen, I found myself at the foot of the staircase, where I looked up to see a tall form encased almost entirely in shadow.

Unlike in my dream, he hadn't yet reached my room. The figure paused, seemingly having sensed my presence, and turned towards me. Although the darkness continued to cover most of his features, I could see his body shaking with what I imagined to be a spiteful rage.

The raspy voice was unmistakably my father's, if slightly deeper and rougher than I remembered. "*Daddy's girl has been bad.*"

I responded as firmly as I could manage. "L-leave me alone."

I shivered as he took one step down towards me. "*You promised you would be a woman of character, of purity, until the day came when God guided you to your husband.*"

He took another step. "*And I recited my own promise. That I would lead you to that day, and protect you along the way from all who wish to diminish you. Like the sinner who lays in your bed at this very moment.*"

He was close to me now. I wanted to fight back, or at least, to scream and warn Aaron. But I felt frozen, paralyzed. I'd never fought back against dad before. He was bigger than me, and he was so much stronger.

"*You broke your word,*" he hissed. "*You made a liar of me. I was going to punish him first. But I see that you need to learn your lesson now.*"

In a sudden burst of speed, he lunged forward, jumping several steps at once. I ran. I burst out the door where, thankfully, dad wasn't waiting for me as he had been in my dream, and sprinted into the woods.

What happened next passed as a blur. I recall hopping stumps, bushes, and roots. Falling, getting up, falling again. Eventually, when

I was out of breath, I dropped to the ground, crawled next to a fallen tree, and curled up in a ball.

I'd done this so many times before. Hidden away from him – in a cupboard, under the stairs, in the narrow space between a bookcase and the wall. I'd hoped his anger would pass; that, in the morning, he'd have forgotten about whatever imaginary transgression had enraged him.

Sometimes, I'd get lucky, and he would, in fact, forget. But I was never free of him, and it was never long before the next time he snapped.

"*Maria,*" he called. He was in the woods, though not particularly close to me. "*Come back, Maria. Daddy's calling you. It'll hurt less if you give up now.*"

I shuddered. *I'm in a good hiding spot. All I have to do is wait here.* But what good would that do? He'd still be looking for me, and if he couldn't find me, he'd go back for Aaron.

This had to stop, I realized, and I had to be the one to stop it. I couldn't do that by being a coward.

I got up as quietly as I could. Keeping low, I crept carefully back towards the house.

When my dad's voice next rang out, it came from less than a few yards away. "*Maria, come to papa,*" he repeated. I held my breath as I leaned against a thick oak tree that I used for cover. I waited there for several moments, until the shuffling sounds of movement drifted far in the opposite direction.

When I reached my property, I went straight for dad's shed, where I took hold of the only weapon available to me. *I can do this*, I told myself, as I gripped the axe with two shaking hands.

I needed a plan. If I played my cards right, surprise would be on my side. Dad expected me to hide, not to fight, after all.

~

I took my position behind the large rocking chair in the living room.

As I'd hoped, the kitchen light I'd flipped on drew dad in from outside.

From a narrow gap between the chair's cushions and the wall, I watched as his dark silhouette stepped through the backdoor. His head bent down as he gazed upon the dirty shoe prints I'd left for him, which led into the kitchen cupboard. *"Found your hiding spot, darling."*

It wasn't a great ruse, and I knew that he wouldn't be fooled for long. I only had a moment to act.

Gathering my courage, I stood up and stepped silently across the carpeted floor as dad reached for the handle for the cupboard door. As he opened it, I held the axe above my head.

Mustering my courage, I swung its blade it into his back with all my might.

~

I'd assumed the figure stalking me resembled the antagonist from one of those movies Addie had shown me – movies during which I covered my eyes for much of the runtime. An evil being that possessed superhuman strength, even invincibility. Who hacked and slashed his way through his victims. And who could only be defeated by, well, somebody with whom I no longer shared a critical quality.

But something strange happened when I ran the axe through my undead dad's back: it easily severed his skin. Not quite like a knife through warm butter, but close.

He whimpered and abruptly collapsed. Worm-ridden sod spilled out of the gap I'd made in him, falling in clumps across the kitchen floor.

I watched, my jaw dropped, as he crawled away from me out into the backyard.

Not wanting to miss my chance to finish him off – to end this, I ran after him and pulled the axe out of him.

When he raised his head to look at me, he wasn't the strong, muscular man I remembered, nor the threatening figure from my dream. Instead, he was frail and weak, held together only by brittle bone and bits of flimsy, heavily decomposed flesh.

*"Maria,"* he mumbled, more worms falling out of his mouth as he spoke, *"I love you. Don't..."*

With a shriek, I swung the axe again, this time digging a long gash into his should blade that severed his right arm from the rest of his body.

"What the fuck is wrong with you?" I screamed, my anger over what he'd done to me, to mom, boiling over. "Why are you so fucking obsessed with - with *nonsense*? I was eleven years when you made me make that stupid pledge. *Eleven*."

"*Maria, daddy's girl, don't do this-*" He raised his left arm, futilely, in an attempt to shield himself from my blows.

"I'm an adult. Why do you give a shit who I chose to sleep with, or when? It's none of your goddamn business, you fucking pervert." I let out an animalistic cry as I swung again and again

When I calmed down, dad's body lay before me in pieces: a knee here, a hand there. At the center of it all was his skeletal head, and it appeared stuck in a permanent expression of agonized disapproval.

~

Roughly two hours later, I pulled up to the cemetery in my old sedan.

I knew I was taking a risk. The sun was peaking over the horizon, and if someone saw me, there'd simply be no way to explain what I was doing. But, I wasn't going to walk again, not after what I'd been through, and not in light of what I needed to bring with me.

My hands covered by thick work gloves, I lifted each garbage bag from the trunk and tossed them over the wall. Once I reached the other side, I carried them to dad's grave, where I dropped them into the hole and pushed them until they slid down to the cedar coffin below. With his joints disconnected and in separate bags, dad wasn't going to crawl back up again.

Using the shovel I'd brought with me, I sealed the hole's narrow entrance with the dirt that had been knocked loose around it. Last, I patted the dirt as neatly as I could to cover any signs that a hole had been there in the first place.

At home, I cleaned up much of the mess dad had made until nothing remained but a few stains on the carpet. Finally, I stepped into the shower, where, under hot water, I scrubbed off the layer of sweat, dirt, and filth that, by this point, had covered my body.

When I stepped out, I stared at myself in the bathroom mirror, slowly taking in the fact that the face looking back at me belonged to a fundamentally different person than before.

For so long, I'd assumed that sex would change me – that it would set in motion some grand new phase of my existence – but that hadn't happened at all. Rather, I'd left that experience as meek, confused, and afraid as before. What had changed me was, well...I think that's obvious by now.

I dried myself off, threw on some night clothes and, at long last, crawled into bed, where I wrapped my arms around Aaron. I tried to be gentle, but Aaron nonetheless stirred and yawned when I touched him.

He turned towards me, his face lighting up at my sight. "Good morning," he murmured in a drowsy voice. "Looks like you showered?"

"Yeah. Sorry to wake you."

"It's fine," he said. "I slept *so* well. How about you?"

I shook my head.

"Sorry to hear that."

"It's alright," I replied.

"Look, I, um," he said, pausing to yawn, "I wanted to talk to you about last night."

"Okay."

"I just, um, I want to say that, like, it means a lot to me to have shared that experience with you. I know it didn't happen the way we thought it would, but, I...I'm glad that we did that."

I felt myself grow a little red as I tightened my grip around him into a light embrace. "It means a lot to me too."

"But, I, uh, also want to talk about something I'm feeling, um, kind of guilty about."

"Oh. Alright." For a moment, I braced myself for a confession I desperately did not want to hear: that last night had been a mistake, that we'd sinned, or that we needed to repent. But, thankfully, the words that followed were quite different.

"It's just that, it may have meant a lot to us both emotionally, you know? But, like, I know you didn't get a lot out of it in other ways. Physically, I mean."

"It's okay," I said, a blush overtaking my face. "Neither of us knew what we were doing. It's normal for it be like that."

"No, I mean, it *shouldn't* be normal. You deserve to enjoy it too, just as much as I do. I just want to say that, like, moving forward, if there's anything I can do to make it better for you, then I want to do that."

I had a few ideas about that, thanks to the material Addie had sent me earlier. I nodded as a warm feeling spread through me, one of comfort and trust. "Thank you."

"I love you, Maria."

"I love you too." I kissed him on the forehead.

For a moment, the events of the night swam through my mind. I was exhausted, and I'd soon be sore all over. I'd witnessed unnatural, horrifying things, and I'd been afraid for my life more than once. I had every reason to spend the day alone, processing what had happened.

But, I was a new person now. Someone who embraces herself, who faces her anxieties instead of running from them. I felt *alive* in a way that I'd never felt before.

I glanced at the clock behind him. It was only a little past 7 a.m. Mom wouldn't be back from her boyfriend's for at least another hour.

I looked back at Aaron. A mischievous smile spread across his face, just as I felt one spread across mine. "Are you thinking what I'm thinking?" he asked.

I nodded. "Yes, I am." I kissed him again before whispering gently, "I think it's time for round two."

# EPILOGUE

"You've been awake for, what, 36 hours now?" I whispered to Emma. "You need to take a rest, especially if you're driving them home in the morning. I can handle things tonight."

It was April's second night in the postpartum unit. Harper had just fed, and they were both asleep. Emma, Mae, Olivia, and I had been with them all day, but the hospital only permitted one visitor to stay overnight. Emma, naturally, had done that previously.

The nurse, a young woman with a wiry frame and a name tag that read "Agnes," tiptoed inside. She spoke softly. "Which one of you is staying?"

Emma sighed and gestured towards me. "Thanks, Casey."

~

As I sat on the couch in the gloomy, quiet hospital room, I couldn't help but stare at the beautiful baby girl. Harper filled my heart with joy. So, too, did seeing the love Emma and April felt for her, which mirrored the love they clearly felt for each other.

It had been over a year since I'd helped vanquish an imposter from their lives. Much had changed since then.

For starters, there was the financial windfall from Olivia's lawsuit against her former employer, which enabled her to finally escape the crummy half-house she'd been stuck renting with us for years. When the townhouse adjacent to Emma and April's went on the market, she consulted with them about it and, with their encouragement, closed on it. To our surprise, she even offered to let Mae and I stay there with her. "Months, years, as long as it takes for you all to find your own place. It'll be like old times, but with twice the space."

Then there was the evening when Emma and April showed up unprompted at our door and asked to have a private conversation with me. I'd then had a private conversation with Mae, and we ultimately agreed to the request. The weeks that followed were full of tedious meetings with doctors and lawyers, questions, tests, forms, waivers, the drawing of strict boundaries, and the dropping off of samples.

But it was all worth it to be here, now, with this perfect girl. As true as that was, I was also grateful to be a step removed from parenting her. My own father was an absent drunkard, and I'd always been terrified on some level that I'd do as bad a job as he did.

When Agnes returned to check in on April and Harper, I asked her if there was a vending area I could use. "Main level, by the cafeteria."

"Gotcha," I replied, eager for some caffeine to push me through the remainder of the night. "I'll be back before you're done."

I found my way there easily enough. There were several machines, and they contained the products I wanted. But, when I tried entering my selection, the words "Service Mode" flashed upon the screen.

"Goddamn it," I muttered. To my frustration, the others gave me the same result.

I took a closer look at one of the machines. It was older than the rest, and its surface was partially covered by a layer of graffiti that felt out-of-place in this setting. On the bottom row, a drink labeled *Timothy's All Night Concoction* hung precariously near the end of a metal coil.

I put two hands on the machine. It was heavy, but, with enough effort, I could rock it sufficiently to dislodge the drink.

I decided against it. I didn't want to get into trouble with the hospital, after all, and I'd never even heard of the brand.

When I returned to the postpartum unit, I noticed a door labeled "Break Room." It had three refrigerators inside. Two were empty, but the third, which was dark green in color and half the size of the others, was stocked with cartons of fruit juice. A note next to them read, "*For patients only.*"

I brought one with me back to April's room, where Agnes was wrapping up her check-in. "It's okay if I drink just one of these, right?" I asked. "I could really use the sugar."

She shrugged. "They won't mind if you take just one."

"Who won't mind?"

"It's not important. April and the baby are still doing great. I'll be back in a few hours."

~

In the morning, I helped load Harper, buckled securely into a carseat, into Emma's Crosstrek. Agnes, meanwhile, assisted April in walking out of the building.

When April reached the car, she tried to climb into the front passenger's seat, but lacked the energy to lift her legs.

Agnes and I simultaneously sprang to help her, accidentally crashing into each other in the process. I managed to keep my balance, but Agnes fell.

"I'm *so* sorry," I said. "Are you okay?" I reached out my hand, which she gripped and used to stand up.

"It's okay," she replied. "I'm totally fine."

Emma, meanwhile, got up from the driver's seat and gave April the assistance she needed. After checking in with us, she returned and started the car.

*They just left the hospital and are on their way back,* I texted Mae.

*Great, honey,* she responded. *Olivia and I just got back from walking Tessa. We'll be here waiting for them, and we'll help out once they get here. See you soon.*

As I watched their car disappear into the distance, Agnes said something unexpected. "You're going to be a good influence on her, Casey."

"Huh?"

"It's going to work out. It won't be like you fear."

"Um, thanks."

She patted me gently on the back and returned inside.

For a few moments, I just stood there, gazing into the early morning light. I thought about what life had in store for Harper, and the loving, responsible parents bringing her home. As I walked to my car, a joyful feeling swept through me: the knowledge that many golden days were ahead.

# BONUS CONTENT

**The Proposal**

As he holds out the ring and proposes to me, the crowd around us forms into a surprise flash mob who dance and sing in unison to the melody of one of my favorite songs.

I've never seen this man before in my life, and the dancers are blocking every exit.

**The Inheritor**

The family members around my deathbed gasped in shock when, with my final breaths, I made the long-awaited announcement: "I leave my fortune not to any of you, but to my loyal companion Rusty, as he is the only one in this room to show me true devotion."

"As was my plan all along," cackled the shapeshifting demon as his canine body reverted to human form.

~

## Escape from the Haunted Cemetery

The school bullies have gone too far! Not only did they leave you, gagged and bound, in a hot trunk for hours, but you now awaken inside the notoriously haunted local cemetery. The moonlight reveals a distant figure. Approach him (H) or search for an exit (B).

A. You follow him up several flights of stairs, through a window, and onto the roof. "I'm sorry. I served my time, why won't you leave me alone?" he cries. You watch, bewildered, as he leaps to his death.

B. A locked gate lined with tall, sharp spikes blocks the main entrance. Climb it (I) or look elsewhere (E).

C: Before you can speak, he charges with surprising swiftness. A swing from his shovel sends you sprawling. You feel his strong grip as he drags you across the cool grass. Go to (G).

D: The door slams shut behind you. A phrase engraved in marble above a burial vault built into the floor reads, *"Qui meam pacem conturbant, peribunt."* The walls shake, then close in. You are crushed into dust.

E: You pass three statues of angels who slowly rotate their heads and whisper, *"You don't belong here."* To your astonishment, one takes flight and grabs ahold of you. Go to (G).

F: You land with a 'thud' on a dirt road. What to do now? Get revenge on the bullies' ringleader Roger (J) or return home (L).

G: Your captor sends you tumbling into a pit. You struggle helplessly as dirt rains down onto your permanent resting place six feet under.

H: It's none other than Old Man Halloran, the infamous gravedigger.

"What're ya' doin' skulkin' about *my* graveyard?" he snarls. Reason with him (C) or flee (M).

I: As you near the top, you hear commotion behind you. You turn to see dozens of undead figures emerging from graves, all staggering in your direction. The distraction causes you to lose your grip. You fall. A zombie in a red jacket drags you away. Go to (G).

J: A figure stands outside Roger's family's tall Victorian house. He's pale and sickly, but otherwise looks like Roger's dad. Upon seeing you, he screams and runs inside. Follow him (A) or just return home (L).

K: You crouch behind the tree trunk as, thankfully, Halloran scurries past you. Your relief is short-lived, however, as the tree begins to swing its long branches at you. You dodge one, but another sends you flying – up, over the fence, and out of the cemetery. Go to (F).

L: When you knock at the front door of your house, a girl opens it. She resembles your little sister, but she's much too old, and she has a horrified expression. You try to form comforting words, but only worm-ridden dirt pours out of your exposed jawbone.

M: As you run away, the heavy 'thumps' of Halloran's footsteps follow. You consider two hiding spots: a brooding oak tree (K) or an ornate mausoleum (D).

# PAST PRINT APPEARANCES AND AUDIO ADAPTATIONS

*After the Surgery (Part 1)*: Adapted on *Creepy* on July 2, 2023.

*Class of 2013*: Adapted on *Creepy* on August 20, 2023.

*Straw Men*: Adapted on *Creepy* on October 23, 2021. Appeared in written anthology *Halloween Horror: Volume 3*, published by DBND Publishing on October 6, 2021.

*Muck*: Adapted on *The NoSleep Podcast*, Season 15 Episode 2 (paid version).

*Blood Money*: Adapted on *The NoSleep Podcast*, *Suddenly Shocking Vol. 18* (available to paid subscribers only).

*Transformations*: Adapted on *The NoSleep Podcast*, Season 15 Episode 9. (The last third of this version was heavily rewritten for this compilation).

*Zippers*: Narrated by YouTuber Mr. Creeps on February 19, 2021.

*The View from the Sunroom*: Adapted on *Creepy* on September 30, 2021 (available to Patreon members only).

*Galápagos*: Adapted on *Creepy* on January 28, 2024. Appeared in written anthology *Angela's Recurring Nightmares*, published by Great Lakes Association Horror Writers on May 23, 2022.

*Agnes*: Adapted on *The NoSleep Podcast*, *Suddenly Shocking Vol. 17* (available to paid subscribers only).

*First Heat*: Adapted on *The NoSleep Podcast*, Season 22 Episode 17.
*Revenging Machine*: Adapted on *The NoSleep Podcast, Suddenly Shocking Vol. 14* (available to paid subscribers only).
*There's No Leaving Evergreen*: Adapted on *Creepy* on March 1, 2023 (available to Patreon members only).
*Countdowns*: Narrated by YouTuber Mr. Creeps on August 24, 2023. (This version was heavily rewritten for this compilation.)
*Madeline*: Adapted on *Creepy* on July 14, 2024.
*Before They Were Scarecrows*: Narrated by YouTuber *Horror Stories with the Barron*, featuring *Dodge the Grave*, on September 23, 2021.
*Autoreply*: Adapted on *Creepy* on August 25, 2024.
*Always a Teacher*: Adapted on *Creepy* on September 11, 2024 (available to Patreon members only).
*Are You Running from Your Refrigerator?*: Narrated by YouTubers *Horror Stories with the Barron* and *Lighthouse Horror* on June 23, 2021.
*Night Drive*: Adapted on *Creepy* on October 16, 2021 (available to Patreon members only).

# ACKNOWLEDGMENTS

I first thank my loving wife, who has been endlessly supportive of my writing.

I owe a debt to *The NoSleep Podcast*, which taught me to love short-form horror fiction, inspired me to write some of my own, and took a chance on me by adapting several of my stories. Thank you to David Cummings and the whole crew for your hard work and the countless hours of entertainment you have provided.

Last, this book would not have happened without the many readers who took the time to leave thoughtful comments about my work. To each of you who take the time to compose helpful, constructive feedback, your efforts are greatly appreciated.

# ABOUT THE AUTHOR

B.A. Ries resides in Alexandria, Virginia with a perfect and brilliant wife and a somehow even more perfect and brilliant daughter. All three take orders from a dog who believes she can climb trees.